THE COLONEL
OF CHICAGO

*Photograph on title page courtesy
Mrs. Maryland McCormick*

ROBERT RUTHERFORD McCORMICK

THE COLONEL OF CHICAGO

By JOSEPH GIES

E. P. DUTTON · NEW YORK

CONTENTS

ACKNOWLEDGMENTS

THIS book was researched at the Library of Congress and the McKeldin Library of the University of Maryland.

Former *Chicago Tribune* archivist (and former correspondent and editor) Harold Hutchings and present archivist Lee Major provided valued assistance by suggesting and making available source material. Both read the manuscript and made corrections and suggestions, and Mrs. Major answered numerous questions that baffled research.

Arthur Veysey and Gwen Morgan Veysey, former *Tribune* foreign correspondents now in charge of Colonel McCormick's Cantigny estate, were most helpful.

Walter Trohan, former Washington bureau chief of the *Tribune,* source of many anecdotes about the Colonel, also supplied information.

Israeli scholar Dina Goren gave permission to use her thesis on the *Chicago Tribune*'s Battle of Midway dispatch.

James Boylan, professor of history at Columbia University and editor of *The Columbia Journalism Review,* read the manuscript and suggested many valuable corrections and improvements.

Mrs. Maryland Hooper McCormick lent pictures and contributed information.

Finally, Frances Gies made decisive contributions to the book's conception, research, and structure, and only by her own choice does she not share the by-line.

THE COLONEL OF CHICAGO

CHAPTER ONE

Colonel McCormick's Tower

CHICAGO, where much architectural history has been made, is richly furnished with landmark buildings, from new high-rise champions—Hancock, Standard, Sears—to such aging charmers as the sprawling Merchandise Mart, the wedding-cake Wrigley, the curious Rookery, the massive-walled Monadnock. Yet the building everybody who has ever visited Chicago knows and can locate, a hundred paces north of the Michigan Avenue Bridge, is Colonel McCormick's cathedral-inspired Tribune Tower.

Thirty-six stories high, the Colonel's creation makes no pretensions as a skyscraper, and the twelve-story annex added in 1948 slightly impairs its symmetry.

Nevertheless, it remains one of the truly distinctive city office buildings, vindicating the design of New York architects John Mead Howells and Raymond M. Hood against some contemporary criticism, possibly jealous. Louis Sullivan derided the functionless Gothic buttresses that, for less severe aesthetes, lend a flourish to the Tower's top. To the medieval sculptural ornamentation of the exterior, Colonel McCormick added his personal decorative touch. Commandeering his corps of foreign correspondents and making use of his own and his newspaper's clout, he collected over a hundred souvenir fragments—bricks, stones, bits of masonry—from famous buildings and sites all over the world and embedded them in the facade, with identifying plaques: St. Peter's, the Great Pyramid, Notre-Dame-de-Paris, the Houses of Parliament, the Great Wall of China, the Parthenon, the Inner Temple of Peking, the Dublin Post Office, the Kremlin.

The cosmopolitan element in the Colonel's taste was balanced by native American fragments with historic or other significance, chosen state by state: for Pennsylvania, a brick from Independence Hall; for Ohio, a stone from Put-in-Bay, site of Commodore Perry's victory; for Iowa, a rock from Louise City, where Marquette and Joliet landed in 1673; for Texas, a piece of the Alamo; for Missouri, a rock fragment from Mark Twain's "Injun Joe" cave; for Connecticut, a bit of Yale, the Colonel's alma mater.

On the Tower's south facade, facing Pioneer Court, the open space before Miës van der Rohe's austere Equitable Building, is a row of newspaper-size

1

bronze plates. These reproduce famous *Tribune* front pages with their venerable headlines: PRESIDENT LINCOLN ASSASSINATED! GREAT FIRE! DEWEY SINKS SPANISH FLEET, REVENGE FOR MAINE! EUROPE'S WAR IS ON! TRIBUNE HAS TREATY! TRUMAN PROCLAIMS V-E DAY! KENNEDY ASSASSINATED!

On the north side, in a miniature court fronting Michigan Avenue, stands a statue of Nathan Hale, author of immortal last words and a Yale man.

The visitor entering the Tower lobby finds himself immediately given something to read. Many buildings, especially those devoted to publishing, education, and similar cerebral pursuits, display an inscription bearing on the enterprise, but the Tribune Tower does not know when to stop. The lobby walls are incised almost top to bottom with ringing phrases, from John Milton to John Marshall, from Euripides to Daniel Webster, all bearing on a single theme, the freedom of the press. The conclusion is inescapable that the man who breathed his spirit into this building thought freedom of the press an issue that could not be overemphasized.

The working floors of the Tower are filled with the anticipatory tingle of the newspaper business—pressrooms, editorial offices, city room—with their natural rhythms of tension and posttension, and occasional bursts of larger excitement. In a way, the working heart of the building is anticlimax, since it could be any major metropolitan newspaper, for example, Marshall Field's *Sun-Times* across Michigan Avenue, whose trim blue-gray horizontal mass seems designed to contradict the vertical, white, Gothic Tribune. The Colonel's old office on the twenty-fourth floor, once again inhabited by the *Tribune*'s chief executive after remaining unoccupied for two decades, is off limits to tourists. Clothed by rumor in the Colonel's lifetime with fictitious bizarreries, from secret wall panels to a machine gun in the ceiling, it is large and pleasant, though on no Hollywood scale, with a fine panorama of the city and the lake.

When Colonel McCormick died in 1955 the Tribune Tower remained upright and the *Tribune* continued to appear on Chicago newsstands. Yet something became past tense. The Tower and the newspaper began the subtle process of ceasing to reflect a living personality and beginning to memorialize a vanished one. Though press eulogies were extensive and at least partly sincere, a discernible note in many was the condescension one bestows on an old rival or enemy who, one now feels comfortably assured, has been proved wrong. Many who remembered back a decade and a half did not even feel very forgiving. Resentment not short of hatred still smoldered from the years when Colonel McCormick and his *Chicago Tribune* were perceived by the majority of literate, educated, politically conscious Americans as the chief fountainhead of a doctrine whose poison compared only with that of the Copperheads in the Civil War. The emotion was not confined to Chicagoans. No publisher and no newspaper were ever so well known, let alone so unfavorably known, to millions of people who never saw or read them. Even foreigners who scarcely knew where Chicago was knew about the terrible *Chicago Tribune.* Traces of the old hostility still abound in and out of Chicago. A recently published Chicago architectural guide expresses the gratuitous suspicion that the souvenir fragments in the Tower facade are fake (the Colonel went to extreme lengths to secure authentication) and adds that even if they are real they "can hardly be said to enhance the beauty of his building."

McCormick and the *Tribune* were already anathema to liberal Democrats before World War II, mainly because of their hostility to Franklin D. Roosevelt and the New Deal, and especially their openly partisan bias in coverage of the election campaigns of 1936 and 1940. To a lesser extent, liberals were outraged by the *Tribune*'s long hostility to organized labor, especially the CIO, and to various other liberal causes. These issues, however, hardly separated the *Tribune* from the rest of the 1930s–1940s press. Big-city daily newspapers and rural weeklies in the East, Midwest, South, and Far West almost uniformly shared the same prejudices, varying only in tone and not much in that. A single issue separated out Robert R. McCormick and his *Tribune:* "isolationism," their tirelessly argumentative resistance to the step-by-step advance of the country toward the brink of World War II. Against them on this momentous question were ranged, for the first and only time, the great bulk of their press compeers, together with an extraordinarily broad coalition of influential opinion that included liberals and radicals, but whose hard core was composed of affluent conservatives.

Colonel McCormick's bellicose grandfather, Joseph Medill, had used the *Tribune* in 1861 to revile as a traitor the Colonel's great-uncle, Cyrus McCormick, for favoring a negotiated peace between North and South. For advocating a similar course eighty years later the Colonel and the *Tribune* were in turn accused of treason, along with fascism, Nazism, cowardice, and un-Americanism. Other newspapers broke journalistic tradition and etiquette by attacking the *Tribune* and its publisher by name. McCormick and Samuel Emory Thomason of the *Chicago Times* sacrificed a lifelong friendship to an exchange of editorial civilities that included the terms *jackal* and *feisty dog.* The *Montreal Star* and other Canadian newspapers called on their government to shut off the *Tribune*'s supply of newsprint, and a crowd of angry Chicagoans met to demand a boycott of the paper and to burn it in the streets.

Following Pearl Harbor, most isolationists were received back into the fold like repentant sinners, but Colonel McCormick was not. On the contrary, he was nominated in Washington as a candidate for hanging or shooting, the government sought ways to harass him and harm his paper, and a grand jury was assembled in Chicago to indict him for treason.

An attempt to defend himself only made him an object of derision. A letter from a former employee named Jacob Sawyer asked him how he could keep on criticizing the government when there was a war on. The Colonel answered courteously, thanking Sawyer for a "very temperate letter" (which gives an inkling of some of the other mail he was getting). But in defending himself against the charge of harming the nation's security he listed rather fulsomely what he regarded as his achievements in promoting it—mechanization of the army, establishment of ROTC, machine guns for the army, offshore bases for the navy—and regretted that he had not succeeded in persuading the navy that airplanes could sink battleships. Sawyer, apparently dazzled and incredulous, took the reply to the rival *Chicago Daily News,* which published it under the rubric "Whatta Man!" and appended a witticism by Carl Sandburg, a former *Daily News* staffer: "And on the seventh day he rested."

The Colonel's letter was picked up by other newspapers and by *Time* magazine, and its author held up to vast ridicule. He had, indeed, exaggerated a bit. Yet the effect of his letter to Sawyer derived less from the excessiveness of his claims than from everybody's ignorance of the validity of most of them. The one about machine guns was endlessly quoted as a claim to having "invented the machine gun," a fairly preposterous assertion to put in the mouth of a man who was an expert on the history of the Civil War. What Colonel McCormick claimed was that he had "introduced the machine gun in the army," which he had indeed done on the Mexican border in 1916.

Though Sawyer had no business turning over a personal letter to a newspaper, Colonel McCormick should have known better than to write it, or at least, as someone said of Harry Truman's hot letter to the Washington music critic about daughter Margaret's concert, he should have known better than to mail it. The episode revealed McCormick's ego less than his innocence, the unguarded openness that allowed him to come right out and say whatever he thought. It also reflected his notorious impatience, which rarely permitted the native hue of resolution to be sicklied o'er by the pale cast of thought.

The bitterness with which his isolationism was viewed by many related closely to a charge against him that antedated the war, but that only acquired its virulence after the war's outbreak. This was the accusation of being "anti-British." So insistently was the epithet fastened to him that it may be the thing many veterans of the ink war of 1940–1941 remember best. Recondite explanations were offered, involving ancestry, Freudian psychology, and political geography. In the end everyone was baffled by the mystery, but belief in McCormick's anglophobia had become an article of faith. The governor of Jamaica once held a frantic conference with aides over the picture of George III that the Colonel would be facing during lunch. The picture couldn't be moved; the moment came for toasts, the governor proposed, "His Majesty the King," and McCormick, unmindful of the problem he had caused, but remembering that the current president was Harry Truman, spotted George III and blandly countertoasted, "To the father of my country."

A 1977 magazine article repeated a silly tale that pilots of the *Tribune*'s corporate plane had installed Pratt & Whitney nameplates on the aircraft's Rolls-Royce engines to guard against offense to "McCormick's all-American passions"—overlooking the fact that the Colonel had long ridden to work in a Rolls-Royce, spoke with a mild British accent, sported a British-style moustache, had a London tailor, hatter, and shoemaker (inherited from his ambassador father), and expressed undying affection for his English boarding school. His three favorite authors were Rudyard Kipling, Arthur Conan Doyle, and P. G. Wodehouse.

Besides being labeled "anti-British," Colonel McCormick was widely dubbed "eccentric." Such quirks as arriving at the office accompanied by his dog, and occasionally dressed in riding habit, were cited, as well as the report (true) that he kept a mechanical exercise horse in the Tower, and another, endlessly repeated but false, that he once emerged on horseback from a van during an office picnic. He himself connected the story with a prank of his youth—on returning from a polo match he responded to a hail from Alice Roosevelt by riding his pony up a dozen front steps. As he pointed out, the horse-van story would have required cutting a hole in the roof of the van to accommodate his head, since he was six feet four inches tall.

The *Tribune* lent corroboration to McCormick's nonconformist reputation. So far from unvarying support for Republican officeholders, it fought its most unyielding battles with two great Chicago Republicans, Boss William Lorimer and Big Bill Thompson, both of whose scalps it eventually tucked in its belt. The most Republican of presidents, Herbert Hoover, failed to please McCormick, who did not wait for the end of Hoover's inaugural address to notify his Washington bureau telegraphically: THIS MAN WON'T DO. Despite his veneration for the birth of American independence, McCormick stuck fanatically to a crusade initiated by his British-born *Tribune* predecessor, James Keeley, and incredibly succeeded in making the nation give up its Fourth of July fireworks.

But contributing most by far to his reputation as an eccentric was the *Tribune*'s decades-long campaign to reform the spelling of the English language. In the *Tribune,* for varying periods of years, *island* lost its *s, jazz* dropped one *z*, *freight* was compacted to *frate*, *though* and *through* were truncated to *tho* and *thru*, and some seventy-five other words were similarly rationalized. The idea of simplified spelling, which he had inherited from Grandfather Medill, was one of two he shared with George Bernard Shaw, the other being his suggestion in 1943 that Britain apply for membership in the United States. The *Times* of London pointed out that the latter proposal had been put forward twenty years earlier by Shaw in *The Apple Cart*, though the pained *Times* seemed not to realize that Colonel McCormick's tongue had been in his cheek as much as had Shaw's, or that the 49th state idea had originated with American anglophiles and had drawn *Tribune* derision in an earlier editorial.

Someone cleverly observed that there was a difference between the Shaw and McCormick commitments to improved English spelling. Shaw bequeathed his fortune to the cause, but did not jeopardize acquisition of the fortune by employing simplified spelling in his writings. The *Tribune* practiced what it preached, though surrendering to an incurably traditionalist public on one word after another. In 1974, with Colonel McCormick long dead, the newspaper finally announced editorially that "thru is through and so is tho," though retaining *catalog, synagog*— and certain others that have caught on with a considerable section of publishing.

Finally, Colonel McCormick is remembered, especially by Chicagoans, for the imperious color of his whims, such as the time he ordered a star removed from the flag in the Tower lobby to stigmatize Rhode Island for a piece of arrant Democratic political chicanery (told that the act constituted illegal defacing of the flag, he hastily had the star restored). Contributing to the aura surrounding a celebrity in a city that had few was his native aloofness, which many who knew him attributed to a patrician's shyness with subordinates rather than arrogance. His childlessness may have lent his public personality an avuncular, or grandfatherly, character that came through in the radio talks he was fond of giving, for example, in his advice to Girl Scouts to carry "a compass, a watch, and an electric torch" (one of the British usages left over from schooldays) when walking in the woods.

A widely cited proof of his vanity was the *Tribune*'s old slogan, "World's Greatest Newspaper," which a San Francisco columnist in the 1970s explained as "just in case you had any doubts about who the world's greatest writer, editor, and publisher might be." McCormick never claimed to be any of those things, and furthermore, did not invent the slogan, which he inherited from his predecessor Keeley. He accepted it, and did his best, according to his lights, to sustain it. *The New Yorker*'s A. J. Liebling found evidence of megalomania in a piece of alleged copy-editing on the obituary of McCormick's cousin, Joseph M. Patterson, publisher of the *New York*

Daily News. According to Liebling, a tribute from General Douglas MacArthur, calling Patterson "the most brilliant natural born soldier that ever served under me," was cut from the *Tribune* version of the obit because McCormick fancied the superlative belonged to himself. McCormick, however, never served under MacArthur, in whose Forty-second Division Patterson was an artillery officer in 1918. The *Tribune* morgue's Patterson obit differed in many details, but not in eulogistic tone, from the *Daily News*'s. The remarkable thing about McCormick and Patterson was their lifelong mutual respect and friendship despite widely divergent political views.

Occasionally cited as evidence of the Colonel's ego is one of the bits of masonry embedded in the facade of the Tower: a russet brick whose plaque identifies it as from "150 Ontario Street, birthplace of Colonel Robert R. McCormick." The Colonel, however, is not responsible; the brick is a mark of esteem placed there two years after his death by his successors at the *Tribune.* His own references to the house on Ontario Street were jocular, based on its metamorphosis around 1940 into a key club—he told a Jewish Welfare Fund dinner that as a result his birthplace was visited by more people than Lincoln's.

Older Chicagoans still remember the Colonel's regular Saturday-night broadcasts of travelogues, history lessons, and memoirs during the intermissions in "Chicago Theater of the Air," a popular radio show on WGN-Mutual Broadcasting System. In 1951, when he was testifying in a Washington lawsuit (columnist Drew Pearson was suing the *Washington Times-Herald,* then owned by McCormick), a smart-aleck lawyer pressed him on what motivated him to air his recollections and opinions. "Egotism," he conceded genially, and, according to the account in the *Washington Evening Star,* enjoyed the laughter that rocked the courtroom.

CHAPTER TWO

McCormicks, Medills, and Pattersons

THE Robert McCormick who was born at 150 East Ontario Street in Chicago was the fifth Robert McCormick in his family's American history. The first, son of an Ulster emigrant to Pennsylvania, fought in the Revolution under Nathanael Greene and helped bottle up Cornwallis in Yorktown. During the war the family moved to the Shenandoah Valley of Virginia where a second Robert was born. Land being cheap and farming easy, Robert McCormick II prospered and married a neighbor named Mary Ann Hall who brought him a dowry of horses and cattle.

A capable tinkerer, Robert tried to build a mechanical reaper. His son Robert (III) died of the "flux," but another son, Cyrus, took over the reaper and made it work. He proved to be an even better businessman than inventor. Moving to Chicago in 1847, Cyrus created a manufacturing and sales empire that helped make the prairie town queen of the rich new Middle West.

As a transplanted southerner, Cyrus McCormick sympathized with the South over the slavery controversy (his father had owned nine slaves) and tried to help arrange a compromise settlement to head off the Civil War. His peaceful sentiments found few adherents in Chicago and were treated with especially caustic disdain by one of the town's morning newspapers, the *Chicago Tribune*.

Born in a loft in 1847, the *Tribune* had nothing to distinguish itself from any other frontier-town news sheet until it acquired a combative editor named Joseph Medill. Tall, angular, red-bearded Medill, a true journalistic son of the free-spirited Middle Border, liberally mixed news reportage with editorial comment. A typical Medill news item was headed simply "A Brute":

> James Wheeler was yesterday fined $5 for abusing his wife. Mrs. Wheeler is the woman who has twice attempted to commit suicide, once by throwing herself into the lake and again by taking laudanum. Both those attempts resulted from injuries inflicted upon her by her husband. A few months' experience in breaking stones in the bridewell would do this Wheeler "a power of good," and he ought to have been sent there.

A founder of the Republican party (it owes him its name) and an early admirer of Abe Lincoln, Joseph Medill covered the 1858 Lincoln-Douglas debates in full, an unheard-of newspaper feat (though he intentionally garbled some of Douglas's oratory, at least according to Edgar Lee Masters). The *Tribune* reports were widely copied, and two years later Medill was one of the little band of manipulators who secured Lincoln's nomination at the Chicago convention, an event that put the brash new city (109,000, up from a village in twenty years) on the national map. In his impassioned indorsements of Lincoln, the Republican party, and war to preserve the Union, Medill was explicit and personal. Editors who perceived the nation's problems in another light, like the *New York Herald*'s James Gordon Bennett, were "liars" and advised to keep their "copperhead slime" to themselves. Politicians were treated with equal liberty, sometimes leading to consequences. On a visit to Washington, Medill was knocked to the ground and slugged by an Illinois congressman, and during the war the *Tribune* at one point needed federal troops to protect it from angry citizens.

For fellow Chicagoan Cyrus McCormick, Joseph Medill reserved his most cordial loathing: "Like all the poor white trash of Virginia, he left that state a better friend of slavery than the slaveholders themselves, and the prejudices of his youth have built upon a defective education a perfect monomania in behalf of man-stealing." So far from having invented the reaper, McCormick had not contributed a single idea to it, according to the *Tribune,* but had stolen them all from somebody else. McCormick, a formidable battler himself, tried to fight back with Medill's own weapon, but the newspaper he bought failed and so did his bid for a seat in Congress.

Yet history never tiring of ironies, McCormick's reaper, to whose technical success he had indeed contributed significantly, was credited by Secretary of War Stanton with saving the Union by freeing northern farm boys to fight for it, and a dozen years later Joseph Medill's daughter Katherine married Cyrus's nephew Robert Sanderson McCormick. From this unexpected alliance came the son born on Ontario Street July 30, 1880.

In the interval several things had happened to the two families and to Chicago. A Cassandra-like editorial in the *Tribune* on September 10, 1871, had warned the city that its "everlasting pine, shingles, sham veneers, stucco, and putty" invited a holocaust, which swept Chicago barely a month later. As flames licked the building that housed the *Tribune,* Medill and his staff double-teamed as fire brigade and press crew, but were finally frustrated by the bursting of gas and water mains. Resourceful Medill collared a job printer on Canal Street in the unburned part of town, leased his shop, found a press and bought it just ahead of a rival, rounded up his exhausted staff, and got out a half-sheet containing the first news account of the fire. The same truncated *Tribune* carried Medill's most famous editorial. Titled "Cheer Up," it began:

> In the midst of a calamity without parallel in the world's history, looking upon the ashes of thirty years' accumulations, the people of this once beautiful city have resolved that *Chicago shall rise again.*

The next year Joseph Medill was swept into office as mayor on a "Fire-proof" ticket. His administration was a success until for some reason he ordered the police to enforce a forgotten blue law closing beer parlors on Sunday. The resulting revolt among Chicago's Central European ethnics drove him from City Hall. He retreated abroad, but came home to gain full control of the *Tribune*—previously he had been only a partner—with the aid of a loan from Marshall Field, the department-store king. For the remainder of the century Medill kept the *Tribune* literate, competent, Republican, and well-informed on national and international issues. On foreign policy he was frankly a chauvinist, and in strict accord with George Washington on the danger of foreign entanglements. Like most editors of the era, he readily waxed violent on the subject of the "anarchists" and "communists" who were agitating for the eight-hour day and other alarming reforms. "If the chief end of man," he wrote, "is to become a lazy lout, a shiftless vagabond, a brawling, long-haired idiot, a public nuisance, and an enemy of the human race, let him turn Communist." To foil such enemies he did not shrink from advocating real violence. An 1875 editorial warned Chicago's Communists, whom it identified as "the very scum of the European cities," that they might bring a war of extermination on themselves. Another recommended that the better element in the city organize military companies "for the common defense." Still another reminded agitators that "Judge Lynch" was an American "by birth and character."

One *Tribune* flight of 1877 was dug up and used against Joseph Medill's grandson in the 1940s. The article (not an editorial) suggested that the best way to get rid of the ragged tramps infesting the suburbs (there was a depression on) would be "to put a little strychnine or arsenic in the meat" given the tramp in charity, a solution that would serve as a warning to other tramps, "puts the coroner in a good humor, and saves one's chickens and other portable property." In context the piece seems to be a clumsy but characteristic example of Artemus Ward-type journalistic black humor.

Besides the Katherine who married Robert Sanderson McCormick, Joseph Medill had another daughter, Elinor, who also made a marriage significant to the future of American journalism. Like Katherine a tall, handsome, strong-minded redhead, Elinor married Robert W. Patterson, Jr., son of the Reverend Robert W. Patterson, pastor of the Second Presbyterian Church. The wealthy Second Presbyterian was also the church of Cyrus McCormick, which may have helped break the ice between the two old enemies. Elinor had two children, Joseph Medill Patterson and Elinor (who later changed the spelling to Eleanor), nicknamed Cissy. Katherine had three children. The middle child, a girl, died in infancy, leaving older son Joseph Medill McCormick and younger son Robert R. McCormick.

The sisterly rivalry implied by two sons named after Grandfather Joseph Medill was already of long standing and flourished ever more greenly with the passing years. Katherine gained an edge by using her older son's middle name as his Christian name, making him a euphoniously aristocratic Medill McCormick, whereas Elinor's son became merely a plebeian-sounding Joe Patterson. Katherine originally gave her second son his father's name, but a few years later improved on this mediocre inspiration by substituting in the middle Rutherford for Sanderson, on the grounds of the discovery of a genealogical connection with Sir Walter Scott, whose mother was Anne Rutherford.

The Ontario Street McCormicks hardly mixed with the rich McCormicks of "McCormickville," the Gold Coast neighborhood a few blocks north and west where the reaper clan built their mansions (only two remain, converted into restaurants). Patriarch Cyrus McCormick modeled his, which stood until 1955 on the northeast corner of Rush and Erie, after a pavilion of the Louvre. The narrow townhouse at 150 East Ontario, cheek-by-jowl with its neighbors, was something of a contrast. In Robert's early childhood the family moved three blocks west to Ontario House, at the corner of State, one of the city's first modern apartment buildings. Katherine's uncle, Samuel J. Medill, was a fellow tenant, and Joseph Medill's own mansion stood a block east, at Ontario and Cass (now Wabash). The two little McCormick boys rode their high-wheeled bicycles as far as the Water Tower, the Gothic minaret that had risen alone above the smoldering ruins of 1871, and perhaps more amazingly stands today amid the towering splendors of North Michigan Avenue.

A later malicious tale attached significance to Robert's childhood wardrobe of dresses, ascribed to his mother's having wanted another girl to replace the lost child, but whoever started it was apparently unaware that Victorian toddler fashion was unisex. Childhood pictures of both McCormick boys, cousin Joe Patterson, Franklin Roosevelt, Harry Truman, and other male children of that era show them in skirts and curls until they were old enough to complain.

"My first vivid recollection," McCormick told his radio audience sixty-five years later, "is the day that the anarchists were hanged in Chicago, November 11, 1887. Children were not allowed out of doors because riots were feared. The police were armed with rifles."

The "anarchists" were the last victims of the Haymarket Riot, which grew out of a strike for the eight-hour day at the McCormick reaper plant. Somebody threw a bomb that killed a number of policemen who had come to break up a workers' meeting, and since the bomb thrower could not be found, several militant leaders were arrested, tried, and sentenced to death for their incitements. Their fate became a burning issue not only in Chicago and Illinois but also nationally and internationally. European socialists like George Bernard Shaw pleaded for their lives, and so did some sensible Chicago businessmen, who were overridden by autocratic Marshall Field. Four men were hanged. The others were later pardoned by liberal Democratic governor John Peter Altgeld. Among those executed was August Spies, who had organized the meeting in the Haymarket. While in prison he had married by proxy a young woman who lived in the Ontario Street neighborhood, where she became an object less of pity than alarm: "We were deadly afraid of the poor woman," recalled Robert McCormick, "and I am afraid shouted at her in the street."

The disparate grandeur that separated the Ontario Street McCormicks from their wealthy cousins of McCormickville derived from the unequal division of the reaper profits, which had piqued Cyrus's younger brother Leander into publishing a tract claiming that Cyrus had stolen the invention from their father. In the series of financial settlements that separated the two younger brothers' families from the reaper business, the heirs of William Sanderson McCormick did not do well. William Sanderson, afflicted with a "nervous disorder," had dropped out of the firm and died in a sanitarium. His son, Robert Sanderson McCormick, the Colonel's father, had less than a hundred thousand dollars to stake him for what proved to be a short-lived business career on the Chicago grain exchange, where he was either unlucky or fleeced by the pros.

Forced to seek employment, but not wishing to descend in the social scale, he got help from his father-in-law, Joseph Medill, in landing something with suitable class. New Republican President Benjamin Harrison had just appointed as minister to Great Britain Robert Todd Lincoln, son of Medill's old protégé, Abe, and now a lawyer for the *Tribune*. Lincoln was persuaded to take on R. S. McCormick as second secretary of the legation in London.

Nine-year-old Robert Rutherford McCormick enjoyed the crossing on the *Adriatic*, an early liner equipped with sails as well as steam. In London he and his brother Medill were enrolled at first in a boarding school whose proprietor stood in front of the fireplace on chilly mornings and blocked the heat from the shivering boys, and one of whose masters displayed the brutality common in English schools—"I have remembered it for sixty years," McCormick recorded. But not all English schools were so bad, and a second proved wholly congenial. Ludgrove was a modest version of Eton or Harrow situated in Hampshire, just southwest of London. Its headmaster was "a splendid and kindly man" and star athlete who had captained the All-England football team. Six days a week, winter and summer, the boys played football (soccer), squash, rounders (ancestor of baseball), and especially cricket, of which McCormick became a rare American devotee.

Robert once saw Queen Victoria. "She was driving in an open carriage with postillions on the horses, a little old woman in a black bonnet. The people threw their hats in the air, as the merry villagers sometimes do in our operas, and she bowed in return. I was told that the old lady really was sitting in a rocking chair, as she was too old to bow in the customary way."

Vacations were spent on the Continent where on one occasion at a German spa Robert met the Prince of Wales, the future Edward VII, and his nephew the new German Kaiser Wilhelm. The prince noted the boy's sailor hat, which bore the name of a British warship, and commented, "Ah, a nice little English boy," provoking the response, "I am not. I am an American." That made the kaiser guffaw, "Haw, haw, haw." At his insistence Robert's parents sent for American hatbands for his own and brother Medill's sailor hats.

When he was ten he turned real sailor, learned to navigate a sloop in Nice, and boldly set out with another boy to cross the Mediterranean, "but [we] were overtaken and brought back." At eleven he was sent home unaccompanied to London from a vacation in southern France. His parents arranged to have an adult meet him in Paris to conduct him from one railroad station to another. "I avoided the man . . . and had a day of fun, stopping at the Hotel de Hollande on the Place Vendôme, where my family and I were known." Part of a year spent at a pension in Versailles had given him a command of French. He paid a visit to a circus in the Rue St. Honoré, among whose performers was an American black called Chocolat "whom I was, of course, glad to see. He talked me out of my only five franc piece."

At twelve he was transferred to another English school, Elstree, where he was impressed with the good manners of the English boys and by the tact of the masters, who while expatiating on the glories of England "always explained to me that my duty was to my own country." English, Scottish, and Irish boys "picked on each other a good deal, but the American was exempt." To guard against seduction by their foreign education, the McCormick boys read *Tom Sawyer* and *Huckleberry Finn,* but were seduced anyway, becoming addicted to the novels of G. A. Henty *(Under Drake's Flag, With Clive in India),* whose perfervid English chauvinism makes Kipling seem a pacifist cynic. Robert corresponded all his life with his British schoolmates and with Mrs. Dunne, the widow of the Elstree headmaster.

In 1893 the family returned to Chicago for the World's Fair, for which McCormick senior had served as commissioner to London, and which introduced electric power and the Ferris Wheel to the world. The following year, as his parents returned to England, Robert R. followed brother Medill and cousin Joe Patterson to Groton.

Founded by Massachusetts textile tycoons to gild the sons of Boston businessmen with the glitter of aristocracy, Groton was designed as an instant imitation of Tom Brown's Rugby. Its earnest headmaster, Endicott Peabody, son of a J. P. Morgan partner, copied his British model to the point of prescribing stiff collars and patent leather shoes at dinner. The British accent, with its broad *a* and vanishing *r,* was also a Groton staple, Boston boys coming by it naturally, and others (possibly including Franklin D. Roosevelt) adopting it via peer pressure. The McCormick boys had it from their English schooling, but their cousin Joe Patterson, a born rebel, stoutly resisted it.

Peabody, who had been converted at Cambridge to the true elitist religion, Episcopalianism, perceived the mission of the school as the instillation of "manly Christian character." In their mature years many of his boys, including both Robert McCormick and Franklin Roosevelt, thought he had been successful, though not necessarily with each other. Rather more obviously, the Reverend Peabody achieved a measure of the British ideal of distinguishing the upper class of society from the reeking herd by conferring, along with the indispensable diction, some light but runic intellectual baggage such as the names of the Latin poets.

The sense of Groton is best illustrated by an exchange of snobberies between the McCormick boys and their Boston and New York classmates. The easterners (possibly miffed by the McCormick accent) tried to put down the Chicagoans by insinuating that the Midwest lacked class. Robert informed his visiting father, who armed him with a reproof valiant: "Tell them they are descendants of Boston tradesmen and you are descended from Virginia gentlemen." McCormick senior, a University of Virginia Cavalier, grounded his own snobbery in his mother's family, the Grigsbys, a notch above the merely respectable McCormicks in the Shenandoah Valley social pecking order. The squelch was so successful that the eastern boys complained to the Reverend Peabody, who fussily told McCormick that he "didn't like sectional arguments."

Eastern parochialism also infected the curriculum. In history "we learned of Washington, of course, and Lincoln, but I think all the rest of their heroes were New Englanders." In retrospect McCormick also found fault with Groton's emphasis on "mediocre New England poets." Since in 1895 there were few non-New England poets in America, the offense apparently amounted to an emphasis on Longfellow and Whittier at the expense of

Keats and Shelley, and what McCormick looked back on as sectionalism the Reverend Peabody probably viewed as healthy American nationalism.

Once a boy was caught cheating in Latin by using a crib. Dr. Peabody solemnly called on any other boy who had a crib to come up and say so. Robert went forward: he had a copy of the new translation of the *Aeneid* by Secretary of the Navy Breckinridge Long that his grandmother had given him for Christmas, and that someone had packed in his luggage. He had purposely left it visible on his night table. To his surprise, the headmaster told him, "You had better put it in your drawer. It might tempt some other boy." In narrating the anecdote to his radio audience McCormick added his own thought about cribs—they could be useful in learning a language, as he had found in teaching French to Pershing's staff in 1917.

Robert's best subject was mathematics, where he finished second in his class and would have won the top prize except for a mistake in drawing a geometry problem. He recalled one master with irritation for discouraging him in music and writing, but the truth was, his talent did indeed lie in the math-science-engineering direction.

During an absence from school due to a bout with pneumonia, he added something to his education that was not on the Groton curriculum. His great aunt, Nettie Fowler McCormick, widow of Cyrus, arranged to have somebody teach him and some other boys "what was then known of electricity." McCormick and a neighbor boy built a telegraph line between their houses and "also made considerable money hanging electric bells in a day before there were either electrical contractors or electrical unions." He noted that the experience served him well later.

Another vacation, in the winter of 1894, was spent at Thomasville, Georgia, where Senator Mark Hanna, powerful leader of the Republican party and friend of Joseph Medill, had an estate. There he met notable guests, such as a Chicagoan named Herman Kohlsaat who after making his fortune baking bread and serving sandwiches to the masses had bought a newspaper, the *Inter-Ocean,* to indulge a taste for politics; and William McKinley, who was the choice of fellow Ohioan Hanna for the Republican nomination in 1896. Kohlsaat was helping clear up McKinley's debts. Other Republican leaders visited Thomasville to offer support, but fourteen-year-old Robert McCormick found more entertainment in Mrs. McKinley, who had epilepsy and sometimes "threw a fit" at the dining table. Older brother Medill McCormick fell in love with Hanna's daughter Ruth, to whom he became engaged the next winter.

Aside from Mrs. McKinley, recreation for Robert included quail shooting and archery, in which he experimented with techniques for increasing the power of the bow. Finding that he could attain maximum range by lying supine and bending the bow with his legs, he shot an arrow entirely out of the Hanna grounds and through a neighbor's window, a feat that terminated the sport for the summer.

Other vacations he spent with Grandfather Medill either at Medill's new Red Oaks Farm west of Chicago, whence Medill commuted to the Loop by carriage and train as easily as Wheaton residents do today, or at San Antonio, where he was with the old gentleman in his last months in 1898–1899. The rough quarter of San Antonio, not across the tracks but across the river, had nightly shootings, which Robert "of course . . . had to look at." He was a witness to "one rather large killing" for which nobody was arrested. He was also a witness to the fact that the Confederacy still lived. At the theater the orchestra played "The Star-Spangled Banner" in honor of army officers back from the Spanish-American War and nobody stood up except the officers themselves in the boxes, and in the pit, Robert R. McCormick all alone.

Grandfather Medill, a keen supporter of "the war to free Cuba," sent his grandson to the telegraph office one night with a message to Washington advising President McKinley to annex the Philippines (by coincidence, according to McKinley's account, God also gave him the same message). Next morning when Robert visited his room, Medill inquired, "What is the news this morning?" and died immediately, creating great last words.

In young McCormick's mind, the winter of 1898–1899 marked the end of boyhood. In the fall of 1899, again following the academic footsteps of brother Medill and his cousin Joe, he entered Yale.

In comparison with Groton, Yale was a little more democratic, with a sprinkling of boys from public high schools in New York and New England, a little less parochial, and more fun. McCormick had already fallen in love with Yale via the Frank Merriwell novels, and reality did not disappoint him. He remained a true Old Blue all his life. It took him five broadcasts in 1952 to ramble through his undergraduate years. Looking back on freshman year he could find no better way of illustrating how caught up he and his classmates were with the heady whirl of college life than to recollect that Kitchener's victory over the Sudanese in the battle of Omdurman failed to attract their notice. What Yale freshmen had on their minds was coloring meerschaum pipes, drinking beer at the Tontine, singing Yale songs ("For God, for country and for Yale" came out of sincere young faces), Bottle Night, when everybody threw bottles of water out of residence windows, and Freshman Rush, on Washington's Birthday, when the freshmen wore old plug hats to be snowballed by the upper classmen as they battled to seize the Sophomore Fence. The freshmen then graduated to silk hats, Mory's (McCormick became a member of the Cup Committee with the privilege of calling for the fabled Velvet Cup of champagne, ale, and liqueurs), going to class in evening clothes the morning after the junior prom, getting arrested, and heckling Democratic presidential candidate William Jennings Bryan (the class was 80 percent Republican).

McCormick was never arrested, but he once had to hide from the New Haven police. He had grown to his full six four, and one convivial evening had a "boyish row" with "a local politician" who evidently did not consider the row all that boyish, since he swore out a warrant for assault with intent to kill. But the policeman to whom the warrant was given remembered McCormick for helping him quell a disturbance among the current freshmen and sent a warning via one of McCormick's friends. The fugitive from justice escaped stylishly on a sailboat to Greenwich.

He joined Alpha Delta Phi fraternity and in senior year made Scroll and Key. Yet college had a serious side—he abandoned card-playing as a waste of time and did not slight classwork, though neither did he strive for academic distinction. "Membership in Phi Beta Kappa . . . we treated with contumely," he recalled. It was the heyday of "a gentleman's C's," a tradition rooted in patrician disdain for exam cramming. Yet the patrician did not seek out pipe courses. Electives had just been introduced at Yale, and among McCormick's choices were physics, mechanics, economics, and accounting, the last of immediate service in his role as treasurer of the University Club. In history he enjoyed an "excellent course in modern European history down to the death of Bismarck," in other words, to contemporary days, but a course in British constitutional history was a disappointment because the lecturer was old and feeble. English and French literature were taught, "but of American history and American literature . . . not one page."

Yale's treatment of history was standard in the East, though a yeasty change had already taken place farther west. The University of Michigan had introduced the study of America's own history to the college curriculum, and by 1903, when McCormick graduated, Harvard was gingerly borrowing Frederick Jackson Turner from the University of Wisconsin to teach Franklin D. Roosevelt and his classmates about the effect of the frontier on U.S. development. Turner was a rare academic bird in his emphasis on the social and economic instead of the political and military. Roosevelt was far more enthralled by Alfred Thayer Mahan, the scholarly naval officer who had become the prophet of the age of imperialism. McCormick too knew all about Mahan, whose son had been a Groton schoolmate. Mahan's massively erudite *The Influence of Seapower Upon History* perceived the annals of mankind as a sort of athletic tournament among the armed forces of the various ancient and modern nations. Even within this narrow focus Mahan distorted grossly, viewing the cartographically overwhelming British Empire as the ultimate trophy of the competition, a notion destined to influence the global concepts of both Roosevelt and McCormick.

During summers McCormick's education was furthered in several directions. That of his freshman year he spent hunting in Idaho. The following summer he explored Hudson's Bay where he shot two polar bears on his twenty-first birthday. In his junior year his parents insisted that he visit them in Europe. Robert McCormick senior had just become one of America's first ambassadors, the nation's foreign service having been upgraded as a result of Europe's startled reaction to the facile U.S. military-naval victory over Spain. The Emperor Franz Joseph of Austria-Hungary was the last of the European heads of state to make the change, out of either conservatism or sympathy with his fellow Hapsburgs in Spain. His delay benefited Robert S. McCormick, whose presentation as U.S. minister apparently reminded the old monarch about the new American status, because he ordered the coach-and-four in which McCormick had arrived at the palace to be replaced by an ambassadorial coach-and-six for the return trip to the legation, forthwith raised to an embassy.

The McCormicks' house in Vienna had belonged to the family of the Baroness Maria Vetsera, tragic heroine of the Mayerling episode in which Archduke Rudolf killed himself and his mistress. Young Robert occupied the baroness's former apartment, separated from the royal castle by a stone wall over which Rudolf had clambered nightly twenty-five years earlier. Somebody challenged Robert to duplicate the feat, which he did, without stopping to think that the archduke might have had assistance on his own side, where the ground dropped off. "I found myself on the other side of the wall, the top well beyond my reach. I had to jump several times before I was able to get back."

With his father he visited Constantinople, whose sights included veiled women, filth, wild dogs, and the Sultan Abdul Hamid driving to the mosque followed by carriages filled with his harem. Together with a Russian, an Englishman, and another American, Robert swam the Hellespont.

En route home he stopped off in Paris, saw Santos-Dumont fly his new dirigible, and with friends rented a balloon that carried them to the village of Tournon, earning on their return a small parade up the Champs Elysées and election to the Aero Club of France.

But the time had come for serious decisions. What to do after Yale? In the light of his admiration for Grandfather Medill it might have seemed natural for him to gravitate to the *Tribune,* where brother Medill McCormick and cousin Joe Patterson were already employed. Not so, however; his parents, and evidently his mother in particular, had decided that the family interest in the paper belonged to Medill McCormick alone. Possibly too the professor who disparaged his writing skill (he was actually a reasonably competent writer) made him think himself unsuited to the newspaper business.

Whatever the reason, he never entertained any intention of becoming an editor or publisher. Impressed by the navy's heroics in 1898, McCormick considered entering the Naval Academy, but his eyesight fell short of navy standards. Another direction was presented to him by accident. A geology course at Yale had failed to interest him (it was mostly about fossils) and his indifference led to his failing the exam. When most of the back row in which he sat was flunked in disgrace for cribbing, an idea occurred to him. He appealed to the professor: If he were not passed, everybody would think he had been one of the cheaters. Rewarding him with a passing grade, the professor told him that though he was not much of a geologist, he "would make a good lawyer." When not long after, Justice Brewer of the Supreme Court spoke at Yale and reminded the boys of all the famous Yale law graduates, such as William Howard Taft, McCormick decided to become a lawyer. The decision elevated him to a new class of supereducated Americans. In the 1890s only 4 percent of the college-age population went to college at all, and few lawyers learned their law at a university. The idea of crowning a liberal-arts education with a professional degree, rather than substituting one for the other, was still brand new.

Briefly he considered Yale Law School, but his father thought he should enroll at Northwestern because his practice would be in Chicago. He accepted the parental recommendation, though leaving New Haven was a wrench: "In senior year we were lords of creation and were quite oblivious of our approaching end. . . . We were like gods of mythology, blessed with eternal youth. . . . And then, like a blast of lightning, the blow fell. College days were over!"

A College Boy in Politics

TO the advantage of Northwestern Law School that Robert's father had pointed out, that of introducing himself to the Chicago community, Robert added one of his own—living in Chicago would enhance his opportunity to play polo, a cultural refinement in which Chicago excelled Cambridge and New Haven. After an invigorating autumn of law books and polo he chose for his winter vacation a trip to Panama, where Teddy Roosevelt was causing things to happen. McCormick and a friend arrived at the moment of the landing of the U.S. Marines. Only later did he learn what Teddy was up to, and when he did, he did not approve, judging it "a questionable deal," and the canal treaty "very burdensome to Panama." In Chicago, though, the *Tribune* joined most of the press in enthusiastic indorsement of TR's coup.

Back home he was well into his spring term when one day Republican boss Fred Busse called on him. Busse had a flattering proposal: Would he like to run for alderman of his native Twenty-first Ward (today the Forty-second), the Gold Coast plus the slums and dives of North Clark Street to the west?

A twenty-three-year-old candidate for public office was unusual, but less so if he had a well-known name and some money. In McCormick's case there was also the *Tribune,* where Medill was now serving as treasurer. Robert's Groton-Yale, English boarding-school background was viewed by some as a handicap, but might instead have been a refreshing change from the political fashion of the nineties when, according to Mayor Carter Harrison, Jr., another Yale man though a Democrat, Chicago's civic affairs had been "the exclusive appanage of a low-browed, dull-witted, base-minded gang of plug-uglies, with no outstanding characteristics beyond an unquenchable lust for money."

The *Inter-Ocean* took note of the elitist image of the young candidate:

"What are we going to do with two silk stocking aldermen?" was the question that agitated citizens of the 21st Ward yesterday who wear cotton socks or no socks at all.

The *Record-Herald* observed that "Rutherford R. McCormick" would tower over his colleagues in the city council in at least one respect, since he had been the second tallest man in his class at Yale. Though not exactly handsome, his features were attractive in an open, honest, college athlete sort of way and, though not an orator (his voice was deep but gruff), he came across well in small groups.

Kicking off his campaign on St. Patrick's Day with "music, red fire, and oratory," McCormick announced his intention of meeting every man in the Twenty-first Ward before the election. He set out next morning with a party of aides and reporters, sticking out a hand to each male passerby and informing him: "My name is McCormick. I am a candidate for alderman for this ward and I want to meet you." When they reached Rush Street, already renowned for its bars, one of the aides wondered if they shouldn't pass it by. "Not on your life," said the candidate, well aware that under universal male suffrage the saloon was the citadel of democracy. Inside he began by shaking the hand of the saloonkeeper, and gratified both him and his morning clientele by the invitation, "Everyone step up and have a drink on me." The assembled breakfast club watched to see what the big college boy would drink. It was straight rye, which he poured himself. "Have another, boys," he urged, and soon they were calling him Mac. "I won't miss a man from Lake Shore Drive to the soap factories if I can help it," the *Inter-Ocean* quoted him as promising.

In more formal campaigning he addressed a crowd estimated at three thousand in the North Side Turner Hall, pledging settlement of the traction question, a new city charter, a North Side bathing beach, and a new bridge over the river. Striking a reform posture, he got the police to raid the small "levee"—brothel district—on the Near North Side, and was deluged with calls for help from other parts of the city.

The Democrats won city-wide in 1904, reelecting Carter Harrison to a fourth term as mayor. Bathhouse John Coughlin, boss of the vice-and-crime-soaked First Ward, congratulated Harrison: "Mr. Mayor, you won because of the well-known honesty which has caricatured your every administration." But the Twenty-first Ward returned Republican R. R. McCormick, who took his seat on the council alongside the alumni of the streets and saloons. He got along all right, though arousing a certain restlessness on one occasion when he hastened to City Hall direct from the polo field and strode into the council chamber in jodhpurs.

The burning issue of the day was transit—private versus public ownership. Named to the Transportation Committee, McCormick took a moderate position in favor of private ownership (making him a "traction company alderman" in the Hearst *Examiner*'s eyes), but succeeded in pleasing neither side. He must have pleased Fred Busse, however, because at the end of the year he was summoned out of a committee meeting by Busse and two other bosses who startled him by offering him the nomination for president of the Sanitary District.

The Sanitary District was a giant engineering project that formed Chicago's answer to the ominous public health problem of the day, contaminated drinking water. The problem was by no means confined to Chicago, but Chicago had a rather special form of it. The very convenience of Lake Michigan created the city's dilemma—how to prevent storm and sewage water from being carried by the Chicago River straight into the very part of the lake that the drinking water was drawn from. A daring early solution, a tunnel six hundred feet under the lake driven without a tunneling shield (invented in Britain but not yet known in America), saved Chicago for several years. But as the city grew, its flood of pollution—the river was lined with slaughterhouses—engulfed the intake crib. A second crib was built farther out, but after a storm nobody wanted to drink the dark and dubious liquid coming out of the water taps.

The ultimate solution, the reversal of the current of the Chicago River to make it run backward into the Mississippi system, was undertaken in 1889 with the help of a strong campaign in the *Tribune*, and was followed by the laying of giant interceptor sewers and a canal to collect all the sewage, industrial and domestic, and deposit it in the river to be carried westward. This work was in an advanced stage when Robert R. McCormick ran for president of the Sanitary District in 1905.

Undertaking two Chicago-style campaigns in two years meant strenuous politicking: "If you were to say that I have felt obliged to spend 90 percent of my time in saloons, and the remaining 10 percent in barrooms," he wrote the secretary of his Yale class, "you have it about correct." All the same, he campaigned in style and relative comfort—a picture in the *Record-Herald* showed him in the rear seat of an open limousine.

According to his own account he would not have run at all if a letter from his parents in Europe had reached Chicago in time. In Russia McCormick senior had won plaudits for inducing the czar's government to accept the passports of American Jews, and (according to his son) had gotten the Russian-Japanese peace talks started, but Teddy Roosevelt, gunning for the Nobel Peace Prize, apparently found him in the way, and transferred him to Paris. From there Katherine wrote offering Robert McCormick a gift of $20,000 as an inducement to come keep his parents company. Kate might better have offered the money to son Medill, but she had made up her mind that Medill was destined to take over the *Tribune* (whence, incidentally, her money came—the paper was now very profitable). Son Robert explained that he was committed to running for office, but despite what he said later it is hard to believe he would have accepted anyway. Whatever he was ready for, it was not retirement.

Campaigning for the presidency of the Sanitary District, he had to struggle to separate himself from the rich McCormicks of McCormickville. Democratic precinct workers told voters that he was the McCormick who had just married Edith Rockefeller (that was his cousin Harold Fowler McCormick), and the *Examiner* claimed "Rich McCormick Family Hopes to Save $150,000" through his election. But aided by a local Republican sweep, he won election. In office he proved not only refreshingly incorruptible but highly competent and zealous to a fault. Though the demagogic *Examiner* called him a "political Romanoff with autocratic powers," he reorganized the accounting system while completing the various construction projects, tramping through the mud in high boots and one night swimming ashore when his rowboat capsized in the Illinois River. The laboratory he established to study bacterial purification of sewage, a brand-new concept, eventually grew into the immense and technically innovative Chicago sewage treatment system.

The project that interested him most was the hydroelectric power plant at Lockport, where the water flowing through the Sanitary Canal en route to the Mississippi system dropped thirty-four feet. As he noted, "The normal thing would have been to sell the power in bulk at the powerhouse to the Chicago Edison Company." But McCormick was not about to give anything away out of respect for the principle of private enterprise. The price offered by the Chicago Edison Company was "so far below its value . . . that he compelled us to go into local distribution." "He" was Samuel Insull, a British immigrant who had served as right-hand man to Thomas Edison at Menlo Park and was on his way to building an electric-power empire. As McCormick prepared to sell power for streetlights and water pumping directly to the city, the vexed utilities magnate attempted an end run, sending aides to Springfield to bribe the legislature to vote against completion of the necessary works, but a bond issue to pay the costs gained voter support and put an end to the battle.

McCormick's attitude won him respect and ink. The University of Chicago invited him to address its midyear graduating class, which he treated to some Teddy Rooseveltian rhetoric. He asserted that when he had graduated from Yale he had already known that Charles Yerkes (protagonist of Theodore Dreiser's novels *The Financier* and *The Titan* and an old *Tribune* target) was "a scoundrel who had been trying for years to corrupt the City Council of Chicago and the [state] legislature," but was shocked to discover that Yerkes had enjoyed the collaboration of "some of the best-known bankers of Chicago." He further accused of malfeasance the presidents of insurance companies and other princes of LaSalle Street. Outright attempts to bribe the Sanitary Board were rare, he said, but there was widespread intimidation by "plutocrats who believe the government must and shall be run as they direct." He even threw in a knock for Chauncey Depew, defender of the railroad trusts and Republican party stalwart. Should Chauncey visit Yale again, McCormick predicted the students would carry him home once more as they had in his own day, but this time it would be "on a rail."

Such unexpectedly Populist language caused the Hearst *American* to send an interviewer, who reported under a three-column head with a full-length photo, "Rich Man Tells How to Crush Rule of the Rich." Elaborating on the intimidation charge, McCormick told the interviewer that he had been "the repeated target for veiled threats in letters and conversations."

"Has wealth itself a degrading or dangerous influence on the possessor?" the interviewer asked (a much debated point in muckraking 1906). McCormick, who scarcely thought of himself as a "rich man," held "no such view. The fact that there are anarchists among the plutocrats is not an indictment against all persons of means. I am no Socialist. I do not feel my conscience pricking me on to any attack on wealthy men merely because of their wealth, any more than to attack the poor because some may be bomb throwers." He thought a rich man could make it into heaven, but, answering a question about rich U.S. senators, indorsed the Populist proposal of direct election of senators by the people, a major reform in which he had no idea that he himself was to play a part.

The morning Hearst *Examiner* also gave him some friendly coverage in his fight with the City Council over supplying power to local industry:

3 ALDERMEN BLOCK CITY COMPETITION
WITH ELECTRIC LIGHT TRUST

Sanitary District President Charges
Committee Is Aiding the Trust

Meantime he ran into problems on the engineering front. In the work at Lockport, the contractor failed to meet his deadline. After sufficient warning, McCormick took decisive action. Getting the board of trustees to order the contractor to cease work, he hired his own day labor, which he armed with the contractor's machines. The pained contractor cried socialism, but McCormick retorted that it was "a necessity to preserve the public interest."

On the Evanston canal, a subsidiary work, he encountered a technical problem, the determination of the most economical cross section, to provide even flow where the height of the banks varied. He had enough mathematics to prepare the equation but not to solve it. Neither could his engineers. While they were scratching their heads, a young man named Ralph Burke, fresh out of college, came in to ask for a job. McCormick gave him the problem. "In his embarrassment among so many older men, he asked if he could retire to the other room. When he applied his calculus, he brought in the solution." Burke was hired, beginning a long Chicago career.

Another young engineer who got his start on the Evanston canal came to McCormick's attention when he punched a recalcitrant worker in the jaw. Though the engineer was a Democrat, McCormick rewarded him with a promotion. Later he recommended the ready-fisted supervisor for the job of chief engineer of the Sanitary District, lending a valuable boost to the career of Edward J. Kelly, future mayor of Chicago and power in the national Democratic party.

The problem of disposing of sewage in the Indiana sand dunes improbably led to what McCormick described as "the greatest thrill of my life." An engineer consulted on the dunes question was Octave Chanute, the French-American glider pioneer. From Chanute McCormick learned that "two men named Wright" were planning to demonstrate heavier-than-air flight at Fort Myer, near Washington. The Wrights' historic Kitty Hawk adventure of three years earlier had passed unnoticed by the press, as had their more recent development of a plane that could turn and remain aloft for a substantial period of time. McCormick journeyed to Washington, where he had lunch in a party with Alice Roosevelt, who drove everybody to Fort Myer in her electric automobile. There was a long wait for the too strong wind to subside. Then, in the gathering shadows, the Wright brothers brought their machine from under cover. It rose, circled the field, and landed safely, to the applause of the small throng of spectators. Decades later McCormick could "recollect no other incident that has affected me as much."

While still directing the Sanitary District, McCormick completed his law courses and, though never taking a degree (a common practice), passed his bar examination. He then opened a law office with a Northwestern classmate, Samuel Emory Thomason, and a third partner, Stuart Shepard. The location of the new firm's office, in the seventeen-story *Tribune* building erected in 1902 at Madison and Dearborn, implied that it would get some law business from the paper. That, however, was as far as McCormick's ambitions went at that moment with respect to the *Tribune,* still reserved by his mother for older brother Medill.

For the time being, Medill and Kate were marking time, imperious Kate rather more impatiently than convivial Medill. Grandfather Joseph Medill had sought to keep the *Tribune* in his family by setting up a corporation with two thousand closely held shares and three trustees, the husbands of his two daughters and his own lawyer. That did not overcome the problem of sisterly rivalry between the McCormicks and the Pattersons. Upon Joseph Medill's death, management of the paper had passed into the hands of Robert W. Patterson, the Presbyterian minister's son who had married Elinor Medill. Patterson proved himself a competent and industrious newspaperman, not lacking in courage and integrity. During the bitter Pullman strike of 1894, Joseph Medill, in a paroxysm of strikebreaking fury, had ordered the city editor to preface every mention of Eugene Debs, the heroic strike leader, with the epithet *Dictator*. Next morning Patterson found the front page sprinkled with the term *Dictator Debs*. Obtaining an explanation from the city editor, he countermanded Medill's order and pronounced the day gone by when news columns could be suborned to editorial bias. The luckless city editor put out a paper without the word *Dictator* and was called to account by Medill, who, however, after a discussion gave in to Patterson.

Patterson got along better with his father-in-law than with his wife, his marriage proving to be one of those tight-lipped Victorian domestic calamities that imply awkward problems with sex. The couple addressed each other as Mr. Patterson and Mrs. Patterson, Robert W. turned to the Chicago Club, and Elinor established a second home in Washington, where she built a classic-revival mansion at 15 Dupont Circle.

Meantime Elinor's son Joe Patterson had finished with Groton-Yale a couple of years ahead of Robert R. McCormick and after an adventure in China, covering the Boxer Rebellion for the Hearst papers, had gone to work for the *Tribune* where, inevitably, he became the rival of Medill McCormick.

Neither of the two actually won the competition. First of all, they simultaneously disappointed their parental backers. Medill was victimized by a drinking problem that may have started at Yale, and that discouraged the directors from enlarging his title from treasurer to publisher. Joe Patterson showed an even more shocking tendency. In appearance a plain-as-an-old-shoe midwesterner with a trace of stubbornness in his jaw, he entered politics not as a normal Republican but as a Democrat, first getting elected to the legislature and next winning an appointment as Mayor Dunne's Commissioner of Public Works. Much worse followed. Finding it impossible to work within the establishment, Joe in 1906 flabbergasted family and friends by writing an open letter to the nation's press (he was temporarily living at his mother's Dupont Circle palazzo) announcing his conversion to socialism:

> Our laws . . . are ridiculous and obsolete . . . designed always to uphold capital at the expense of the community. . . . I realized soon after I took office [as

Commissioner of Public Works] that to fight privilege under the present laws would be a jest.

Promptly invited to join the national executive committee of the Socialist party, he addressed Chicago proletarians in a midwestern twang that he had rebelliously preserved against the diction prescribed by Groton:

> You will never get anything from us capitalists by coming along with your hats in your hand and asking for it. The only way you can get it is to fetch us down.

He pained family and fellow patricians even more with a book, *Confessions of a Drone,* in which he described his start in life:

> I do not think that it was entirely natural aptitude that marked me out for a university education, since I remember that frequently I had to pay money to tutors to drill into my head information of a remarkably simple character. I was fond of a good time, and that I had. . . . Having in this pleasant fashion achieved my education, I went to work in my father's business. I "started at the bottom," as the saying goes. I became a reporter at $15 a week. If my father had been a broker, I would have started in to sweep out the office at $3 a week. Most of my college friends who went into Wall Street seem to have done just that. But I knew I was playacting all the time, just as they did.

The following year Patterson published a novel, *A Little Brother of the Rich,* a reverse Horatio Alger tale in which the hero, a poor but honest youth from the Midwest, enrolls at Yale and gets corrupted by his classmates into spending his days making money in Wall Street and drinking cocktails at the club. "My whole life is a horrible lie!" he concludes. A similar facile cynicism characterized *The Fourth Estate,* a play Patterson wrote in collaboration with a woman named Harriet Ford, which ran successfully on Broadway in 1909.

The year *A Little Brother of the Rich* was published (1908) the Patterson-McCormick feud exploded. As if having a Socialist son was not a sufficient cross, Robert Patterson found himself simultaneously oppressed by a madcap daughter. Cissy Patterson had acted out a popular fiction and movie charade by marrying a worthless European aristocrat and becoming an unhappy American countess. Her count was a Polish subject of the czar, and in her fight over custody of their child, Cissy appealed for help. In Europe to mediate, Robert Patterson ran into sister-in-law Kate McCormick, seething with a conviction that Patterson was responsible for Teddy Roosevelt's having retired her husband from his ambassadorship. But Kate was Machiavellian too: She offered to use her husband's connections with the St. Petersburg court on behalf of Cissy Patterson in return for the *Tribune*'s influence toward landing them a new diplomatic post.

Kate was a poor judge of men. Outraged, Patterson turned around and penned a blistering letter to new President Taft telling the whole story, including the fact that Kate had earlier misrepresented herself as owning the *Tribune*. Taft intervened with the czar to get Cissy her child, and left the McCormicks permanently retired.

Baffled, embittered Kate McCormick stayed in France and paid only fleeting visits to Chicago, as on the occasion of installing her ailing and probably alcoholic husband in a nursing home in Hinsdale. One morning in April 1917 John McCutcheon was accosted from behind by Kate while looking in a bookstore window on Michigan Avenue. Kate's query: "What do you think of this god-damn war?" To sustain competition with sister Elinor, Kate bought a palace of her own on Massachusetts Avenue in Washington (today the Brazilian Embassy) but spent most of her time in Paris, where she had an apartment at the Ritz, Place Vendôme. Around the *Tribune* a jest ran that if either of the sisters was in Chicago and the other appeared, the cashier had a standing order to buy the earlier arrival a train ticket out of town.

Poor Kate was not born to be happy, or even placated. As long as Medill remained alive, she stubbornly refused to switch her maternal hopes from the unpromising to the promising son. Her favoritism had no discernible effect on Robert, who remained dutiful and even affectionate, corresponding and visiting throughout her life, and spending Christmas in Washington whenever she was there. She had no use for any of the other McCormicks, and joined enthusiastically in promoting the tale that Cyrus hadn't really invented the reaper. The illusion of which Robert Patterson complained, that she owned the *Tribune* (she owned substantial stock), persisted, and she even sometimes meddled in the newspaper's affairs in small, mischievous ways. Some thought Kate might better have been a man. Her womanly feelings were evidently frustrated. She once told Maryland Mathison Hooper (later Robert McCormick's second wife), "You're so lovely—you must have many temptations. Take them. My only regret is that I didn't take all of mine."

Kate's intrigues in favor of son Medill were in vain. On his return to the paper from a European stay in 1909 the board of directors named him first vice-president, but next year he was back in Europe to dry out. Medill's lawyer, Levi Mayer, conceived the idea of Kate's buying out Robert Patterson, who was having problems with the bottle himself. Kate lacked the resources to purchase a majority of the stock, so presumably Mayer intended to organize some sort of consortium. Robert McCormick perceived the scheme as designed to win a major role in the corporation for the lawyer, and advised his mother against it. Did he also see a possible future for himself in the *Tribune* in the light of Medill's problem? Possibly, but he also turned down a proposition by his cousin Joe Patterson, with whom, family feud and Joe's socialism notwithstanding, he got along excellently. Joe's father had followed Medill McCormick to Europe to take the cure, so Joe proposed that he and Robert move into the power vacuum left by the departed drinkers. With the backing of their two mothers the coup seemed feasible, but McCormick held back: "Aside from the fact that we had no voting powers I felt Mr. Patterson's long service in the paper entitled him to great consideration, and that he should not be removed."

Patterson senior presently returned from Europe and made moves to propitiate some of his critics and to keep Medill blood in the top management of the paper. He made son Joe secretary of the *Tribune* and nephew Robert treasurer, the post his brother, Medill, had briefly held. This last appointment came about following a curious incident related by McCormick:

> I was accustomed to box at the Chicago Athletic Club and afterwards take a plunge in the swimming tank. One day a friend told me there was a man in the hot room, evidently intoxicated, signing *Tribune* checks. I found this to be so and told Mr. R. W. Patterson, president of the Tribune Company. . . . He said, "We will correct that by making you treasurer and you can sign the checks." He had the board elect me treasurer, but neglected to attach a salary to the position.

All the same, Patterson took McCormick's role seriously, as was indicated by his selling the new treasurer ten shares of the closely held Tribune Corporation stock at three thousand dollars apiece, giving him the voting power he had lacked.

In the spring of 1910 McCormick happened to visit Washington. At Aunt Elinor's Dupont Circle palace he encountered Uncle Robert Patterson making a rare call on his wife, and received some words of encouragement on enlarging his function at the *Tribune*. His brother, Medill, had just handed in his resignation. McCormick returned to Chicago to think about it. A couple of days later his office telephone rang. It was the chief switchboard operator, with a message: Mr. R. W. Patterson had died in Philadelphia.

McCormick went at once to Patterson's office to seek information. To his surprise, he found assembled there the principal corporate stockholders: William G. Beale, Joseph Medill's elderly lawyer and (along with Robert W. Patterson and McCormick's father) a trustee of the Medill Trust; Alfred Cowles II, son of Medill's business manager; Horace White, ancient Medill associate and long editor of the *New York Post;* Azariah T. Galt, trustee for the Bross-Lloyd estate; "and one or two of the very small stockholders."

The meeting was not concerned with Robert Patterson's death. It had been called by Patterson himself for a momentous purpose: to consider an offer for the purchase of the *Tribune.* The offer was from Victor Fremont Lawson, publisher of the *Record-Herald* and *Daily News,* and the price bid was $10 million.

Had Patterson lived a couple of days longer, McCormick was certain the sale would have gone through and the *Chicago Tribune* would have had a different history. But though he stood to make $20,000 personally on the deal, "the idea of selling the *Tribune* appalled me"—and at length he won agreement to postpone the decision to sell. Alfred Cowles stipulated that McCormick enter actively into the management of the paper. McCormick expressed himself as willing, though he wondered uneasily what his mother and her sister, who had agreed to the sale, would think.

After a number of meetings and discussions, McCormick found himself delegated to break the news to Victor Lawson. Lawson, a bearded editorial autocrat thirty years his senior, did not react kindly. He "was very angry and said that unless we carried out the sale, there would be a newspaper war; that he would reduce the price of the *Record-Herald* to one cent, and that his great experience in newspaper publishing and our disorganization would destroy the *Tribune.*" In his nervousness during the highly charged interview, McCormick found himself lighting one cigarette after another. He made a resolution, and quit smoking for life, though apparently he backslid, because he later attributed his abandonment of the habit to a throat irritation from getting gassed in World War I. Lawson ended by sweetening his offer. McCormick promised to convey the new terms to his mother, his aunt, and lawyer Beale, all of whom were now in Europe. He had made up his mind, however, and was confident that he could persuade the others.

Combining two missions, he took with him George W. Wisner, assistant chief engineer of the Sanitary District, to check out the new sewage disposal plants in Berlin and Birmingham and to inspect the new Manchester Ship Canal. They sailed in August (1910) on the *Lusitania.* The journey was satisfactorily negative on all counts—none of the European engineering works offered technical insights unknown to the Americans, and mother, aunt, and Beale agreed to let the answer to Lawson stand. Lawson promptly carried out his threat and lowered the newsstand price of the *Record-Herald* (which he had intended to merge with the more prosperous *Tribune*) from two cents to one.

Coupled with the pressure from the other morning competitor, Hearst's *Chicago Examiner,* which already sold for a penny, the price war posed genuine danger to the *Tribune,* even though it was the richest of the three in ad revenue.

McCormick was confident the paper could ride out the storm, and he foresaw a future intimacy between its career and his. But exactly what form the union would take was unclear, because his term of office as president of the Sanitary District was ending and he had to run for reelection. Not only did the post satisfy his taste for practical and constructive work, but it threw open a wide political gate. At twenty-nine he was a power in the Illinois Republican party and was becoming well known to voters ("Shows City Way to Save Million in Electricity," and "Wants All Chicago Lighted from Canal," the *Tribune* typically said of him, though the Democratic *Examiner* claimed: "Sanitary Tax Is Swelled Over $32,624,000 by GOP Board" and "Do Nothing Is Called Policy of President McCormick"). He had already been tempted to run for mayor. A reelection victory in November 1910 held out the promise of a stepping-stone to Congress or even the governor's mansion.

Democrat Ed Kelly thought Robert McCormick so sure of winning that he declined to run against him, but Teddy Roosevelt and William Howard Taft split the Republican party into liberal and conservative wings and in November the Democrats had their biggest inning in years, winning twenty-six governorships and the presidency of the Chicago Sanitary District. MCCORMICK, TRIBUNE CANDIDATE, BEATEN chortled the *Examiner,* which claimed that its own groundless charges of "waste and corruption" had decided the election. There was more than party ideology involved in the *Examiner*'s jubilation. The newsstand war was on, or more precisely on once more. Yet the *Examiner* would have been better off if McCormick had gone to Washington or Springfield.

CHAPTER FOUR

Competition, Chicago Style

WHILE *Tribune* president Robert Patterson and first vice-president Medill McCormick shuttled between the cure in Europe and the disease in Chicago, the *Tribune*'s management was left in the hands of the second vice-president. This executive was a man not only able, but also very willing to shoulder the responsibility. Bulldog-faced James M. Keeley, like his wealthy friend Samuel Insull, was an immigrant Britisher endowed with talent and a driving energy fueled by plenty of ambition. He had worked his way up from reporter to city editor to managing editor and along the way had scored historic scoops. In 1898 Keeley had arranged with the *New York World* to share a correspondent with Commodore Dewey's Pacific squadron, and when Dewey sailed secretly to attack the Spanish fleet in Manila Bay Keeley held the presses at the *Tribune* night after night hoping for a flash. The Spanish governor refused to let Dewey use the Manila cable to report his victory, and the three correspondents with him (two represented Chicago papers) raced for Hong Kong on the same dispatch boat. The *World* and *Tribune* man beat the other two by an expensive ruse, filing a very terse dispatch at the "urgent" rate—$9.90 a word. His wire reached New York too late for the *World,* which had just finished its press run and failed to get out an extra. Telephoned on to Chicago it gave the *Tribune* a terrific world beat, one of the bronze front pages on the Tower facade today. When Keeley had his paper on the street he telephoned the White House to wake up President McKinley and give him the news.

A few years later (1906) Keeley executed a coup single-handed when he followed an absconding Chicago banker to Africa, captured him, and brought him back. En route home Keeley and his prisoner became friends, and when the banker was paroled Keeley got him a job working for Samuel Insull, who many years later himself fled abroad. Still another Keeley claim to fame was his initiation of the *Tribune*'s long crusade against July 4 fireworks, which ultimately saved thousands of children's lives and limbs while ruining the Fourth of July for all the others.

Like so many old-time newspaper editors, Keeley was an unbridled autocrat, inspiring fear in top subordinates and awe in reporters. When he wished to make a direct assignment, he employed the third person, addressing the city editor in the reporter's presence. His ascendancy at the *Tribune* was scarcely limited by ineffectual Medill McCormick or faltering Robert Patterson even before the former's resignation and the latter's sudden death in 1910. In 1909 Keeley himself came close to leaving. A messenger bearing an attractive offer from another publisher stopped off at the Chicago Athletic Club for a game of billiards and by the time he reached the *Tribune* Keeley had signed a new contract as managing editor.

The publisher who had sought to hire Keeley away was the same Victor Fremont Lawson, guiding genius of the *Record-Herald* and *Daily News,* who tried to buy the *Tribune* (and Keeley along with it) in 1910. Lawson's father, one of Chicago's many immigrant Norwegians, had made a million dollars in garment manufacture, printing, real estate, and other enterprises and lost most of it in the Great Fire. Victor went to work in the family printing plant, which published the only Norwegian daily in the United States and also printed, among other jobs, the struggling *Chicago Daily News,* started on a shoestring by an ex-*Tribune* newsboy and reporter named Melville Stone. When the *News*'s failure to pay its bills brought up the possibility of a takeover by the printer, the Lawson family lawyer advised him, "Fremont, don't touch it with a ten-foot pole." Later, when the paper was a success, Lawson chided the lawyer, "What do you think of the *Daily News* now?" The attorney replied glumly, "I think, Fremont, that fools have all the luck."

Lawson was no fool and neither was Stone. Borrowing the idea and some of the crew of Joseph Pulitzer's trend-setting *New York World,* Stone introduced the first graphics—drawings on chalked plate—into Chicago journalism. Two years later, in 1885, Lawson and Stone copied a Pulitzer promotion stunt by renting a battery of artillery and firing a one hundred-gun salute over Lake Michigan to celebrate the *Daily News*'s achievement of 100,000 circulation, far above that of its competitors (the *Tribune*'s was 36,000). Lawson also pioneered many newspaper advances, such as full-page ads (the first was placed by Marshall Field executive Harry Selfridge, later founder of Selfridge's of London), branch advertising offices, mechanical typesetting (Lawson and Stone invested in Ottmar Mergenthaler while he was still getting bugs out of his Linotype), and wire service (with Joseph Medill they helped start the Western Associated Press, parent of the modern AP).

The *Record-Herald,* Lawson's morning paper, was the offspring of amalgamations of a number of unsuccessful and semisuccessful ventures that he had acquired in payment of printing bills. It was Chicago's largest morning paper, as the *Daily News* was the largest evening. The Lawson papers, like the *Tribune,* were distinguished by strong news coverage, somewhat more sedate than such scandal-prone rivals as the *Times,* forever memorialized in journalistic history by its headline over a story concerning the hanging of four tardily converted sinners: JERKED TO JESUS! The *Times* filled columns with the crime and vice that were indeed a conspicuous part of the Chicago scene. The "resorts" of the South Side "levee" covered many blocks, and ranged in opulence from sordidly functional rooming houses to the pretentious "Everleigh Club," run by the hilariously named Everleigh sisters, who went so far as to publish an illustrated advertising brochure.

But when it came to sensational news presentation, turn-of-the-century Chicago discovered that up to now it had seen nothing. In 1900 William Randolph Hearst opened the *Chicago American* on Madison Street with effects that reverberated through Chicago's twentieth-century history. Rich, aggressive, a born maverick, untroubled by tradition or ethics, Hearst came to Chicago not to make money—his father had been the luckiest prospector ever to pickax into a Nevada silver lode—but to get himself elected president. He proved an indifferent politician but a born newspaperman. Hearst senior had bought a U.S. senatorship from the California legislature and for PR purposes had picked up a grubby San Francisco newspaper, the *Examiner,* which son William Randolph, expelled from Harvard, cajoled as a sort of graduation present.

Like Victor Lawson, Hearst learned much from Joseph Pulitzer, but proved a daring and creative innovator himself. His single-minded devotion to selling the largest possible number of newspapers every day accorded with his political ambitions, since every newsstand purchaser was a prospective voter, but his manic devotion was rooted in something deeper, the true editor's passion for attracting readers merely for the sake of attracting them. He sold his papers for a penny and made them generous in size (sixteen pages whether the advertising was there or not). He printed multiple editions and numerous extras, flooding newsstands at all hours of the day and night. He hired the best people he could get—Ambrose Bierce in San Francisco, Arthur Brisbane and Stephen Crane in New York—at whatever it cost. He stressed the kind of news that he sensed, with a sure instinct, would grab the passerby, via headlines nobody could miss, such as HUNGRY, FRANTIC FLAMES LEAPING HIGHER, HIGHER, HIGHER WITH DESPERATE DESIRE. He crusaded both pro bono publico, denouncing the trusts, and atrocity-peddling jingo, demanding war with Spain. He got the war but despite dogged efforts never won election to anything except two terms in Congress from New York, and a near-miss at mayor of New York (he was jobbed out of it by Tammany men who dumped bales of Hearst ballots in the East River).

When he launched his invasion of Chicago, he sent right-hand man Arthur Brisbane ahead with an advance crew from New York. The dilapidated building they rented on West Madison Street presently won a nickname earned earlier by Hearst's *San Francisco Examiner*—"the mad-house." At the *Chicago American,* reporters and editors were hired, fired, and rehired daily, news was reported, distorted, and invented, headlines varied from large to gigantic (the 480-point filled the top half of page one) and from black to red.

The heads were designed to make the *American* highly visible on down-town newsstands, but in Chicago a slight problem developed. Though in accordance with Hearst's now established pattern, his evening paper came out at midday, hours ahead of the competition, it had trouble finding room on the stands. The other publishers ganged up to keep the interloper out. There was something personal about it—not only did they not want the added competition, but they found Hearst objectionable. He soon became so.

Hiring personnel from competitors was a standard Hearst technique. The *Tribune* and other Chicago papers were driven to protect themselves with higher pay for editors and reporters, but when the *American* found the circulation man it wanted in the person of a twenty-five-year-old assistant at the *Tribune,* it offered enough to get him, and the unbelieving *Tribune* let him go. The robust son of Prussian-Jewish immigrants, Max Annenberg had grown up peddling newspapers and fistfighting on the streets of the West Side. He knew the newspaper business from the gutter up and had fewer compunctions than Hearst himself. To persuade the news dealers to find room for the *American* on their stands he recruited prizefighters, bouncers, muggers, and other street athletes, armed them with blackjacks, brass knuckles, and handguns, and sent them out in the *American* circula-tion wagons with instructions to give each news dealer a fair choice—he could either sell the bundle of papers tossed to him or he could eat them.

Naturally, Annenberg stirred some resistance, first from the news dealers and next from the other newspapers, who found the unlucky news dealers cutting down on their orders to make room for the *American.* Street-corner battles became a daily sight throughout the Loop. The public was bewil-dered, because the papers never printed a word about the fights. Gradually, accommodation and stability set in, though hardly peace. The *American* spawned a *Morning American,* soon renamed the *Examiner,* with Max Annenberg's little brother Moe as circulation manager, and launched an editorial barrage to support the street-corner storm troops. The *American* told Chicago readers that the *Tribune* and the *Daily News* had cheated the city in leasing the land on which their plants stood in the heart of the Loop (the land belonged to the Chicago Board of Education and the newspapers had the favorable terms of lease typical of mortgage holders in a developing area, though nothing scandalous). Hearst's Democratic politics also col-lided with the Republicanism of the *Tribune* and *Daily News*—Hearst was widely believed to have poisoned the mind of Leon Czolgosz, McKinley's assassin. Both causes were united when Democratic Mayor Dunne sought to get the leases canceled.

Joe Patterson, at the moment working within the system as Dunne's Commissioner of Public Works, considered banning newsstands from the sidewalks to halt the circulation war, but resigned before doing anything. The *Tribune, Examiner,* and *Record-Herald* were left to fight it out, and a lively decade of competition had cooled to a simmering truce in 1910 when Victor Lawson cut the price of the *Record-Herald* to one cent. Caught between Lawson's price cut and Hearst's thugs, the *Tribune,* rich though it was, appeared to be in imminent danger. Cutting its own price to one cent was inescapable, but Keeley proposed another measure: hiring Max Annenberg back from Hearst. McCormick and the stockholders agreed, and back came Annenberg, bringing with him Moe, his troop of thugs, and his arsenal of weapons. The *Examiner* and the *American* cried foul and sued Annenberg for breach of contract, but the *Trib*'s lawyers got a ruling that Annenberg's contract with Hearst was void because it was a contract "to commit illegal acts." Nobody mentioned what kind of acts the *Trib* wanted Annenberg to commit.

In October of 1910 the *Trib*'s new army began touring the Loop in a "big black limousine truck," according to the *Chicago Socialist,* the only newspaper that reported renewal of the war. The "limousine truck" adopted the tactic of parking near a newsstand and awaiting the arrival of the delivery truck of the *Examiner,* which they greeted with a fusillade of shots. Hearst's people promptly recruited a new guerrilla army and counterambushed, using delivery trucks as decoys. Dozens of thugs, news dealers, and passing citizens got hit, and an indeterminate number killed. The *Socialist* called for a grand jury investigation, but the police and the prosecuting attorney, friends of either the *Tribune* or Hearst or both, treated the problem with detachment. Arrested sluggers were released. If their depredations caused too much damage to innocent parties, as when a pair of *Tribune* bravos wrecked an Ashland Avenue saloon, the paper paid. Max Annenberg had himself deputized by the sheriff's office, a detail noted by the *Socialist* in reporting one incident:

> Sluggers employed by the trust newspapers this morning beat into unconsciousness Alexander Hickey, a newsdriver . . . and then kidnapped him in an automobile under the pretense of taking him to a hospital. . . .
>
> A warrant will be sworn out charging [Max] Annenberg and his accomplices with attempted murder. Annenberg was dressed as a typical tenderloin representative. He wore a flaming red sweater and over his low brow was pulled a soft cap. With a malicious leer upon his countenance he swaggered

around the elevated station . . . using foul language in the presence of women.
. . . Carrying in his pocket a commission as a deputy sheriff he kept raging
around the elevated station . . . flourishing and brandishing his revolver like
a maniac.

On another occasion Annenberg and a rebellious lieutenant named Whipple fought a predawn duel in the Loop in which ten shots were exchanged
and Whipple was finally subdued by the intervention of Moe with a freshly
loaded gun. The police, till then spectators, arrested Whipple and saluted
Max Annenberg, who waved them a friendly acknowledgment.

Once Max was indicted by a jury for shooting an enemy in the chest, but
McCormick's law firm successfully pleaded self-defense. Many underlings
on both sides landed in court and some even in prison, mostly as a result
of extracurricular activities. Hearst thug Vincent Altman was shot dead in
the bar of a hotel in an argument over profits from a chain of brothels, and
Hearst's Dutch Gentleman was gunned down in a State Street saloon by
McCormick's Mossy Enright, who eventually went free despite confessing
to the shooting. Neither Mossy's confession nor his connection with the
Tribune ever appeared in the paper.

Looking back across the years, McCormick in a 1952 broadcast expressed
only nostalgic satisfaction with the outcome: "Max Annenberg . . . proved
to be much the best circulation manager in town. It was the *Tribune* that
gained in circulation at the expense of the *Record-Herald* and Hearst's
Chicago Examiner." Since the *Daily News* had broken the 100,000 barrier
twenty-five years earlier all circulations had shot up, even faster than the
Chicago population. In 1910 the *Tribune* led the morning field at 241,000
(though still trailing the evening *Daily News*).

That same year circulation was aided by a sensational new scoop from
the news department. Keeley had sniffed a fishy aroma from Springfield
when a number of Democratic legislators helped elect Chicago Republican
boss William Lorimer to the U.S. Senate. *Tribune* bird-dogging paid off
when a Democratic legislator named Charles White called one day and
asked to see Medill McCormick, absent on cure, then offered Keeley sensational information on a massive bribe—"not chicken feed," he specified.
The appeal of the case was heightened by the fact that Lorimer controlled
the *Chicago Inter-Ocean,* a *Tribune* competitor whose candid slogan was
"Republican in everything, independent in nothing." White, who had first
tried to blackmail Lorimer for $75,000, wanted $50,000 from the *Tribune,*
but Keeley, a tough bargainer, got him to spill his guts for $3,250. Keeley
splashed the story on page one (April 30, 1910) under the largest headline
ever used in the *Tribune* to that time: DEMOCRATIC LEGISLATOR CON-
FESSES HE WAS BRIBED TO CAST VOTE FOR LORIMER FOR UNITED STATES

SENATOR. Keeley followed up on the editorial page with an insinuation that Lorimer got his bribe money from lumber and meat-packing interests.

It was a gloves-off battle. Lorimer, whose political origins were in the slaughterhouses of the Southwest side, regaled the Senate with a six-hour speech denouncing his enemies, among them President Taft, Theodore Roosevelt, and William Jennings Bryan, but the most sinister, according to Lorimer, were Robert R. McCormick and Joseph M. Patterson. In Chicago the *Inter-Ocean* defended Lorimer and denounced the *Tribune,* which followed up its exposé with a barrage of news stories, editorials, and cartoons. Several legislators were indicted, but the juries somehow didn't convict. The *Tribune* then exposed alleged bribing of jurors, and again indictments were obtained, but again no convictions.

The Senate finally voted on Lorimer's right to be seated in March 1911. By a narrow margin (46–40) the clubby upper house declined to see evil in its new member. The *Tribune* attributed the vote to the influence of "big business," and next to its openly slanted Washington story ran a cartoon by artist John T. McCutcheon knocking the Senate ("Although we've admitted seven of your votes [in the Illinois legislature] were corrupt, we think your election is honorable and legal enough to suit us").

It looked, though, as if Keeley had made a rash blunder and McCormick and Patterson were stuck with it. Lorimer supporters organized a parade in Chicago that climaxed with a derisive serenade outside the *Tribune.* Lorimer told his supporters that he was out to "smash Bob McCormick." He filed a succession of libel suits against the newspaper, but McCormick and Patterson refused to quit. Suddenly the *Record-Herald* came to the rescue. Bakery king Herman Kohlsaat, who had just bought the paper from Victor Lawson, disclosed, first in his newspaper, then in testimony in Springfield, that he had personal knowledge of $100,000 in bribe money paid to elect Lorimer. Springfield and Washington reopened hearings and Kohlsaat named his informant: Clarence Funk, general manager of the Cyrus McCormick family's International Harvester Company. Funk had been approached by Lorimer's bagman, lumber magnate Edward Hines, who had asked him to help out to the extent of $10,000 to meet the unexpectedly large bill for sending a reliable friend to Washington. Prodded by Progressive Republican Bob LaFollette of Wisconsin, the Senate reluctantly dropped Lorimer, who in turn dropped his libel suit against the *Tribune.* The general public began to see the sense of a long-advocated liberal reform, which soon followed: direct popular election of U.S. Senators.

In the course of the Senate hearing James Keeley was summoned to Washington (July 1911) to testify. Keeley was doubtless nettled by Lorimer's crediting the exposé to McCormick and Patterson, who had merely countenanced it (McCormick himself gave credit to Keeley in his memoirs: "The responsibility for the Lorimer fight was mine, but the executive work was done by James Keeley"). Recounting the threat of a lawsuit by Hines, Keeley quoted himself as valiantly telling the lumberman to "sue and be hanged," that the Tribune Building, worth $1,500,000, stood bond and that "doubtless he could use it in his lumber business." The Tribune Corporation's worth he estimated as between $7,500,000 and $10,000,000, with stock held by a small group of which he was not a member. Nevertheless, he was at pains to assert, he was the boss: "My authority is absolute." "In all departments?" "In all departments." He had directed *Tribune* editorial policies since February or March of 1910 (in other words, since Robert W. Patterson's death). Before that "I was managing editor—subordinate to Mr. Medill McCormick." But since then, "My authority is absolute."

Such a declaration, however literally true, could not help vexing Robert McCormick and Joe Patterson. It was nice of Keeley to take the responsibility for the Lorimer libel threat, but after all the Tribune Building, which he had so airily wagered, did not belong to him, and his assumption seemed to have more of the character of a boast than of an admission.

Not unconnected with Keeley's testimony in Washington was the ambiguous election of McCormick, four months earlier, to the presidency of the Tribune Corporation. In many ways the elevation seemed natural enough, a follow-up of stockholder Alfred Cowles's stipulation that McCormick enter actively into management. But Keeley, who had had to put up with the presence of Medill McCormick while awaiting the demise of R. W. Patterson, could view the intrusion of a second McCormick only with hostility, and the fact that the new McCormick failed to share the family antipathy to the Pattersons, and on the contrary reversed it in his close friendship with Joe Patterson, made things worse.

Keeley's views carried weight with the stockholders, including even Kate McCormick, who apparently adopted a passive role toward the question of the elevation of her second son. Did she still hope to get Medill sobered up long enough to take over the *Tribune?* Sister Elinor also seems to have put forward no effort in behalf of her own son, who together with McCormick lobbied the other stockholders. McCormick himself believed that his appointment was intended simply as a stopgap to fill the vacuum created by the loss of both the president and first vice-president.

Yet his behavior that summer and fall (1911) seemed to imply a rather longer view of his tenure. In what could only be taken as a slap at Keeley he ordered a halt to the puffs the paper had been giving Commonwealth Edison, the utilities company headed by Keeley's friend Samuel Insull. Next he seized an opportunity presented by the departure for South America of the Sunday editor in flight from alimony payments, to make Joe Patterson

Sunday editor. Finally, he liberated business manager William H. Field, an appointee of his brother's, from the oversight of Keeley, allowing Field a free hand in reorganizing the advertising department. Field launched a novel campaign of advertising promotion, in the *Tribune* and through ads purchased in rival papers, that proved highly effective in stimulating both circulation and advertising, whose already healthy rates were steadily increased.

But McCormick's most important move as president did not impinge on Keeley at all—quite the contrary. It carried him entirely out of Keeley's sphere, and in fact out of Chicago, and showed him to be much more of an engineer than an intriguer. The war with Lawson and Hearst, even if won, promised terrific strain on the critical weak point shared by all the mass-circulation dailies, the cost of newsprint per copy. Paper was getting more expensive just as newspapers were growing thicker. Hearst held a trump card in his multiple ownership of newspapers—he now had eight— that gave him the bargaining power with the pulp industry to get paper at five dollars less a ton than his competitors.

"This discrepancy, if continued, would have starved us to death," McCormick observed, leading to a fairly startling conclusion: "With my experience in electricity and canals and a general instinct for machinery, I decided that we should build our own paper mill, which could be done under a charter granted to the *Tribune* in 1861."

CHAPTER FIVE

Taking Over the Tribune

A DEMOGRAPHIC study done for the Sanitary District gave McCormick a basis for projecting future *Tribune* circulation. It predicted a steady, rapid increase in the population of Cook County over the ensuing four decades to a figure of 4,500,000 by 1950. Such projections are subject to all the imponderables of demography, and neither McCormick nor the board could have known that this one would hit within a fraction of a percentage point of the 1950 census. Nonetheless, McCormick used the study to sell the board on a potential *Tribune* circulation of 500,000 if the newspaper was well managed and the price kept low. To help keep it low, he proposed that the *Tribune* should build its own paper mill, at an investment cost of $1 million.

The sum was staggering, and the enterprise dubious—other papers had tried to run their own mills and failed. But Keeley lent his support—partly, perhaps, to get McCormick occupied somewhere else—and with one nay vote the plan was approved.

Business manager William H. Field had just met a man on a fishing trip whom he thought might be of help. Warren Curtis was a rotund, jolly, knowledgeable pulp engineer who had recently explored for Hearst the feasibility of a large mill in Canada. Wood was growing scarce in the eastern United States and the tariff on Canadian newsprint had just been removed. Curtis had an ambitious proposal: instead of simply building a paper mill and buying pulp from somebody else, build a combined pulp-and-paper mill and do the whole job. Enormous power would be needed, but the Niagara Falls generating capacity could supply it, provided that it could be used at twelve thousand volts. No twelve-thousand-volt electric motors were made in the United States, but they could be imported from Sweden. The proposal had the element of challenge and McCormick accepted it. In the winter of 1911–1912 rangy, taciturn McCormick and chunky, voluble Curtis reconnoitered the Ontario wilderness, ultimately settling on Thorold, ten miles from Niagara Falls, where a mill could take advantage of Niagara power and Welland Canal-Great Lakes transportation. Nailing down site acquisition, machinery purchase, and other details used up many months, during which the option McCormick had taken on Niagara power neared its term.

He and Curtis were on a train to Wilmington, Delaware, to negotiate with paper machinery manufacturers when McCormick, nervously pacing the aisles, learned that the president of the Ontario Power Company was on board without a seat. By inviting him to share his compartment McCormick picked up a tip—he should sign the contract when the option expired or the directors would not extend it. McCormick decided to sign, though for years afterward he wondered if the president had bluffed him.

Through 1912 and 1913 work went forward on the mill, with Curtis assisted by two engineers McCormick recruited from the Sanitary District: George S. Brack, who became chief engineer of the mill, and George W. Wisner, who had sailed with McCormick on the *Lusitania* in 1910, and who now acted as consultant to the paper mill while retaining his post with the Sanitary District. Novel problems were encountered and overcome. The twelve-thousand-volt motors, imported from Sweden, burned out and had to be replaced, with extra copper added. Construction difficulties in the wilderness delayed completion of the mill building, in which McCormick and Curtis often slept on cots. The steam turbines gave trouble. Through the fall of 1913 the machinery started, sputtered, failed, started again. McCormick fretted and lost patience with the tireless Curtis, fearing that the *Tribune*'s board of directors would appoint a committee and that the committee would turn the project over to its own expert. But early in 1914 Curtis got everything synchronized and the mill began turning out virtually the entire *Tribune* paper supply.

Meantime in Chicago the rivalry between Keeley and the two cousins slowly heated up. Keeley wanted the title of editor and publisher. McCormick and Patterson kept him from getting it, though letting the board name him "general manager." Keeley seized on Theodore Roosevelt's Bull Moose resurgence in 1912 to propose hiring TR as editor, a coup that he somehow felt would strengthen his own hand. McCormick and Patterson (whose socialism was fading to pale pink) were united in their admiration for TR (the *Tribune* had campaigned successfully for a special session of the legislature to pass a presidential primary law helpful to him), but they did not go for Keeley's proposal. Instead, they came up with another way to spend the $15,000 that would have gone to the new editor's salary—to add the popular German-dialect "Katzenjammer Kids" to the paper's new collection of Sunday comics.

When the Thorold mill settled into serious production in the spring of 1914 it raised the problem of assuring a reliable source of wood pulp. McCormick had been making forays into the wilds of Quebec and Ontario looking for lands to lease or purchase, and he and Curtis were exploring the Saguenay region of northern Quebec when Curtis, whose short legs had trouble keeping up with McCormick's pace, collapsed from exhaustion.

McCormick and the guides built a fire and made camp, and a guide was sent to the nearest town to find a doctor. Curtis recovered, but the guide brought back a Quebec newspaper that gave McCormick a different scare. Keeley had resigned from the *Tribune* to assume control of the *Record-Herald.* McCormick's instant apprehension was that Keeley would kidnap all the best *Tribune* staff.

Hiking to the nearest railroad station he inquired for a message from Keeley. There was none, heightening his fears. He sent a telegram to business manager Field with the names of key men to be kept at all costs, mainly Max Annenberg and managing editor Ted Beck, and hitched a switch engine ride to the main line and a train to Chicago.

An extra tremor of alarm was his knowledge that Joe Patterson was not in Chicago, having shipped out as correspondent with the U.S. Marines whom President Woodrow Wilson had just sent to Vera Cruz. On his interminable forty-eight-hour journey McCormick had plenty of time to worry, yet his concern must have been mixed with some degree of relief or even exhilaration. Two years earlier he had rejected a proffered nomination for Congress, turning his back for good on a political career, and now, abruptly enough, the *Tribune* was his.

The situation in Chicago turned out to be not so bad after all. Keeley had lured only two top *Trib* staffers—night editor Leighton Reilly and Washington correspondent John C. O'Laughlin—to the *Record-Herald.* On the other hand the *Record-Herald* had powerful financial support. Its chief owner was Herman Kohlsaat, but though Kohlsaat had purchased a controlling interest, Victor Lawson retained a role. With Lawson's help Kohlsaat had obtained backing from other magnates and the Continental National Bank, and Keeley himself brought in his friend Samuel Insull. At Keeley's suggestion Kohlsaat bought up the tottering *Inter-Ocean,* which had never recovered from its embrace of Lorimer, retitling the whole combination simply the *Herald.*

"It was widely thought that Keeley's competition would be too much for us," recalled McCormick, "but that opinion was not shared in the *Tribune,* " which not only lost few staffers in the shuffle but picked up a valuable one in James O'Donnell Bennett, characterized by McCormick as "perhaps the best newspaper writer who ever lived," and remembered by many others as at least among the ablest of his day.

But what all Chicago newspaper people wanted to know was, what about James Keeley himself, recognized all over town as Chicago's No. 1 newsman? Who could replace him?

The answer—and it must have been to Keeley's own astonishment—was a couple of amateurs, or semipros, named Robert R. McCormick and Joseph M. Patterson. What was perhaps even more surprising than their lack of self-doubt about being able to run the *Tribune* was their unconcern about being able to run it together. They divided the top editorial job between them, and to keep from getting into arguments over day-to-day decisions they hit on an expedient nobody in the business would ever have suggested—alternating the top responsibility month by month. Some old *Tribune* watchers thought they could discern reflections of who was running the paper by whether the editorials favored an inheritance tax (Patterson) or knocked public ownership of transit (McCormick), but reading the paper today for those McCormick-Patterson years, variations in tone seem mostly too subtle for detection.

The *Tribune* staff had for some time been acknowledged to be the best in Chicago. Burton Rascoe, later the paper's drama critic, recalled in his memoirs some of the exceptional talents of his early days:

"Bert Leston Taylor ('B.L.T.') was conducting his column, 'A Line o' Type or Two' [a *Trib* editorial page feature till 1969 that pioneered the use of reader contributions]; Finley Peter Dunne was writing a Mr. Dooley story every week for the *Sunday Tribune;* H. E. Keogh was conducting the column on the sports page, 'In the Wake of the News,' to which Ring Lardner . . . succeeded in 1913; Clare Briggs [subsequently creator of one of the great comic strips, 'Mr. and Mrs.'] was sports cartoonist; Lillian Russell [aging but fabled entertainment celebrity] was beauty adviser. . . ." There were columns on cooking, health, housekeeping, advice to the lovelorn, a "swap column." Nearly all were innovations of Keeley, one of the first editors to sense the importance of non-news features. "The newspaper," Keeley wrote, ". . . must enter into the everyday life of its readers and, like the parish priest, be guide, counselor, and friend."

Many *Tribune* news staffers made names later—Lucian Cary as a fiction writer, Mark Watson as editor of the *Ladies' Home Journal* and *Baltimore Sun,* George T. Bye as a New York literary agent. In the art department toiled several young men who through talent plus being in the right place at the right time became creators of long-lasting comic features—Frank King ("Gasoline Alley"), Sidney Smith ("The Gumps"), Harold Gray ("Little Orphan Annie"), Carl Ed ("Harold Teen"). Garrett Price became one of *The New Yorker*'s long-lived regulars.

For the time being, however, and for many years thereafter, the graphics star of the *Tribune* remained chief cartoonist and veteran newsman John T. McCutcheon. A Purdue (1889) alumnus, McCutcheon first had a career as a war correspondent, covering the Boer and Spanish-American wars for Lawson's *Daily News* and *Record-Herald.* In 1898 he had been one of the three correspondents with Dewey at Manila Bay. Turning cartoonist, McCutcheon had revealed a natural touch, especially at invoking rural nostalgia. Five years later, when McCutcheon's cartoons had become a talked-about feature of the *Record-Herald,* Keeley had hired him away at an unheard-of two hundred fifty dollars a week. Equally appreciated by McCormick, McCutcheon remained an independent creative presence at the *Tribune* for half a century.

"In charge of the news [continues Rascoe] was the perfect combination —E. S. Beck, managing editor, and Walter Howey, city editor. Beck was a man of education and natural refinement, a graduate of the University of Michigan . . . an excellent governor for that amazing engine of energy, Walter Howey." Howey was the original of the immortal Walter Burns of *The Front Page,* whose stage description contains the wonderful line, "Nerveless and meditative as a child, his mind open to all the trouble he can find or create. . . ."

Hired away from Hearst by Keeley in 1910, Howey was in Rascoe's words "a journalistic genius of the kind which began to disappear with [World War I]. He insisted on news stories being written in a colorful, dramatic, or humorous fashion; they had to be readable and entertaining first. Their strict news value . . . was unimportant. . . .

"Howey's character as a city editor was best reflected in one of his first admonitions to me, 'Don't ever fake a story or anything in a story—that is, never let me catch you at it.' "

Once Howey told Lucian Cary to write the front-page lead on a train wreck, and not satisfied, told him to do it over. Still not happy, he gave it to somebody else, and then to Rascoe, and finally, with the deadline minutes away "sat down at a typewriter and, writing at incredible speed, tore off a news story that was a classic of newspaper writing."

In 1917, after a silly fight with Joe Patterson over a puff for a D. W. Griffiths movie, Howey went back to the *Examiner.* Coming home from lunch with Brisbane to close the deal, Howey saw a limousine drive up. Robert McCormick got out: "I'm glad you told Joe Patterson what you did. He had it coming to him. I have a check here for three months salary, which I've brought as a bonus to you, and I have lined up a job for you on the *Minneapolis Tribune.* " Howey appreciated McCormick's gesture but preferred his new spot at the *Examiner,* where his two star reporters were Hilding (Hildy) Johnson and Charles MacArthur. When MacArthur quit the *Examiner* and took the train to New York with his fiancée, Howey had him arrested in Gary and brought back to Chicago on the charge that "the son of a bitch stole my watch," a line MacArthur and Ben Hecht used to ring down the curtain on *The Front Page.* Though in the play Walter Howey was altered to Walter Burns, Hildy Johnson remained Hildy Johnson and the *Examiner,* of which Hecht was also an alumnus, the *Examiner.*

Howey's assistant city editor on the *Tribune* was another arresting exemplar of old-school journalism, Frank Carson, who reputedly knew every policeman and every politician's mistress in Chicago. When he left the *Tribune* Howey missed Carson, and after playing a succession of pranks on the *Trib*—such as tricking it into promoting an *Examiner* serial story by planting a fake "mystery millionaire" in the Bismarck Hotel—he determined to bring Carson back to the *Examiner*. Carson had a contract, but Howey got him drunk and induced him to sign a letter of resignation to Joe Patterson designed to terminate relations:

> I address you as "Mister" Patterson because your phony pretensions to democracy, urging the help to "Just call me Joe," turn my stomach as they do all who must lick your boots for pay. I could stand your cousin because the man is honest according to his lights. He is a Twentieth Century Quixote, tilting at windmills visible to no eyes but his own. You are a common pander, catering to the meretricious tastes of the masses.

The letter freed Carson from his contract, but perhaps to Howey's surprise did not prevent Patterson from later hiring him to come to New York to edit the *New York Daily News.*

Howey notwithstanding, Patterson was also a journalistic genius. From Sunday editor he readily branched into newspaper features in general, among other things fathering most of the comic strips that originated in the *Trib*'s art department and spread through syndication across the country. An exception was "Gasoline Alley," McCormick's inspiration, rooted in the typically McCormick idea that such a strip could help people learn to take care of their automobiles, just becoming a national middle-class problem. Both Patterson and McCormick had senses of humor, but in different veins. McCormick appreciated dry urbane wit, perhaps exemplified on the comic-strip level by low-key "Gasoline Alley," whereas Patterson was knocked off his seat by the slam-bang foolery of little Hans and Fritz Katzenjammer.

Patterson's great contribution to the comics was the idea of continuity, something that made the *Tribune*'s first daily strip, the otherwise forgettable "Gump" family (from a word Patterson's mother used for someone stupid), into a national mania and that in "Little Orphan Annie" created a new genre, the non-comic, or soap-opera, strip. For "Gasoline Alley" Patterson conceived a refinement of continuity which, though little imitated, had value—the characters were made to age naturally along with the readers. Skeezix, found on Uncle Walt's doorstep, ultimately became a grandfather.

Patterson's "Bright Sayings of Children" feature, which paid parents a dollar on top of the gratification of seeing their tots' drolleries in print, lasted many years in the *Tribune* and even longer in the *New York Daily News.*

Together with McCormick, Patterson pioneered a new printing technology by importing one of the first rotogravure presses from Germany (the *New York Times* had the first) to print the "brown section," a form of Sunday supplement that used coated stock and the gravure press to give superior photo reproduction in sepia.

Accepting a suggestion from a bright assistant named Mary King, Patterson pained *Tribune* snobs by establishing a motion-picture department that exploited the new medium in a variety of imaginative ways, including the profitable one of publishing a movie directory made up of compact, paid-for ads by the exhibitors. Another idea was narrative versions of the film serials that had seized the fancy of the moviegoing public. For regular serialized fiction, a cut above that of Hearst and Victor Lawson, Patterson paid premium prices to get such names and talents as Booth Tarkington and E. Phillips Oppenheim, and sold the product to some sixty other papers. So successful was the Patterson-King Sunday feature collaboration that they ended up getting married, after he divorced the daughter of the president of Marshall Field.

Yet valuable as were Patterson's many contributions to the *Tribune*'s fight for supremacy in the morning field, they were not as decisive as McCormick's single sustained effort in Canada. What rendered the newsprint problem critical was World War I.

Foreign news was by no means neglected by metropolitan dailies of 1914, but the *Tribune*'s coverage of the assassination of Archduke Franz Ferdinand was phenomenal: all eight columns of page one, including pictures of the slain archduke and archduchess, a highly detailed cable from Sarajevo, and an exhaustive backgrounder by-lined "Ex-Attache," which jumped inside. Several more pages included cables from Vienna, Rome, and London, a map of the Balkans, an explanation of "Where Bosnia Is and What It Is," a bird's-eye view of Sarajevo, a feature on the tragedies of the reign of old Emperor Franz Joseph, photos of the archduke's family and castle and a sketch titled "The Crown of Austria," featuring tragedy and assassination, by Sidney Smith, the artist on the threshold of fame as creator of "The Gumps."

Yet despite the journalistic revel in the assassination, nobody had much inkling of what was coming. A terrific but fleeting sensation, Sarajevo vanished from the front pages as quickly as it had appeared. Readers were hardly prepared when one month later, with the publication of the Austrian ultimatum and the Serb reply, the diplomatic crisis suddenly loomed. The threat of war was at first less interesting than the assassination. On Sunday, July 26, the *Tribune* gave five columns to

AUSTRIA AND SERVIA BREAK: TROOPS MOVE

and indicated the likelihood of a general European war. The same day the *New York Times,* more conservative in makeup, headed the story in four columns, but more daring in forecast, virtually promised the engulfment of Europe.

Still no one grasped the extent of what was happening or its effect on America, including its effect on the American newspaper business. The Spanish-American War had given the *Tribune* its Manila Bay scoop, and the Russo-Japanese War had inspired O. Henry to a brilliant satire of cliché-ridden journalistic style in "Calloway's Code," but August 1914 created a news revolution. Dependably violent headlines day after day sold newspapers faster than the wagons could deliver them. The circulation gangs were disbanded, their members drifting off to pimping, thievery, and extortion. Max Annenberg took up golf, and rode horseback in Lincoln Park.

As demand for newspapers rose, and war prosperity fueled advertising, the price of newsprint soared. The combination made Robert R. McCormick look like a certified genius, and he did indeed deserve credit for his foresight, enterprise, and execution. The Thorold mill would eventually have given the *Tribune* a decisive competitive edge over other Chicago morning papers. The German invasion of Belgium merely shortened the process.

CHAPTER SIX

To the Russian Front

WALTER MILLIS, distinguished editorial writer for the *New York Herald Tribune,* in a book looking back on 1914 from the very different American atmosphere of the 1930s, described the press's response to World War I:

> Long before the great war propagandas began to develop from abroad, the leading organs of American opinion, through the interplay of haste, ignorance and their own psychological necessities, had begun to distinguish in the German Empire a vast, malignant power which alone and for its own atrocious ends had plunged the world into this stupendous catastrophe.

That was true of a very important section of the press, but there was some variation, and it had a geographic sense. The *Chicago Tribune* and the *New York Times* had significantly different reactions. The *Tribune,* in an editorial by Clifford Raymond of which McCormick was inordinately proud, bitterly ridiculed the appeals to religion on the part of the two kaisers and the czar, and made a forecast:

> This is the twilight of the kings. Western Europe of the people may be caught in this debacle, but never again. Eastern Europe of the kings will be remade and the name of God shall not give grace to a hundred square miles of broken bodies. . . .
> It is the twilight of the kings. The republic marches east in Europe.

In contrast to the abstract antiwar, antimonarchical sentiment of the *Tribune,* the *Times* enlisted categorically on the side of the Allies. For the kaiser's claim that "the sword has been forced into our hands," the *Times* had nothing but contempt, going so far as to utter a *Times*ian "forsooth," in light of the fact that

> from many sources it has been disclosed that German mobilization has for days been under way.

The *Times* did not disclose any of its "many sources," but its busy London bureau was headed and mainly staffed by Britishers. The information was wrong—Russian mobilization had preceded, and triggered, German mobilization.

Most newspaper readers, like most newspaper editors, favored the *Times* view of German war guilt because it gave fundamental satisfaction. Something this big and bloody, it seemed, had to be deliberate. Only a handful of European insiders were aware that Germany's violently aggressive opening posture was simply the product of an irresponsible and out-of-date strategic plan that did not reflect the political attitude of the German government. The famous "Schlieffen Plan" not only helped bring on the war and made Germany look bad, but had the further disadvantage of drawing Britain in and thereby arousing the emotions of the most powerful of America's numerous ethnic groups, the lordly Anglo-Saxon Protestants. The acronym WASP had not yet been invented, but in 1914 the racial cohort that thought of itself as "native American" was in command of the country—press, pulpit, school, and government—and anything it felt strongly about became a national policy.

Lesser groups with their own prejudices were not entirely devoid of influence. The Irish were bitterly anti-British, the Germans and Scandinavians pro-German, and even such low-status immigrants as the Italians, Hungarians, Poles, and Jews chose sides in the cataclysm across the sea, sometimes for, sometimes against their "old country." Russian Jews were anticzarist Russia, but German Jews felt much as other Germans. Prussian-born Max Annenberg, returning from vacation in Europe, gave an interview disparaging France and extolling Germany.

McCormick and Patterson, cosmopolitan conservative and ex-socialist cynic, cast more sophisticated eyes on the scene in Europe and refused to commit themselves to either side. Patterson shipped over to get a firsthand look, taking with him John T. McCutcheon. In their Paris hotel McCutcheon introduced Patterson to a new journalistic phenomenon, the London *Daily Mirror,* a picture-filled half-size "tabloid." Patterson was fascinated, and squirreled the idea away for the future. Meantime he concentrated on a series of articles for the *Tribune* that gained fame, or notoriety, under the title *Notebook of a Neutral.*

Patterson's basic thrust, to which McCormick adhered, was a plague-on-both-your-houses, American-interests-must-come-first line. Yet strangely enough, and despite his title, he did not advocate neutrality. Expressing a cynic's admiration for Britain's success at power politics, he proposed that America take a leaf from the British book and strike a profitable bargain. This he proposed to do by entering the war on the Allied side, demanding as payment a free hand for annexation in Mexico and Central America. Thus if McCormick and Patterson foresaw the extinction of monarchy, they anticipated a continuing future for imperialism.

The Patterson series caused a sensation because of the sour note it sounded amid the swelling press concert of anti-German propaganda. Patterson, who had visited Belgium, on both sides of the battle line, flatly contradicted the lurid atrocity stories being fabricated by the AP and others. McCutcheon, James O'Donnell Bennett, and four other correspondents then with the German army wrote an open letter to the same effect, but Belgian atrocity stories continued to enjoy popularity. For the Germans to have set out to conquer Europe and then to be lenient, or merely rather strict, with the conquered did not suit the psychological need of either the press or its public.

Patterson's tour stimulated McCormick's own impulse to gratify an old longing to be a war correspondent. There was also a strictly personal motive behind his sudden departure for Europe in February of 1915.

One year earlier, in February–March 1914, the Chicago clubs had buzzed with a scandal that did not find its way into local print, either in the *Tribune* or its rivals. Mrs. Amy Irwin Adams sued her husband, Edward S. Adams, for divorce, and Adams countersued to collect $100,000 damages from Robert R. McCormick.

Adams was known chiefly for two things: He possessed one of Chicago's most unslakable thirsts, and he was a nephew of Cyrus McCormick, thus a second cousin of Robert R. McCormick. His wife was the good-looking and accomplished daughter of General Bernard J. D. Irwin, a Civil War army surgeon and early Medal of Honor winner. When McCormick had finished his first year at Northwestern he had spent a summer at the Adamses' Tower Court residence, and later had lived with them in Lake Forest (his principal address at the time was 1440 Dearborn, the Union Club). Love had blossomed, with the resulting divorce suit, countersuit, and divorce decree (March 6, 1914). Adams appealed the decree, keeping the scandal alive while the lovers endured the year-long waiting period prescribed by Illinois law and finally seized the opportunity of the war to get out of Chicago.

McCormick had the idea of visiting the Russian army, little covered by the American press. To get there he enlisted his mother's clout with the Russian foreign office and obtained permission from Foreign Minister Sazonov himself, who wrote Katherine in Washington that the Grand Duke Nicholas, commander-in-chief, "preserved the best remembrance of the late ambassador, Mr. McCormick," and "consents, as a unique exception, to admit your Mr. McCormick on the field of active fighting." Mr. McCormick was not to be accredited as a war correspondent, but merely "a distinguished foreigner personally known to the Grand Duke," an identification which, however, would not prevent him from writing dispatches.

To give himself some military coloration McCormick hit on the device of asking Governor Dunne (former mayor of Chicago) for a commission in the Illinois National Guard. Although the governor was a Democrat, the *Tribune*'s crusade against Senator Lorimer had been good for the Democrats and Dunne was glad to oblige by naming McCormick a colonel on his personal staff. After getting a uniform fitted, the new colonel departed at once for New York, sailing for Liverpool on the S.S. *Adriatic* on February 10, 1915.

Much more quietly, if not surreptitiously, Amy Irwin Adams followed him over on another liner and on March 10 they were inconspicuously married. The ceremony was performed in St. George's Church, Hanover Square, not in the nave or chapel, but in the registry office, with only two witnesses, Amy's sister from Chicago and a British major of McCormick's acquaintance. Meantime back home the court of appeals did not get around to throwing out Adams's suit until nearly three months later.

McCormick had already filed his first dispatches from the *Adriatic,* aboard which he interviewed two young Englishmen returning home from South America to enlist and members of the ship's crew. He found a striking difference in viewpoint between Britons "of rank and wealth," personified by the two émigrés, and the lower-class crewmen: "The former are insistent on war to a finish, the latter anxious for peace." The young aristocrats were indignant that the victorious German naval squadron in a recent engagement had failed to rescue British survivors, but one of the *Adriatic*'s own sailors commented, "The poor German people are not responsible for this war, and they are losing two boys to our one." In London he obtained interviews with Prime Minister Asquith and other leaders, and filed a dispatch containing what a lead-in written in Chicago called "the most authoritative pronouncement yet made in England for America" to the effect that

> Britain will never make peace unless utterly defeated or until Germany evacuates Belgium and pays Belgium full compensation for damage done. It is felt that the permanence of the empire demands these terms.

If the statement sounded a little irrational, it was not the fault of McCormick's reporting. From Asquith he obtained permission to visit the British front in Flanders, which was necessary because the Allies had foolishly imposed a blanket exclusion of all correspondents from forward areas.

Asquith asked a question of his own: What was the state of American public opinion? McCormick told him that so-called society was strongly pro-Ally, but that the German-Americans were pro-German and most of the country was pro-American and "inclined to be critical of all the nations involved in the war." Asquith expressed surprise, reasonably enough, since this information did not accord with what he was getting from his own sources. Spring Rice, his ambassador in Washington, describing an unsatisfactory interview with pacifist Secretary of State William Jennings Bryan, asserted that "I didn't believe there was a man in the country not a German or a Jew who could advocate such a cause [as peace without compensation for Belgium]." Spring Rice was obviously acquainted only with eastern sentiment, as McCormick was principally with midwestern.

McCormick also talked to Foreign Secretary Sir Edward Gray and First Lord of the Admiralty Winston Churchill, whom he pleased by a compliment on his "master stroke" in having "the fleet ready mobilized at the time of the outbreak of the war."

McCormick crossed the Channel to Paris and called at the Quai d'Orsay, where Foreign Minister Delcassé remembered his father and procured him a pass to visit the front. He was taken to Arras, where the cathedral and other medieval buildings had been hit by German shells, damage thought to be of propaganda value with Americans. McCormick pocketed a stone fragment, which started him on what became the collection in the Tribune Tower.

He came under fire for the first time as German artillery shelled the road from Arras to St. Omer, where he called at British headquarters. The sergeant on duty, identifying him as a newspaperman, ordered him to get out, but "having been brought up in England, I knew how to browbeat a member of the lower classes," and he refused to leave. When an officer appeared, McCormick remembered a letter he had been given in London by a young woman who knew Sir John French, the British commander-in-chief. He was promptly invited to dinner with the staff, assigned quarters, and over the next several days escorted to various sectors of the front. During one of these excursions, the automobile broke down, with a curious social-cultural consequence. Both the British major and the chauffeur, who was the owner and had volunteered for service with his vehicle, disclaimed all knowledge of automobiles. Could the American perhaps fix it? McCormick was no more expert at auto repair than his British hosts, but lifted the hood and found a disconnected wire. "I fastened it and we completed our journey, but I was aware I lost social standing because I knew mechanics' work."

He also met Sir Douglas Haig, then a corps commander, and visited an advanced observation post where he was impressed with the coolness of an officer at pains to acquaint his relief with the exact situation, despite shells falling close by. "I came near to disgracing my country," he later admitted. "I didn't ask to be taken away, but I wasn't miles from it." Returning to Calais in Sir John French's own staff car, he quit the British army "very much in its debt. . . . I had been the associate of very gallant gentlemen."

He and Amy sailed for Russia via Malta and Greece, taking along a large box entrusted to McCormick by the Russian ambassador in London. It contained, according to the embassy, the flag signals of the British navy, to be used when the Allied fleets joined forces in the Black Sea or the Bosporus. The explanation sounded fairly incredible to begin with, but McCormick accepted the charge. He was told that British or Russian nationals could not safely carry out the mission because of the pro-German regimes in Greece and Bulgaria. With the clumsy box added to their baggage, the honeymooners boarded a British vessel bound for India via the Mediterranean. At Malta they were put surreptitiously ashore by small boat, met and taken to a hotel by a British agent. A few days later they sailed for Piraeus, the port of Athens. There the box became a nuisance. After registering as "Robert R. McCormick," its guardian checked it in the hotel safe, but upon ascending in the slow-motion lift he found the hotel proprietor and two porters at his room door, with the box. "This is not the Ritz Hotel, and I cannot be responsible for Mrs. Robert Rockefeller McCormick's jewelry!" the excited innkeeper told him.

The man's conviction that the couple belonged to the rich McCormicks was unshakable, and the tale that they were carrying around a trunkful of jewelry followed them to Russia. McCormick already had reason to be concerned about thieves: He was wearing a money belt containing a thousand gold pounds, which it turned out he had no use for—everyone on his itinerary preferred his American letter of credit. The railroad journey through Serbia, Bulgaria, and Romania was replete with Agatha Christie touches—a mysterious "little man with lemon-colored hair" who kept turning up in different clothes but who never spoke a word, an altercation with a police officer on the platform at Sofia mediated by an army doctor who turned out to be a fellow Northwestern alumnus, a police interrogation at Bucharest prompted by suspicion of McCormick's National Guard uniform, and a party of men in the dining car who seemed intent on picking a quarrel and who vanished just before the train crossed the Russian border.

At Kiev McCormick telegraphed St. Petersburg to inquire whether it wouldn't be a good idea to send the box of signal flags to Odessa, headquarters of the Black Sea fleet. He was told no, bring it to Petersburg. In the capital he turned the box over to the assistant minister of foreign affairs, who proved to be married to a San Francisco girl Amy knew. They never did find out the actual contents of the mysterious box.

Next day McCormick called on Foreign Minister Sazonov, who treated him to a discussion of "international affairs and American affairs with a facility that aroused my admiration," and arranged for him to interview the czar at the palace at Tsarskoye Selo. He journeyed there by train and imperial carriage from the railroad station, improbably dressed, according to instructions, not in uniform but in white tie and tails. In due course he found himself alone in a large anteroom whose double-paned windows had thermometers outside, in between, and inside—McCormick noted the temperatures, 8 degrees Celsius, 12, and 15 respectively. He had time to inspect the oil paintings, the books on a table, the "large, carved, egg-shaped decoration" (probably a Fabergé creation), and the Turkish carpet before, as the clock struck two, a door opened and a pair of figures in scarlet uniforms festooned with medals entered. For a moment they stood solemn and "straight as ramrods" before the baffled American, then one announced, "The Emperor is waiting." Passing through the door McCormick found himself face to face with Nicholas II, whom he remembered thirty-seven years later as having had "the largest eyes I have ever seen in living mortal." The czar addressed him in faultless English: "I cannot remember just what year it was your father left us." They chatted briefly, and Nicholas promised that his brother the Grand Duke would permit McCormick to visit the "extreme front."

His Majesty then excused himself for lunch, and his American visitor retreated to the hall where he was handed first hat, then coat, then cane. He returned to the station the same way he had come, by carriage. In the station restaurant, he picked four dishes at random from the Russian menu and found he had ordered two kinds of caviar, a cheese sandwich, and a bottle of kvass (Russian beer).

Leaving Amy in St. Petersburg, he was soon off to the headquarters of the Grand Duke Nicholas in Poland. Here his National Guard title and uniform proved providential. Anything with *guard* in it sounded elite to the Russians, and at headquarters mess he was given precedence over all the other colonels. His lack of Russian did not handicap conversation, which was carried on in French. On one occasion the Allied and U.S. heads of state were toasted and their national anthems played by a band, but the officer in charge had not kept up with American politics and instead of toasting Woodrow Wilson toasted Theodore Roosevelt, while the bandmaster led what McCormick alone recognized as "There'll Be a Hot Time in the Old Town Tonight."

Passing through army, corps, and division headquarters, McCormick visited a sector of the front where the Russians were striving to drive the Austrians off a Carpathian peak. He suggested to the division commander that artillery fire could do the job, and the general asked him to tell that to the army commander, General Brusilov, whose reply he remembered: "Men and shells may be used interchangeably. We have few shells but many men." McCormick later thought the callousness of the reply "had much to do with the revolution," but did not grasp the real significance of it, that

World War I was a war of mass production that put industrially weak Russia at a terrific disadvantage.

Leaving the front he stopped in Warsaw, where a visit to a base hospital showed him that "it is in the hospitals that the horrors of war are found." A wounded soldier who spoke English turned out to have worked in the South Chicago steel mills. "Thinking to cheer him up," McCormick told the man he would be glad to see him in Chicago after the war. In reply the poor fellow revealed two stumps of legs and "over his face came an expression that I would not describe if I could."

A sinus infection, for which Russia offered no medical specialists, caused him to leave for home by way of Stockholm. Quitting the Ritz Hotel with Amy he was following the Russian custom of saying good-bye individually to waiters, maids, desk clerks, and cooks when he inadvertently included a lady whose function in the hotel had been indicated by her succession of dinner companions—a grand duke, admirals, generals, "even a bishop." "Good-bye," began McCormick, and re-collecting himself, "Oh, I beg your pardon. We have not met." "No," agreed the lady cheerfully, "you are on your honeymoon. But the next time you come. . . ."

He never set foot in Russia again, though a few years later he met the Grand Duke Nicholas at Cap d'Antibes. The grand duke was too proud a man to make the request, so the grand duchess asked McCormick for help in peddling his jewelry. "There was one very large yellow diamond, a gift from the Sultan of Turkey, which I was able to dispose of, but a pink diamond, the size of a man's thumbnail, was valued at a half million dollars, which, of course, I could not obtain."

CHAPTER SEVEN

The Issue of War

WHEN the McCormicks arrived home in midsummer by way of Scandinavia, London, Paris, and Joffre's headquarters at Compiègne, they could not miss a change in the American atmosphere. "So-called society," in McCormick's phrase to Asquith, was more passionately pro-Allied than ever and was now joined by the overwhelming majority of the respectable middle class. Largely responsible for the swift maturing of American partisanship was the torpedoing on May 7 of the *Lusitania,* the Cunard liner on which McCormick had sailed to Europe in 1910. Unlike the Belgian atrocities, the *Lusitania* was no fairy tale, going down with the loss of 1,198 lives, 128 of them American.

Until the sinking of the *Lusitania,* the "pro-Germans," as neutralists·of all political coloration were labeled, had been able to argue that the British were violating American rights as flagrantly as the Germans. International law permitted only a close blockade of enemy ports, something 1914 geographical, military, and political conditions made as impracticable for the British as for the Germans. Consequently the British navy adopted a quite different tactic, occupying the Channel and North Sea approaches to northern Europe, halting all shipping, escorting it to British ports, and freely labeling the cargoes "contraband," that is, war-related material subject to seizure.

The Wilson government by no means acquiesced in the illegal British blockade, and even the sinking of the *Lusitania* did not silence U.S. protests. What it did was to cancel the effect of the protests by robbing them of the support of public opinion as expressed in the newspapers. Editors ransacked their Roget's in search of epithets for the U-boat commander, his admiral, the kaiser, and Germans in general ("savages drunk with blood," was the *New York Times*'s description).

The *Chicago Tribune* was more sober, but agreed that the nation faced a choice, either to submit meekly to Germany's new rules of war or "to fight to the best of our power," and concluding, "There is no more argument about it. Further words merely abase, dishonor, and humiliate us."

The Germans were able to weather the crisis by promising not to sink any more *Lusitania*s, an easy promise to make in light of the freaky charac-

57

ter of the sinking—a tiny, slow submarine needed all the luck in the world to bring down a giant, swift liner (the *Lusitania*'s sister *Mauretania* made scores of unescorted crossings in the two wars). Beyond that the Germans actually employed a degree of restraint over the next year and a half. So did America's editors and publishers, who kept calling the kaiser and the Germans names, but avoided anything further. Taking sides was one thing, getting involved something else.

There was even a continuing opposition, mostly passive and defensive, to the pro-Allied hysteria. In the many pages of coverage the *Tribune* gave the *Lusitania,* the most unusual piece of copy was one headed "Appeal to German Ministers to Present Their Side of Case." A lead explained that what followed was an appeal published by Chicago German newspapers, which the *Tribune* gave in the original German gothic type and in translation:

> As apparently the sinking of the *Lusitania* has brought the unjust opposition among our American people against the country of our forefathers and our German people to the highest mark, as further not only the pro-English press is making capital out of this feeling but hundreds of English-speaking ministers will support this hostile press from their pulpits tomorrow and widen the breach between us and the old fatherland, we the undersigned feel it our duty to call upon all the German pastors in the interest of truth and justice and request them most emphatically to explain to their congregations during the service tomorrow the danger of the situation and call their attention to the fact that the German government has been forced by England to this horrible step and according to international law is not responsible for the loss of American life.

As the Midwest's Germans and Scandinavians settled into sullen opposition, Chicago, rich in both ethnic groups ("the sixth German city in the world" was a civic boast), in fresh-from-oppression Irish, in anti-Russian Poles (Chicago was a "suburb of Warsaw" according to Arnold Bennett) and Hungarians, became the neutralist capital. By coincidence it had just the mayor for the job. William Hale Thompson was a patrician immigrant from Boston, son of a Yale man who had made a fortune in Chicago real estate. Discovering in himself a talent for demagoguery, the younger Thompson got elected to the City Council, where he served with fellow-Republican Robert R. McCormick, and where he sponsored a bill creating the first public playground in America. But when Thompson joined the Republican faction headed by Boss Lorimer, he automatically became an enemy of the *Tribune,* which he accused of avoiding property taxes, and which published his name at the top of a list headed "Do Not Vote for These Men: They are the Puppets of Lorimer." It was the beginning of a long, cordial loathing that defied ideology. When Thompson ran successfully for mayor in the spring of 1915 the normally Republican *Tribune* sat on its hands.

Thompson's neutralism on the war, which gained him support in the German and Scandinavian wards, took the form of a blustery American nationalism despite which he was dubbed "Kaiser Bill" by the pro-Allied party. He had the support of the two Hearst papers, half-liberal and ever maverick Hearst having turned around from 1898 to adopt a militant antiwar posture in all his (now nine) papers, provoking threats to quit from his editors, who did not, and to cancel from his advertisers, many of whom did. The *Tribune* remained anti-Thompson, and kept its neutrality sedate enough not to provoke much anger.

In the fall of 1915 McCormick set forth his own ideas on the war in *With the Russian Army,* half memoir of his journey to a war and half reflection of his mixed feelings about the dangerous new world on which the curtain had risen. His perceptions were orthodox both in their accuracies and their misconstructions. He now accepted the *New York Times* theory that Germany had gone to war deliberately, and Patterson's view that German motivation lay in thwarted colonial ambitions.

Besides missing the political significance of the Schlieffen Plan, he did not appreciate its military sense. From his Russian hosts he had picked up the idea that the German invasion of Belgium and France had "revealed" enemy strategy to the Grand Duke Nicholas, who had then "decided" on his invasion of East Prussia. In actual fact, the Russian invasion of East Prussia had been planned years earlier by the French and Russian staffs as a counter to Schlieffen, and by placing a premium on early Russian mobilization had contributed to triggering the war.

The principal message of *With the Russian Army* was a long disquisition on "Modern Fortifications" illustrated by an elaborate pull-out diagram, based on the Russian version of the ring fortress, a central fort girdled by independent outworks. The information the Russians had supplied him he called "an evidence of friendship of the Russian government for the American people," adding, "I consider it particularly desirable that I should publish it because our government has forbidden American army officers to educate the American people in military affairs." This slap at Wilsonian pacifism may have related to a comment elsewhere in the book, "When will some far-seeing college president furnish a similar training [to that of the Russian Guard cadets] for our youth, so we will not be without officers when the time comes that we have to fight for our institutions and our firesides?"

In other words, ROTC. McCormick was among the first, but not the very first, to advocate it. General Leonard Wood, who had commanded the Rough Rider regiment in which Teddy Roosevelt was second-in-command, had organized a summer camp for college boys in 1913, less with the thought of training them to be future officers than with that of converting them into missionaries in the cause of a larger American army. The outbreak of war in Europe had not inspired either the idea of an expanded army or of a reserve officers' corps, but it had provided a wonderful stimulus. By mid-1915 Wood and Roosevelt were strenuously calling for "preparedness," a clumsy but shrewd word that did not embarrass by spelling out what the country was to prepare for, defense at home or adventure abroad, and so supplied a ground on which defensive nationalists like McCormick and Patterson could join with warmongers like Teddy Roosevelt. Many college presidents accordingly organized ROTC units in the fall of 1915.

For McCormick "preparedness" was not a piece of hypocrisy. Confronted with the overwhelming European military spectacle, bristling with novel weaponry and sinister in the suddenness of its appearance, any American who could read a newspaper might be moved to a degree of alarm. The country was totally outclassed at sea by both Britain and Germany, had practically no army and literally no air force. Without being fanciful McCormick could depict American vulnerability in arresting terms:

> I take it as a matter generally admitted that in the event of war, if any military power should obtain command of the sea, it would be impossible to attempt to hold our seacoast States. Our whole object would be to keep the hostile army from the centre of the nation during the years that it would take us to organize sufficient forces to retake the lost provinces and buy arms and ammunition abroad.

He advocated construction of forts at Albany, Buffalo, Pittsburgh, Atlanta, Vicksburg, Houston, and the passes of the Sierra Nevadas and the Rockies, these last precautions aimed at the Japanese, who also had a sizable fleet and a large army.

To illustrate the difficulties faced by a democracy without conscription engaging in a modern war, McCormick cited the experience of the British. He expressed admiration for the British Liberal government, which stood for "all that is best in our Progressive and . . . liberal side of our Democratic parties" but pointed to the shortcomings in equipment of the British Expeditionary Force of 1914 and the problems of training and arming a mass army after war had begun.

With the Russian Army was soberly received and its author treated with the respect due a man who had actually witnessed twentieth-century war. McCormick was invited to lecture to the officers at Fort Sheridan, an army post on Lake Michigan that owed its founding to the fears inspired by the Haymarket Riot.

A few months later he again appeared as an author, this time in collaboration with a writer named Edwin Balmer. Their product was a serialized novel on a theme that had become sensationally popular, the invasion of America. In the McCormick-Balmer *1917* (serialized in 1916) the invaders were frankly German, and drove to the Mississippi before getting stopped. Such journalistic scenarios helped rouse enthusiasm for the big-navy program that was being assiduously pushed by bellicose Undersecretary of the Navy Franklin D. Roosevelt behind the back of pacifist Secretary Josephus Daniels. Roosevelt joined in the game by arranging to have the fleet maneuvers enact a mock invasion of the northeast coast by an enemy readily identifiable as German. President Wilson finally indorsed the Roosevelt program in a speech in St. Louis in which he declared that the United States should possess "incomparably the greatest Navy in the world." Apparently reconsidering the superlative, Wilson amended the official version of the speech to "incomparably the most adequate Navy in the world," possibly setting a record in the department of rhetorical qualification.

McCormick planned a return to Russia as a correspondent, but other business intervened. In October he made a fresh foray into the Canadian wilderness, this time to the Rocky River, near the broad mouth of the St. Lawrence, in search of a good tract of timber. Surveying the huge boulders in the water, he told Curtis, "If we call this place Rocky River no ship captain ever will come in here to get our wood. Let's call it Shelter Bay."

They had a number of adventures in the wilderness. Once McCormick and Curtis stayed out too long on a reconnaissance and were caught by nightfall. They could make their way back only by one man crawling in front on hands and knees to feel for the trail. The two were nearly exhausted when they reached camp, at which point a flashlight he had forgotten about fell out of McCormick's pocket. "The incident did not increase goodwill," he recalled thirty years later.

Another time McCormick set out with two companions carrying canoe and provisions on a three-mile portage around falls and rapids, finally reaching the south end of Fifteen Mile Lake. He sent his companions across the lake in the canoe to make camp while he reconnoitered the timber. Clearing a path through the dense brush with an ax, he kept his bearings by counting his strides and jotting his changes of compass heading in a notebook. Heavy snow began falling, visibility blurred, and he suddenly experienced the uncomfortable conviction that he would never be able to find the tiny campsite. Using the notebook to retrace his steps he made his way back to the lakeshore where he had earlier spotted a Tsibasse Indian hut. The dozen Indians inside shared their meal with the stranger and invited him to sleep in the hut. McCormick admired the Tsibasses as guides. On his timber reconnaissances, he supplied the bread, the Tsibasses the meat.

His favorite guide was Francis Tsibasse, a powerful man of "impeccable manners," who cut a trail through the brush, pointed out the best places to step, and gave his hand where necessary. McCormick, in fact, found himself a little nettled at the Indian's easy superiority in woodsmanship, and once at the head of a familiar fourteen-mile trail he rashly set off in front at a five-mile-an-hour clip. Panting and sweating, his heart pumping, he was gratified to reach the fork where he and Francis parted company. With a cheery, "Bon soir, Monsieur," the Indian left him. As soon as he was alone McCormick sat down on a log and rested. "The experience was good for my ego," he recorded.

In Chicago after arranging to purchase the timber tract and getting port construction under way he once more planned a return to Russia, but again something intruded: Mexico's irrepressible half-bandit, half-revolutionary Pancho Villa. All shades of opinion toward the war in Europe were united in their reaction to Villa as he progressed from outrage to nervy outrage, killing Americans not only in Mexico, but even in Texas. Joe Patterson followed Hearst in calling on the United States to annex all of Mexico, plus Central America down to "the Panama Canal and beyond."

When Villa killed seventeen people in Columbus, New Mexico, on March 9, 1916, President Wilson called up 150,000 National Guardsmen to seal the border while General Pershing crossed it with the regular army to capture and hang Villa, a mission that proved one of the army's less successful enterprises. Among the National Guard units ordered to Texas was the First Illinois Cavalry, one of whose officers was Major Robert R. McCormick. He had traded in his temporary commission as a colonel on the governor's staff for a permanent line commission two grades lower.

McCormick had noted the army's deficiency in automatic weapons (even the Mexicans had them). He induced a fellow officer, banker Charles G. Dawes, to raise enough money to buy six machine guns, along with several mobile field kitchens like those he had admired in the Russian army. Chicago meat-packer Ogden Armour threw in four mules and an Armour & Co. wagon. When McCormick reached Texas, his commanding general welcomed the machine guns and asked McCormick to position them to cover the Rio Grande bridge.

Joe Patterson had also joined up, as a private in fashionable Battery C of the First Illinois Artillery. On departing for the Mexican border the two cousins entrusted the *Tribune* to business manager William H. Field and managing editor Ted Beck. It turned out the cousins were missed no more than James Keeley.

More important than the management was the paper supply, which despite Ontario production was threatened by the increasingly tight market and the steadily rising size of circulation and daily editions. McCormick was able to buy a ship that became the foundation of a *Tribune* Great Lakes cargo fleet, on which he put his own stamp by introducing decent living quarters for the crew, even providing shower baths.

On leave in August to negotiate a deal for newsprint in New York, he called on Charles Evans Hughes, whose nomination as Republican presidential candidate the *Tribune* had supported. McCormick regarded Hughes's election as a certainty, since Wilson had won in 1912 thanks strictly to Teddy Roosevelt's splitting the party with his Bull Moose Progressives. The Republicans were again ideologically riven in 1916, but the two wings, interventionist and neutralist, found common ground in despising Wilson for his alleged failure at preparedness and his alleged weakness in defending American rights. In a *Tribune* cartoon, John McCutcheon drew Wilson composing a diplomatic note in verse addressed to "Mexico, England, Germany, France, Ireland or Patagonia":

> *I take my pen in hand to say*
> *I hear you're very rude today.*
> *If you don't stop, I do insist,*
> *Perhaps I'll slap you on the wrist.*

Hughes campaigned under the cumbersome slogan "America First and America Efficient." An old *Tribune* sportswriter named Robert W. Woolley, recruited to Wilson's campaign staff, countered with a winner: "Thank God for Wilson, he kept us out of war." Shortened on most billboards to simply "He kept us out of war," it gave Wilson a powerful shelter under which he could damn the "hyphenates," meaning the German-Americans, who were Republicans to begin with and had pledged their support to Hughes.

Few outside the Socialist Left commented on the strange campaign that saw both major-party candidates pledging to defend American rights to sail into the war zone and simultaneously promising to keep the country out of war. The candidates' hypocrisy mirrored that of the press and echoed the irrational psychology of the country. Everybody hated the Germans and nobody wanted to fight them.

McCormick spent the remainder of the summer and fall in Texas growing a moustache, playing polo, and drilling his cavalry in maneuvers that he said later convinced him that cavalry had no future against automatic weapons. He won a pistol competition, finished near the top with a rifle, and fired his first shot in combat. As part of an army effort to provoke a fight with the Mexicans across the river he rode along the shore and drew a shot from a Mexican horseman opposite. "I slid off my horse, steadied up my arm on his saddle and fired my Colt .45 revolver with a six-inch barrel, making allowance for the range. The Mexican went out of his saddle and his horse ran away. He then crawled under some cover or was concealed in the grass because I could not see to shoot him again."

The guardsmen were sent home just before the election, though McCormick noted that "many northern troops did not return in time to vote." Whether that made a difference or not, the race went down to the wire and past. The East was solid for Hughes, the Midwest almost equally so. The South and West went for Wilson, who also won squeakers in Ohio and Minnesota. On election night, the New York and Chicago papers plastered Hughes's handsomely bearded face on their front pages but in the morning, as Ohio fell to Wilson and the Far West was heard from, there were second thoughts. The *Tribune* got out a 9 A.M. extra to report WILSON NOW IN THE LEAD—STATES IN THE WEST MAY GIVE HIM A RE-ELECTION. But Hughes's picture, with the title "The Probable President-Elect," had merely been shifted from page one to page two as the paper strove to hedge its bets. In New York Pulitzer's *World* ingeniously modified its headline of HUGHES ELECTED IN CLOSE CONTEST by adding a question mark. The *Tribune* had to get out another 9 A.M. extra on Thursday to announce, WILSON THE WINNER, with a tardy portrait of the President.

On the momentous question of America's entry into the war, the Wilson-Hughes election made not the slightest difference. At the very moment of the election a much less public debate in Berlin over the pluses and minuses of "unrestricted" submarine warfare—that is, the torpedoing of all ships approaching Britain and France—was taking the issue out of the hands of U.S. politicians and editors. Announcement of the German decision, which curtailed a neutral shipping right that everyone still believed to be fundamental, logically moved McCormick and Patterson, with the whole bloc of nationalist-neutralists, into camp with the war hawks. Once committed, the *Tribune* was not slow in jumping into the front line. McCormick wrote old schoolmate Franklin D. Roosevelt a letter promising *Tribune* support for the navy, and asking advice on what sort of naval preparedness the country should be told it needed. Roosevelt expressed the opinion that universal military training and further large appropriations on the eve of war "would probably be of no value to the navy," since such things "must be provided beforehand." McCormick did what he could by contributing his own seventy-five-foot yacht, which Roosevelt accepted. The correspondence was chummy, the two old Grotonians saluting each other as "Frank" and "Bert," and the Republican editor assuring the Democratic official that he would like nothing better than to keep in touch.

McCormick joined the *New York Times* and the other pro-war newspapers in embracing the European allies. "We cannot sit in smug and snug security while other men die for our common cause," the *Tribune* asserted. It even went so far (May 17) as to advocate Wilson's League of Nations scheme,

> We have entered into a brotherhood of nations. It will last. . . . At bottom it is not a brotherhood leagued against Germany. At bottom it is a brotherhood of man that will in the end include Germany.

The *Tribune* thus came over to the war program of the more enlightened hawks. The neutralist Left, however, refused to be moved, and was joined by a handful of the conservative pacifists. Six senators, led by Wisconsin Progressive Bob LaFollette, and fifty congressmen, including majority leader Claude Kitchin of North Carolina, voted against the War Resolution. Representative Fred A. Britten, Illinois Republican, drew applause from gallery and floor when he referred to popular opposition to the war, exaggerating that "ninety percent of your people and mine do not want this declaration of war and are distinctly opposed to our going into that bloody mire on the other side."

On that last point there remained not only profound disagreement, but profound misunderstanding. Nobody—McCormick, Roosevelt, Wilson—realized how large the American commitment was going to be, or in McCormick's case, how it was going to affect him personally.

CHAPTER EIGHT

The First Division

THE nation's psychological transition from arsenal of democracy, a phrase not yet invented but appropriate, to full combat role was accomplished in 1917 with astonishing ease. The passage of the War Resolution and the unanimity of press opinion created overnight an atmosphere of unrestrained ardor for military victory, sweeping along the hesitant and silencing the dissenters.

Looking back on the phenomenon two years later, McCormick was impressed by the role played by an Allied mission whose outstanding figure was Marshal Joffre. "Of all the strangers who ever came to our shore," wrote McCormick, "Joffre exercised the greatest influence over our people and upon our destiny. He captured public opinion at once, and the people imposed his recommendations upon Congress, President, and army alike." In Washington, Medill McCormick, elected to Congress in 1916, translated Joffre's sobering phrases for the press, which treated the message with sympathy not short of enthusiasm. When Joffre arrived in Chicago, Mayor Thompson refused to extend an official invitation. The City Council indignantly voted the invitation (the socialist members opposed), the Rotary Club expelled Thompson, and Bishop Kinsolving of Texas recommended that he be shot. The *Tribune* contented itself with a gibe—perhaps Thompson could preserve his neutrality by also inviting Von Hindenburg.

McCormick personally was "so affected by a meeting in honor of Joffre that, upon returning to my office, I dictated a letter to General Pershing offering my services in any capacity." He left the letter unsigned, the thought occurring to him that he was already an officer of the National Guard and likely to be included in the Joffre-proposed American army. However, his secretary sent the letter off to Washington unsigned, and he at once received an invitation to join Pershing's new headquarters in France. In retrospect McCormick thought he might have been lucky, since his eyes had not improved in the twenty years since the Naval Academy had turned him down.

Apparently only one eye was affected, because he purchased a monocle for overseas wear, to which he presently added a cane in deference to an old athletic knee injury. A photo shows him with Sam Browne belt, one

hand on hip, the other resting on gloves and cane, the pip-pip British officer
image popular with 1917 Yanks.

Only two *Tribune* friends saw him off at the station, Joe Patterson and
Henry J. Reilly. Reilly was an ex-army officer for whom McCormick had
obtained a commission as colonel in the Illinois National Guard; at the
same time, he got the governor to make Patterson a lieutenant.

Once more he took Amy along. They sailed in war-shrouded secrecy from
New York on June 30, 1917, on a French Line ship aboard which McCormick was the recipient of a curious and thoughtful gift. The manager of the
French Line, M. Kosminski, was aboard and at dinner one night McCormick expressed an apprehension at finding himself lying helplessly wounded
in no-man's-land. Next day he received several morphine capsules—Mme.
Kosminski was dying of cancer—which he had sewn into his uniform.

Landing in France on July 12, he reported to American general headquarters in Paris, where Pershing greeted him with a copy of the new army
edition of the *Chicago Tribune.* Joe Pierson, an enterprising member of the
Chicago staff, had conceived the idea and McCormick had sent him to Paris
to implement it. Pierson had arrived in Paris less than a week before July
4, the target date McCormick had set for the first issue. Speaking no French,
he hired a pretty secretary-interpreter, two linotypers who spoke no English, and a proofreader, and took an office in the Rue Royale two flights
above Maxim's. The paper thus inaugurated had a remarkable postwar
career, but its immediate value, besides serving the American troops with
home news, was to give the home *Tribune* a European base. Chief war
correspondent was daredevil Floyd Gibbons, who had deliberately courted
U-boat danger on his way over, gotten torpedoed and sunk, and survived
to write a great eyewitness story. In Paris, McCormick met and hired Peggy
Hull, a Texas reporter who became, briefly, the first woman war correspondent. Her career ended when jealous male correspondents successfully
protested that the *Tribune* should not be allowed to have both her and
Gibbons accredited to Pershing's headquarters. Still another *Tribune* correspondent was Ring Lardner, who appeared at the office in the Rue Royale
one day with the improbable announcement that McCormick had assigned
him to cover "the funny side of the war." Lardner had already found a
funny side in the training-camp adventures of his fictional baseball hero,
Jack Keefe.

Visiting the U.S. Army's press headquarters in Castellane House, Rue de
Constantine, McCormick found that chief press officer Frederick Palmer
was desperate for an aide who could deal competently with the correspondents. McCormick suggested Mark Watson, a *Tribune* man who had just
finished officers' training in Illinois, and Palmer got him assigned.

When McCormick reached Pershing's new headquarters at Neufchateau, in eastern France, he started off as liaison officer with the French war department, and soon learned that the American troops were the subject of a spirited inter-Allied debate. Invited to the home of the U.S. counselor of embassy, who had previously been counselor under McCormick's father, he found himself engaged in conversation by "a charming English major general." The general wanted McCormick to convey a suggestion to Pershing. The British, he said, considered American soldiers "every bit as good as their colonial troops, but this was not a colonial war and it would be wise for us to place the American army under British command."

The State Department man evidently thought McCormick would share the State Department's point of view and agree with the British. When he did not, "the counselor's wife asked me rather scornfully if I thought our generals from the Philippines and Mexico were in a class with the British generals." The question was not as silly or subservient as it might sound, but when McCormick reported his experience to Pershing, he was told, "You acted exactly right, McCormick, as I would have expected you to do."

The French were as eager as the British to take command of the American army, but at first were reticent about giving any information about their own, a large part of which had recently been in a state of mutiny. To find out how many Allied divisions there were in line, McCormick ascertained where his French liaison kept the list in his desk and surreptitiously copied it. Competing with the British for American favor, however, the French turned cooperative and gave the Americans many pieces of information, ranging from terms of the secret treaties among the Allies to decoded German radio messages from Spain giving their U-boats information on troop convoys. "This was a real act of friendship, as the French staff was so anxious to keep secret the fact that it could decode the German dispatches that it had never given any decoded information to its other allies or even to its own navy." When he looked into the problem of transmitting the French information to the U.S. Navy, he found that the American army and navy were as disconnected from each other as the French and found it expedient simply to call on the naval attaché at the U.S. Embassy.

Another piece of information divulged by French intelligence gave McCormick an insight into the psychology of generals: The Catholic party in Germany had made a secret peace overture via Switzerland. "When I told this to General Pershing, he was terribly disturbed that peace might come before he could have his war."

McCormick credited his old Chicago banker friend Charlie Dawes with striking a blow for American liberation from British psychological ascendancy. "General Pershing and his regular army staff were very formal . . . but could not begin to be as formal as the British who finished their dinners with after-dinner coffee and did not smoke until after they had proposed the king's health." Dawes, a brigadier general and purchasing agent, began his first formal dinner with the British by lighting a cigar with his soup and followed up by drinking coffee American-style all through dinner. "He asked the lady next to him what her name was, and when she said Lady Anne Rutledge, he replied: 'How nice of you to let me call you by your first name, Anne. Call me Charlie.' He completely wrecked the British ascendancy and was the dominating influence in interarmy relations throughout the war."

At GHQ McCormick had been appointed chief of the Russian section of Intelligence. When Russia dropped out of the war following the October (Bolshevik) Revolution, Captain Billy Mitchell, future air war prophet, recommended him for chief of the aviation section. Mitchell helped indoctrinate him for the post by teaching him to fly, but after Mitchell's transfer elsewhere the job was given to a graduate of the War College, and though McCormick still had high seniority on the staff, he asked to be transferred to the line. A newly arrived artillery brigade included his old National Guard cavalry outfit, now the 122nd Field Artillery. He needed an automobile and obtained one by getting a friend to buy a secondhand Model T Ford in England. He had it shipped to Le Havre, whence a "wild reporter"— future *Front Page* author Charles MacArthur—drove it to Paris for him, though nearly wrecking it in the process.

Every month throughout his stay in France he received a letter from Bill Field in Chicago detailing the newspaper's situation and problems—coal shortage, power curtailment, Canadian government orders to supply newsprint from Thorold for the *London* (Ontario) *Free Press,* and the painful squeeze the paper shortage placed on newspaper prosperity in the winter of 1917–1918.

Meantime at the American artillery base at Valdahon, in Burgundy, McCormick joined fellow officers in studying under French instructors, and himself translated a French book on orientation, the location of batteries by map, to which he added some forest craft he had learned in his Canadian timber-cruising. He also translated mathematics lessons that the non-West Pointers needed. Discovering that the French had no plans to teach the Americans tactics to go with their firing technique, on the grounds that tactical command of American artillery would remain with the French, he protested to Pershing and to Pershing's chief of staff, General Harbord, who told him to learn all he could about batteries and let tactics be learned at the front. His natural bent and strong academic background made him an exceptionally good artilleryman. A fellow officer later inscribed a book to "R. R. McCormick, who could aim his 155s by the North Star."

In January 1918 the First Division moved up to Lunéville, in the quiet sector of Lorraine, with Major McCormick in command of a battalion of

155-mm. howitzers. As the division was ordered into line, he came down with a bad cold. "The division doctor said I would never get rid of it in those surroundings and [ordered] me to the South of France," but he stayed with his outfit and "was never warm or dry for several weeks. . . . A French priest, who was also a major, gave me a small barrel of wine and a big demijohn of rum. He said to drink the wine regularly and take the rum just after I had gone to bed. I followed his prescription and came into perfect health."

On March 21 the Germans launched their win-the-war offensive against the British at the northern end of the Allied line. French troops were quickly switched northward and in the scramble to fill out the line the U.S. First Division was ordered to a position north of Paris. On the road to Amiens they passed through a flood of refugees and the debris of discarded knapsacks, blankets, and weapons of the routed British Fifth Army. Miles short of where the front was supposed to be McCormick spotted barrage balloons and halted his battalion of 155s. Not knowing where the division infantry or the other artillery outfits were, he kept the guns "in battery" with the men sleeping around them and the horses picketed close by. He sent his two noncoms, Sergeant Cohen and Corporal Janette, to the local telephone station, and went to bed, only to be awakened by the regimental commander, who gave him orders for next day. He was to proceed to French division HQ at Mesnil-la-Tour, get breakfast and a guide, and locate the outpost line, the main line of resistance, and the reserve line. Because this was supposed to be a "stabilized section" the heavy artillery was moving in first in the process of relieving the French division holding it.

As soon as the colonel left, McCormick assembled his battery commanders and gave the orders. Because the command post of the French division was in a château in sight of the Germans McCormick started out in time to get there before daybreak. He and his driver located the château, but were surprised to get no challenge from a sentry. It turned out there was no sentry; the door was opened by a servant. The French general who presently appeared was very elderly, sleepy, and clad in a worn dress uniform, having been summoned out of retirement for the emergency. He did not know exactly where the front was, and could spare no officer as a guide. For breakfast he could offer nothing but coffee and brandy, which McCormick accepted to try to stay awake.

Guided by the sound of the guns, McCormick found a French battery firing, horses close by, not looking very much like a "stabilized section." The commanding officer assigned a lieutenant to show him the front line. They arrived at a wall on the near side of which stood a number of French soldiers.

"Let's push on to the front line," said McCormick in French.

"This is the front line," his guide told him.
"Then let's find the outpost line."
"It is also the outpost line."
"And the main line of resistance?"
"It is the only line we have."

Finding the situation a little too casual for comfort, McCormick sent word back to his commanding officer by his driver, leaving him without a car. When he learned that the French general of corps artillery was a few miles off to the left, he walked there to ask for orders, but the general knew nothing about Americans coming into the sector and said he had no authority to give them orders.

That night McCormick's batteries arrived. He no sooner had them in position than he received a message from the French corps commander: though disclaiming the right to issue an order, he would be obliged if the American officer would fire on a certain target on his left flank. McCormick expressed curiosity at the target's being on the left instead of in front, and the officer bearing the message explained that the British were still falling back toward Amiens and the fire would be in their support. He complied with the request.

The French infantry now was ordered out without waiting for the First Division infantry to reach the all-purpose front line. A sleepless, worried McCormick moved his antiaircraft machine guns to the front of his battery in case German shock troops showed up, ordered his guns to fire at anything suspicious, and stayed awake on coffee and brandy. When the infantry finally arrived, he turned in, exhausted, and slept through a visit from the brigadier general. As a result he found himself in receipt of charges of being asleep on duty and smelling of liquor. McCormick dispatched a message answering the charges "with more eloquence than tact," but a friendly sergeant major intercepted his answer and nothing further came of the incident. McCormick was later gratified to hear that the brigadier general had failed as a commander and had been sent home reduced in rank.

Over the following days, as the French finally wrestled the German attack to a halt, the First Division held its position on the flank of the main combat, with McCormick's 155s firing continuously. "We fired on enemy batteries," McCormick recalled later, "we fired on enemy machine gun nests, we fired on any points where enemy troops were, or were supposed to be. If we could locate their kitchens, we killed them while they were eating. If we knew where they slept we killed them in their sleep. We did not indulge or gratify ourselves by war worker platitudes about Huns and noble causes. We expected to die.

"We were savage and saturnine and took prisoners more for information than for mercy. . . . The Germans did the same to us. They knocked our little town about our ears and we had to go elsewhere. I took up my abode in a hedge. It was not rainproof but it furnished concealment."

He had a dugout made for his command post and had the men dig foxholes. The Germans never spotted the position, but the constant fire they kept on the railroad to the rear frequently dropped short rounds on it. McCormick's gunners worked in shifts, the officers continuously "until they were played out and then they were replaced.

"Every night the burying parties worked. Every night the ambulances went out with the wounded. Every night the ammunition wagons brought up the replacements."

Once McCormick wanted to open fire, but was told not to by division headquarters. He used his own judgment and fired. Ordered to report to General Summerall, the artillery brigade commander, for a reprimand, he was embarrassed at arriving during lunch and reporting before the whole staff, but Summerall rose and shook his hand: "Thank heavens, there is somebody in this brigade who knows when to disobey an order."

Early in May, the First Division was hit by double disaster. On the night of May 3 the Eighteenth Infantry got a massive bath of gas shells mixed with high explosive. Two hundred infantrymen were killed, another eight hundred wounded or incapacitated by gas. Long lines of doughboys were evacuated like blind men, hands on the shoulders of the man ahead, retching and coughing, eyes stuck shut. At about the same time the virulent "Spanish influenza," just beginning its devastating sweep of both armies and most of the world besides, struck the division. McCormick got a whiff of the gas and a serious case of the flu, but was ordered by his commanding officer to stay on as one of the few senior officers familiar with the sector. Wrapping himself in his blanket roll, he commanded from a telephone at his bedside.

He was in this state when the First Division was ordered to launch the first American offensive of the war, against the German-held town of Cantigny directly opposite. Major McCormick had to be assisted to the meeting of field-grade officers at which Pershing gave a football coach's pep talk. McCormick made a last-minute check of his dug-in batteries, and narrowly missed death when an enemy shell burst close by, knocking him down and leaving him stunned. Lieutenant Arthur Schmon, an eager beaver fresh out of Princeton whom he had made his adjutant, helped him back to his command post.

D day was May 28. On the morning of the twenty-seventh the Germans sent over a heavy barrage followed by two raiding parties, but evidently learned nothing from the prisoners taken. The Allied barrage the next morning was supplemented by several batteries of French heavy guns. General de Chambrun, descendant of Lafayette, who took charge of the combined artillery, assigned McCormick's 155s the German frontline trench. The lines were so close together that McCormick realized that some short rounds from his guns would inevitably fall in American trenches. He explained the situation to the colonel commanding the Twenty-eighth Infantry and early in the morning took personal charge of registry fire. The full barrage began at 5:15 to such effect that "there was not a living German in the trench when we attacked." The infantry charged across the narrow no-man's-land behind a scattering of French light tanks and captured the ruined town against slight resistance.

Next day the victory of Cantigny was trumpeted in the French and American press out of proportion to its strategic value. Part of the reason was that elsewhere the news was bad, the Germans having scored a major breakthrough against worn-out French and British divisions in Champagne.

In the middle of the battle, McCormick's monthly letter from Bill Field brought news of the end of Keeley's *Herald* in the face of the newsprint shortage (it was taken over by Hearst's *Examiner*), and shortly afterward the Spanish flu finally knocked him out. In a base hospital in Paris he slept for two days and awoke "to find a friend, Cornelia Armsby of Evanston, sitting by my bed." Another visitor was Amy, who was directing a branch of the American Duryea war relief fund. As soon as McCormick was able to get out of bed the two of them went to visit *Tribune* correspondent Floyd Gibbons, whose frontline coverage of the Second Division's assault on Belleau Wood had cost him his left eye. Out of feeling for Gibbons' wounds the censor had allowed his last dispatch to go through despite his breaking rules by naming Belleau Wood and the U.S. Marines who formed one brigade of the Second Division. Gibbons had already foiled one censor in Britain with a dispatch beginning, "Major General John J. Pershing landed at a British port today and was greeted by the Lord Mayor of Liverpool." His scoop on the marines helped create a legend, much to the annoyance of the army.

McCormick also drove out to Château-Thierry to offer his enfeebled services to the commanding general (evidently of the U.S. Third Division, which had come into line there), but "they could not have been very useful," as he admitted, and were politely declined.

Eventually McCormick was reassigned as adjutant to the Twenty-sixth Division. In August he was promoted to full colonel and as one of the oldest officers in point of service ordered home by Pershing to help organize troops for the Allied offensive of 1919. Though reluctant to leave Europe, he had visions of returning at the head of his own division, doubting no more than anyone else that the war would be going strong next year. Before leaving he looked up Joe Patterson, whose battery was part of the Forty-second

(Rainbow) Division that, like McCormick's First, had played a conspicuous role in the Second Battle of the Marne in mid-July. At Forty-second Division headquarters McCormick borrowed a helmet and gas mask from the assistant division commander, General Douglas MacArthur, and found Patterson at a regimental command post at the village of Mareuil-en-Dole. To find a place to talk, the two climbed out a window of the farmhouse in which the CP was quartered and seated themselves on what McCormick originally described as a manure pile, though for his radio audience he later amended it to a straw pile. There Patterson unfolded his dream of the postwar world. If he made it through to peace he wanted to launch a tabloid newspaper in New York modeled on the London *Daily Mirror,* to which John McCutcheon had introduced him in 1914, and whose founding genius, Lord Northcliffe, Patterson had visited on furlough. McCormick, who felt a little guilty about going home and leaving Patterson in combat, promised to get Bill Field going on the preliminary work.

He and Amy landed in New York August 22, and returned to Chicago, McCormick having been assigned to Fort Sheridan. There he commanded a battalion of cavalry converting to artillery, a regiment of National Guardsmen, and "a large number of doctors." The Spanish flu was raging: "A man who attended officers' call in the morning would turn black and die before night."

On October 18 the papers reported him heading back to France. He looked forward to commanding his own division, in which he planned to save a post as major for Joe Patterson, who had just made captain. The Armistice on November 11 intervened. He was put in for the Distinguished Service Medal, and was offered a commission as brigadier general.

He accepted the medal but declined the commission. The peacetime army held little appeal. Yet his war experiences in France were a high point in his life. Years later he attributed the "dourness" of which he was sometimes accused to his exposure to the realities of battle, but his memory of the First Division was more complicated than that. When he renovated Joseph Medill's Red Oaks Farm at Wheaton he renamed the place "Cantigny," a bit of romanticism, anachronism, and egotism that recalled Marlborough's "Blenheim" and McClellan's "Antietam." In 1938, at Pershing's request, he represented the First Division at a memorial celebration at the original Cantigny where he delivered an old-fashioned martial oration that emphasized not the grimness but the glory. He was so infatuated with the sound of his own peroration—"March on! March on, First Division," etc.—that he had it incised among the innumerable inscriptions on the Tribune Tower (far up on the Gothic facade, where no one can read it) and in the library hearth at his own Cantigny. There he also found a prominent place for the First Division's citation from Pershing, contemplation of which reminded him of "what a priceless experience it was to serve in that division."

At the same time there was the disillusion, the sense of the futility of the slaughter, which he shared with the rest of the country. Nearly all Americans, stay-at-home as well as veterans, felt the ambivalence expressed in the school Armistice Day assemblies that combined one minute of silence with heroic flag-and-gun tableaux. Fueled in no small part by the mischief-making "war debts," an antiwar, anti-European cynicism competed with a hangover romantic militarism (characteristically in the stage hit *What Price Glory?*). Slowly the first sentiment won ascendancy, with a universal agreement among all parties, old war hawks, old neutralists, and the new generation, that whatever the merits of the crusade to save the world for democracy, it had been a failure and should never, never be repeated, a consensus achieved just about the time Hitler came into power.

CHAPTER NINE

"Tribune Has Treaty!"

THE year 1919 marked a major transition in McCormick's life as in that of the country. The dream that Joe Patterson had unfolded on the manure pile in France was swiftly translated into the *New York Daily News,* which beat Hearst's rival tabloid, the *Daily Mirror,* to the starting gate, and soon left all competition behind, achieving the largest circulation in New York and far surpassing even its parent *Chicago Tribune.*

Patterson's paper, it is true, seemed to substantiate Walter Howey's indictment of him as "a common pander, catering to the meretricious tastes of the masses"—with Frank Carson, for whose drunken letter of resignation Howey had dictated the phrase, as the chief assistant caterer. Nevertheless, the *Daily News* had verve and wit. A few publishers, notably Bernarr McFadden, copied the whole format. Many more were influenced by the glib and grabby style. *Time* magazine was a sort of glossy, intellectualized version, and newspapers everywhere, after seeing a few copies of the *News,* brightened up their head and caption writing.

The fact that Patterson did not immediately transfer his complete attention to New York underlined the remarkable degree of concert between the two cousins in Chicago. The *Daily News* was founded not to allow them to part company but to permit each a sufficient sphere of his own. On the other hand, the fact that Patterson at once took Max Annenberg and Bill Field to New York added to McCormick's weight of responsibility in Chicago. To replace Field he hired his old law partner and Northwestern classmate, Samuel Emory Thomason, who soon became vice-president and general manager at a salary and bonuses amounting to $250,000 a year, believed to be the highest pay of a newspaper employee in the country and certainly an indication of the *Tribune*'s affluence.

Moe Annenberg having also left, McCormick hired Louis Rose, a brother-in-law of the Annenbergs who proved to be another circulation genius with a fine sense of what sold newspapers. Managing editor Ted Beck joked that he was going to title his autobiography *The Colonel Told Me,* and that Louis Rose could write the sequel, *I Told the Colonel.*

Another personnel move of 1919 that turned out happily was hiring McCormick's wartime adjutant, young Arthur Schmon, to take charge of the suspended Shelter Bay construction. Schmon arrived, still in uniform, in time for a fiasco. McCormick had conceived the idea of sinking an old hulk loaded with worn-out millstones as part of the foundation of a wharf. He had picked up a war-surplus subchaser to use as a headquarters boat, naming it the *Mareuil-en-Dole,* after the village where he and Patterson had planned the *New York Daily News.* Aboard the *Mareuil,* McCormick and Schmon watched the millstone-laden *Egan* run onto a shoal. "Good thing we found that," McCormick commented nonchalantly. "We'll have to mark it with a buoy." He was the second explorer to find the shoal—Jacques Cartier found and reported it in 1534, but failed to mark it with a buoy.

High tide floated the *Egan* and she was towed to the wharf site and sunk. McCormick, Warren Curtis, and Schmon went ashore to celebrate, but at three in the morning a storm came up and slowly pounded the *Egan* to pieces, scattering her and her millstones uselessly. Curtis and Schmon were downcast—the boss's idea hadn't worked. But McCormick told them, "Cheer up, this has only cost us about twenty thousand dollars."

He didn't abandon the idea, and the following year it worked.

Back at the *Tribune* he divided 1919 between editorial problems and reflections on the war. He was not the only person trying to make sense out of it, but he may have been the only one to do his thinking while practicing polo shots aboard a mechanical horse on the roof of a seventeen-story building. In *The Army of 1918* he got his thoughts down on paper. Their focus was the military lesson he felt America should learn from the war. The nation had corrected its most glaring defense weakness by almost overnight building a navy that amazingly not only displaced the kaiser's scuttled fleet as the British navy's chief rival, but promised to achieve parity with the British. Nevertheless, McCormick felt that despite Armistice and victory the war's chief effect on American defense was to spotlight its shortcomings.

The nation's ground forces, he thought, should be maintained in a much better state of readiness. The Draft Act of 1917 he termed "one of the great milestones in our national evolution" and thought future historians would class it with the Constitutional Convention and Civil War. He did not revert to his idea of fortifying inland cities or indeed to fortification at all, indicating a realization that the fixed fortifications that had played a conspicuous part in 1914–1915 seemed to have lost their value in 1918. At the same time, and despite his flying lessons from Billy Mitchell, he resisted the postwar infatuation with air power that made Mitchell, Italian general Giulio Douhet, and other enthusiasts see airplanes virtually replacing armies and navies. "From the point of view of military attack," he wrote," airplane bombing is not effective. . . . As a weapon of destruction the airplane cannot compete with the artillery in accuracy or volume of fire." Of the four principal innovations in military technology—airplanes, tanks, trucks, and poison gas—he pointed out that airplanes had "practically monopolized public attention." Least appreciated of the four was the homely truck, whose military advocacy by the *Tribune* in the next few years brought recognition in 1940 from Lieutenant General Hugh A. Drum, who credited McCormick with "a very definite and prominent influence in the adoption by the army of the general proposition of mechanization."

The army itself he sharply criticized on several counts; the Ordnance Department's aversion to the machine gun, an American invention (Hiram Maxim) that had been offered the army gratis in the improved version of Colonel Isaac Lewis; the Quartermaster Corps' absurd uniform design which dressed the infantry doughboys in riding breeches and handicapped them with poor footwear; the unchallenged reign of seniority that assumed "that a soldier was senile at 64 but at the height of his power at 63 years, 11 months and 30 days."

He blamed the failure of many American officers on their arrogant disdain of French advice (something Pershing was as guilty of as any, though McCormick tactfully refrained from saying so). He cited France as a model of preparedness—"equal at the front and stronger at the rear" even than Germany. He missed something there. The superready state of French and Germany military preparedness in 1914, created in large measure by the mischievous Schlieffen Plan, had led to Europe's going to war over nothing. The great conundrum was, how prepare an adequate defense without risking having the preparation itself cause war? *The Army of 1918* did not face the problem.

In 1919 McCormick also found time to revisit Paris and make a decision that shortly paid a sensational dividend. American tourists were already flocking to Europe and McCormick decided to keep the Paris *Chicago Tribune* going for this new clientele. Though the little paper never quite managed to compete with the *New York Herald*'s rival version, McCormick took pride in the fact that it exercised an unexpected influence on art and literature by promoting such little-known geniuses as Rilke, Céline, Kafka, Aymé, Mauriac, Stein, and Joyce.

The Paris *Chicago Tribune* also played a role in a scoop that may have altered history.

The closed-door peace conference at Versailles had become an object of intense journalistic interest. Woodrow Wilson had made the cardinal blunder of failing to take a delegation of Republican senators with him, while many of Wilson's own constituents suspected the Allies of plotting to ditch the president's Fourteen Points in favor of harsher treatment of Germany. Wilson's strategy was to keep the terms of the treaty secret until he could bring it home and explain it point by point to the Senate.

Liberals who objected to an imperialist peace, nationalists who objected to the League of Nations, pro-German ethnics, and people who couldn't see what America was getting out of the war all had their fears and suspicions fed by the six-month travail at Versailles.

Naturally, there were leaks. On May 8 the *Tribune* published a twelve-thousand-word summary of the treaty, and other newspapers got hold of similar reports. By June a copy of the text was known to be in the possession of the State Department, but under lock and key until Wilson got home. The Senate was seething, the Republican opposition furious, the press frustrated and overheated, and the whole country cynically suspicious. In this atmosphere, the *Tribune* banner of June 9, 1919, was a stunner:

TRIBUNE HAS TREATY!

The story ran under the by-line of Frazier Hunt, one of the paper's best and most adventurous correspondents, but over his own protests, because Hunt had merely played the role of messenger. After covering the Russian Revolution and the Allied intervention, he was passing through Paris on his way home when the scoop happened, partly by luck, partly by the efforts of Henry Wales, a correspondent whom Hunt described as "a natural gumshoer," and Spearman Lewis, editor of the Paris *Chicago Tribune* and bureau head.

Wales had planted with various dissatisfied delegations the notion that the *Chicago Tribune* was critical of the way the peace conference had been run in secret, contrary to Wilson's pledge of "open covenants openly arrived at." The tactic paid off when one morning a Chinese official took the bait and made a wary contact. Lewis and the Chinese (identified many years later as a certain George Chen) had a series of clandestine meetings in the parking zone outside the Crillon, on the Place de la Concorde, sometimes in the *Tribune* car, sometimes in the embassy limo, sometimes in a taxi. Lewis swore eternal secrecy and pledged that the *Tribune* would take note of the Chinese objection to Section XV, Article 156, giving Japan the former German mandate of Shantung. At last the Chinese brought a copy of the treaty to a rendezvous, only to drive Lewis crazy by taking alarm and decamping, treaty clutched in hand. Next day, however, he called at the *Tribune* office in the Rue Royale and brought the document, wrapped in paper. Before entrusting it to Frazier Hunt for the journey home Lewis made Hunt take an oath that he would never disclose the source of the scoop, because if he did Lewis might have to leave France.

Hunt took the treaty through customs hidden in an old dressing gown, then wired McCormick and Patterson from New York. Next morning he met them in Patterson's office. A question arose: Now that they had the treaty, what exactly should they do with it? The focal point of the national controversy was the floor of the Senate, and it was decided that Hunt should take the text to Washington and present it to Senator Borah, leader of the opposition to the treaty's most controversial section, the League of Nations. On the morning of June 9 the *Trib* had its scoop, and that afternoon Hunt presented his package to Senator Borah, who inserted it in the Congres- sional Record. Next day the *New York Times* did a neat piggyback scoop of its own by getting out an eight-page special section containing the whole 75,000-word text.

The effect of the *Tribune*'s coup is hard to explain, since the full text of the treaty contained no startling, previously unknown information. Ver- sailles, in fact, was not a bad treaty—after all, most of it is still in effect. Somehow the tension and aggravation of the waiting period and the drama of the revelation seemed to mix with other elements to produce a violent reaction, perhaps akin to that of the Pentagon Papers half a century later. The storm that broke was so large that Spearman Lewis in Paris changed his mind and accepted public credit (along with a one thousand dollar bonus). Senators, congressmen, and editors loyal to Wilson denounced the premature publication, and Wilson himself blamed it for the ultimate defeat of ratification.

That seems farfetched, in the light of the breadth and intensity of the debate, especially since the controversy centered so largely on the league issue. Prominent in the opposition was Medill McCormick, elected to the Senate in 1918. The *Tribune* supported the "reservations" on the league, yet the newspaper's posture was moderate. American opposition to the league in fact grew much stronger after the issue was settled.

The summer of 1919 also saw Colonel McCormick defend himself and the *Tribune* against a charge of libel lodged by one of the *Tribune*'s biggest advertisers, Henry Ford. Getting sued was no novelty for the *Tribune.* Bill Thompson had sued the paper three times in the previous two years for a total of $1,350,000, claiming libel in its unfriendly reportage of his attitude toward the war. (Thompson also sued Victor Lawson's *Daily News,* the *Chicago Evening Post,* and the *New York Herald Tribune* for libel, losing every case.)

Consequently McCormick's old law firm, now headed by a capable attor- ney named Weymouth Kirkland, had plenty of experience in libel suits involving the alleged impugning of somebody's patriotism when the case of *Henry Ford* vs. *Chicago Tribune* reached the courtroom, not in Chicago, but in Mount Clemens, Michigan (north of Detroit).

Back in 1916, at the time of the Mexican trouble, Ford had publicly opposed calling out the National Guard and had termed the looming war against Mexico "organized murder." McCormick might have told him the campaign wasn't that well organized, but the *Trib* had published a news story charging that Ford workers who volunteered for service faced loss of their jobs, and had followed up with an editorial beguilingly titled "Henry Ford Is an Anarchist." The text repeated the news story's statements and declared that

> If Ford allows this rule of his shops to stand he will reveal himself not merely as an ignorant idealist but as an anarchistic enemy of the nation which protects him in his wealth. . . . The proper place for so deluded a human being is a region where no government exists except such as he furnishes. . . . Such a place, we think, might be found anywhere in the state of Chihuahua, Mexico. Anywhere in Mexico would be a good location for the Ford factories.

The editorial was written by Clifford Raymond but shown to McCormick, who was momentarily in Chicago between a trip to Canada and his National Guard service. Ford issued a denial of the news story, and the *Trib* printed the denial, which probably would have ended the affair except for that word *anarchist*. Thanks to the "anarchist," batteries of lawyers and armies of witnesses—Texans for the *Tribune,* Mexicans for Ford—flooded Mount Clemens in May 1919, for a trial that was enlivened by the personal testimony of both Colonel McCormick and Henry Ford.

On the stand McCormick frankly admitted his approval of the famous editorial—he had given it a quick reading and told Raymond, "Go ahead." He recalled that his mind had been occupied by the lack of machine guns of his First Illinois Cavalry, adding, "Mr. Ford was one of the reasons we could not get them," a comment promptly stricken from the record.

Ford counsel William Lucking tried to discredit the Colonel with insinuations about his motivation as a correspondent and a soldier:

"Captain Patterson had made a little name for himself as a war correspondent," he remarked.

"I would say that he made a very good name for himself," McCormick corrected.

"And you thought you would go over and make a little name for yourself?" the lawyer inquired. McCormick denied any such ambition, explaining that his mother's friendship for the Russian ambassador made possible his trip, which he was eager to make because "I had never seen a battle."

The lawyer switched his sarcasm to McCormick's Mexican service:

"Where did you live down there?"

"In a tent."

"Bring your wife down there?"

"Later, yes. I rented a house, as most of the other officers did after the crisis had passed."

"Bring your cook down, too?"

"No, like other officers, I had a soldier cook."

On the subject of anarchists and anarchy, Lucking quoted some of the *Tribune*'s 1917 editorials in support of the brotherhood of nations, and inquired if they might not be construed as anarchistic, but the witness did not think so.

Henry Ford's testimony produced the never-to-be-forgotten, but mis-quoted, line "History is bunk," derided as revealing the Neanderthal bent one might expect of an auto mechanic, even if he was a production genius. What Ford really said was not bad—"History is more or less bunk. We want to live in the present, and the only history that is worth a tinker's dam is the history we make today."

Ford in fact came off well on the stand and probably repaired his wartime reputation, which was not that of an anarchist but of a crackpot—his antiwar activism had extended to a fairly strenuous attempt in 1915 to get the European governments to listen to reason, though it had not prevented him from manufacturing gun carriages and airplane engines in 1918. No-body took the anarchist issue seriously and the Michigan jury sensibly found for Ford and awarded him twelve cents—six cents damages and six cents cost. Colonel McCormick thought the *Tribune* had got its money's worth in advertising promotion—its lawyers had even drawn glowing, quo-table responses from Ford's advertising manager on the value of the *Tribune* as a medium for selling cars. Years later, in World War II, he took an opportunity to write Ford a nice letter. Ford had probably already forgiven and forgotten, having himself written the *Tribune* an urgent letter on the occasion of Little Orphan Annie's loss of her dog: "Please do all you can to help Annie find Sandy."

That did not conclude the *Trib*'s postwar litigation. Bill Thompson, who had lost the Republican nomination for senator to Medill McCormick in 1918 but managed to get reelected mayor of Chicago in 1919, was madder than ever as the *Tribune* added exposure of corruption to its charges of aid and comfort to the kaiser. When it accused him of bankrupting the city he spotted what looked like a great legal opening and had his corporation counsel file a suit in the name of the city on the grounds that the *Tribune* had damaged Chicago's credit. Cited among other articles was one in which the *Tribune* had roundly asserted that the city's government was "bank-rupt, insolvent, broke, in a bad financial condition, and so improperly and corruptly administered by its officers that its streets were not properly cleaned and its laws not efficiently enforced." Thompson wanted the *Trib-une* to pay the city $10 million in damages. The idea of a government suing for libel was completely novel in the United States, but corporation counsel Samuel Ettelson, a gift to Thompson from utilities magnate Samuel Insull, cited as a precedent a suit against the Manchester Ship Canal in England.

McCormick brought to bear on the case not only his background in publishing and the law, but in canals. Inspecting the Manchester Ship Canal on his 1910 trip he had become acquainted with its corporate character, which was more that of a private enterprise than a public agency, and Weymouth Kirkland was able to argue that the Thompson suit was "libel upon government," a legal form once permitted but long since repealed in Britain and never introduced in the United States. Yet no court had ruled on its legality, and McCormick was worried. He "delved deeply into the origin and history of the freedom of the press" to help Kirkland come up with convincing precedent, and in the end Judge Harry M. Fisher of the Cook County Circuit Court found for the defendant.

Thompson appealed, and ultimately the *Tribune* was vindicated by a unanimous decision of the state supreme court. The case became a landmark in press jurisprudence. The essence of the courts' view was expressed by Judge Fisher: "The harm [the press] can do has its own limitations. The press is dependent for its success, for its very existence, almost, upon public confidence. . . . It cannot long indulge in falsehoods without suffering the loss of that confidence from which alone comes its power, its prestige and its reward. On the other hand, the harm which would certainly result to the community from an officialdom unrestrained by fear of publicity is incalculable." In February 1923 the Illinois Supreme Court sustained Judge Fisher. Chief Justice Floyd Thompson asserted that "history teaches that human liberty cannot be secured unless there is freedom to express grievances," a sentiment that found its way to the north wall of the Tribune Tower lobby.

McCormick now came up with a legal novelty of his own. Colonel William Judson of the corps of engineers told him the new double-decker Michigan Avenue lift bridge had cost a million dollars more than it should have because of huge fees paid to "expert consultants." *Tribune* reporters discovered that the "consultants" were expert only in needling the beer in their speakeasies and getting out the vote on election day. The *Trib*'s exposés did not prevent Thompson from winning the next Republican primary, but Daniel M. Deininger, whom McCormick had brought into the newspaper as auditor, suggested having the *Tribune* sue Thompson as a taxpayer, and after talking it over with Kirkland, McCormick did just that. A taxpayer's suit filed in circuit court charged Thompson and his cronies with conspiracy to defraud the city of $1,732,000. The case was postponed for several years, but partly because of it, Thompson decided not to run for reelection in 1923.

The year 1919 in Chicago was further marked by a shocking, days-long race riot on the changing South Side, a major part of the first nationwide steel strike (Chicago's part was memorialized by John Dos Passos in *1919*), and by the Black Sox World Series scandal that shook the sports world. The *Tribune*'s coverage of the race riot was restrained in the face of a hysteria that swept the city after an incident on a South Side beach exploded in the summer heat into hundreds of battles with guns, knives, clubs, and fists all over the South Side. On July 30 the *Tribune*'s editorial denied that the "violence done thus far is the result of deliberate organization," as some people obviously thought it was, and concluded evenhandedly:

> The whites of the lower order must be restrained by law from mob attacks. . . . The thinking Negroes must use their influence with their race. . . .

The next day's editorial, written when the appalling extent of the battle (at least twenty-six dead, hundreds injured) was known, began, "Chicago is disgraced and dishonored," and called the tragedy "the most horrible race riots in American history."

The steel strike, which took the paper much less by surprise, was also treated with moderation, though the city was in a state of considerable tension, with suburban Gary, Indiana, under martial law.

Reporting the World Series, sports editor Ring Lardner wrote of White Sox pitcher Eddie Cicotte's strange fielding performance in the first game, "I don't like what these old owl eyes are seeing." Old Owl Eyes was only thirty-four, but his suspicions, among the first, were finally confirmed in the investigation the following year, when a gambler payoff to several White Sox players was proved. An ex-*Trib* sportswriter named Sherman Duffy later lamented a lost opportunity. During the Series he was assigned by the *American* to help Cicotte write a daily article, and had a hotel room across the corridor from the star pitcher. The night before the first game one of the gamblers entered Cicotte's empty room and left $10,000 under the pillow. "I could have taken the $10,000," wrote Duffy, "I would have had a bundle, Eddie Cicotte would still be an honest man, and no one would have been in a position to complain."

The Black Sox World Series was not the last bad news for Chicagoans in 1919. On October 28 the *Tribune* disclosed to its readers the gloomily anticipated information that Congress had passed the Volstead Act over Wilson's veto, meaning that beginning January 16 no American could legally get a drink containing more than one half of one percent alcohol. The *Tribune*'s editorial comment was pessimistic:

> The United States Congress, under the influence of zealous opinion, is guilty of disorderly and dishonest processes. Good public morals do not grow out of such procedure. When contempt for legislation begins with the nation's legislative body, it will be found elsewhere.

But no newspaper, politician, or clergyman on either side of the Prohibition issue had the slightest inkling of what was really going to happen when the government and its law-enforcement agencies sought to take away everybody's booze. Certain Chicagoans had ideas, though. Among them were several veterans of the Hearst-McCormick circulation wars, which thus played a role in the city's history not easily foreseen.

CHAPTER TEN

Al Capone and Jake Lingle

ON the morning of May 12, 1920, commuters picking up the *Tribune* at Northwestern or Union Station or at the newsstands and cigar stores in the Loop were rewarded with a sensational banner set in two sizes of type. The big type on the left read COLOSIMO SLAIN, followed by two lines in half-size, SEEK EX-WIFE, JUST RETURNED.

The dead man's name was so well known to Chicagoans that no identification was needed in the headline. Big Jim Colosimo owned one of the city's largest restaurants, but much more than that, he was vice and gambling lord of the South Side, where most of this activity went on. He had been shot down, as the column head noted, in his own café at 2126 South Wabash, a place where the Gold Coast often went slumming. The story, which filled the right-hand column and a lengthy turn, disclosed that a lone gunman had ambushed Big Jim as he reentered the empty foyer from the kitchen in midafternoon. A drawing reconstructed the scene, with dotted lines to indicate the victim's approach and the killer's escape path. The exhaustive coverage included a verbatim account of the police interrogation of Colosimo's recent bride, under the heading "Dale Sobs Story."

Yet the *Tribune*'s reporters and editors entirely failed to grasp the significance of the crime, as did the police, whose theories the *Tribune* put in a series of rhetorical questions:

> Was the murder committed at the behest of Vittoria Moresco, former wife of Colosimo, in revenge for fancied ill treatment?
> Or was it committed by a disgruntled admirer of Dale Winter, Colosimo's present wife . . . ?
> Or was it but a manifestation of the workings of the deadly Camorra, that underworld society of little Italy to whom so many crimes of a like nature can be traced?
> Or did someone who had thought himself ill-treated in business dealings with "Big Jim" use assassination as his method of "getting even"?
> Or was Colosimo killed as a sequel to the gang war between the battling elements in Chicago labor circles, who already are responsible for the death of Maurice Enright and Edward Coleman?

In the last guess the writer had just a glimmer of the truth (Maurice "Mossy" Enright, though not so identified in the story, was one of Max Annenberg's thugs). Although Prohibition was four months old, the story casually disclosed that a suspicious late luncher in Colosimo's restaurant had enjoyed an apricot brandy, while a photo showed a table with several bottles and glasses. It was no news to reporter, editor, or reader that restaurants still served booze. But few yet tumbled to the significance of illicit commerce in a mass-consumption commodity.

Among those who did was Dion O'Banion, who quit his job as circulation manager of the *Herald-Examiner,* took some of his bullies with him, hired drivers and contracted with distillers, and organized the distribution of liquor for the affluent homes, restaurants, and hotels of the North Side and lake shore. Among them also was Johnny Torrio, a dapper gunman Big Jim Colosimo had imported some years earlier from New York to help keep his vice and gambling circuit running smoothly. Torrio quickly perceived that the existing Colosimo organization was the natural vehicle for distributing beer and liquor in the Loop and on the South Side. Aging Big Jim was slow to grasp the potential, so up-and-coming Torrio had him removed.

A new era in Chicago, and American, crime had begun. Colosimo's was the first of more than seven hundred gang murders to blacken, or brighten, Chicago front pages in the fourteen years of Prohibition, averaging out to one a week. Not that murder was unusual in pre-Prohibition Chicago—a smaller head in the same edition that reported Colosimo's death read "5 Face Noose as Brislane Is Doomed to Die." But up to 1920 killings were unspectacular—holdups, domestic spats, fights in bars—with rarely more than a single weapon fired, and with no planning involved. The Prohibition murders were more like war, and had much of war's journalistic appeal. And though Chicago gangsters conducted their business no differently from their co-professionals in St. Louis, Kansas City, Detroit, New York, and elsewhere, from the beginning the Chicago mobs had more flair and made more news. The first man "taken for a ride" was a Chicago hood named Steve Wisiewski whose body was found in Libertyville, a northern suburb, in the summer of 1921. The phrase was credited to Big Tim Murphy, a racketeer who in due course was himself gunned down.

Colosimo's dead body set a precedent that passed into American folklore: the gangster funeral. As the *Tribune* put it, "Pretentious obsequies marked the interment." The mile-long cortege numbered five thousand mourners, including three judges, eight aldermen, a congressman, a state legislator, an assistant state's attorney, and stars of the Chicago Opera. En route to the cemetery it paused in front of Colosimo's restaurant on Wabash while the band played a number. The *Tribune* editorialized under the title "The Vice King's Funeral," "A cavalcade such as moved behind the funeral car of

Caesar . . . a strange commentary upon our system of law and justice."

It was stranger than Colonel McCormick and his editorial writers realized. Expert and comprehensive as the *Trib*'s coverage of Colosimo's death might have been by old-fashioned standards, the city staff would soon look back on it as an amateur operation. The staff, however, learned quicker than did the Colonel, who was engrossed in loftier matters such as the 5–5–3 U.S.-British-Japanese naval ratio. Before the Prohibition era ended he received a shock that forced him to pay it tardy but concentrated attention.

Down on the fourth floor the *Tribune*'s city news people quickly became conversant with the technology and vocabulary of the new age—bootlegging, Tommy gun, alky, blind pig—and its geography, which segmented Chicago into a South Side (Torrio-Capone) territory, a North Side (Dion O'Banion, later Bugs Moran) territory, and some smaller pieces labeled Klondike O'Donnell, the Gennas, the Aiellos, and other lesser mob names. Yet though they did not fall into the error of a British correspondent who marveled innocently at the sudden popularity of ice cream parlors in Chicago, they had to grope their way to a full command of the new crime scene. They were at first as puzzled as the public by the behavior of eyewitnesses to a brazen killing committed by a young thug Torrio had imported from Brooklyn and whom the *Tribune* identified as "Alphonse Caponi." One after the other, the witnesses swore to the coroner's jury that they could not remember a thing.

Reporters felt more at home with the ethnic angle, the South Side mob being mostly Italian and the North Side predominantly Irish. "That's one more Dago to my side," star reporter Jim Doherty kidded an Italian colleague upon returning from a killing, and next day the colleague reciprocated: "It's leveled, Jim—we chalked up one on our side last night."

The Irish-Italian aspect lent venom as well as color to the gang war and may have contributed to the sensational murder of Dion O'Banion in 1924. Partly as a cover and partly by avocation O'Banion operated a florist shop on North State opposite Holy Name Cathedral. One chilly November morning a Jewett sedan pulled up outside and three men entered the shop. The porter in the back room told the reporters afterward that he heard five shots, then after a pause a sixth, the *coup de grace.* Unable to reach any of his own three guns, O'Banion crumpled amid his chrysanthemums. Because the story broke for the afternoon papers the *Trib* sought a next-day angle and found a far-fetched *femme* to *cherchez*—"Girl an O'Banion Death Clue." The story, however, admitted that the dead man had provoked "the enmity of more than one rival gang in bootlegging" [it made no mention of his past as a circulation manager]. Sob sister Maureen M'Kernan covered the funeral in detail half loving, half sardonic:

Silver angels stood at the head and feet with their heads bowed in the light of the ten candles that burned in the solid golden candlesticks. . . .

Vying with that perfume [of the masses of flowers] was the fragrance of perfumed women, wrapped in furs from ears to ankles, who tiptoed down the aisle escorted by soft-stepping gentlemen with black, shining pompadours.

A few months later a step forward in sophistication was evident in Genevieve Forbes Herrick's interview with the widow of slain Angelo Genna, reporting that she "doesn't know that he was a bootlegger, that he may have been cutting in on somebody else's territory, or that he with the [other] Genna boys, may have been trying to usurp too much power in that Sicilian society [the *Unione Siciliano*]."

Press indignation with the mobs developed only slowly, inhibited by the popular shrug, "They only kill each other." Not till the summer of 1925 did the *Tribune*'s front page show a sense of outrage, when two policemen were slain in a bizarre shootout that grew inadvertently out of an intramural gang skirmish-on-wheels along Western Avenue. A prosecutor's confidence in getting a conviction (an ironclad rule said you couldn't kill a cop and get away with it) was reported in the *Tribune* with a satisfaction that proved premature. The mobsters' escape via bribes and intimidation was followed shortly by a new killing that first raised press outrage to a new high, and then plunged press cynicism to a new low. A young assistant state's attorney named William McSwiggin was machine-gunned "from a curtained auto-mobile" in Capone-dominated Cicero. At first McSwiggin appeared to the *Tribune* (and the other papers) a martyred hero. The front-page cartoon depicted Organized Crime slapping The Law in the face. But over the next few weeks it developed that McSwiggin had been corruptly involved with Cicero saloonkeepers who were resisting Capone. One of the two companions killed with him had been a gunman, the other a beer salesman (and Republican precinct captain). Capone was all injured innocence ("I liked the kid," and more disarmingly, "I paid him plenty").

Without letting up on the criminals, the press turned its investigative fire on the law-enforcement agencies. Hilding Johnson, real-life original of the Hecht-MacArthur hero, phoned the *Herald-Examiner* daily from the sheriff's office: "City desk? I'm here in the office of John P for Prick Anderson to ask him who killed Billy McSwiggin and why. The bastard says he doesn't know."

The heat drove Capone from Chicago for four months. On his return he gave welcoming reporters a great plaintive quote: "I've been accused of every death except the casualty list of the World War."

Despite the press, and despite seven grand juries, nobody was indicted for the McSwiggin killing. More miraculously, Capone survived an incredibly bold attempt by his rivals to rub him out. As he finished lunch in a Cicero restaurant one noon, an unhurried cavalcade of ten cars drove by, pouring ten successive broadsides through the facade. Tumbled to the floor by an alert bodyguard, Capone was unscathed. A wounded henchman who had had an unobstructed view of the assault battalion was unable to identify a single enemy.

Next morning the *Tribune* revealed its new grasp of current history with a sidebar narrating in accurate detail the story of the Torrio-Capone mob's takeover of Cicero.

By now the frequency and piquancy of Chicago's gang-war news had given the city national and international renown. Not only the *Tribune,* but papers in New York, Los Angeles, London, and Paris now spelled Capone's name right. He was Chicago's most famous citizen. When his custom-built armored limo rolled down Roosevelt Road, scout car in front, gun-laden touring car behind, everyone turned to look: "There he goes! There goes Al!" Big Bill Thompson, who retired under *Tribune* harassment in 1923 and let a reformist Democrat take over City Hall, made a comeback in 1927 aided by Capone's thugs. The mayor's esteem for the mob lord was later shown when Capone was first to greet Commander Francesco de Pinedo, Mussolini's flying good-will ambassador.

Colonel McCormick met Capone once himself, as the result of a labor dispute with the mob-linked Newsboys' Union. According to the Colonel's own version, he peremptorily ordered Capone to leave a meeting between publishers and union, but another version, authored by an ex-Capone henchman and Thompson bureaucrat named Danny Serritella, pictured the Colonel as polite to the gangster, addressing him in a rather credible quote, "You know, you are famous, like Babe Ruth. We can't help printing things about you, but I will see that the *Tribune* gives you a square deal." More indisputably, and perhaps more to the point, Colonel McCormick and his fellow publishers and editors owed Capone one of life's chief comforts. "When I sell liquor, it's bootlegging," Capone commented sardonically. "When my patrons serve it on silver trays on Lake Shore Drive, it's hospitality."

To his undoubted executive ability Capone even added a dimension of statesmanship. Thompson's return to City Hall, so far from setting off a new crime wave, was accompanied by an eerie calm, the result of a secret peace treaty engineered by Capone at the Sherman House. The armistice lasted several months, until a new alliance of his enemies offered a $50,000 prize for a "Capone notch." Capone's security department proved a tough nut to crack. One after another, four bodies were found, each with a derisive nickel clutched in a hand. Going on the offensive, the Capone killers knocked off six of the enemy Aiello brothers, one after another, and then

seven Bugs Moran men all at once in the never-to-be-forgotten St. Valentine's Day massacre (1929). The *Tribune* showed an insider's perception:

> . . . The gangsters who were killed paid the penalty for being followers of
> George Moran [whose antagonist] . . . is Al Capone. . . . A more immediate
> reason lies in a campaign of Moran's alcohol sellers to take liquor from
> Detroit sources and with it penetrate the Bloody Twentieth Ward, the booze
> territory of the Capone gang.

Inside, a photo cutaway depicted the massacre technique, victims lined
facing the wall, hands over heads, killers in cops' uniforms moving by
dotted line from Cadillac touring car at curb to position inside garage.

Six of the seven were dead when the police arrived, the seventh, Frank
Gusenberg, surviving to deliver famous last words. In response to a detective's query, "Who shot you, Frank?" he explained, "Nobody shot
me."

A page one sidebar from Washington bureau chief Arthur Sears Henning
reported on progress of a bill in Congress introduced by Illinois' Adolph
Sabath to facilitate deportation of "the alien gangs that have been terrorizing Chicago." At the moment, federal government action did not look very
alarming to Capone, who had to remain more concerned about his Chicago
competitors.

On May 17 (1929) the *Tribune* carried a surprise story:

Jail Al Capone and
Bodyguard in Philadelphia

Next day the story grew into a banner:

CAPONE TAKES COVER IN JAIL

The story was doubly surprising. For the first time in his life, the gang
chief was in prison, with a stiff one-year sentence for the almost absurd
crime of carrying a concealed weapon. It was obvious to the *Tribune* that
Al had sought jail in Philadelphia as asylum. But there was more: secure
in his cell Capone revealed that he had just engineered another peace pact
among the mobs, this one including not only the Chicago gangs but others
around the country. The treaty site had been the President Hotel, Atlantic
City:

> The compact parceled out the territory to be controlled by the various gang
> chieftains. All "signed on the dotted line," Capone said, to quit shooting. An

arbiter was chosen to settle all future differences. This man is to be a sort of "Judge Landis" of the underworld racket.

The story explained the recent gun-and-bludgeon deaths of three of Capone's top hit men in an Indiana roadhouse as a prelude to the Atlantic City meeting, necessitated by the insistence of Moran and other rival leaders that these three be eliminated. The story did not, however, speculate on the identity of the proposed "Judge Landis" (a reference to the baseball commissioner appointed following the Black Sox scandal).

For the next several months Capone was safe in his Philadelphia cell, but eventually he had to come home to Chicago where in August (1930) the papers reported a grimly funny incident: he was on the golf course when a car backfired. Al dived into a sandtrap while his bodyguard-caddies yanked Tommy guns from their golf bags. But in the end what did Capone in was not rival machine-gun slugs but publicity. In this Colonel McCormick, so aloof in his new Michigan Avenue Tower from the sordid goings-on in the streets, played a totally unexpected role.

Reporters had always mixed some with the criminals, who provided so much of the news, but the gangs had distinctly increased the tendency. For the first time known criminals were public personalities who could give interviews. The *Tribune*'s Jim Doherty told British writer Kenneth Allsop, "I spent a lot of time with the mob and saw Capone often. . . . I'd accuse him of a murder today, and meet him tomorrow, and neither of us would mention the subject. I'd see him at a funeral, or in a speakeasy, or down at the DA's office and he'd always give me some quotes. . . . [He] didn't volunteer information [but] the more I wrote about him, the more he liked it. . . . He liked the advertising. . . . It made it easier to intimidate the customers."

Reporters drank in speakeasies frequented by gangsters, partly by natural accident, since all the speaks were part of the mob empire, and partly because they could pick up information in them. One midnight a *Herald-Examiner* reporter named Don Mathieson was alone in a little joint called the Tunnel when a Moran collector named Hymie the Slob came by to complain that the Tunnel didn't buy enough Moran beer. Two gunmen entered, shot Hymie the Slob dead, and departed. Mathieson locked the front door, turned out the lights, telephoned his desk, and sat down with the proprietor to wait till the *Tribune* had gone to press. Four hours passed. Then he telephoned the police.

Another reporter helped Capone's brother Ralph to gain the publicity he coveted. The reporter suggested that Ralph be given charge of the bottle-beer business—not a major component of the enterprise, since most Capone beer was sold by the barrel. Next time Ralph was arrested the reporter identified him by the sobriquet "Bottles" Capone, which stuck, and afterward Ralph got his share of ink.

Harry Read, reporter and later city editor of the *American,* was close enough to Capone to receive a friendly warning that "Mike de Pike blames you for that fall [conviction] he took. Watch out for him. He's a rat." Read asked Capone to arrange an interview, at which he told Mike de Pike that if he made good on a threat to "toss a pineapple" through the window of Read's house, "I will shoot you dead." When the *American* got the only pictures of the St. Valentine's massacre before the police cordoned off the area, Read's intimacy with Capone came to the attention of the grand jury. Read swore there was no connection.

Thus the existence of amicable relations between the press and gangsterdom was no secret in the summer of 1930. Yet the killing that took place on June 9 shook Chicago journalism to its foundations, with reverberations that reached far beyond.

The police radio message received at the city desks was routine, except for the locale and time of day (1:30 P.M.): "Shooting in the Illinois Central underpass, Randolph and Michigan." The only idle reporter on duty at the *Tribune,* John Boettiger, left the Tower, walked across the Michigan Avenue Bridge and south three blocks, and descended into the Grant Park tunnel, which provided a pedestrian underpass below the busy avenue and a station for the Illinois Central. Flashing his press card and elbowing through police and onlookers Boettiger saw the body sprawled on the cement and to his horrified amazement recognized *Tribune* legman Jake Lingle.

A copy of the *Racing Form* was clutched in Lingle's hand. As numerous witnesses in the crowded underpass attested, he had been sauntering toward the platform for the train to the Washington Park track, a cigar in his teeth and a program in his hand, when a blond man wearing a straw hat, walking at his side as if in companionship, suddenly stepped back, drew a gun with his left hand, and fired a single round upward into the back of Lingle's head. As Lingle plunged forward, his killer tossed away the gun, dashed ahead, then doubled back past the body to disappear up the stair. Though chased by a policeman, he escaped in the crowd on the street.

The hit man had not acted alone. Several witnesses reported a dark-haired man in a blue suit who had walked briefly on Lingle's other side, and who had dropped away just before the shooting. One witness had even chased the second man, but had been bumped off course by a priest, or, as the police quickly concluded, an accomplice in priest's attire. A trio of men whose car had been parked at the curb and who had waved a greeting to Lingle as he approached the underpass may have acted as finger, suggesting that the killers were imports.

At the morgue Boettiger got another shock. Lingle, sixty-five-dollar-a-week legman, had fourteen hundred-dollar bills in one pocket and was wearing a diamond-studded belt of a kind Al Capone was known to bestow on special pals.

Colonel McCormick may not have been informed of these telltale hints. He took little interest in crime news, despite a fairly preposterous though funny allegation in *The Front Page* that seems to refer to him—Bensinger, the *Trib* reporter, asking the sheriff as a favor to "a certain party" to move the hanging from seven to five o'clock so "we can make the City Edition." If the Colonel took in the suspicious details of Lingle's murder, he lost them in his overpowering outrage at the murder of a *Tribune* reporter. His reaction to the news astonished even the staff. Descending from the twenty-fourth floor he moved into the fourth-floor newsroom and took personal command of the handling of the story. His first order was for the posting of a $25,000 reward offer by the *Tribune*. Next he contacted fellow publishers and solicited their cooperation. The following morning the *Trib* banner read:

OFFER $30,000 FOR ASSASSIN

Gunman Slays Alfred Lingle in I.C. Subway
$25,000 for Capture Is Tribune Offer

The story carried no by-line, indicating the work of several hands:

Alfred J. Lingle, better known to his world of newspaper work as Jake Lingle, and for the last eighteen years a reporter on The Tribune, was shot to death yesterday in the Illinois Central subway at the east side of Michigan Boulevard at Randolph Street.

The Tribune offers $25,000 as a reward for information which will lead to the conviction of the slayer or slayers.

An additional reward of $5,000 was announced by the Chicago Evening Post on the same terms, making a total of $30,000 offered.

The Press Club of Chicago issued a statement that it stood ready to post another $10,000 reward for the slayers.

The story had broken for the previous day's late afternoon papers, which turned out to be not the only unfortunate aspect of the case from the *Tribune*'s point of view. For the moment, however, though the story stated that no direct motive was apparent, the implication of the killing seemed clear:

Jake Lingle for years has been "covering" the underworld for The Tribune. He has come to know gang leaders and he has sifted the crimes they committed in his efforts to bring about solutions. He probably knew more policemen than even any policeman on the force, and he was an intimate friend of Commissioner Russell and of Chief of Detectives Stege.

The story then recalled the 1926 murder of Don Mellett, a Canton, Ohio, editor shot by gangsters, and commented that "these two are the only outstanding cases in which newspapermen paid with their lives for working against organized criminals."

In a slight but pregnant non sequitur, the next paragraph mentioned that Lingle's was the twelfth gang slaying in Chicago in ten days. A couple of paragraphs later, an intriguing disclosure was made:

> Because of his close friendship with Commissioner Russell and with other officials and leading politicians, Lingle was frequently besought by his hoodlum and racketeer acquaintances to use his influence to obtain concessions for them to pursue a profitable lawlessness. Invariably he told them that he could gain no such permission for them if he tried; that if they attempted to go ahead with their plans, they would surely be brought to answer before the law.

Next day's banner (the *Herald-Examiner* having responded to McCormick's appeal with its own $25,000 reward) raised the ante:

SET $55,000 PRICE ON KILLER

A McCutcheon cartoon showed "Chicago's Gangland" challenging law enforcement with a glove across the face. Echoing the cartoon, the *Tribune*'s lead editorial was also titled "The Challenge." After describing the killing it said:

> The meaning of this murder is plain. It was committed in reprisal and in attempt at intimidating. Mr. Lingle was a police reporter and an exceptionally well informed one. His personal friendships included the highest police officials and the contacts of his work had made him familiar with most of the big and little fellows of gangland. What made him valuable to his newspaper marked him as dangerous to the killers.

The assumption was not unreasonable, that is, that a broad-daylight killing in a crowded downtown location, close to the *Tribune,* was designed to intimidate. The next paragraph frankly expounded the difference between the Lingle killing and all the others:

> It was very foolish ever to think that assassination would be confined to the gangs which have fought each other for the profits of crime in Chicago. The immunity from punishment after gang murders would be assumed to cover

the committing of others. Citizens who interfered with the criminals were no
better protected than the gangmen who fought each other for the revenue
from liquor selling, coercion of labor and trade, brothel house keeping and
gambling. . . .

And the editorial concluded: "The Tribune accepts this challenge. It is
war. . . ."

Next day, June 12, the page-one pressure continued with another banner
(GANGS RAIDED: CHIEFS FLEE) and another McCutcheon cartoon ("The
Nation's Eyes Are on Chicago," showing a determined giant rolling up his
sleeves amid the Loop skyscrapers while pigmy mobsters hoped that "this
will soon blow over"). The story announced that police "sharpshooter
squads" made up of officers who had killed "from four to eleven criminals
each" were being organized to "carry the war into the enemy camp."

The following day's front page changed key with a story whose familiar-
ity was faintly troubling. Though the column head, "Throngs Honor Alfred
Lingle at Last Rites," and Kathleen McLaughlin's cover of the services at
Our Lady of Sorrows and Mount Carmel cemetery were straightforward,
her very listing of city notables in attendance carried echoes of the obsequies
of Big Jim Colosimo, Dion O'Banion, Hymie Weiss, and the rest.

Tribune staffers who had known Lingle best had from the first taken a
reserved attitude toward the assumption that he was a martyr in the war
against crime. The diamond-studded belt, residence at the Sherman House,
hundred-dollar bills, and habit of spending afternoons at the track did not
come as news to some reporters and desk men. Diffidently they clued in
their superiors, and gradually word filtered to the top of the Tower. Among
other things, Colonel McCormick learned that he had not been the only one
at the *Tribune* to arrive at work in a Rolls. Lingle had also rivaled the
Colonel in his taste for expensive suits and haberdashery. A curious and
now arresting incident stuck in someone's memory: riding around Chicago
late one night Lingle had remarked, "I fixed the price of beer in this town."

One of the *Trib*'s follow-ups on the McSwiggin murder had disclosed a
price debate in Cicero over Capone's sixty-dollar-a-barrel charge for nee-
dled beer. More recently Capone and the rest had settled on fifty-five dollars
a barrel.

Was Jake Lingle the "Judge Landis of the underworld" the *Tribune*'s
story on Capone's Philadelphia jailing had mentioned? Nobody ever found
out, but slowly Colonel McCormick was forced to accept the fact that his
dead reporter had been something rather different from what he had innocently assumed. Many a publisher would have dropped the whole thing.
Characteristically, the Colonel made up his mind to see it through. In a
forty-five-minute meeting of the news staff he got across a message which

reporter Fred Pasley summarized: "When he had finished we knew what he meant. We knew the search for Lingle's slayers would never abate."

A new plank appeared in the *Tribune*'s Platform for Chicago—"End the Reign of Gangdom"—and an investigative committee headed by *Tribune* lawyer Charles F. Rathbun, whom McCormick got named special assistant to the state's attorney, went to work. At first it merely added further embarrassments by exploring Lingle's large, active checking accounts and large, active and recently calamitous stock-market transactions. Many of these latter proved to be in partnership with Police Commissioner William F. Russell, who admitted that he and Jake were old buddies from days when Jake was a semipro baseball player on Sundays and a *Tribune* office boy during the week.

The *Daily News* and *Herald-Examiner* came up with revelations: two North Side (Moran) mobsters had recently sought a police fix to open a high-class gambling club, and a police official had referred them to Lingle, who had demanded a 50-percent cut on the profits. In another incident, a former state senator had threatened Lingle if he failed to get Commissioner Russell's approval on a West Side gambling joint, and in still another Lingle had complained to a D.A. assistant who had raided a Northwest joint: "You've put me in an awful jam. I told them they could run."

At least Lingle supplied a lot of copy for his old colleagues. The St. Louis papers sent reporters, who came up with their own discoveries. The *Post-Dispatch* man, John T. Rogers, had the bright idea of interviewing the Sherman House management, from whom he learned that Lingle had been on the "private register," meaning he got no phone calls except from people on a list he supplied. The house detective explained: "How could he get any sleep [otherwise]? His telephone would be going all night. . . . Policemen calling up to have Jake get them transferred or promoted, or politicians wanting the 'fix' put in for somebody. . . . He had a lot of power. I've known him twenty years. He was up there among the big boys and had a lot of responsibilities. A big man like that needs rest."

St. Louis Star reporter Harry T. Brundidge dug into the friendship of Capone and *American* city editor Harry Read, who defended himself by printing vouchers to show that when he visited Capone in Miami he paid his own way. A *Daily News* reporter, Leland H. Reese, wrote a story revealing his employment of a racketeer named Julius Rosenheim as an informer, which seemed to help explain Rosenheim's getting shot dead the previous February, and to shed possible light on a sideswipe auto collision just a few days earlier in which Reese himself had escaped an apparent gang hit. Colonel McCormick backed a grand jury investigation of the links between the mobs and the press, but the *Herald-Examiner* and *Daily News* copped out, telling the grand jury they had just been playing games with the St. Louis reporters.

A long *Tribune* editorial of June 30, titled "The Lingle Murder," showed the embattled Colonel at bay. It recalled the *Trib*'s earlier reasoning that the killers either wanted to shut Lingle up or intimidate the press, and went on:

> Alfred Lingle now takes a different character, one in which he was unknown to the management of The Tribune when he was alive. He is dead and cannot defend himself, but many facts now revealed must be accepted as eloquent against him. . . . The reasonable appearance against Lingle now is that he was accepted in the world of politics and crime for something undreamed of in his office. . . .
>
> The Tribune, although naturally disturbed by the discovery that this reporter was engaged in practices contrary to the code of its honest reporters and abhorred by the policy of the newspaper, does not find that the main objectives of the inquiry have been much altered. The crime and the criminals remain, and they are the concern of The Tribune as they are of the decent elements in Chicago. . . .
>
> That he is not a soldier dead in the discharge of his duty is unfortunate considering that he is dead. . . .
>
> The murder of this reporter, even for racketeering reasons, as the evidence indicates it may have been, made a breach in the wall which criminality has so long maintained about its operations here . . . The Tribune . . . has gone into the cause in this fashion and its notice to gangland is that it is in for the duration. Kismet [Fate].

There was substance for admiration in the determination voiced by the editorial, and some sense in the idea that the exposure of Lingle's strange secret life made the investigation of his death only the more urgent. To State's Attorney John A. Swanson, McCormick wrote in a similar vein:

> We wish the matters exposed had never occurred. We tend to wish that soiled linen be not washed in public, but out of so much evil a greater good may come. The activities of Lingle and men of his stripe are like paths leading into the forest of crime. . . . By following them the whole criminal organization which has Chicago by the throat may be surrounded and destroyed.

Despite jeers and sneers, McCormick and the *Tribune* had accomplished something; they had set in motion a public furor that put pressure on police and politicians and produced some erratic action. A fresh roundup of hoodlums included Jack Zuta, a top Moran lieutenant, who was being transported through the Loop in a squad car when at the busy intersection of State and Adams a sedan opened fire, missed Zuta, and killed a streetcar motorman. The hit car then escaped by employing a new tactic borrowed from the navy: laying down a smoke screen. Zuta survived only briefly, getting it a month later in a Wisconsin resort. His office in the Loop yielded four safe-deposit boxes filled with records of payments to police and officials (there was even a loan of "four C's" to the police chief of Evanston).

Nothing much happened as a result of the Zuta disclosures, but the *Trib* was nevertheless right in believing that "the day of reckoning is measurably nearer." Zuta stimulated further investigating, more people volunteering information, and more ink about politicians and gangsters, in short, more heat. Badgered and beleaguered, Capone made a plaintive offer to Assistant State's Attorney Pat Roche: He would have his hit squad deal with Lingle's killer and turn in the dead body. It was an offer Roche couldn't accept, and Capone played his second card, revealing (if that is the word) the identity of the killer. It was, Capone told the *Tribune*'s Rathbun Committee, a St. Louis torpedo named Leo Brothers, a member of the same Egan's Rats gang that had supplied two gunmen for St. Valentine's Day. (One of those two, Fred Burke, was suspected of being the "priest" in the Lingle job.)

Brothers was arrested and brought to trial. Some witnesses said he was the blond-haired killer, some said they didn't think so, and the jury came to a fairly weird verdict—guilty, but not all that guilty, with a sentence of fourteen years. Brothers delivered another memorable one-liner, ascribed to many other mobsters over the next decades: "I can do that [fourteen years minus good behavior] standing on my head."

Colonel McCormick felt sufficiently vindicated to indorse the verdict and lent the *Tribune*'s clout to the political ambitions of Assistant State's Attorney C. Wayland Brooks, who wound up in the U.S. Senate. The Colonel also rewarded young reporter John Boettiger with a top assignment, Franklin D. Roosevelt's presidential campaign in 1932.

If Capone imagined that tossing Leo Brothers to the *Tribune* lions would end his own problems, he was mistaken. The forces of decency, and/or hypocrisy, were too fully aroused to go back to sleep. The Chicago Crime Commission, a civic body that had been in unobtrusive existence since 1919, came up with a winner of an idea: a listing in order of importance of the top Chicago gangsters. Capone, naturally, was No. 1. The list was sent to judges, state's attorneys, the sheriff of Cook County, and the police commissioner (no longer Lingle's pal Russell, who had resigned) with a letter urging that the hoods be harried in every legal way, as tax evaders, aliens, vagrants, and patrons of illicit gambling and drinking places. The title given to the names on the list—Public Enemy—was itself a publicity triumph, catching on at once with the press (and even the mobsters—Dago Lawrence Mangano voiced his chagrin at being rated only No. 4). What had at first looked like a comically feeble slap at the underworld showed remarkable muscle as the legal harassment paid off in arrests, sentences, and deportations.

The best tactic, though the one that at first drew the most incredulous smiles, was the tax-evasion rap, which in the summer of 1931 caught up with Capone and, with the aid of a barefaced double-cross by the judge, sent him to prison.

The decision to pursue Capone via the Internal Revenue was made by President Hoover in response to a number of representations from Chicago's civic-minded citizens, including McCormick's wartime buddy Charlie Dawes, who had brought Chicago's crime problem to the attention of the Senate when he was Coolidge's vice-president. Colonel McCormick exaggerated in a later radio broadcast when he in effect claimed sole credit for Capone's downfall. Nevertheless, his determination to pursue Lingle's killers, courageously maintained despite the embarrassing discovery of the truth about Lingle, played a definite part.

Furthermore the version the Colonel told his radio audience pithily reflected the tardiness of the pro-dry administration of Herbert Hoover, inaugurated three weeks after the St. Valentine's Day massacre, in recognizing the problems Prohibition had created:

> President Hoover asked me why I didn't give him more support in his effort to enforce the Prohibition law. I told him that government agents were always arresting the little fellows and letting the big ones go, like Al Capone, for example.
> "Who is Al Capone?" President Hoover wanted to know. . . .

CHAPTER ELEVEN

The World's Richest Newspaper

EVEN in Chicago the 1920s were not exclusively devoted to gang warfare. During the city's most flamboyant decade the *Tribune* grew into, if not the world's greatest newspaper, indisputably the world's richest. Circulation nearly doubled (436,000 in 1920 to 835,000 in 1930, Sunday circulation to over a million), putting it ahead of all U.S. dailies except its New York tabloid offshoot. The *Tribune* moved into its new Tower on Boul' Mich, helped pioneer radio, joined a tiny newspaper elite with its own foreign coverage, fought Big Bill Thompson to the death (his, politically speaking), and covered all the big stories of a newsy era from the Scopes monkey trial in Tennessee to Lindbergh's flight, seeking always either to beat or outcover the competition and usually succeeding.

The front page was fixed in a characteristic format. Max Annenberg had suggested during the war that the *Trib* use an eight-column banner every day, and the practice was continued after the war, even when the news story was a little weak (Prohibition and gang war kept that from happening often). In editorial outlook the paper remained true to the principles of Joseph Medill: combative, censorious, sarcastic, Republican, antilabor, and antisocialist. Oswald Garrison Villard, editor of the liberal *Nation,* wrote in 1922 that "You can never be certain . . . whether [the *Chicago Tribune*] is going to be reactionary and vicious, or whether it accidentally will be found on the side of progress and enlightenment." The paper's sectional patriotism, inherited from Medill, had led it into bitter opposition to the Federal Reserve Board, which it viewed as a benefit to the South at the expense of the North and East, an adventitious opinion which (according to Villard) gave the *Tribune* an adventitious popularity with "intellectuals of the colored race." In foreign affairs it also followed the Medill tradition, which it emphasized by flaunting on the masthead Stephen Decatur's stirring but jingoist toast: "Our Country! in her intercourse with foreign nations may she always be right; but our country, right or wrong."

It also revived Medill's dormant crusade for spelling reform. Despite the eminent good sense of simplifying the awkward and difficult spelling of modern English, McCormick was under no illusion that success would be easy, and it wasn't. Over a period of years a list of words was gradually

101

expanded, with lengthy articles to explain the reasoning and the advantages of starting *phantom* with an *f,* like *fantasy,* or eliminating the doubled consonant in such forms as *patrolled, skillful,* and *tranquillity,* and of clipping the silent *ue* from *dialogue, analogue, pedagogue,* and *catalogue.* In most of these the public did not object, but it did not adopt. In more radical modifications—*telegraf, frate, iland* (which readers said reminded them of an African antelope), it complained.

Typically the *Tribune* answered questions, such as that of a schoolgirl over *frate,* by expressing the belief that in time the new spelling would catch on, but on word after word its hopes were disappointed. Even the rather attractive *tho* and *thru* got only a limited acceptance. One of the *Tribune*'s most rational crusades, simplified spelling encountered extraordinarily obstinate resistance from both the masses and the elite, and was universally regarded as a flat failure. Yet Colonel McCormick may have merely been a few decades ahead of his time. Today's dictionaries not only accept the truncated *og* but such *Tribune* neologisms as *skilful, drouth, fantom, harken,* and *canceled.*

A memorial to Joseph Medill that proved more immediately successful than simplified spelling was the Medill School of Journalism. A staff member suggested a training program for future *Tribune* reporters, and when Dr. Walter Dill Scott, president of Northwestern, was approached, he sensibly proposed expanding the project into a journalism school. The idea won from McCormick approval backed by solid financial support, for which Northwestern thanked him with an honorary LL.D. in 1947.

Meantime the *Tribune*'s rapidly increasing bulk and circulation outgrew the 1902 Madison and Dearborn building, and in 1920 McCormick and Patterson laid the cornerstone of a new plant on a site that surprised some by its location outside the Loop, where all Chicago newspapers had always dwelt. The new site was across the river, fronting on as yet undeveloped North Michigan Avenue. The six-story building whose cornerstone McCormick and Patterson laid on June 7, 1920, occupied the eastern part of the lot, leaving room on the Michigan Avenue side for the future main building. In December the mechanical and editorial departments were moved across the river, but advertising, circulation, and everything else remained on Madison Street awaiting completion of the two-level Wacker Drive-Michigan Avenue construction, in partial fulfillment of Daniel Burnham's visionary plan for the Chicago riverfront. This and the new Michigan Avenue double-decker lift bridge provided easy access for circulation trucks, while a railroad line running east-west through the area made it possible to bring paper by rail to the plant door. A few years later the deepening of the Welland Canal facilitated direct shipping all the way from the Canadian mills, with the aid of a tunnel from the river to the pressroom.

The Tower itself was built in 1923–1925 following a $100,000 design competition that attracted 285 entries from all over the world. While modernists, especially of the form-follows-function Chicago school, scoffed, the committee chose the neo-Gothic design submitted by the New York firm of Howells and Hood. One of the modernist proposals, that of Eliel Saarinen of Finland, received second prize. The winning design, which owed something to the Malines Cathedral in Belgium and something to the famed Butter Tower of Rheims, rose twenty-four full stories topped by another twelve of Gothic stonework, with gargoyles and grotesques. The medieval whimsy was echoed below on the Michigan Avenue level: an "Aesop's screen" above the main entrance to the building was sculptured with caricatures, including Colonel McCormick and Captain Patterson in World War I uniform and the two architects in the shape of Gothic puns—a howling dog for Howells and Robin Hood for Hood.

When the newspaper moved into its new home in May 1925, the pressroom was organized in a new pattern designed by McCormick. The traditional layout grouped five or six presses together to produce a certain number of pages, which were assembled with the other sections to form a whole paper. McCormick installed his twenty-five press units and six folders in a continuous line, connected mechanically and electrically, a system that became standard for newspapers and on which he was granted three patents.

Following experiments by John Yetter, superintendent of the pressroom, and Otto Wolf, his mechanical expert, the rotogravure process was ingeniously turned to color printing in 1920, the first time anywhere that more than one color was printed on a continuous web of paper. The *Trib*'s new "Coloroto" section, four pages of color and eight of mono, appeared for the first time on Sunday, April 9, 1922, the forerunner of the modern newspaper Sunday magazine. The *Tribune* long maintained a lead in color technology, scoring significant firsts later with the first color shot of a spot news event (a 1939 grain elevator fire) and the first color wirephoto (King George VI arriving in Washington, also 1939).

In the aftermath of World War I the paper had to weather a newsprint crisis just the opposite of the one that had sunk Keeley's *Herald*. The postwar depression of 1921–1922 hurt ad sales, thinned papers, and produced a glut of newsprint just as Arthur Schmon succeeded in building up a handsome backlog of pulpwood. McCormick's solution was to push his space salesmen to a superhuman effort. The strategy worked, mainly because the depression dissipated in 1922.

Recovery permitted McCormick and Patterson to be seduced by Coloroto into a magazine venture that proved their first failure. *Liberty* was conceived as a mass-appeal newsstand weekly, a "less stodgy Saturday

Evening Post." Technically, the roto process did not work well for *Liberty,* and though circulation leaped at once to over a million, putting the magazine among the leaders, advertising support remained permanently soft, and the *Saturday Evening Post,* stodgy or not, was unassailably tough. *Liberty* was moved from the Tribune Tower to New York and kept going by Patterson and Max Annenberg, but it never did more than survive, until the Great Depression put an end to it.

The 1920s witnessed the arrival of the newspaper promotion stunt. The *Tribune* had already done some circulation and advertising promotion, as had a few other papers, and Joe Patterson launched his New York tabloid on a wave of contests. Hearst's *New York American,* a morning competitor, tried a lottery, printing "Lady Luck" coupons and giving away cash prizes. Patterson promptly responded in kind, with richer prize money. Both papers gained circulation, and Hearst directed the *Herald-Examiner* in Chicago to try the lottery. Though in New York the stakes built up to $25,000 a day, it was in Chicago that the stunt went wild. The *Herald-Examiner*'s "Smile" coupons, given away by the millions but requiring purchase of the newspaper to ascertain the lucky numbers, sent circulation jumping and caused Louis Rose to importune McCormick for a counterweapon. He considered litigation—the lottery was pretty surely illegal—but decided to fight silliness with silliness. The *Trib* issued millions of "Cheer Checks" with, naturally, a fatter payoff. Drawings were held in the heart of the Loop; the *Herald-Examiner* got Bill Thompson and other city fathers to do the drawing; the *Trib* cleverly countered with Chinese laundrymen, street sweepers, and other picturesque proletarians. Circulation results were instantaneous and slightly astounding. In one of the editorials that accompanied the daily promotion page the *Trib* frankly confessed that "it is difficult to feel so keenly the scruples of past weeks. . . . We could have easily sold a million Tribunes yesterday. . . . Such profitable philanthropy."

Postmaster General Will Hays, future motion-picture czar, put an end to the giveaways, rather to the relief of the participants, and promotion took a less frivolous turn. Joe Patterson, still dividing time between Chicago and New York, was mainly responsible for organizing the Golden Gloves amateur boxing tournament, which spread nationwide and became part of the U.S. Olympic program. It also set a precedent for the later All-Star baseball and football games fathered by sports editor Arch Ward against inertial opposition from inside the conservative-minded sports establishment.

The *Tribune*'s primacy in coverage of baseball, football, and boxing was more a reflection of McCormick's editorial sense than of his recreational taste, which lay in the direction of polo and fox hunting. Also strong on sports coverage was McCormick's pioneering radio station WGN, which was first to broadcast the World Series (Pittsburgh Pirates vs. Washington

Senators, 1925), the Indianapolis 500, and the Kentucky Derby. WGN also had the enterprise to take its microphones into the courtroom for the Scopes monkey trial in Tennessee (1925) and to pioneer extensive coverage of national political conventions (1932). It launched what turned out to be radio's all-time hit show, a comedy serial in which actors Freeman Gosden and Charles Coryell impersonated "Sam 'n' Henry," later changed, when the program went network and WGN wouldn't surrender the name, to "Amos 'n' Andy." Another highly successful WGN-originated serial was McCormick's own suggestion—converting Joe Patterson's best comic-strip idea, "Little Orphan Annie." A trailblazer for the future of radio and television was Floyd Gibbons as a news commentator. Gibbons's punchy, breathless delivery contrasts with the dégagé air of latter-day practitioners, but it went over big in 1926. "News on the hour" was a New York innovation by Joe Patterson.

More important than its program pioneering, or its supply of the first police radios to the Chicago police department, was WGN's legal battle to protect its frequency from intrusion by a competitor, out of which grew the Radio Act of 1927, creating the Federal Radio Commission, refined in 1934 into the Federal Communications Commission.

Despite the loss of Walter Howey, Charles MacArthur, Percy Hammond, Lucian Cary, and others to opportunity elsewhere, the *Tribune*'s news and feature staff remained outstanding. One of its salient characteristics was sophistication. It carried regular coverage (by Burns Mantle) of the Broadway theater, while Mae Tinee, a by-line derived from "matinee," won fame and imitation with her saucy movie critiquing. Westbrook Pegler, son of an old *Tribune* star reporter, practically revolutionized sports writing with a sour and witty iconoclasm that made fun of sports writing itself. "White Sox Open Pennant Drive—Only 42 Games Behind League-Leading Yankees" read a Pegler cover of a last-week-of-the-season baseball game. The narrative featured a base-running blunder in which, according to Pegler, one Yankee told another as he passed him between first and second, "Get out of the way and let a guy run who can run." From 1924 to 1929 H. L. Mencken was a *Trib* weekly columnist, his superficial audacity bedded in safe conservatism fitting the paper nicely.

In addition to new popular comic strips "Winnie Winkle," "Harold Teen," and "Moon Mullins," and the new adventure strip "Dick Tracy," improbably inspired by the Chicago police department, the *Tribune* carried higher-level graphic wit in the form of European cartoons. *Punch* was the favorite source (melancholy Cockney explaining to friend: "Baby set hisself on fire playing wiv matches and the missus put 'im out wiv the supper beer."). A unique Sunday feature by W. E. Hill was a full page of sardonic drawings and captions on some aspect of the age—suburban living, cocktail parties, European travel.

Gang killings did not monopolize the crime news. For one thing the ironclad mob tradition of never squealing practically ruled out courtroom drama, in which other kinds of murder were so rich. In *The Front Page,* Walter Burns, threatened with arrest, commands Hildy Johnson: "Get me a lawyer! Get Clarence Darrow!" Darrow provided the *Tribune* and the rest of the press with thousands of columns of excitement, from the Leopold-Loeb kidnap murder (the *Trib,* along with Hearst, vainly tried to hire Sigmund Freud to help with the coverage) to the Scopes trial. The crime passionnel was by no means left to the tabloids and Hearst. Possibly the first appearance of the immortal line "I shot him because I loved him" came in a *Tribune* story by sob-sister Maureen Watkins about a girl who killed her lover, phoned the police, and put a blues record on the phonograph. Maureen was inspired to turn the incident into a play, *Chicago,* that had a Broadway run and was revived in the 1970s as a musical.

Newsgathering competition continued razor-edged and produced a thousand anecdotes. Old Chicago newsman and chronicler of *The Front Page* era Jack McPhaul records this one: A *Herald-Examiner* reporter and photographer followed a tip to the apartment of a North Side playboy who was supposed to have been shot, getting admitted by flashing a fake detective badge to the super, and stuffing a nice cache of letters and photos in their pockets just as the playboy walked in. The reporter, still pretending to be a detective, told the man he must call the police right away to let them know he wasn't dead. Without waiting for questions reporter and photographer hastened out and hailed a taxi. What to do with the now embarrassing letters and photos? An inspiration. They directed the taxi driver to "Tribune Tower," and when they arrived, handed the cabbie the bundle and a tip, told him to return them to the owner with the *Tribune*'s apologies, and sauntered across the Michigan Avenue Bridge to their own shop.

A major postwar development was the founding of the *Tribune* foreign staff, or more precisely the conversion of "war correspondents" into "foreign correspondents." Only six other newspapers maintained regular foreign staffs *(New York Times, New York Post, New York Herald Tribune, New York World, Chicago Daily News,* and *Christian Science Monitor).* The war origin of the foreign correspondents skewed their role. War remained a surefire news favorite. The *Tribune* even sent a correspondent to cover the Chinese-Russian border skirmishing of 1929, whereupon the *Chicago Daily News,* not to be beaten, sent one too. Revolutions were good, famines OK. Difficult and daring exploits had been popularized in the big war, above all by irrepressible, torpedoed, shot-up, decorated Floyd Gibbons. In 1918 *Tribune* correspondent Frederick Smith hitched an airplane ride to become the first newsman into Berlin after the Armistice. Dick Little was wounded covering the Russian civil war with the White Army. Larry Rue reported the famine in Russia in 1921 by penetrating the ravaged and chaotic country from Turkey without benefit of passport. Vincent Sheean had hair-raising adventures covering the Rif insurrection in Algeria, disappeared completely, and was given up for dead. When he made it back to Tangier and Paris he was wined and dined by Colonel McCormick, and his interview with celebrated adventurer "Hadj Aleman" was turned into the Broadway musical *Desert Song*. Floyd Gibbons also had a desert adventure, brought on by a telegram from the desk in Chicago ordering him to "obtain true picture sheiks and their appeal Anglo-Saxon and American women," in the light of Rudolph Valentino's sensational film success. Gibbons obediently crossed the Sahara, encountering plenty of hardship but no sheiks who looked appealing to him. Back in Paris, his safari was sufficiently unusual, and he himself well enough established as a hero, to win a citation from Marshal Foch.

A more substantial accomplishment was that of John Steele, who, using George Seldes as a messenger, brought about the contacts between Dublin and London that ended the civil war in Ireland.

The *Trib*'s foreign correspondents were characteristically young men in their twenties, many of whom became famous: William L. Shirer, George Seldes, Edmond Taylor, Jay Cooke Allen. In addition to the regulars, the paper used the services of a score of stringers, providing it with coverage second only to the *New York Times*. The paper's membership in AP and UP circumscribed the mission of a *Tribune* correspondent, who was often needed less to report major events than to do background, interpretation, and features. Seldes, a somewhat humorless idealist, chafed under the preferences of the Chicago desk for what he considered trivia, such as favoring entertainer Josephine Baker's marriage to an Italian count over a scuffle between French royalists and the police.

In his extensive writings after leaving the *Tribune,* Seldes recorded only two instances of censorship. When he first moved into the Berlin bureau he got a request addressed to each European correspondent for a piece on the "failure of government ownership of railroads in his country." Seldes cabled a story that reported, truthfully, that German railroads were prospering under government operation, and received back a cable signed "McCormick" making it clear that what was wanted was a negative report—at home the government operation of war-seized rail lines was a hot issue. So detailed were the Colonel's specifics of what he wanted that Sigrid Schultz, Seldes's colleague, suggested that he simply "change the tenses, sign your name, and cable it back." Seldes instead wrote a much longer account corroborating the facts in the first story. He never heard back from the

Colonel, and further, "the Colonel never again in the next five or six years tried to dictate what I was to write or how I was to report the news. I wrote as I pleased."

Writing as he pleased he was suppressed only once. From Mexico, with whose revolutionary government Washington was having a prolonged bicker, Seldes conceived a both-sides series, with matching articles giving the Mexican and the State Department views. After the first few pieces the Mexican side of the story vanished from the *Trib*'s columns and the State Department prevailed. Despite that and doubtless some other instances, there was considerable validity in the claim of a *Tribune* "Book of Facts" in 1927 that "On no other paper is a reporter more free to write what he sees as he sees it and to have the story appear uncensored."

The *Tribune* had one of its best correspondents in China in John Powell, editor of the *China Weekly Review* in Shanghai. It did not, however, have a correspondent in Russia. Following coverage of the great famine of 1921 Floyd Gibbons stationed Seldes in Moscow, but the bureau was short-lived. To evade heavy-handed Soviet censorship, Seldes tried smuggling dispatches in the mail pouch of Herbert Hoover's American Relief Commission and got caught. Notified of the problem in Chicago, Colonel McCormick fired off a cablegram, which Soviet foreign commissar Chicherin showed Seldes:

YOU MUST ABANDON CENSORSHIP AND GUARANTEE FREEDOM OF EXPRESSION OTHERWISE OUR CORRESPONDENT WILL BE WITHDRAWN AND SO WILL CORRESPONDENTS OF OTHER AMERICAN NEWSPAPERS SO THAT RUSSIA WILL FIND HERSELF WITHOUT MEANS OF COMMUNICATION WITH THE OUTER WORLD

R R McCORMICK

"Your Colonel McCormick," remarked Chicherin, a worldly diplomat with a sense of humor, "he addresses me as an equal power, he sends me an ultimatum."

With a smile he added, "There are two trains a week to Riga; if you can't make Wednesday's—we are not a cruel people as your newspapers say— you can take the Saturday."

Over the next few years several correspondents and other visitors wrote pieces for the *Tribune* on Russia, but the regular Soviet correspondent was stationed in Riga, Latvia. Donald Day's post outside the then Soviet border was not his fault; he had even married an American Communist woman in 1920 in an attempt to get admitted to the tightly closed country as a Hearst representative. When that failed, he was fired by Hearst and presently caught on with the *Tribune,* in whose service he was destined to have a remarkable career.

Riga was a rich fount of anti-Soviet rumors, and when the *Tribune* refused some, Day sold them to Lord Rothermere, brother of tabloid pioneer Lord Northcliffe and scruple-free proprietor of the *Daily Mail.* Day's judgment of the Soviets accorded closely with Colonel McCormick's own: a dictatorship whose viciousness was exceeded only by its incompetence. The judgment was widely shared. The Russian people were perceived by Americans as bearing, and in a sense meriting, their Communist dictatorship out of what a *Tribune* editorial called "the Russian capacity for suffering and inaction in the face of suffering." Stalin's historic first Five-Year Plan, far from drawing acclaim for laying the foundation of industrialization, was judged to have caused economic ruin, abetted "by the incompetence of the Russian masses." The *Trib*'s Wasp American view that Russians were fitted only for "plain husbandry, crafts and arts" was widely echoed, as was the attribution to Communists, Russian or other, of superhuman powers in the realm of political intrigue.

The young foreign correspondents were special pets of the Colonel, who paid them well, fortified their egos with compliments, and rewarded good stories with bonuses. Further, he ordered them always to go first-class, train, ship, and hotel, and to hire the most impressive cars available. He set an example for Waverley Root in front of the Ritz in Paris, inviting him to share a ride in a limousine that looked as long as the Place Vendôme, then instantly dismissing it and commanding a second because he found a dirty ashtray.

More than any other group of employees, the correspondents gave the Colonel the happy sense of still being a military commander. His orders were typically peremptory. Shirer in London received a cable: "Fly Ethiopia." When Shirer cabled back that he would leave in three days, after getting his shots, he was queried: "What are you, a newspaperman or a historian?" Larry Rue thought the cables always arrived just as he was planning a holiday, and he pictured the Colonel in his Tower office studying his globe, turning to his secretary and saying, "Miss Burke, send this cable to Rue." Whereupon Rue "would jump across seas and continents, wherever a revolution, a national disaster or some other spot news" was popping. Once he received a cable in Vienna: "Proceed to Afghanistan and interview Abdullah," an outwardly placid assignment practically impossible to fulfill since revolution and civil war were raging in Afghanistan and there was no way to get there to begin with. Amid a train of adventures, ex-wartime flyer Rue was frustrated by his inability to rent an airplane in India and cabled his intention to head for Kabul overland, a dubious enterprise that would have taken weeks. He got a return cable: "Proceed to London and take delivery of your own airplane." His mission, when he finally accomplished it, won a gratifying accolade: "Your story of Afghanistan greatest *Tribune* story for more than a year."

Sometimes the Colonel gave an order by way of testing untried mettle. In London he once commandeered Waverley Root, junior member of the four-man bureau, to accompany him on a shopping trip. The Colonel, like royalty, carried no money, and Root, supplied with cash by the bureau, hastily paid clerks and pursued the Colonel down Regent Street to his next stop. He was rewarded by being invited to lunch with the Colonel and bureau chief John Steele, but was suddenly told to get the next train for Cardiff and check out the unemployment situation in Wales. Root toyed with the idea of relaxing and catching a later train, but wisely caught the early one and fifteen minutes after checking in at his Cardiff hotel received a phone call from the Colonel's secretary.

While giving the correspondents a free hand, the Colonel worried about their ideology, fearing their American viewpoint might be distorted by long sojourn abroad. From time to time he brought them home for "re-Americanization" in the healthy climate of Chicago, where Poles, Czechs, Germans, Ukrainians, and Hungarians jostled each other on the El. Commonly the prodigals were treated to a stint on the police beat, under the tutelage of Jake Lingle.

Once McCormick summoned all European hands to Paris for a special meeting to pick a replacement for Floyd Gibbons. Gibbons had been fired for spending $20,000 on a safari to Timbuktu, for which the only excuse he could offer was that he had promised his mother to some day send her a postcard postmarked Timbuktu. His playful misfeasance might have been overlooked save for the watchfulness of Kate McCormick, who was living with a bottle at the Ritz and keeping one red eye on the Paris *Tribune* and the foreign staff. George Seldes once was drafted to accompany her, along with maid, nurses, and interpreter, to Karlsbad, a journey that did nothing for his incipient ulcer, as she cursed French, Germans, and Japanese, Jews and Catholics, doctors and nurses, and bragged of her imaginary power at the *Tribune.* Seldes managed to get something out of the experience by selling it as a fiction story. An office boy from the Paris bureau, sent up one day to keep her company, got drunk at her invitation; she then escorted him to the head of the stairs and kicked him down it.

To reassign Gibbons's post of roving correspondent, a coveted plum, McCormick interrogated the assembled corps on their language abilities— who spoke French, who German, etc., then left them speechless by picking Larry Rue, the only self-confessed nonlinguist. His explanation, according to Seldes: "I don't want my American boys ruined by these damned foreigners." The anecdote seems to defy logic in either direction, since it might be considered good sense to keep German-speaking correspondents in Berlin and Vienna, French-speakers in Paris and Brussels, and let a nonlinguist do the roving, while on the other hand the rover might seem the least susceptible anyway to being seduced by the Europeans. The Colonel may merely have been exercising a boss's prerogative of startling the help.

Seldes, who told the tale to A. J. Liebling for his Wayward Press column in *The New Yorker,* apparently thought it illustrated McCormick's parochial nationalism, but the Colonel's own European-flavored background leaves room for mystery. It may be that the Colonel's much reiterated American nationalism included overcompensation for something he felt vaguely missing in himself. Whether as a result of his cosmopolitan childhood or not, he apparently did not react to Continental Europeans with the automatic negative that came with being an American Wasp. His anti-Europeanism lay on a more abstract and intellectualized level. A *Tribune* editorial of August 18, 1929, illustrates:

> The whole structure of Europe is grossly materialistic. All society has to be occupied with material things, but European society has made this a gross preoccupation for centuries of acquisitive wars and struggle for peace, of peonage and villenage, of profligacy at the top and stolid plotting at the bottom with a culture, a scholarship, and a civilization which has not had much meaning for the masses of the people in several hundred years.

Echoing here is not the American tourist resentment of the maître d', suspicion of the shopkeeper, and condescension toward the hotel maid, but rather the Yale 1900 depiction of history, with its overemphasis on war, its negative view of revolution, its ignorance of technology, and its disregard of economic progress.

The European quality the Colonel most exaggerated, and in fact feared, was diplomatic skill. Here he was in congenial touch with the man in the street, who was deeply persuaded that Americans were no match for Europeans in what was conceived to be the paramount diplomatic trait: guile. The idea appealed to all classes and viewpoints—Americans were gullible nice guys, Europeans shrewd operators. How else could America's massive participation in World War I and failure to get anything out of it be explained?

Perhaps more than specific prejudices or tangible objections, the feeling accounted for the now settled American opposition to the League of Nations and the World Court, which Bill Thompson found so general in some Chicago wards that he made it an issue in the mayoral campaign of 1927. The *Trib* gibed at that, but nevertheless agreed with Thompson that the United States could get little profit and might suffer loss from the World Court.

What proved to be the most futile of all foreign-policy issues of the post-World War I period was the "war debts," the portion of the inter-

Allied debt complex that consisted of borrowings (mainly in 1918) from the U.S. government by Britain, France, Italy, and Belgium. The European view that the war was a joint enterprise to which all had contributed in blood and treasure was not accepted in the United States. "The sick man is well," said the *Tribune,* overlooking the depressed European economy. "He hates all the expenses of his illness." To the problem of the British debt, McCormick offered an ingenious solution that had a curious sequel many years later: The British could hand over some of their Caribbean possessions. Hoover went so far as to mention the idea to Prime Minister Ramsay MacDonald who received it in frosty silence. The *Tribune* later suggested a pair of British battleships as payment of the $100 million due in 1932.

The State Department and its diplomatic service were a target of many editorials and cartoons. McCormick perceived the diplomatic service, filled with men of his own prep-school-Ivy-League background, to be more concerned with advancing their private social prestige than in defending the country's interests. A March 26, 1929, editorial regretted that "high grade men, strongly American, strongly democratic in their instincts, have not emerged in the diplomatic service in numbers. . . . The day of imitation and of toadying to foreign castes and titles . . . should have been over since the time of Ben Franklin."

The fact that the State Department was governed throughout the twenties by the Republican party did not mollify the Colonel, whose enthusiasm for the decade's Republican presidents remained tepid; the last president or presidential candidate for whom he felt genuine admiration was Theodore Roosevelt.

A faithful delegate to every Republican national convention, more or less enthusiastic about the nominee at the moment of his nomination, McCormick was regularly disillusioned by performance in the White House. He had two main criticisms of Harding, Coolidge, and Hoover—their support of Prohibition and their weakness on the navy. The Teapot Dome scandal did not bother him much, as indeed it scarcely troubled any of the press. Senators Thomas Walsh and Burton K. Wheeler experienced frustration in getting reporters to come to their hearings until Washington correspondent Paul Y. Anderson, backed by his newspaper, the *St. Louis Post-Dispatch,* shamed the rest into coverage. The *Washington Post*'s playboy publisher, Edward B. McLean, turned out to be a party to the scandal. The *Chicago Tribune*'s verdict on the acceptance of a bribe by the Secretary of the Interior to give away government oil land to an oil company was that the whole thing was really the fault of Prohibition, which had turned the United States into a nation of lawbreakers. Most of the rest of the press adopted a similar tone of cynicism.

Colonel McCormick's attitude toward Herbert Hoover chilled with the new president's inaugural address. As a result Arthur Sears Henning, courtly and conservative chief of the *Tribune* Washington bureau, returning from the White House lawn to the bureau (then in the Albee Building, corner of Fifteenth and G), received the famous telegram, THIS MAN WON'T DO, which reflected no unearthly prescience on the Colonel's part but an apprehension that Hoover planned an enlarged role for the federal government—dam-building; favored naval reduction, which the *Tribune* opposed; thought well of the World Court, of which the *Tribune* thought ill; and pledged enforcement of Prohibition, for which the *Tribune* had no use at all.

Interestingly enough, McCormick was one of the few observers to express a foreboding of the stock-market debacle, in a letter to his mother that he recovered and saved. But he had no more inkling than anyone else of the scope of the depression that followed. His old friend Samuel Emory Thomason, who had quit his $250,000-a-year position as general manager of the *Tribune* in 1927, after a disagreement neither he nor McCormick ever explained, had the ill luck to found a new tabloid, the *Chicago Times,* in the summer of 1929.

Meantime, on another front, the *Tribune*'s taxpayer suit against Big Bill Thompson had finally come to trial and 100 witnesses, 3,000 exhibits, and 11,000 pages of testimony established beyond anybody's reasonable doubt that the *Trib*'s allegation was true enough—the Thompson machine paid extravagant fees to unqualified "expert appraisers" of its building projects who kicked back most of the cash to the machine. Thompson was ordered to return nearly two and a quarter million dollars to the city. "The sons of bitches have ruined me!" he protested, but his appeal to the state supreme court was ultimately rewarded by a liberal judgment to the effect that he had been merely negligent rather than criminal. After Thompson's death in 1944, Colonel McCormick took satisfaction in the discovery of safe-deposit boxes containing nearly a million and a half in gold certificates and another half million in stocks and bonds.

The judicial decision permitted Thompson freedom to once more harangue the hoi polloi (and, as somebody said, there were plenty of them in Chicago) with the added power of a demagogue who has passed beyond the limits of ridicule. "A buffoon in a tommyrot factory" in the *Trib*'s words, he had run against the World Court, the Chicago school board (whose textbooks he said disparaged Von Steuben, Pulaski, and Kosciusko, all great Chicago heroes), and Prohibition, promising constituents that "no cop will invade your home and fan your mattress for a hip flask." He had run against crime in North Side wards while on Election Day Capone's hoods roamed South Side and West Side wards terrorizing reformers and Democrats. He had run against the Rhodes scholars (whose anglophilism also drew *Trib-*

une gibes), and King George V for the benefit of Chicago's Irish, though his celebrated promise to give the poor king a "crack in the snoot" if he ever came to Chicago was, according to some, craftily ambiguous; Thompson is said to have referred to the snoot's owner simply as "George" in order to allow Protestant bigots to think he was talking about George Cardinal Mundelein.

Finally, he had always run against the *Tribune,* but for the 1931 campaign he went to new lengths. He advertised a special noontime speech at the Apollo Theatre in the heart of the Loop where he promised shocking revelations about the *Tribune.* On the eve of the speech Thompson was stricken with appendicitis and his words had to be read by Richard Wolfe, his Commissioner of Public Works. The message heard by the crowded theater (free, and at noon) was that the *Tribune* planned to assassinate Thompson. The paper's slogan, according to Thompson, was not "World's Greatest Newspaper," but "We always get our man." He cited Mayor Carter Harrison, Sr., who had been shot by a "weak-minded newspaper boy" who might have been incited by reading the *Tribune*s he was selling —an obvious echo of Czolgosz, McKinley, and Hearst. The *Trib* also might have been responsible, Thompson thought, for the death of a Thompson crony who had fallen into the Chicago River, and the death of the wife of corrupt governor Len Small. He even thought that old man Medill might have had a finger in Lincoln's assassination. For his windup, he pulled out one more stop:

> I am doing today what I conscientiously believe is my duty, and if the Lingle wrecking crew kill your mayor for telling you the truth for the good of our future generations, I will ask of you that some citizen with equal courage see to it that the present editor of the Chicago Tribune is properly punished. I leave the matter in your hands and I will accept the consequence of telling the truth and from my nine years' experience on a ranch and my ability to handle a gun I confidently believe that I will not go alone should one of their cowardly attacks be made upon me.

The *Tribune* treated the speech with its usual raillery, implied that Thompson was habitually drunk at council meetings, and quoted him as saying, "The clerk will call the roll and all the wets will answer aye." Nevertheless, when McCormick noticed that he was being followed on the street by hoodlums he took precautions. He purchased a bulletproof limousine and hired as a chauffeur-bodyguard an ex-cop named Bill Bockelman. Thompson had already taken similar precautions, and Chicago was regaled by its three leading celebrities, Capone, Thompson, and McCormick, tooling down its avenues in three armored limos.

Since McCormick was still dogged afoot, Louis Rose assigned a trio of strong arms from the circulation department. Next time the hoods turned up, Rose's men clobbered them. It did not apparently occur to McCormick, telling the story to his WGN audience years later, that the *Tribune*'s continued employment of strong arms might lend a tint of color to Thompson's fears.

Thompson's Democratic opponent in 1931 was Anton J. Cermak. The *Tribune* had rarely supported a Democrat, and Cermak was no fragrant violet, but McCormick held his nose and backed him: "We think," said the editorial, "that any honest man must conclude that Cermak will be a better city executive than the incumbent."

The campaign was further enlivened by a fresh Thompson stroke against McCormick. Somehow he got hold of a *Trib* obituary of him that was unexpectedly sympathetic, the result of a fit of kindness on McCormick's part when he thought Thompson's appendicitis would be fatal. Along with the obit and other material, in a brochure entitled "The Tribune Shadow —Chicago's Greatest Curse," Thompson published the "Serritella letter," disclosing McCormick's single meeting with Capone in terms that made the Colonel seem overcourteous to the mobster. That Serritella himself was a for-real Capone buddy and had been boss of the news-handlers' union that brought on the meeting was nowhere indicated. Serritella was now a top Thompson patronage staffer, with the title of City Sealer. But he was unable to give up old habits, and before the campaign ended the *Tribune* had a last laugh when Serritella was indicted for stealing Christmas funds collected for the poor.

Thompson's defeat in the election was saluted by the *Tribune* as riddance of a demagogue who had given the city "an international reputation for moronic buffoonery, triumphant hoodlumism, unchecked graft, and a dejected citizenship." His successor was unlikely to duplicate the moronic buffoonery, but had potential for equalling Thompson in the other qualifications. Foreseeing the end of Capone and also the end of Prohibition, Cermak, at least according to one theory, decided that gambling was the economic wave of the crime-politics future and sought to assure himself a position of power through control of Capone's successor. The thug he chose to back was Ted Newberry, Capone's designee to take over the old North Side territory of O'Banion and Moran. A rival, Frank "the Enforcer" Nitti, objected. Killings jumped to one a day. Somebody tried to kill Nitti, and somebody did kill Newberry.

By that time the 1932 Democratic National Convention was in town. Cermak had a secret deal on with New York's Tammany Hall, whose bosses Jimmy Hines and Albert Marinelli, sharing rooms at the Drake with New York mob chiefs Frank Costello and Lucky Luciano, were pushing the candidacy of Al Smith. But the wheeling and dealing for Smith fizzled and Cermak had to do a quick clamber aboard the Franklin D. Roosevelt bandwagon.

It may have been in order to edge a little closer to the new powerhouse that Cermak visited Roosevelt in Miami in January. A nut named Giuseppe Zangara, who had already tried to shoot the king of Italy and Hoover, fired at Roosevelt, missed, and hit several other people including Tony Cermak.

When Cermak died a month later, Carey Orr did a front-page cartoon showing History adding Tony's alleged last words ("I'm glad it was me instead of you," that is, FDR) to those of Nathan Hale and other heroes. Not all Chicagoans believed Tony said the words, and some even thought Zangara wasn't that bad a shot. The *Tribune* printed a rumor from the underworld that mobsters, presumably from the Nitti faction, had hired Zangara to hit Cermak.

Laying the cornerstone of the new *Tribune* plant on North Michigan Avenue in 1920. Joseph M Patterson (*left*) and Robert R. McCormick (*right*).

LEFT: PRESIDENT LINCOLN ASSAS-
SINATED! GREAT FIRE! DEWEY SINKS
SPANISH FLEET—famous *Tribune* front
pages are memorialized in bronze on the
south façade of the Tribune Tower.

BOTTOM LEFT: In the 1920s the Tribune
Tower, although condemned by Mod-
ernists for its non-functional Gothic, immediately joined the Wrigley Building
across Michigan Avenue as a major Chicago landmark. (*Chicago Aerial Survey
Company*)

RIGHT: Robert R. McCormick (*left*) and
older brother Medill, about 1899, the
year the family moved to England.

BELOW: Ambassador and Mrs. Robert
Sanderson McCormick. McCormick Sr.
served as U.S. ambassador to Austria-
Hungary, Russia, and France.

Grandfather Joseph Medill, founder of the dynasty, with his grandchildren in 1898. Seated, Robert R. McCormick (*left*), Joseph M. Patterson (*right*); standing, Eleanore M. Patterson (*left*), Medill McCormick (*right*). (*Mrs. Maryland McCormick*)

Robert R. McCormick, Yale
class of 1903.

Amy Irwin Adams McCor-
mick, first wife of Robert R.
McCormick, portrait by Glen
Philpot.

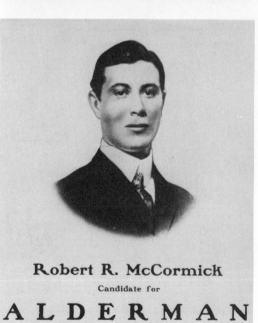

Election poster, 1904 style.
The Twenty-first was Chi-
cago's silk-stocking ward.

ABOVE: On the Russian front, 1915. McCormick is the tall figure in the center.

TOP RIGHT: Recruiting poster for World War I, published in the *Tribune* April 7, 1917, the day after war was declared.

BOTTOM RIGHT: In France. Probably at Valdahon, an AEF training base, before going into line with the First Division.

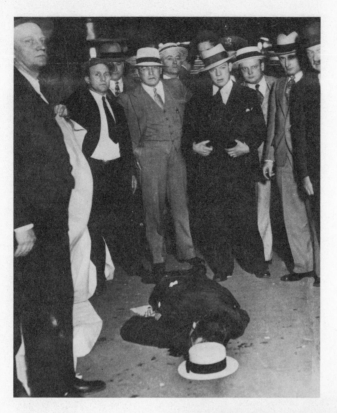

TOP LEFT: The body of Alfred (Jake) Lingle, *Chicago Tribune* reporter and secret intimate of Al Capone, gunned down in the Randolph Street underpass in midday, June 9, 1930.

BOTTOM LEFT: Big Bill Thompson, demagogue, buffoon, and bitter *Tribune* enemy, votes in the 1931 primary.

ABOVE: Colonel McCormick in the 1920s. (*Mrs. Maryland McCormick*)

A famous McCutcheon cartoon.

TOP LEFT: Colonel McCormick at Shelter Bay in the 1930s. Behind him, bareheaded, Captain Patterson.

TOP: Colonel McCormick with Alf Landon, whose nomination he had just helped secure, June 1936.

ABOVE: In 1943 Colonel McCormick made peace with Henry Ford (*left*), who had once sued the *Tribune* for libel for calling him an anarchist.

The Colonel's second marriage, in 1944, was to Maryland Mathison Hooper, a former Baltimore belle.

In Edinburgh in 1948, the Colonel listens from the parapet of City Chambers as the proclamation is made deleting the words "Emperor of India" from the King's title. (*Mrs. Maryland McCormick*)

CHAPTER TWELVE

Colonel McCormick Meets the New Deal

IN the watershed year of 1932–1933 ·Colonel McCormick was a happy, successful fifty-two-year-old benevolent despot. Though he was annoyed by the "radicals" sent to Congress by the disgruntled electorate of 1930, the depression did not bother him much. It had amazingly little effect on newspaper circulation, the *Tribune*'s declining only to 770,000. Ad lineage fell by half (32 million lines in 1929 down to 15 million in 1932) but figuring in the deflation, revenue was hardly affected. According to *Fortune,* net profits to *Tribune* shareholders for 1933 were $2,900,000. The Colonel profited personally from the sharp drop in interest rates by his ownership of preferred stock in the *Tribune*'s paper subsidiary, mainly acquired from *Tribune* executives who had received the stock as bonuses and had requested conversion to cash. The stock paid 8 percent, a glorious figure in 1933, and in fact one that McCormick felt was excessive. He therefore arranged to have all the preferred stock retired.

The *Tribune* skipped its Christmas bonus in 1931, but resumed in 1932 and never missed another of these jolly events. Colonel McCormick presided over the celebration in the Tower lobby not in Santa Claus suit but in morning coat and striped trousers.

Poor Kate McCormick died in 1932, drunk and disorderly to the last, followed by sister Elinor Patterson in 1933. Medill McCormick, whose constitution perhaps withstood booze less manfully than his mother's, was already gone. The reorganization of the corporate structure to avoid inheritance taxes was carried out just in time, in 1932, with the formation of a McCormick-Patterson trust that secured permanent control to the two cousins. Elinor's revenues, but no share in control, went to her daughter Cissy, who that year became editor of Hearst's Washington *Herald.* Cissy presently used her *Tribune* wealth to first lease (1937) and then buy (1939) the *Herald,* which through merger became the *Washington Times-Herald,* giving the three Patterson-McCormick cousins ownership of the three largest papers in Washington, New York, and Chicago just as certain other events were converging.

Meantime, Colonel McCormick used his *Tribune* profits for some purchases of his own. In 1926 he and Amy had bought an attractive town house in fashionable Astor Street (No. 1519, now gone), a long stroll from the Tribune Tower, or a short limo ride, and in the early thirties began the expansion and refurbishing of Grandfather Medill's Red Oaks Farm, renamed Cantigny. "I want the new house to last a very long time and possibly become one of the showplaces of Chicagoland because of its sheer beauty," he wrote architect Willis Irvin, an expert on famous American homes. With the Colonel's enthusiastic concurrence, Irvin introduced elements of Monticello and Montpelier in the form of a Jefferson porch and a Madison porch. The Madison porch was given distinctive McCormick touches. Bricks from Old North Church, Appomattox, Lincoln's tomb, and Fort Sumter were implanted in the wall, and the exterior lintels were decorated with the names of illustrious Americans: Jefferson, Washington, Patrick Henry, Lincoln. After getting stung by a bee, the Colonel had the porch enclosed, the lower space with glass and the upper with Fourdrinier screening, a fine wire mesh he knew about because its normal function was squeezing the water out of pulp in a paper mill.

He decided he didn't like the red brick Irvin chose for the new facing, and had it whitewashed. When he found that the white didn't suit him either, he had it scraped, resulting in a soft rose that turned out to be perfect. Two new wings included a library with a movie theater below, and new living quarters. Between the library and the drawing room a large bar was concealed behind butternut paneling which opened to pressure on a carved rose. Another gadget reminiscent of Monticello raised firewood from below to the firebox in the library.

Cantigny became one of America's first air-conditioned homes when the Colonel circulated chilly water from the well through a system of pipes; later, when modern air-conditioning became available, he used his lily pond to cool the condensers. Not long after, Tribune Tower became one of the world's first completely air-conditioned office buildings, a reflection of both the Colonel's paternalism and his interest in technological innovation.

The fifteen hundred acres of the estate provided room not only for riding but for fox hunting, a recreation the Colonel also carried on in a spread he later bought near Aiken, South Carolina. He also picked up a place at Boynton Beach, Florida, for deep-sea fishing. This sport, however, failed to enlist his passion because of its requirement of fisherman's patience. Waiting for a marlin strike proved as fatally taxing to the Colonel's forbearance as watching a baseball game at Wrigley Field.

Besides frequent vacation or semibusiness trips to Europe, mainly Paris and London, the Colonel traveled extensively in the United States, often in his own plane. Sometimes he flew the plane himself, but normally he left the flying to a hired pilot. The planes all had names—*Buster Boo* and *Tribby* (after his bulldogs), *Arf Pint,* and, a favorite, *'Untin' Bowler,* after a hat.

He had asked a London hatter for a cork derby to ride to hounds in and had been informed that the item he sought was "a 'untin' bowler, so if you fall off the 'orse you won't 'urt your 'ead." *Arf Pint* and *'Untin' Bowler* were amphibians, preferred for their ability to alight on lakes in the Canadian wilds. The planes had short lives. Of five that cracked up, the Colonel was aboard three, but was able to "walk away from one, run away from one, and swim away from one." He took pride in the safety precautions he enforced on his pilots, four of whom were killed after they left his employ, "doing things I would not have countenanced." Nevertheless, he was a notorious optimist on weather conditions, an attitude Amy strove for years to moderate. One of his European correspondents once found himself flying with the Colonel from London to Paris in a raging storm. Over the din and his own state of alarm the correspondent became aware of the Colonel's voice shouting at him from the seat behind. Fearing the worst, he cocked an ear and made out: "When you translate an editorial from a French paper you oughtn't to follow the grammatical structure of the original. Break it up into smaller segments."

At home, on Astor Street or at Cantigny, he rose early, dressed in his English tweeds, breakfasted European-style on juice, coffee, and rolls, and read the morning *Tribune,* cutting out items and stuffing the clips in his pockets for reference when he got to the Tower. The six-day-a-week trip was made in these years by Rolls, supplanted during the war by Buicks and Packards equipped with telephones. The Colonel sat in front with the chauffeur.

He enjoyed dining out and fancied himself a bit of a gourmet and wine connoisseur, though he was not really all that interested in either food or drink. Winston Churchill, a guest of the McCormicks at Astor Street, entertained the Colonel in London. No admirer of the American cocktail custom, Churchill complimented the visiting Colonel McCormick on his preference for Old Fashioneds, but rather overcame him by the profusion of the wine service through dinner, at whose end Churchill insisted on port, over McCormick's protests—"This port was laid down by Father in the last century. You would insult any British host by not drinking his port." But McCormick drew the line at a "spot of brandy"—"I don't care whether I insult the king, the queen, and the whole British Empire, no thank you." "Good," Churchill agreed heartily, "then we'll proceed to Scotch and soda."

In New York, the Colonel was an inveterate but impatient Broadway addict. Often he imposed on the *Tribune*'s New York business office to get him last-minute tickets for friends he had met on the train. Once the New York office head managed through strenuous efforts to obtain four tickets to a hit, and later asked the Colonel if he had enjoyed the show. The Colonel pronounced it "the greatest I ever saw," and after a moment inquired, "How did it come out?" He had left before the last act. In Chicago Amy talked him into taking her to *Romeo and Juliet* but at the first intermission he recalled that he had seen the play twenty years earlier, and departed, sending the chauffeur back to keep Amy company. For a while he regularly patronized the Chicago Civic Opera, to which he contributed generous support both financially and in the columns of the *Tribune,* but predictably he vanished from his box at the first opportunity.

The Colonel enjoyed public speaking. An *Editor & Publisher* writer called him "the most agile publisher in America" and noted that in a space of ten days he spoke in Chicago, St. Louis, Oklahoma City, several western states, and twice in New York. His favorite topic was freedom of the press, on the history of which he had become perhaps the nation's leading authority. His legal battle with Bill Thompson had intensified his interest and when he came to the aid of a small Minneapolis publication, the *Saturday Press,* which had been shut down under a new state libel law, he won national acclaim. Entering the litigation as an amicus curiae, and bringing in the American Newspaper Publishers Association, of whose Committee on Freedom of the Press he was chairman, he had fought the case to the Supreme Court. There he ultimately won a 5–4 decision. The majority opinion, delivered by Charles Evans Hughes, now Chief Justice, became a landmark.

The Colonel was moderately famous and regarded as powerful. Former ambassador to Germany James Gerard, in a 1930 magazine article, listed him among the sixty-four men who "ruled the United States," a list headed by Rockefeller, Morgan, Mellon, the Duponts, etc., and containing six publishers: Hearst, Roy Howard (head of The Scripps-Howard chain), Adolph Ochs of the *New York Times,* Cyrus H. K. Curtis of the *Saturday Evening Post,* Joe Patterson, and McCormick, whom many still confused with the rich McCormicks. It was easier to do the confusing now that he had become a millionaire himself. This contributed to a slight embarrassment when a *Tribune* campaign against big property owners who avoided payment of taxes turned up the fact that McCormick had been assessed only a modest $1,115 in 1931. He defended himself on the ground that at least he had paid it. The search for scapegoats for the depression caused embarrassment to many, from the New York bankers quizzed by a Senate committee to Samuel Insull, whose dizzy pyramid of utilities holding companies had collapsed. Amid cries of rage from ruined shareholders, Insull took it on the lam, as they now said in Chicago, and was extradited all the way from Turkey for an anticlimax in court—it turned out that he had done nothing illegal. Allowed to leave Chicago a second time he settled in Paris where he died leaving $1,000 in cash and $14 million in debts.

The *Tribune*'s analysis of the cause of the depression was high taxes, the result of federal government extravagance. Weird though the notion was, it accorded with what the business community thought, and few argued against it. The country in general agreed at least to the extent of blaming Hoover. When the off-year election gave the Democrats victories all over the country, the *Tribune* editorialized (under the title "1928 and 1930") on what two short years had done politically:

> Mr. Hoover and his advisers looked at the election returns [of 1928] and came to some conclusions. They decided to reorganize the party under the tutelage of [Methodist, Prohibitionist] Bishop Cannon for the further conquest and occupation of the Democratic South; to make it the party of Georgia and South Carolina, of the hills and the swamps, the Klux, the fundamentalists, the primitives and the holy rollers. . . . It was decided to make the Republican party the party of Bryan, dry with all the teeth of prohibition in it, pacifist and internationalist and economically satisfactory to the radicals who are elected as Republicans and conduct themselves as Bryanistic Democrats. . . .
>
> Mr. Hoover was not responsible for the disillusionment of American business men as to the new era, and its permanence, but when the illusion cracked he had nothing in his medicine chest for it. Another man might not have had, but another man would not have had the reputation for miracles. And another man might not have had his party so far away from its home.

The editorial ended by pointing out with indignation that in the recent vote Illinois was "wet and Democratic" and so were New York, Massachusetts, and even Ohio, "home of the Anti-Saloon League and mother of Republican presidents." The immediately following editorial demanded, "Modify the Volstead Act—Now."

As for nostrums against the worsening depression, the *Tribune* recommended a moratorium on European immigration to benefit the unemployed, but knocked the ultra-protectionist Smoot-Hawley tariff of 1931.

A daily editorial conference was held in the Colonel's twenty-fourth-floor eyrie, where the editorial team gathered facing the boss's huge desk, or rather table, of red-and-white marble that Amy had bought in Paris, and that caught the eye of every visitor. The marble table may be only the second most famous desk he ever owned. The "huge, ornate, black walnut rolltop" in which Walter Burns and Hildy Johnson conceal Earl Williams is described as being "the former property of Mayor Fred Busse," McCormick's old political patron, and at the time of *The Front Page* it belonged to the *Chicago Tribune*. It may have gravitated to the City Hall pressroom as a result of being replaced as the Colonel's own desk by Amy's gift. Yet McCormick's Tower office still displayed a rolltop desk, and a historic one, that of Joseph Medill. From it McCormick borrowed a heavy fixed magnifying glass and pair of long-bladed shears for his own desk, next to which stood a large globe on a pedestal.

One detail of furnishing that the office lacked contributed much to the legends it inspired. It had no doorknob, the Colonel's delight in gadgetry having dictated a brass kickplate which permitted him to depart with dog leash in one hand and briefcase in the other.

In attendance at the daily conference were Tiffany Blake, Clifford Raymond, Leon Stolz (a new star recruited from the Paris edition), and several other writers and artists. Dean of cartoonists John T. McCutcheon had won a Pulitzer in 1931, and the daily cartoon, by McCutcheon or Carey Orr, was a page-one fixture (and widely syndicated). Though McCormick took great interest in the cartoons, he did not, like Hearst, dictate their content, and McCutcheon sometimes differed with the *Tribune* on policy. His antiwar sentiments did not always synchronize with the paper's championing of a big navy, and his sympathy with Prohibition was at odds with the editorial column's diatribes on the noble experiment.

The editorials received careful consideration, and when the conference, which might last three hours, was concluded, the writers had clear notions of what the Colonel thought. He seldom if ever wrote an editorial himself, but Tiffany Blake and the others acted as expert amanuenses. What McCormick thought and what the *Tribune* said on its editorial page were in total harmony.

By the staff in general the Colonel was regarded as an awesome but benign autocrat. No one questioned his decisions; his orders were obeyed like those of a general or a czar. Yet he was not surrounded by yes-men, and Blake and the others, as well as the editors in the newsroom on the fourth floor, were not too terrified to ask questions, raise difficulties, and even express negative opinions. One writer given to such opinions McCormick seated directly in front of himself as "my no-man." But though he listened, in the end he decided, and what he decided was done.

Very rarely did he descend to the newsroom, which, nonetheless, was never oblivious of his presence twenty stories above; or at home in the evening—he called in regularly via a "hot line" phone on the news desk; or at the theater—he sometimes sent his chauffeur-bodyguard to the Tower with a correction; or out of town (editorials were read to him over the phone). When the transatlantic telephone cable made it possible he even called from abroad, on one occasion to ask the desk what the weather was in Chicago. The notation "R. R. McC." appeared frequently on assignment sheets, signifying that the Colonel had a personal interest in the story. He offered endless criticisms, corrections, and ideas, all of which had to be taken with utmost seriousness. "If the Colonel wants a drink of water we turn the hose on him," explained one editor. Despite his background in law and engineering, despite his preoccupation with politics, war, and history, McCormick had an instinctive feel for the news business.

Walter Trohan recollected that when he won the coveted Washington bureau assignment in 1934, "telegrams signed 'McCormick' and letters signed 'McC' began to explode over my life like Roman candles . . . [and when] I became executive director and later bureau chief . . . these explosive missiles set the tempo of an existence that makes James Thurber's *The Years with Ross* as uneventful as the meditation hour in a Trappist monastery."

Trohan must have expressed the feelings of many *Trib* editors and correspondents when he told the Illinois Historical Society:

> Some [experiences with the Colonel] drove me to exasperation, so that while I loved him I could cheerfully have strangled him many times. But I never could neglect him because in the midst of the most trivial and exasperating flow of suggestions, requests, and unrelated inquiries, he would come up with the most accurate information and the most penetrating observations.

The *Tribune* in 1932–1933 was not a very controversial newspaper either in its news or its editorial columns. Despite the national economic crisis, there was little editorial controversy in the nation's press. The *Tribune*'s attitude toward the Great Depression was typical—impassioned demands for reduction in government spending and taxes, and bland appeals for national unity. The cartoonists depicted the depression as a ragged tramp, typically (January 17, 1933) commenting over squabbling congressmen, "They're still fightin' about the best way to lick me." The title of the cartoon was "After three years it's time we got together," but neither cartoonist Carey Orr nor the editorial page could specify what everybody should get together and do.

Occasionally a depression-caused news event stirred brief *Tribune* alarm or anger, as in the rent-eviction riot on Chicago's South Side in August of 1931. REDS RIOT; 3 SLAIN BY POLICE, the *Tribune* bannered, reporting that "2,000 communists, mainly colored, abandoned a parade and started a battle to prevent the legal eviction of a family. . . ." But next day brought a sympathetic report of the Cermak administration's decision to give "every humane consideration [to] the hundreds of penniless families" who had been evicted and to suspend further eviction notices. It observed with satisfaction that there was "no report of the slightest trouble." Exposure by the inquest of alleged Communist leadership in the "rent strike" and riot brought a stern editorial calling for "foreign agitators" to be "run down and expelled" and their "American allies" to be "punished under our laws." But the paper felt no apprehension, foreseeing for the Red invasion "no prospect of any results except the fomenting of futile but tragic violence."

The basic meekness of America's unemployed reassured McCormick and other conservatives, and few besides Hoover panicked over the 1932 veterans' Bonus March on Washington. The *Tribune* assumed Communist leadership (a not unfounded assumption) and the veterans' brutal eviction from their Washington camp was at least condoned in Arthur Sears Henning's coverage (as in most other correspondents'). The entire press joined the *Tribune* in denouncing the veterans' demand for early payment of their promised bonus, as did both presidential candidates and nearly everyone else, showing how little anybody knew about depression economics. (Roosevelt at least expressed sympathy for the evicted veterans.)

The Roosevelt-Hoover campaign oratory scarcely touched the depression. When the *Tribune* addressed a query to both candidates about their views on cutting the federal budget, Roosevelt wired McCormick personally: "Preliminary survey leads me to believe federal expenditures can be cut twenty percent by eliminating many functions not absolutely essential and by complete reorganization of many departments."

The statement was by no means out of character—Roosevelt said the same thing in speeches: "I regard reduction in Federal spending as one of the most important issues of the campaign," and "I shall approach the problem of carrying out the plain precept of our Party, which is to reduce the cost of current Federal government operations by twenty-five percent" —up five percent from his reply to McCormick. He even seconded the opinion of the *Tribune* on the high-tax sins of the Hoover administration: "We had ventured into the economic stratosphere—which is a long way up —on the wings of President Hoover's novel, radical, and unorthodox economic theories of 1928, the complete collapse of which brought the real crash in 1931. . . ."

Naturally, Roosevelt said some things out of the other corner of his mouth, but Colonel McCormick, who at Roosevelt's invitation paid a congenial visit to Hyde Park, could be excused for imagining that he was dealing with a fiscal conservative. When it came to big spending, the man to fear seemed to be John Nance Garner, the Texan Speaker of the House, who demanded a public works program from which Roosevelt diffidently withheld his indorsement. Garner was Hearst's favorite, and Hearst was credited with the convention deal whereby Garner accepted the vice-presidency (though confidentially evaluating the office as "not worth a quart of warm piss"). Hearst's maneuvering was based not on love for Roosevelt but hatred for Al Smith, who had derailed Hearst's New York political career.

Possibly Colonel McCormick would have been more enlightened about the direction a Roosevelt administration would take had he reread a *Tribune* news story that contained this quote:

By next year it will be clear to the American people that the Republican party is the conservative party of the United States and that the Democratic party is the progressive or liberal party. . . .

So we are approaching the campaign . . . with the broad principles settled in advance; conservatism, special privilege, partisanship, destruction on the one hand—liberalism, common sense idealism, constructiveness, progress, on the other.

That was Franklin D. Roosevelt all right, but back in 1920, when he was running for the vice-presidency on a ticket supporting the League of Nations. At that time the *Tribune* editorial line on Roosevelt was that the Democrats had nominated him for one reason only: "He is [there] to put the honey of a name on the trap of a ticket. . . . If he is Theodore Roosevelt . . . Bryan is a brewer."

But in 1932 the paper found nothing much to choose between candidates. Neither did Walter Lippmann and most of the press's deep thinkers. Roosevelt and Hoover were old, apparently firm, middle-of-the-road progressives, ready, after due deliberation, to adopt small reforms if enough people wanted them. What was driving the two candidates into opposite corners in 1932 was not their own inclinations, but new political exigencies created by the tide of history.

Thus Robert McCormick—"Bert"—conservative, but neither blind nor stupid, could believe that as president of the United States old schoolmate "Frank" would not indulge in any very dangerous economic experiments.

In the realm of foreign policy, McCormick felt even more reassured. Foreign policy was the area in which the departing administration had satisfied him the least. Hoover's Secretary of State was Henry L. Stimson, a wispy eastern patrician (Andover, '84, Yale, '88), who like McCormick was an admirer of Teddy Roosevelt but unlike McCormick approved Teddy's swashbuckling activism in foreign affairs. Stimson had favored the League of Nations, a posture Roosevelt had just dropped in deference to Hearst. He had negotiated the London Naval Treaty of 1930, affirming the 5–5–3 U.S.-Britain-Japan ratio of the Washington Treaty of 1922, but in some eyes, including the *Tribune*'s, giving Britain and Japan the best of the deal, since neither could really compete with American naval building. To the Kellogg-Briand Pact renouncing war as an instrument of national policy, Stimson had sought to attach an activist interpretation that, according to the *Tribune*'s interpretation of the interpretation, amounted to a pledge by the United States to "engage in measures to prevent other nations from making war," such as trade embargoes.

In Asia, the *Tribune* favored China over Japan but thought protests against Japan's aggression in Manchuria futile and hypocritical ("Japan, looking about for parallels . . . might observe Texas") and anything stronger, like an embargo, positively dangerous. Strengthen the navy and leave Japan alone, the *Tribune* in essence cautioned in its frequent lectures against the opposite policy of weakening the navy and pinpricking Japan.

In the light of the Hoover administration's "Bryanist" faults—quixotic internationalism, one-sided disarmament, costly public-works projects, and last but far from least, Prohibition—the *Tribune* reported the campaign impartially. Editorially the newspaper depicted Roosevelt as weak and ineffectual, but essentially harmless, as did the press in general. "Now, Cliff," Clifford Raymond remembered the Colonel telling him, "I want you to treat Roosevelt nicely in your editorials. I want that boy that I went to school with at Groton to know I wish him well in his career." On election eve the *Tribune* indorsed Hoover, in a perfunctory way, spending most of its editorial wordage in criticism of Stimson.

Kissing Hoover good-bye the following March, the *Tribune* judged him kindly but sternly: He had "not acquired public confidence" (nobody could argue with that), and though he talked a good game of private enterprise, he had gone in for public works on a scale that made him "the greatest state socialist in our annals. . . . He could praise individualism with eloquence, but he could also build Boulder Dam."

Hoover's all-time championship as a state socialist was not destined to last, but for a while the old Groton-tie friendship between Frank and Bert continued across party lines. A forecast (February 5) by Arthur Sears Henning of the New Deal program ("Maps Fight on Depression") was sympathetic, as was coverage of the inaugural, describing the new president as "a man with lines of pain, of will power, and of courage written into his face," and editorial comment: ". . . the American people, regardless of party or condition, of doctrine or diverse opinion, loyally salute the new President and government and pray for their success."

FDR's first moves were reassuring. His handling of the national banking crisis drew *Tribune* praise as "superb leadership," and an Orr cartoon reversed the *Trib*'s 1920 judgment on the two Roosevelts, using a couple of big sticks as symbols with the depression tramp muttering apprehensively, "Who said they were only distant cousins?" How well McCormick or anyone else understood what Roosevelt had really done is unclear, but there was nothing in his performance to merit conservative criticism. He had turned the banking problem over to Hoover's treasury people and the big bankers, limiting his own contribution to what he was good at, that is, going on the radio and telling everyone that the banks were now OK, and they could bring their money back. Next he sent a bill to Congress cutting $400 million worth of employees off the federal budget, and then called for repeal of the Volstead Act, bringing back legal beer. .

Obviously, the man was too good to be true, and he soon proved it. Tiffany Blake had privately labeled the inaugural speech, with its pretentious "We have nothing to fear but fear itself," as so much "hot air." Colonel McCormick's subordinates in fact were out in front of the Colonel, who, as Blake complained, had plunged into scholarship—a book on Grant's campaigns—and was "leaving us to face the Red Army." So little alarmed was McCormick by the Red Army that he invited its leader to stay at the Astor Street house during his projected visit to open the Chicago World's Fair (Roosevelt's visit did not materialize).

The New Deal's honeymoon with the press lasted about as long with the *Tribune* as it did with any other paper. Among the swarm of new federal creations there were a few the *Tribune* approved, such as the Securities and Exchange Commission, and some it hated, such as the Tennessee Valley Authority (not strictly speaking a New Deal innovation, since Republican Senator Norris had pushed it for years), but the agency that finally estranged Colonel McCormick and most of his compeers was NRA (National Recovery Administration). One title of NRA was a gigantic public-works appropriation to be spent under the rubric of PWA (Public Works Administration) by the Secretary of the Interior. The fact that the new secretary, Harold L. Ickes, was an old *Tribune* reporter did not reassure Colonel McCormick. Neither did the fact that Ickes was an old Teddy Roosevelt progressive who had worked with Medill McCormick among Illinois Republicans. Ickes had despised Medill as a snob, had joined the Democrats, and entirely apart from such trivia, was about to spend a truly unheard-of $3.3 billion of the taxpayers' money. Ickes for the next twelve years was second only to FDR, if that, as a *Trib* dislike. Ironically enough, Colonel McCormick could not have found a man more to his own taste in spending government money—Ickes was so prudent that the PWA remained miraculously free of graft, and the works it produced, from sewage mains to aircraft carriers, were tremendous bargains. But Ickes's splendid record was achieved by being very careful, and being careful meant going so slow that the PWA spending had little impact on the depression, a detail nobody noticed until later economists began dissecting the New Deal. A far better spender was Harry Hopkins, a wisecracking, horse-playing idealist in charge of first CWA (Civil Works Administration), later WPA (Works Progress Administration), who spent like a drunken sailor. The *Tribune* characterized Hopkins in an editorial that Hopkins framed for his office wall:

> Mr. Hopkins is a bullheaded man whose high place in the New Deal was won by his ability to waste more money in quicker time on more absurd undertakings than any other mischievous wit in Washington could think of.

But in the eyes of Colonel McCormick spending was not all that was wrong with the New Deal. Something else loomed even larger. Title I of NRA established "codes of fair practice" for all the various industries. That sounded like the Boy Scouts and Mom's apple pie, and the press along with everybody else turned momentarily starry-eyed. NRA's symbol, a blue eagle with the legend "We do our part," seemed to meet the psychological need expressed by Carey Orr's cartoon about "getting together" to lick the depression. It blossomed on every storefront and every masthead, including the *Tribune*'s. The truth about Title I, that the codes were mainly a way for big business to concert its interests and put the squeeze on small business, without having to worry about the antitrust laws, was slow to dawn, but the *Tribune* was not far off in spotting an analog to Mussolini's fascism.

That, however, was not the real defect in NRA in the view from the Tribune Tower. What bothered McCormick seriously was the imposition of a code on the newspaper business. As chairman of the Committee on Freedom of the Press of the American Newspaper Publishers Association (ANPA) McCormick urged his fellow press lords, at their annual meeting in New York, to take a stand. While the publishers debated, the semi-religious enthusiasm for NRA peaked with a parade of 250,000 believers down Fifth Avenue, and the ANPA settled on a prudent compromise, signing the code while writing in a stipulation, framed by McCormick, reserving First Amendment rights.

As his favorite author, P. G. Wodehouse, would have put it, the NRA caused the scales to fall from Colonel McCormick's eyes. Thenceforward the *Tribune*'s news coverage of the New Deal turned suspicious and its editorial tone caustic. In October John Boettiger, now assigned to the White House, was instructed to interrogate the president on the threat to press freedom. Boettiger put his question about as broadly as possible:

"There has been noted, around the world, a disposition to curb the freedom of the press and I wanted to get your attitude on that."

Roosevelt might have mollified McCormick with a solemn answer, but being Roosevelt, and at the height of his popularity with the White House press corps, he flipped Boettiger a wisecrack: "Well, look, John, you tell Bert McCormick that he is seeing things under the bed." That got a laugh from the correspondents but did not exactly smooth relations with the *Tribune.*

Yet McCormick showed he was not thin-skinned. A month later when the NRA's Newspaper Code came up in a press conference, Roosevelt mentioned "Dave Stern's editorial in the *New York Evening Post* last night," and turning to Boettiger, said, "I commend it to John Boettiger and, John, entirely off the record, I wish you would give a dare to Bert to reprint it."

"You say it is off the record?" Boettiger asked.

Roosevelt: "Yes."

Boettiger: "I will mail you a copy of that." More laughter from the correspondents, but better followed two days later when Boettiger raised his hand:

"May I present the compliments of Colonel McCormick, and tell you that we are running Mr. Stern's editorial on the freedom of the press tomorrow morning."

Roosevelt exclaimed, "No!" and amid laughter told Boettiger, "I think that is perfectly grand."

In January the *Tribune* delivered a lengthy analysis of the "1934 Business Prospect," which proved surprisingly sympathetic to the New Deal. Pointing out that the president and his advisers were applying the reverse of traditional economic theory in their pump priming via the Hopkins and Ickes agencies, it nevertheless in effect indorsed the experiment and reminded readers that the practice had been pioneered in principle with Boulder Dam and Muscle Shoals. If some Chicagoans were troubled by the city's taking $42 million to spend on a new sewage plant, a water filtration plant, completion of the Outer Drive, and improvement of the Art Institute, they should take courage from New York's example of asking and getting $92 million for its under-river tunnels.

> The immediate effect of paying billions for public works and other billions to the city folks for little work, and to farmers for refraining from work, is to make trade active. Whether recovery will then come of its own momentum is a question over which some people may differ from the President. But while the money is being spent retail trade is bound to be active.

This was at least kinder than Huey Long's sardonic capsulization of the New Deal: "We took four hundred million from the soldiers [the defeated bonus bill] and spent three hundred million to plant saplings [the Civilian Conservation Corps]."

Through 1934 the *Tribune*'s Washington coverage turned even more noticeably anti-Roosevelt than the editorials. Stories compared him to Kerenski as an ineffective leader paving the way to bolshevism. Agriculture Secretary Henry Wallace, son of a distinguished family of Iowa Republicans, was compared to Lenin, Mussolini, and Hitler. McCormick saw a coincidence in the birthplace of Felix Frankfurter, which was the same as that of Hitler, Habsburg-ruled Austria-Hungary, a nativity that left him "impregnated with the historic doctrines of Austrian absolutism."

By election time 1934 the *Tribune* was all out to save the country from Lenin, Mussolini, Hitler, and the Habsburgs by electing a Republican Con-

gress. Something went unaccountably wrong and the November 7 banner
read: A LANDSLIDE FOR DEMOCRATS.

Editorially, the *Tribune* commented:

> In effect, these critical times find the United States with a one party govern-
> ment with authority to do exactly as it pleases. That is the outcome of the
> election and for two years it is final. The voters said it shall be so, and for
> whatever comes of it, so it is.

An analysis of the election was sourly titled "Tax Payers Voted Republican." The momentous truth that Roosevelt had accomplished a permanent
tilt in the two-party system from Republican to Democratic preponderance
was as yet concealed from McCormick.

In reporting and interpreting the other historic governmental change that
occurred in March 1933, the *Tribune* was less indecisive. The Weimar
Republic had been a favorite of Colonel McCormick, who saw its democratic character as reflecting the "very high level of character and intelligence" of the German people, "the most stable and orderly" in Europe, just
as chaotic, despotic Communism seemed to him to reflect the traits of the
likeable but less favorably endowed Russians. From the start he saw Hitler
as a calamity, and the *Tribune*'s readers were kept well-informed. The
paper's Berlin correspondent was Chicago-born Sigrid Schultz, one of the
few ranking newswomen of her day. Daughter of an artist, she had grown
up in Paris and Berlin, and started as a cub reporter under *Tribune* correspondent Richard Henry Little on her graduation from Berlin University
in 1919. Schultz ultimately became chief of the Central European Bureau
and Berlin commentator for the Mutual Broadcasting System (a post Shirer
filled for CBS). In 1933 she did a first-rate job of covering Hitler's takeover
under such heads as "German Decree Annuls Liberty and Civil Rights,"
"Rule of Hitler Is Opened with Riots; 4 Slain," "Nazi Terrorism Grows,
Jewish Stores Closed," "Hitler Opens War on Reds, Homes Raided."

McCormick himself (with Amy) visited Germany in the summer of 1933
and wrote a series of pieces in which he tried to explain the Nazi phenomenon. He stuck stubbornly to a thesis already advanced in the *Tribune*'s
editorial columns, that Hitler was the product of the Versailles Treaty, and
that the persecution of the Jews was a sort of national psychological reaction to being officially blamed for World War I. He admitted the economic
factor, but only to distribute blame for Germany's poverty between Versailles and the New Deal-like public works of the Social Democrats.
McCormick perceptively noted that the remarkable thing about Hitler's
speeches was not his words, but their reception, and drew the inference that
Hitler owed his rise to German resentment of Versailles.

In light of the history of the National Socialist party—a decade as a splinter group, then suddenly commanding the attention and votes of millions of Germans—the Versailles interpretation made little sense, but McCormick's view was widely shared in America. The true explanation, the devastating effect on German economic recovery of the Wall Street crash, only occurred to historians after World War II. In May 1934 the *Tribune* sounded another note: Germany was a land of "excitements, repressions, and totem pole enthusiasms, a land of Teutonic Ku Klux, all the more formidable for being efficient." Again the verdict was widely echoed: Germany was a weird country.

An angle that passed strangely unnoticed by Colonel McCormick and others was the significance of Hitler for American security. A much criticized feature of Versailles was the hypocrisy of the Allies on the disarmament clause, strictly enforced against the Weimar Republic while Britain and France indefinitely postponed their own disarmament. The Anglo-German Naval Agreement of 1935, permitting Germany to build a sizable fleet, including U-boats, was accepted with perfect equanimity by the *Tribune* and other papers, many of whom barely five years later would be crying alarm over German potential for invading the United States. In 1935 the whole Hitler drama, though fascinating, seemed to be happening far off, on another planet. Domestic politics was infinitely more compelling.

CHAPTER THIRTEEN

Colonel McCormick Becomes
an Old Reactionary

BY the time the election year of 1936 arrived Colonel McCormick had won recognition as the leading reactionary publisher of the Middle West, failing to win the national championship only because Hearst, despite having had a large hand in Roosevelt's nomination, had soured as swiftly and even more bitterly. In intensity of feeling about the New Deal, Hearst and McCormick were in harmony with their fellow publishers, and may have been outdone by some. The entire press, or very nearly, voiced the same sentiments about New Deal bungling, extravagance, bureaucracy *(burocracy* in the *Tribune),* and government interference with business, commonly in identical metaphors. McCormick's sentiments, like those of Frank Knox at the *Chicago Daily News,* Ogden Reid at the *New York Herald Tribune,* Henry Luce at *Time-Life,* DeWitt Wallace at *Reader's Digest,* and the other publishing giants, were rooted partly in a sense of solidarity with the business community and in loyalty to the Grand Old, if battered and tattered, Republican party. All voiced apprehension of an incipient Roosevelt dictatorship. Yet in Colonel McCormick's perception there seemed to be an especially deep, or more genuine, fear of a New Deal threat to America's political structure. In expressing its satisfaction at the unanimous Supreme Court decision outlawing NRA in 1935 the *Tribune* thought that

> it may not be easy for the American people to see plainly or perceive wholly what has been done for the free democratic structure of the American government. We are all very close to profound events. . . . Later days, later years, and even another generation may understand more clearly how the republic in excitement, if not in extremity, began to consent politically to forms and policies of government which would have revolutionized American society. . . .

Most of his fellow publishers surely nodded sage agreement and perhaps wished their writers could have expressed it so well. Two conspicuous exceptions were the *New York Daily News* of Joe Patterson (known to New Yorkers as Captain Patterson, in defiance of the convention that only field-grade officers keep military rank) and the *Chicago Times,* the after-

132

noon tabloid of McCormick's old friend, law partner, and *Tribune* general manager, Samuel Emory Thomason. Among their trunk murders, Hollywood divorces, and madcap heiress escapades, the two tabloids interspersed straight or sympathetic coverage of Washington, and Patterson even raised money among his readers to build FDR a White House swimming pool.

The press's gratification in 1935 at reactionary Supreme Court decisions on the New Deal proved premature. Roosevelt held Congress in session for a "Second New Deal"—the Wagner Labor Relations Act, Social Security, and a tax bill dubbed "Soak-the-Rich" by most of the press, and "Soak-the-Successful" by Hearst, whose obedient editors henceforth referred to the New Deal as the "Raw Deal."

The *Tribune* reacted less violently, but made clear its apprehensions with a numbered series of editorials titled with variants on the theme of approaching revolution. The core of McCormick's fear was contained in a paragraph of the first:

> [From the New Deal's measures thus far] it is possible to see what sort of a house is to be built . . . for the new Kerensky-Roosevelt state, the socialized democracy. The builders think they are at Runnymede. They may be mistaken. They may have lost their way.

The series gave readers a schoolmasterish lesson in the history of the corporation, starting with Sinibaldo de' Fieschi (Pope Innocent IV), and its adaptation to the purposes of government via the Panama railroad and Hoover's Reconstruction Finance Corporation, over whose vast New Deal growth its creator "now professes amazement." The Roosevelt administration, through its dazzling proliferation of corporate agencies, was constructing a gigantic extragovernmental structure that could not fail to have a profound effect on the republic's future, and that, like Kerenski's Russian democracy, might prepare the way for a Communist or a fascist dictatorship.

So much for the intellectual approach. Taking off the gloves, Colonel McCormick borrowed from Thomas Nast's campaign against the Tweed Ring the slogan "Turn the Rascals Out," which appeared on the editorial page masthead on January 1 as the *Tribune*'s "Platform for 1936" and continued daily thereafter. He tried to give it some justification by ordering a series exposing the graft in Harry Hopkins's WPA, but though Hopkins ran a less taut ship than did Harold Ickes, there was little room for graft in a program that focused on labor-intensive light public works, and the series fizzled. A couple of years later the *Trib* was enchanted with Scripps-Howard writer Thomas L. Stokes's exposé of Hopkins' use of the WPA to help reelect Kentucky New Dealer Alben Barkley to the Senate. The *Trib* applauded the resulting Hatch Act.

Later in the spring McCormick had another inspiration, and at the
bottom of the mast, under its Platform for 1936, Platform for Illinois, and
Platform for Chicago, a bold italic question was posed: "Only 217 days
remain to save your country. What are you doing to save it?" Sinibaldo de'
Fieschi and Harry Hopkins notwithstanding, it seemed an unduly peremptory query to confront a faithful reader with as he unfolded his breakfast
napkin. Chicago Democrats were first incredulous, then entertained, and
amusement redoubled when phone calls to the *Tribune* brought a similar
greeting from the switchboard operators. Either the Colonel decided the
idea wasn't working or simply got tired of it—since after several weeks the
silly slogan was dropped.

Altogether, though the New Deal made plenty of mistakes, the *Trib*
voiced few valid criticisms, mainly because economics was not well understood. (For its claim that NRA and AAA [Agriculture Adjustment Ad-
ministration] had inhibited rather than helped recovery, the *Tribune* could
cite respected sources, such as the Brookings Foundation.) Typically, the
Tribune attacked Social Security in articles as well as editorials, but missed
the one vulnerable aspect of the act: It imposed a heavy regressive tax
during a period of deflation; in other words, it took money out of circulation
when everything else the New Deal was doing was aimed at putting it in.

On the plane of electoral politics, the Second New Deal and its rhetorical
follow-up sealed the advantage the Democrats had gained in 1932 into a
permanent realignment. Crudely put, the bulk of the Left and Center re-
grouped behind Roosevelt, leaving the Republicans stuck with the Right.

From the Tribune Tower the transformation was not clearly perceived.
A handful of defections among old-line Democrats—Lewis Douglas, Al
Smith, John W. Davis, the Du Ponts—made it look to Republican optimists
like Colonel McCormick as if the Democrats were falling apart. Once more,
as in 1916, he looked forward to a big Republican comeback.

Somewhat surprisingly, in view of the scarcity of Republican officeholders of any description, the Colonel found a candidate very much to his
liking. Governor Alf Landon of Kansas was an old Teddy Roosevelt Progressive who had fought the Ku Klux Klan and balanced his budget—what
more could you ask? He had also indorsed large parts of the New Deal, but
the Colonel expansively overlooked that detail.

Roosevelt, a front-page editorial asserted, could not be beaten by "people
who merely hate Roosevelt . . . a question of personal dislike . . . merely
turns in his favor." He could be beaten only by "a better man, a man of
sounder principles and better intentions." Plain-spoken, down-home Landon came across as credible, democratic, common-sensical—virtues Colonel McCormick thought of as especially midwestern. Roosevelt had charm,
a quality behind which might lurk dark ambitions. Nobody could suspect

Alf Landon of harboring dreams of dictatorship, though unfortunately one reason they could not was that he had an uninspired speaking delivery. Though in the aftermath Landon came to be labeled a symbol of reaction, at the time he was more accurately perceived as a moderate, and attracted indorsement from such liberal sources as the *St. Louis Post-Dispatch* and (after prolonged soul-searching) Walter Lippmann.

For vice-president, McCormick liked Arthur H. Vandenberg of Michigan, an outstanding moderate whose equivocation on the New Deal had led the Gridiron Club to portray him in a baseball skit as stepping to the plate with two bats to announce, "I'm Vandenberg—I bat for both sides."

Vandenberg also equivocated on whether he wanted to run for vice-president, and surrendered to Colonel McCormick too late. His less bashful rival was Colonel Frank Knox, a former top Hearst executive who in 1931 had bought into the *Chicago Daily News,* leading Chicagoans to distinguish their principal newspaper publishers as the "morning colonel" and the "afternoon colonel." Between the two there was little love lost. Though a four-square enemy of the New Deal, Knox was in foreign policy a Stimson-type throw-America's-weight-around internationalist, in contrast to neutralist Vandenberg. Like McCormick, Knox owed his military title to service in the artillery in World War I, but his record included a touch of panache—in 1898 he had galloped up San Juan Hill with Teddy, and had a great souvenir to prove it, a broad-brimmed campaign hat with two bullet holes. How much personal jealousy accounted for the animosity between the two colonels is conjectural. Once someone reported to McCormick that Knox had issued orders for the *Daily News* to differ with the *Tribune* on "everything," causing McCormick to comment, "He'll be at a disadvantage next week when we start our campaign against syphilis."

Some thought McCormick himself had coveted the VP nomination, but had been too dignified to chase it. However that might be, he was determined to go down the line for the Republican ticket. When Chicago advertising magnate Albert Lasker passed the hat in Cleveland, leading off with a $50,000 donation, McCormick was the only cat present fat enough, or foolish enough, to top Lasker.

The Cleveland convention was bannered in the *Tribune* as OPEN CAMPAIGN TO SAVE U.S. and suffocated with affectionate coverage. Even cartoonist Orr went to Cleveland, whence his front-page drawings depicting the rout of European-style dictatorship from American shores were transmitted by the new AP Wirephoto technique.

The Colonel issued orders for the news desk to treat the two candidates evenhandedly, as in 1932, but either that was for public consumption (*Editor and Publisher* reported it) or else he forgot, because the *Trib* did anything but. Landon speeches, interviews, sidelights, personals were all over page one and inside, while on some days readers could hardly find out who it was Landon was running against. McCormick justified his course on the grounds that Roosevelt had the radio and the freedom to make news, an argument other publishers also used. Whatever the merits of this argument, it did not seem to cover the more or less subtle bias in actual reportage, whereby Landon's crowds were "enthusiastic," while Roosevelt's were merely "partisan." (John Boettiger was no longer covering Roosevelt for the *Tribune.* He had fallen in love with FDR's daughter Anna, and by the same token out of love with the *Tribune*'s editorial policy. He married her, and somehow ended up editing the *Seattle Post-Intelligencer* for Hearst.)

The most controversial news story of the campaign, and perhaps the most revealing, was a *Tribune* dispatch from its Moscow-at-one-remove correspondent, Donald Day in Riga, Latvia. On January 1 Day had startled *Tribune* readers by departing from his normal rumors of Soviet atrocities and imminent counterrevolution with a highly optimistic report on the new Stalin constitution. The story, which the *Tribune* played prominently on page one, cited the abolition of the bread ration, the restoration of family life, and the promise of elections as a harbinger of a liberal transformation of the Soviet regime. Day was echoed by the editorial page, which described the new constitution as "the most momentous event in Europe . . . since the world war," even though the "fruits of liberty may be slow in ripening." They were far too slow for McCormick's impatience, and Stalin was soon again classed with Hitler as an incorrigible dictator.

Yet the Donald Day story of August 8, headed "Moscow Orders Reds in U.S. to Back Roosevelt," was played inside rather than on page one, as one of a routine batch of foreign items, such as starving Eskimos, a Nazi governor ousted, the Spanish Loyalists shelling Seville. As Day reported it,

> Because the Republican party in the United States must be defeated at the November elections at all costs, according to communist international headquarters at Moscow, instructions have been sent to the American communist party to support the candidacy of President Roosevelt.

Day quoted *Kommunistisceski International,* No. 13, as pronouncing the "common aim" of America's radical groups as the defeat of Landon, "who represents forces which oppose the development of class war and revolution in America." Considering that the Communist preference for Roosevelt over Landon could be read every day in the *Daily Worker* (not to mention the *Tribune* and the rest of the press), the story did not seem to constitute much of a scoop. Yet its authentic-sounding source gave it an amazing impact, and it was seized on and repeated all over the place by Republicans and conservatives.

The LaFollettes' *Progressive* in Wisconsin and Samuel Thomason's *Times* in Chicago were moved to denounce the Day dispatch as a fake, and each offered five thousand dollars if the *Trib* could prove it true. The *Trib* did not deign to acknowledge the challenges, although Day's record made it at least seem possible that the thing was a phony. Day's other patron, Lord Rothermere, had written a page of journalistic infamy in 1924 by doctoring up or forging the "Zinoviev letter" to torpedo Ramsay MacDonald's Labour government. Rothermere had cleverly waited till the eve of election to spring his revelation, something Colonel McCormick was too forthright to do. But Hearst had the gall to try the Rothermere tactic; his own papers picked up Day's dispatch for a rerun just before election. A traitor in the Hearst organization tipped off Steve Early, Roosevelt's press secretary, and Early successfully defused it in a press conference.

Among the Colonel's contributions to the Landon cause was the organization of the Volunteers, a Ladies Auxiliary corps that put on rallies, made speeches, waved flags, and passed out sunflower buttons. Their founder told the Volunteers that they were saving the country, provoking an anonymous *Tribune* employee into a limerick whose rhymes mimicked the Colonel's accent:

> There was a young man from Topeka
> Whose campaign grew weakah and weakah,
> Till the Volunteers came
> And made every old dame
> A bell-ringah, singah, or speakah.

When Roosevelt came to Chicago the throngs on the parade route (police said 500,000) could hardly be overlooked, though the *Trib* did its best to pretend they had been dragooned there by union bosses. At some points the crowds got ugly around the press cars, demanding to know who the *Tribune* and Hearst men were. A *Trib* photographer's hoax backfired when his photo of a streetsweeper clearing away allegedly discarded FDR buttons was happily exposed by the *Times,* which quoted the sweeper as saying the photographer had strewn the buttons and paid him twenty-five cents to pose.

Though editorially pronouncing November 3, 1936, "the most fateful day in the history of the American people," the *Tribune* on its election-day front page bannered a noncommittal U.S. PICKING ITS PRESIDENT and merely urged everybody to vote.

Next day Thomason's *Times* reminded Chicago of the *Tribune*'s discarded "Only X Days" slogan by running a head, "Only 52 Days to Christmas."

The election's outcome surprised many besides McCormick who might have known better. The *Literary Digest* straw vote, which had been right on Roosevelt vs. Hoover four years earlier, had blown it badly this time (the new Gallup poll, which the *Trib* did not buy, correctly forecast the outcome). Arthur Sears Henning had expressed misgivings, and McCormick's old friend Mayor Kelly (the only Democrat present at the dismal victory dinner the Colonel gave election night) had tried to tell him Cook County was going for Roosevelt by 500,000 (it went by 600,000). Nobody except Roosevelt's canny campaign manager, Jim Farley, anticipated the size of the rout.

More striking to 1936 observers than the erroneous forecasts with which the press was filled was the embarrassing contrast between what the press told its readers to do and what they did. A study the *New Republic* made of fifteen cities showed that, omitting the few neutral dailies, 71 percent of the total circulation belonged to Landon papers but delivered only 31 percent of the votes. A Chicago neighborhood weekly, the *West Side Times,* had the bright idea of querying people: "Knowing nothing about him, would you vote for a candidate endorsed by the paper you read regularly?" With the election fresh in their minds, the breakdown among readers of the five dailies was:

Hearst (two papers for Landon)	75% no
Tribune (for Landon)	72% no
Daily News (for Landon)	66% yes
Times (for Roosevelt)	83% yes

It may be inferred that most of the afternoon *Daily News* readers were Republicans and voted that way, and most of the Hearst readers and most of the *Times* readers were Democrats and voted that way. The most striking figure (assuming validity) is the one for the *Tribune,* which had evidently been preaching its Republican sermon to a backsliding audience. Peter Lisagor, longtime Washington bureau chief of the *Chicago Daily News,* once commented that in those days many Chicagoans read the *Tribune* "just to see what that so-and-so paper says today." Certainly among its 813,000 readers there seemed to be a startling number who either did not agree with its Republican slant or thought its partisanship excessive.

The outcome of the election did not alter Colonel McCormick's views. The *Tribune*'s editorial policy did not waver, and if anything grew more conservative and more pessimistic in the year following the election. Once more it was in the press mainstream. Roosevelt's ill-considered attempt to enlarge the Supreme Court and pack it with liberals stirred a storm of hysteria in which even the *Tribune*'s voice was hardly noticeable. Similarly, when the economic results came in on Roosevelt's timid decision to balance the 1936 budget, the 1937 recession was blamed by the press including the *Tribune* (and by the public according to Gallup) on government spending rather than its true cause, the very opposite.

The *Trib* was equally at one with press and public on its negative attitude toward the wave of strikes of 1937–1938, as John L. Lewis's CIO, armed with the Wagner Act, moved into the basic industries. Riga correspondent Donald Day reported that U.S. Communist head William Z. Foster had told Moscow (via a published magazine article) that the CIO was helping prepare the way for an American "Popular Front," with "the sympathy and support of President Roosevelt's administration." Interestingly, though, the tragic riot on Memorial Day at the Republic Steel plant in South Chicago, in which ten strikers were killed and many strikers and police injured, was covered without a single reference to a Red. The inevitable editorial defending the police related the strike, riot, and CIO generally not to the Communist but to the Democratic party:

> The fact that the CIO leaders think they are above the law is easily explained. When John Lewis gave his half million dollar contribution to the Democratic campaign fund he expected a quid pro quo. From the national administration he has been receiving it.

Lewis himself agreed, except with the last sentence. When Roosevelt at a press conference pronounced "a plague on both your [management and labor] houses," Lewis bitterly assailed his presumed benefactor in his own rhetorical style: "It ill behooves one who has supped at labor's table . . . to curse with equal fervor and fine impartiality both labor and its adversaries."

Eventually an investigation by Senator Robert LaFollette (son of Fighting Bob) and stories by the *St. Louis Post-Dispatch*'s Teapot Dome hero, Paul Y. Anderson, brought out the truth, that the police had been the aggressors, though even then the *Trib* gave little ground. Its stubbornness in sticking to the thesis that the strikers were responsible, rather than the character of its original story, made its coverage notorious to liberals and labor.

Oswald Garrison Villard, in *The Disappearing Daily* (1944), summarized liberal strictures on the *Tribune:*

> Since it is a newspaper obviously made, above all else, to sell and not to educate or to convey information, it constantly slights national, state, and municipal matters of great importance. In its local news it is as biased and inaccurate as many of our metropolitan dailies, and it has never hesitated to

reveal malice in its reports of the doings and utterances of those whom it does not like; there are plenty to accuse it justly of falsification; its news reports are not beyond question.

Villard's opinion of the paper had if anything deteriorated since 1922, but his strictures applied roughly to almost any newspaper of the 1930s–1940s (and elsewhere in his book Villard said more or less the same of many of them). If the *Tribune* stood out at all it was probably on the basis of its truculent front-page appearance, with the screamer head and three-column cartoon. It is difficult today to find textual citations to distinguish the *Tribune* from its 1930s contemporaries. Its wealth permitted it to go a little farther afield in slandering the CIO, as in a 1938 story headed "CIO Strangles San Francisco, Industries Die" (in which it erroneously placed the Oakland Chevrolet assembly plant in San Francisco, leading to a pained letter to the editor from the Oakland Chamber of Commerce). Yet even the wire services gave labor news a decisive slant. Among liberals, the growing antipress anger and frustration—"reactionary press" was a top liberal cliché, with implications of conspiracy—led to an interesting though abortive bit of action. Senator Sherman Minton of Indiana called for a congressional investigation of the nation's newspapers, singling out the *Tribune* along with the *Washington Post, Philadelphia Inquirer,* and *New York Herald Tribune.* His idea received predictably sour or silent response from every editorial page save one. Joe Patterson, who had given Roosevelt enthusiastic editorial support (even on Supreme Court reorganization) in his *New York Daily News* and had contributed $20,000 (no mean contribution in 1936) to his campaign, backed Minton and offered the *News* as target No. 1:

> There is talk about the relationship between the New Deal News and the old deal Chicago Tribune. Cynics snicker that this organization's plan is to work both sides of the street, so that in any event it will have a friend in the White House. Let's have that gone into.

Minton's proposal never got off the ground, and the press failed to mend its conservative ways for another generation. Justifiably or not, the *Chicago Tribune* came more and more to be singled out, though usually with Hearst, Roy Howard, the *New York Sun,* or *New York Herald Tribune* for company. A poll of Washington correspondents voted the *Tribune,* except for the Hearst chain, the least fair and least reliable newspaper in the country. The correspondents were thinking mainly of the 1936 election coverage, most being privately pro-Roosevelt Democrats, though from their stories their readers might not have guessed. Ickes fumed to FDR that the *Tribune* was "the rottenest newspaper in the whole United States." Ickes was a parochial Chicagoan, and many liberals would have so described their own hometown papers, but the *Tribune*'s reputation as reactionary was spreading beyond its own "Chicagoland" area.

The *Tribune* still commanded respect as a newspaper, notably among its own staff, many of whom doubtless voted for Roosevelt, and some of whom doubtless enjoyed their employer's discomfiture. There was nothing rotten about the *Tribune* as a paper to work for. It paid the highest salaries in Chicago or New York and gave the best fringes (bonuses, loan funds, sick leave, death benefits, and, a nice paternal touch, silverware wedding gifts). Its Washington staff was the best paid in that city. Top people got contracts for top figures, and sometimes with exceptional throw-ins. Besides being paternalistic by nature, the Colonel was a believer in the philosophical cornerstone of free enterprise, that merit should be rewarded. When critic Claudia Cassidy once thanked him for a trip to Europe, he answered simply, "Why thank me? You more than paid your way." He also saw to it that she got the same cost-of-living raises the rest of the staff got, though her contract didn't require it.

In the 1930s the Colonel's predilection for paternalism was fortified by the very dragons he was combatting, the New Deal and organized labor. When Social Security came in (against the *Tribune*'s opposition) firms that had pension plans canceled them as no longer needed. Patterson, who welcomed Social Security editorially, canceled the plan at the *News*. But McCormick kept the *Tribune*'s plan, which he himself had designed and installed, partly out of suspicion that the New Deal would fritter away the Social Security fund and partly out of the conviction that no government could take care of *Tribune* employees as well as he could. When the Newspaper Guild began organizing the Hearst papers, McCormick learned what their salary demands were for experienced newspeople, and set the *Trib* minimum, for inexperienced people, at that level.

Consequently the *Trib*'s Guild unit never got off the ground, but it left a story. Crusading reporter Virginia Gardner was a union enthusiast and joined the pickets in front of the Hearst Building. Colonel McCormick, outraged at such conduct by a *Tribune* employee, ordered her fired. The Guild complained to the new National Labor Relations Board, which ordered Gardner reinstated, with back pay. The baffled Colonel obeyed the law but, still seething, had Gardner relegated to city news and, cruelest cut, forbade her any more by-lines. For months the former star, who had covered such major stories as the alienation-of-affection suit of Charles MacArthur's first wife against Helen Hayes, did routine assignments and never saw her name in print. But her beat included the archdiocese, at the time occupied by the great liberal prelate Cardinal Mundelein. Out of sympathy, the cardinal gave the reporter a terrific scoop—the beatification of Chicago's famed Mother Cabrini. The story was a page-one lead, and the rule was that a page-one lead carried a by-line.

On the desk, after worried debate, it was decided that a query would have to be sent Upstairs. In due course, down from the Colonel's aerie came the reply: Give Virginia Gardner a by-line.

The story explained that for Mother Cabrini to become a full-fledged saint, she had to be credited with "two authentic miracles."

"Mother Cabrini," commented somebody, "is halfway home."

CHAPTER FOURTEEN

Quarantine the Aggressors?

COLONEL McCORMICK emerged as a leading spokesman for conservative opposition to labor and the New Deal at the same moment that the issue of fascist aggression came to the fore. The coincidence of McCormick's domestic conservatism and his militant neutralism in foreign affairs led many to assume an ideological connection between the two attitudes, but there was none. Neutralism, or isolationism, had its historic roots in anti-imperialism and pacifism and had never been associated with domestic conservatism. The fact that the two attitudes were still unconnected in 1937 was shown by the press reaction to a remarkable speech Roosevelt made in Chicago on October 5 of that year. Dedicating the new Outer Drive Bridge, with Lake Michigan as a backdrop, Roosevelt took press and public completely by surprise with a major foreign-policy pronouncement. He first depicted at length, though in carefully anonymous terms, what he called the "international reign of terror," and then asserted that if the "epidemic" should spread, America itself could not escape, that it would be futile to imagine that "the Western hemisphere will not be attacked, that it could continue tranquilly and peacefully to carry on the ethics and arts of civilization."

> The peace-loving nations must make a concerted effort in opposition to those violations of treaties and those ignorings of human instincts which today are creating a state of international anarchy and instability from which there is no escape through mere isolation and neutrality.

Finally, he came up with a memorable metaphor:

> When an epidemic of physical disease starts to spread, the community approves and joins in a quarantine of the patients in order to protect the health of the community against the spread of the disease. . . .

The idea of talking about fascist aggression as a contagious disease belonged to Harold Ickes, who for a Secretary of the Interior took an extraordinarily active interest in foreign affairs.

In the light of peaking American disillusionment with World War I, Versailles, and the war debts, Roosevelt's quarantine speech was, to say the least, a bold departure. For the first time since Woodrow Wilson's attempt to sell the League of Nations, it introduced the idea that America might play a collaborative international role.

The parallel with Wilson could hardly escape Colonel McCormick. The *Tribune*'s editorial on the speech was titled "He, Too, Would Keep Us Out of War," and began:

> The crowd which gathered at the dedication of the new bridge yesterday heard Mr. Roosevelt deliver what well may prove to be the most important speech he ever will make.
>
> Mr. Roosevelt announced a new foreign policy for the United States. It would be more accurate to say that he readopted the foreign policy of Woodrow Wilson, the policy which brought the United States first into armed conflict with Mexico and then into the world war, the policy which was overwhelmingly rejected by the American people after the war.

Pointing out that there was no mistaking which countries Roosevelt was talking about despite his reticence about naming them, the editorial reminded readers that Wilson's diplomacy, similarly aimed at defending international legality, had drawn support because most Americans had assumed that "our contribution would consist of little more than our navy and our money. They learned differently."

This was a key observation, which McCormick was virtually alone in expressing. The *Chicago Daily News, Chicago Times, New York Times, New York Herald Tribune,* and many other papers hailed the speech as an imaginative and stirring appeal. The *Chicago Daily News* noted that readers of its foreign dispatches would recognize as accurate Roosevelt's depiction of the world, as indeed they would—the *Daily News*'s European correspondents, Paul Scott Mowrer, Edgar Ansel Mowrer, John Gunther, Leland Stowe, and others were renowned for their outspoken antifascism. A few papers expressed timid reservations. "It is hoped that there was no intimation . . . that the United States should take up arms," said the *Rochester Democrat & Chronicle.* Fewer yet joined the *Chicago Tribune* in clearly negative response, except for the Hearst chain, whose reaction provoked Roosevelt to tell Ickes that he meant to remind Hearst one day that he had caused the war with Spain in 1898, not to mention McKinley's assassination. Some thought the posture of Hearst and McCormick owed something to prejudice against Roosevelt, but it continued an editorial policy covering more than two decades. Most of the papers applauding the speech were hard-line anti-New Deal, and one prominent isolationist paper, the *St. Louis Post-Dispatch,* had good liberal credentials.

Even the *Chicago Tribune,* for all its concern with the danger of another 1917, had given extensive and often anti-fascist-slanted coverage to Hitler's repressions (Sigrid Schultz was seconded by Edmond Taylor), to Mussolini's invasion of Ethiopia (the *Tribune*'s Will Barber got a posthumous Pulitzer), and to the Spanish civil war (David Darrah predicted Franco's postwar totalitarianism). Nor did Colonel McCormick's neutralism extend to support of the Neutrality Act, a piece of misguided legislation passed as a result of the prolonged Senate investigation of how the country got into war in 1917. The committee headed by Senator Gerald P. Nye had concluded, with an assurance not shared by contemporary historians, that the large munitions sales to the Allies had been the main cause (or culprit), and Congress passed a law banning such trade with belligerents. When Roosevelt invoked the Neutrality Act in the Spanish civil war, the *Tribune* objected because application hurt the Loyalists (Franco was getting plenty of help from Hitler and Mussolini).

To sustain the *Tribune*'s neutrality in the face of Hitler and the fascist aggressions, McCormick fell back on reiteration of the accusation against the Allies that they were unfairly hogging the world's colonial goods. A December 1936 editorial gave typical expression to the view:

> The whole peace was an act of folly and stripping Germany of its colonies was a part of it. It is conceded that the victors had . . . not expected mercy if defeated. . . . In such a state of mind they sought their future security as well as their revenge by binding the German people to perpetually humiliating conditions. In doing so they destroyed the German republic and produced Hitler, now their chief menace.

The indictment of the Allies for taking over Germany's colonies by no means originated with the *Tribune,* and had been harped on by liberals as well as conservatives. It had little grounding in reality. Imperial Germany had never profited from its colonies, few Germans had any connection with them, and even Hitler made only perfunctory noises about them. (Furthermore, few Americans agreed with the Colonel; 76 percent told Gallup, don't give them back.)

In the Pacific, to which the *Tribune* gave considerable attention in both news and editorial columns, Colonel McCormick was able to find a simpler and more persuasive theme. The very nakedness of Japan's policy of aggression helped to frame straightforward questions: Should the United States fight a war to stop Japan from partitioning China? To prevent her from attacking Malaya and Singapore? From seizing the Philippines? Colonel

McCormick faced all these possibilities and returned a negative answer. American army and navy units in the western Pacific should be brought home. Since the Filipinos had voted in 1936 to sever their connection with the United States, it was folly to station an American military force in the islands and risk being "drawn into a great war across the Pacific by a people who have chosen to part from us." (The public, according to Gallup, disagreed, 76 percent opposing immediate independence for the Philippines.) He objected in advance to a proposal Roosevelt did not press till 1939, the fortification of western-Pacific outpost Guam, advocating instead a defense line across the central Pacific anchored on Alaska, Pearl Harbor, and American Samoa.

The *Tribune*'s views on the Pacific stirred no controversy. Few Americans knew enough about the Pacific to be sure of exactly where the Philippines were, let alone Guam, although in 1939, Socialist party chief Norman Thomas got some mileage on the college lecture circuit with the line "Are you ready to die for dear old Guam?" The whole idea of a war with Japan, which was perceived largely as a supplier of knicknacks for Woolworth's, lacked credibility. Even the sinking of the U.S. China-station gunboat *Panay* by Japanese planes in December 1937 brought no outcry from the public, and instead paved the way for U.S. withdrawal from China, in accordance with Colonel McCormick's precepts. But in Washington Harold Ickes wrote in his diary: "[Secretary of the Navy] Swanson's point of view cannot be lightly dismissed. Certainly war with Japan is inevitable sooner or later, and if we have to fight her, isn't this the best possible time?"

To the public, another war in Europe, and the danger of another American involvement, seemed far more believable. According to a Gallup poll, 70 percent believed that entry in World War I had been a mistake. The mail response to Roosevelt's speech expressed strong fear of another such mistake, but it was also strong on opposition to Nazi Germany. The American public had already adopted the policy of having it both ways—stop Hitler, but stay out of war—that was to carry it triumphantly to Pearl Harbor.

On one thing the whole press, pro and anti, agreed: The quarantine speech was mystifying. Its main point, that fascist aggression threatened the United States, was simply not taken seriously by anyone. Consequently, it was logical to suspect, despite Roosevelt's denials, that there was something or other behind the speech.

As a matter of fact there was, but the press never found it out. Roosevelt and Undersecretary of State Sumner Welles (an old Groton-Harvard chum) had cooked up a scheme for a global diplomatic conference, for which the speech was designed as a trial balloon.

The balloon was shot down by British Prime Minister Neville Chamberlain, who disdained American help in handling Hitler. On the other hand, the British were already showing an eagerness to get U.S. Navy collaboration in the Far East, and a suspicion on Colonel McCormick's part that there might be a secret alliance behind the visit of a navy squadron to Singapore was not as crazy as some people thought.

In its ignorance of the Roosevelt-Welles global summit scheme the press tended to look for extraneous reasons for the quarantine speech. The *Tribune* credited a desire to distract first from the revelation that new Supreme Court Justice Hugo L. Black had once belonged to the Ku Klux Klan, and second from the 1937 recession.

Had the *Tribune* gotten wind of the summit project there surely would have been a freshet of apprehension and sarcasm. The scheme bore all the earmarks not only of New Deal do-goodism but of "Stimsonism"—irritating potential enemies without accomplishing anything.

The fact that Hitler's chief foreign enemy was the Soviet Union reassured Colonel McCormick. The American public, no matter how unstable its passions, was unlikely to press for involvement in a war of Nazis versus Communists. It was the old World War I allies, England and France, who were most likely to stir dangerous sentiments, but not both equally. Despite Lafayette, American folklore was anti-French. Even the war debts, as New Deal economist Rex Tugwell noted, were perceived as mainly French. On the other hand, to most Americans, England remained the romantic ideal among nations, with a lingering sense of "mother country." Consequently, to an American neutrality advocate, a part of the task seemed to be to minimize the difference between Britain and Germany. In adopting this tactic in 1937 Colonel McCormick anticipated the *Daily Worker* and other Leftist publications by two years.

Germany had Hitler and the Nazis, Britain had only a Tory government and the Empire, but in the summer of 1937, before the quarantine speech, McCormick had himself done a series from England explaining the abdication of Edward VIII as a manifestation not of Anglican stuffiness but of British fascism. In support of his contention he could muster only a lame piece of evidence: the self-imposed censorship of the British press during the abdication crisis.

The thesis that Britain was nearly as bad as Germany, or was about to become as bad, never carried conviction, and McCormick fell back on blaming the greedy Allies for the death of the Weimar Republic—"They killed liberalism, culture, intelligence, good will, and liberty. In the place of a friendly society they raised up dictatorship, brutality, ignorance, serfdom, and military power." The *Trib* sympathized with Hitler's demand for "a square deal for Germans, separated from the fatherland through the hoggishness of other European powers." The reference could have been to Germans in Danzig and Poland, but at the moment (February 1938) Hitler was pressing the Czechs over the Germans in Sudetenland, which had never been part of Germany. The *Tribune* had always had doubts about the viability of such "jigsaw nations" as Czechoslovakia and Yugoslavia, no doubt partly because they were products of Versailles and associated with Wilson.

Yet as the Munich crisis deepened, the paper sounded other, and contradictory notes. A McCutcheon cartoon credited Chamberlain with "thankless courage" that might yet save the world from war, while Orr depicted Britain as cynically sacrificing others to Hitler.

The *Tribune* was unaware of a French request (September 8) for American arbitration, but would certainly have seconded Roosevelt's hasty retreat from any such role.

On September 29 the *Tribune* headline read NAZIS TAKE OVER TOMORROW and the editorial, while congratulating the people of Europe on their escape from war, expressed serious misgivings:

> Herr Hitler's goal, it may be assumed, was the complete destruction of Czechoslovakia's capacity to resist. The dispatches from Munich suggest that he has fallen little, if at all, short of achieving it. Indeed, it becomes difficult to understand what Chamberlain and Daladier were contending for if they were willing to concede so much. There is little now to prevent Hitler from dominating and organizing middle and eastern Europe.
>
> Whether Herr Hitler will be or can be content . . . remains to be seen. If the answer is no, then the settlement of Munich is little more than a truce. . . .

The characterization of Colonel McCormick as "one of the finest minds of the fourteenth century" dates from this period. Ex-*Trib* correspondent and fiery antifascist Jay Cooke Allen said it first. The sense of the epithet is interesting, since it implies that McCormick was an old fogy (he was twice Allen's age) who hadn't caught up with the modern world, rather than a sympathizer with Hitler and Franco, which Allen knew he was not. It was a mild enough bit of name-calling, but open to question, since the antifascist premise of Allen and others who urged action was that Hitler could be stopped short of war. McCormick did not agree, and his conviction that Munich was no bluff was vindicated by postwar revelations.

A significant angle of the Munich crisis, overlooked by many, did not escape McCormick: the liquidation of the French-Soviet-Czech alliance. He suspected that the French and British might have been influenced by the weakening of the Red Army as a result of Stalin's purges of the high command. A few months later (May 9, 1939) an editorial on Hitler's intentions, "Waiting the Event in Europe," ended on an exceptionally shrewd observation:

It may be that Russia will offer the solution to Hitler's problem. If he could even neutralize Russia the cost of direct action in taking Danzig might be greatly reduced. An agreement with Stalin might easily persuade Hitler that he was master of Europe. . . . Trustworthy sources of information say that Stalin's policy is for an agreement with Hitler. An honest agreement of ideas would seem absurd, but there is no honesty of idea in Stalin. Hitler is a creature of simpler emotions. He has zealously persuaded himself that he hates communism, although in dictatorship Stalin is his true cousin.

Thus the *Tribune* could claim credit for foreseeing the Nazi-Soviet pact that triggered the war. Perhaps the most significant fact about all the *Tribune* coverage and editorializing of the prewar period is the immense volume of it as compared with pre-1914. Neutralist or isolationist though Colonel McCormick was, he was anything but head-in-the-sand. Rather, he contributed considerably to the preparation of the American public for a role in World War II simply by giving Hitler, Mussolini, and the Japanese so much space. No *Tribune* reader could fail to be concerned about fascist aggression.

That was broadly true of the whole metropolitan press. The influential mass of literate Americans, whatever they thought of the coming of World War II, were this time not taken by surprise.

CHAPTER FIFTEEN

"This Is Not Our War"

ON October 22, 1939, McCutcheon drew a tight-lipped Uncle Sam sitting tensely in the parlor with his worried wife under a sampler reading "Never Again," while a shelf of bottles labeled "Emotionalism, Old 1917 Brand," "War Hysteria," and "Hate Hooch" beckoned. The scene was entitled "She Dreads a Return of His Old Weakness." As McCutcheon perceived, the country was in the grip of a strange new mood. The end of the suspense, the actual outbreak of war, had dissolved at a stroke the pacifist cynicism of two decades in a flood of pro-Allied, anti-Hitler sentiment. No Belgian atrocities were needed; Hitler's record was bad enough already. Meantime the passage of twenty-five years had assimilated the Germans and Scandinavians into the American majority, had softened Irish anglophobia, and via Hitler had turned the mildly pro-German or neutralist Jews around. True, nobody wanted to fight any more than last time, but from the very beginning, there was a Greek tragedy fatalism about the possibility of America's being drawn in.

One result was to isolate the isolationists. Far more than in World War I, the *Tribune*'s neutral posture stuck out. Although Colonel McCormick was widely known for his intransigence toward the New Deal, up to September 1939 only a few Communists and other political sophisticates identified him as isolationist (the word, in fact, was little used). Few thought him anti-British. Now all that changed. Britain's declaration of war altered nothing in logic, but everything in psychology. Neutralism was suddenly embarrassing, shading into suspicious.

By chance the Colonel was at this moment becoming isolated in other ways. Amy Irwin McCormick died on August 14, 1939, after a long illness, ending twenty-four years of happy, close companionship. His tribute to her was touching—a military funeral in honor of her family background and her war work of 1917–1918. A squad from Fort Sheridan fired three volleys over the grave, dug at Cantigny in ground specially consecrated, and a group from WGN sang Amy's favorite hymns.

The Colonel had no children, his mother and brother were gone, and the creature closest to him was probably his German shepherd. It was during

150

this lonely period that his natural reserve began to be referred to as "dourness."

He was also left alone in a different sense. The summer of 1939 saw the passing, among so many symbols of a vanished age, of the roistering old *Front Page*-famed *Herald-Examiner,* leaving the *Tribune* in solitary splendor on Chicago's morning newsstands. Though Hearst was as anti-New Deal and isolationist as McCormick (and still present in Chicago with his evening *American*), the *Tribune*'s morning monopoly lent an emphasis to its editorial bias that could not fail to provoke resentment.

The paper's first statement on the war voiced an uncompromising neutrality consistent with its past attitude:

> This is not our war. We did not create the Danzig situation. We did not sign the treaty of Versailles. The peace America made with Germany did not contain another war. The United States did not take spoils. It did not divide up colonies. It had nothing to do with the remaking of Europe which sowed war on nearly every frontier of the new map.
>
> . . . France and Great Britain are not weak nations. They are great empires. Their pooled resources are enormous. . . .
>
> We may think their side is the better side. But it is their war. They are competent to fight it. Great pressure will be brought to bear on the United States. Americans will be told that this is their fight. That is not true. The frontiers of American democracy are not in Europe, Asia or Africa.

Few readers, or other editors, neutralist or pro-Allied, would have contradicted the Colonel's assertions of fact, but some of them were wrong all the same. Everybody had conveniently forgotten that Danzig and the Polish Corridor, so far from being inventions of Versailles, were No. 13 of Wilson's Fourteen Points, the basis of the Armistice in 1918.

More important, Britain and France were not, in the light of World War I, "competent to fight" Hitler's Germany. They had not been competent to fight the kaiser's Germany without Russia in 1914 and without America in 1918, and Hitler's Germany was substantially larger and stronger than the kaiser's. That absolutely nobody, neutralist or pro-Allied, noticed this, or pointed it out, seems to reflect psychological need or ideological rationalization. Colonel McCormick, who had heard all about the Russian contribution to the battle of the Marne from his Russian hosts in 1915, and knew the American role in 1918 firsthand, wanted to believe the Allies "competent to fight" so that they would not need America.

The pro-Allied press wanted to believe it for the opposite reason, in order to soothe public apprehensions over repeal of the Neutrality Act. Colonel McCormick had never liked the Neutrality Act, which he felt was based on a misconception about what had gotten America into the last war, and consequently the *Tribune*'s opposition to its revision was perfunctory, but he took insufficient early note of a phenomenon reported by his Washington bureau. The lobbying for revision was spearheaded by "The Committee to Keep America Out of War by Aiding the Allies," shortened in the press to the "White Committee" after its chairman. William Allen White, editor and publisher of the much-quoted *Emporia* (Kansas) *Gazette,* was America's favorite country newspaperman. The White Committee had from the start genuine grass-roots support despite the fact that White's chairmanship masked a New York elitist origin. The thrust of its argument to Congress was essentially Roosevelt's quarantine doctrine, that it was in America's self-interest to help nations resisting fascist aggressors.

The White Committee was formed in the immediate wake of the startlingly swift German victory in Poland, which sobered both press and public. General Charles Wesson, chief of army ordnance, made a speech in Chicago in which, though specifically disclaiming any thought of getting into a European war, he called for a munitions reserve sufficient for an army of a million. The *Tribune* reacted with alarm. Such an army, it thought, "goes far beyond the general's stated defense aims [national defense and the Monroe Doctrine], and could be used in but one way:

> That would be as a new A.E.F. in Europe.
> This nation needs a field army of perhaps 100,000 men, equipped with the most modern arms and trained as a unit in their use to make its land defense secure.

The beauty of a small army was that it did not require universal military training, something Colonel McCormick had hailed in 1919 but which he now perceived as a step not only toward war but toward dictatorship.

Did McCormick, who despite his critics had as good a grasp of military affairs as anybody in the press, really believe that a "mobile field army" of no more than 100,000 would suffice to guarantee American security against the potential of Hitler Germany? Once again, wish fathered thought. A national plunge into war under Roosevelt's leadership seemed to him the immediate danger, and he could not find a genuine solution to the problem of creating a purely defensive U.S. armed force.

In November the Soviet attack on Finland again caught the press by surprise and, accompanied by a fury of anti-Soviet hysteria, brought the fantasy of a lineup of democracies versus Nazi and Communist dictatorships that cut across the neutralist-pro-Allied schism. The *Tribune* went a step farther. It suggested "a quick peace" in Western Europe and a "change of front from one which divides civilization against itself to one which again faces the Asiatic barbarism"—in other words, Britain and France should join Hitler and the Finns against the Soviets. Lunatic though the proposal seems in retrospect, it was not only widely accepted, but also halfway adopted. With full U.S. moral backing, Britain and France prepared an expeditionary force for Finland that was on the point of embarking in March of 1940 when the Russians broke through the Finnish Mannerheim Line and ended the war. Hitler delayed another year before following Colonel McCormick's recommendation and allying himself with the Finns.

Yet in advocating a united European front against the Soviet Union McCormick maintained a prudent consistency, warning that the United States must not "let our natural and genuine sympathy for the Finns involve us in Europe again."

The next month (April 1940) the press was again taken by surprise by the invasion of Denmark and Norway. Colonel McCormick now for the first time provoked outrage by blaming Britain for the involvement of the little Scandinavian countries. Nobody agreed with him, but he was right. Admiral Erich Raeder, who persuaded Hitler to launch Operation *Weser Exercise,* much preferred Scandinavian neutrality, and opted for action only when British mine-laying and other activity in Norwegian waters warned of an imminent invasion. The Allied operation, using the troops originally ticketed for Finland, was scheduled for April 5, the day before the German jump-off, but was delayed at the last moment.

The remarkable German success, accomplished with a handful of troops and in the face of an overwhelming British naval advantage (but with the help of Norway's Quisling), further sobered America and prepared it a little for the catastrophe of May–June, when the basic weakness of the Allies, instead of being balanced by some technical or tactical advantage, proved instead to be aggravated by technical and tactical advantages on the side of the Germans.

The British switch of prime ministers from Chamberlain to Churchill (May 10) was applauded by the *Tribune,* McCormick having known Churchill since 1915 and admiring his tough-mindedness and incisive speech. The paper also found a generous word to say of Chamberlain, for "trying to preserve the peace of Europe against a man determined to have world war"—a rather anti-isolationist turn of phrase. But it blamed the fall of France on the prewar Leftist (Popular Front) government—too much social welfare, not enough military preparation—and coldly refused to express any emotion over the fall of Paris or concern over the threat to Britain.

McCormick even professed to see a bright side to the disaster. Going on the air in his avuncular style, he gave WGN listeners what he conceived to be good news: Since there was no longer a battle front in Europe, there was no longer any danger of the United States being dragged in.

That turned out to be an overoptimistic conclusion. As early as May 16 his old friend, First Division buddy, and frequent Cantigny visitor George Marshall had asked Congress for a mass army, to be raised by conscription, though Marshall prudently avoided the word. A clubby group of wealthy New Yorkers, headed by another publishing colonel, Julius Ochs Adler of the *New York Times,* picked up the ball. Meeting at the Harvard Club for the nostalgic twenty-fifth reunion of their officers' training class at Plattsburg, they agreed that the country needed preparedness even more than in Teddy Roosevelt's day, and got New York Republican congressman James Wadsworth to introduce a conscription bill.

Amid the alarm and confusion the Republicans held their national convention in Philadelphia. Colonel McCormick made a speech decrying "the hysterical appeal for immediate conscription" and backed New York district attorney Tom Dewey for nomination. He was overruled on both pleas. Congress passed conscription and the convention nominated Wendell Willkie. Though chagrined, McCormick loyally closed ranks and gave strong *Tribune* support to Willkie in the campaign, since conscription made the election of a Republican candidate "imperative if this country is to be kept out of war." Yet he never trusted Willkie, a tousle-haired utilities magnate whose New York backers stressed his Indiana boyhood (Ickes labeled him "a simple, barefoot Wall Street lawyer"), and events justified his suspicions.

Roosevelt's nomination for a third term was accomplished in Chicago, partly with the assistance of a bit of Chicagoese manipulation that went down in history as "the Voice from the Sewer"—Colonel McCormick's old Sanitary District aide, Ed Kelly, now mayor, stationed his leather-lunged superintendent of sewers in the basement of the hall to launch a "We Want Roosevelt!" chant over the PA system. The *Tribune* gibed at the "draft" with front-page cartoons—"Draft Roosevelt and He'll Draft You," and a kneeling FDR entreating a reluctant FDR, "Pretty please." Editorially it accused Roosevelt of "working up a series of war scares" to justify breaking the two-term precedent.

Roosevelt did not make his third-term candidacy any more palatable to Colonel McCormick by adding two Republicans to his Cabinet. One of the two was Henry L. Stimson, Hoover's activist Secretary of State, who became Roosevelt's Secretary of War, and the other was Frank Knox, Chicago's afternoon colonel, who became Secretary of the Navy when Alf Landon declined (by conditioning acceptance on Roosevelt's not running for the third term). Since Stimson and Knox saw eye to eye with Colonel McCormick on the worth of the New Deal, it was evident that they were in their new posts because they stood with Roosevelt on the war. Stimson, like Willkie, was close to the Century Group, a new superhawk wing that the White Committee had sprouted. Named after the wealthy, Waspy Century Club in midtown Manhattan where they met to talk up the war over cocktails and lunch, the Century Group included *Time-Life* publisher Henry Luce, Morgan partner Thomas W. Lamont, conservative Democrats Lewis Douglas and Dean Acheson, and playwright Robert Sherwood. Sherwood startled many people including William Allen White by placing a full-page ad in New York and Chicago papers calling for immediate entry into the war. (The *Tribune* accepted the ad and ran an editorial opposing the thought.) The Century Groupers, who had good connections inside the government, were aware of a plea Churchill had made to Roosevelt for naval aid to keep the North Atlantic supply route open against the U-boats. They suggested to Roosevelt an extraordinarily ingenious way of giving Churchill the help he wanted—swap him warships for bases in Newfoundland and the West Indies.

Where did the Century Group get its bright idea? From Colonel McCormick and the *Chicago Tribune.* For years McCormick had advocated the acquisition of offshore bases from Britain, proposing to take them in payment for the World War I debt. He had also suggested naval swaps, most recently recommending in May 1940 the exchange of forty U.S. destroyers for four British battleships. (McCormick apparently got wind of the Century Group communication to Roosevelt, because he told his Washington bureau he had heard that FDR was planning a destroyers-for-bases deal. When the bureau checked the Navy Department they drew a blank.)

When the deal (fifty destroyers plus other items for the bases) was finally announced, the *Tribune*'s news and editorial sections got their signals a bit crossed, page one playing up opposition ("Congress Storm Brews Over U.S.-British Ship Deal") while the lead editorial proclaimed its satisfaction under the title "We Get the Bases":

> The Tribune rejoices to make this announcement which fulfills a policy advocated by this newspaper since 1922. In spite of much discouragement, The Tribune persisted, month by month and year by year, in calling for these additions to the national defense. It may be found, as we think it will be, that this is the greatest contribution of this newspaper to the country's history since the nomination of Lincoln.
>
> The agreement is not in terms The Tribune would have preferred. Nevertheless, any arrangement which gives the United States naval and air bases in regions which must be brought within the American defense zone is to be accepted as a triumph.

Colonel McCormick's pleasure in both the deal itself and in taking credit for it apparently blinded him to its potential effect on America's neutrality, which it compromised more dangerously than anyone knew. Hitler was moved to send a general to Tokyo to conclude the alliance the Japanese had been angling for, and whose terms specified that

> in the event of either contracting party entering upon a state of war with the United States, the other contracting party will assist . . . by all possible means.

That virtually guaranteed that if the United States got into the war, it would get in in both oceans at once.

Japan, which McCormick had always advocated treating gently, if not actually appeasing, was irritated by another Roosevelt diplomatic move the *Tribune* applauded and for which it took a share of the credit. A U.S.-Canadian alliance was embodied in the Ogdensburg agreement of August 18, very much in accord with a *Tribune* recommendation of two months earlier (June 19), for a defensive alliance between the two countries. "It would be presumptuous," the *Tribune* thought, "for the United States to offer to protect Canada. What we should do is say to our neighbor: 'Here, we have a common problem. Let us sit down and plan to face it together.' "

While the Century Group was supplying the link between Colonel McCormick and Roosevelt on the destroyers-for-bases deal, an antiwar organization tardily appeared on the field. The makeup of the America First Committee was a fascinating mix. Where the White Committee owed its origin to a middle-aged small-town Kansas editor, America First was founded by a pair of Yale graduate students. A pacifist discussion group under the tutelage of historian Frederick Borchard included Kingman Brewster, Jr., editor of the *Yale Daily News,* and R. Douglas Stuart, Jr., son of an executive in Chicago-based Quaker Oats. The two young men attended the Republican convention in Philadelphia and the Democratic convention in Chicago, making contacts with a number of isolationist political leaders and with General Robert E. Wood, president of Sears, Roebuck. Wood accepted the temporary chairmanship of an "Emergency Committee to Defend America First," soon shortened to "The America First Committee," echoing, though its young founders were probably unaware of it, both Charles Evans Hughes and Big Bill Thompson.

Colonel McCormick played no role in the founding of America First, but gave it press support, the more valuable since it got little elsewhere. Most of the press attacked the organization, alleging connections with far-Right fringers, which it actually did its best to discourage. Its top leadership was by no means far Right, and included Joseph P. Kennedy, Roosevelt's principal financial angel and current ambassador to Britain; Robert Maynard Hutchins, liberal president of the University of Chicago; William Benton and Chester Bowles, Madison Avenue stars now turning to other careers; upstate New York writer Samuel Hopkins Adams; the Progressive LaFollettes of Wisconsin; and liberal-pacifist Senators Bennett Champ Clark, Gerald Nye, and Burton Wheeler. Despite the adherence of several leading businessmen—Wood, Kennedy, Henry Ford, meat-packer Jay Hormel, World War I ace and airline executive Eddie Rickenbacker—America First had much less big-money support than did its pro-Ally rivals, and remained, like the White Committee and unlike the Century Group, a broad-based grass-roots outfit.

The location of America First's headquarters in Chicago and the Century Group's in New York seemed to make the two cities respectively capitals of the isolationist and interventionist movements, and the universal passion for simplifications based on geography created the myth of a Chicago-centered Midwest isolationism that had actually had a basis in reality one war earlier. In 1940–1941, America First and Colonel McCormick notwithstanding, there was only a shading of difference in the polltakers' opinion sampling of East, Midwest, and West. (The East's prowar enthusiasm of 1916, though never measured by pollsters, was pretty clearly not matched in World War II.)

There was, though, one region markedly more pro-British and prowar than the rest. In poll after poll, the South was far out in front, and its congressmen and senators supplied the decisive votes for one pro-Allied, prodefense, prowar measure after another. The South was the one region where America First found it impossible to organize chapters (in New York they had a strong one).

The basic thrust of America First was voiced with a whiskey hoarseness by its first network speaker, General Hugh S. Johnson, well known to the nation as Roosevelt's NRA chief (and consequently a one-time *Tribune* target): Aid to Britain, however desirable, threatened America's own vital defense buildup. This was a departure from Colonel McCormick's view that the country needed only a small army (whose equipping would not interfere much with supplying Britain), but the Colonel did not demur. After all, the draft act was now a reality, the mass army under formation, and the argument a good one. Like a prudent general, he silently withdrew his "small mobile field army" of 100,000 from the field.

The confrontation of the rival committees was a healthy thing for American democracy, which got little sustenance from a presidential campaign that amounted to a replay of Wilson vs. Hughes. Willkie, with incredible effrontery in the light of his Century Group connection, ranted around the country accusing Roosevelt of plotting entry in the war. Battle-wise FDR kept his powder dry, affecting to be too busy with the national defense to spare time for electioneering, thereby contributing to another presidential campaign with one-sided press coverage, in which red-hot hawk papers, such as the *New York Herald Tribune,* backed Willkie right alongside the isolationist *Chicago Tribune*. Picking his time, Roosevelt announced that because Willkie had told so many fibs he would now have to descend to the arena to refute them. He did so very skillfully, and then went on to top Willkie's hypocrisy with a double dose of his own:

> I give to you and to the people of this country the most solemn assurance: there is no secret treaty, no secret obligation, no secret understanding, in any shape or form, direct or indirect . . . to involve this nation in any war or for any other purpose.

A few nights later he promised to reiterate *"again* and *again* and *again"* that "your boys are not going to be sent into any foreign wars." A British purchasing mission was at the moment negotiating for arms and equipment for ten divisions, to be supplied gratis, provoking Colonel Knox to tell Stimson and Hull that "the English are not going to win this war without our help, I mean our military help." That was understating the case, because it was becoming clear to General Marshall and Admiral Stark that Britain was not even going to be able to hang on without United States entry into the war.

That truth was hidden from the press, pro-Ally as well as isolationist, but even without it Roosevelt's speeches sounded suspicious. The very admiration aroused by beleaguered Britain (the London blitz backgrounded the election campaign) served to focus attention on the military problem. Americans saw Britain as the underdog, but if it was the underdog, how could it win? How much help did it need? Colonel McCormick gave his own estimate in a talk over WGN. He stated his opinion that yes, Germany could be defeated by a joint Anglo-American war effort. But a massive landing on the Continent would be required, involving large-scale combat, and the cost would be appalling. He hazarded a guess of one million dead.

In the light of the apparent military logic of the situation, McCormick could not help concluding that Roosevelt's determination to aid Britain at all costs must be rooted in a desire to perpetuate his presidency. When Japan formally joined the Axis on September 27 the *Tribune* blamed Roosevelt's embargo of scrap steel and other "departures from strict neutrality" and editorialized:

> . . . For the first time in our history a foreign alliance against us has been perfected. When and if it suits their purpose to do so, they will make war on us. So far as pretexts for war are concerned they have them already.
>
> Mr. Roosevelt now has the critical international situation which, in his reckoning, his third term candidacy requires. He has it because he made it. Logically, his position today corresponds closely to that of the man who poisoned his mother and father and then pleaded for mercy on the ground that he was an orphan.

Amid the suspicions, protestations, and accusations, stranger and stranger bedfellows embraced. John L. Lewis, head of the CIO and heretofore in *Tribune* eyes a baleful Red ruffian, bear-hugged Willkie and indorsed America First. *New Republic* intellectual John T. Flynn had his anti-FDR book, *Country Squire in the White House,* serialized in the *Tribune* while the *New Republic* canceled his column. The magazine's explanation, that Flynn's views no longer fitted in, caused Oswald Garrison Villard, another liberal isolationist, to wonder what the *New Republic* would say if the *Chicago Tribune* offered such an excuse for censorship.

The *Tribune* predicted Willkie's election, but with less assurance than it had Landon's. Its coverage of the late stages of the campaign grew more evenhanded, with Willkie and FDR trading page one positions (columns one and three) on October 24 and October 31, and Willkie given only the advantage of the banner on election day:

PROSPERITY! NO WAR! WILLKIE

Willkie picked up a respectable 45 percent of the popular vote compared with Landon's 34 percent. The *Tribune* blamed the defeat on Willkie's failure to separate himself enough from Roosevelt, intimating a suspicion of his true attitude on the war that was promptly justified. Staging an instant recovery from his campaign wounds, Willkie astonished most of those who had voted for him by offering his services to his opponent, who commissioned him to make a trip to England ("to confirm the war," according to Walter Winchell), to try to win maximum Republican support for an enormous increase in the aid-to-Britain program.

The Lend-Lease Act created the original "Great Debate" and among other noteworthy participants brought Colonel McCormick to Washington to testify.

CHAPTER SIXTEEN

Colonel McCormick Takes the Stand

ON December 8, 1940, Colonel McCormick publicly and Winston Churchill privately set forth their differing views on the war. In an editorial entitled "American Aid to Britain," McCormick expressed the conviction that Britain should be saved from invasion, something "nearly all Americans" would view as a calamity. Further, he thought the British Empire should be preserved, since despite its faults "nearly all thoughtful Americans" preferred it to "the substitute world power which is within vision."

The question then arose of

> ... What should be the extent of our aid? How far shall we go? At this point reason should have the upper hand of sentiment. We should not be depended upon for an expeditionary force. . . .
>
> America would like to help Great Britain to a peace which would leave it, its dominions, and its empire intact and safe. That this peace should impose other conditions upon Europe is not within our sphere. Europe has been in many forms and in many convulsions. This is only another. We cannot assume that the United States is its guardian. Time has always been the greatest conqueror in Europe. It will take charge again.

Thus McCormick thought that American aid alone could never bring a British victory, but could suffice to keep Britain afloat and permit it to negotiate a peace. Churchill differed, strangely enough, on both counts. In a letter written to Roosevelt the same day, he maintained that Britain could ultimately win the war through bombing and blockade alone, and would therefore never need an American army. Yet at the same time he confessed a British weakness McCormick did not suspect: Despite the destroyers-for-bases deal, Britain was not capable of mastering the amazing little U-boats by herself and needed the U.S. Navy's help. Churchill proposed that Roosevelt resurrect the "freedom of the seas" doctrine that Bryan and Wilson had vainly argued with the British government in 1914. If Roosevelt could not go that far, Churchill requested the loan of a substantial number of additional U.S. warships and a sweeping extension eastward of the U.S. Navy's antisubmarine patrol.

160

In Washington the American military establishment made its own assessment of the war situation in a document called Plan Dog. General Marshall, Admiral Stark, and their staffs sided overwhelmingly with McCormick's judgment. They foresaw American entry into the war as indispensable if Britain was to be saved, though the idea of an expeditionary force was slurred over.

The question of what America would ultimately have to contribute to war against Hitler was one nobody in Washington seemed eager to face. Roosevelt himself may have been somewhat distracted from it by another Churchill confession of weakness, in the financial area. Roosevelt was shrewd enough to perceive that in the current state of public opinion the problem of paying for British supplies was not financial but political, that is, avoiding the entanglement that allegedly got the country into the war in 1917. America First propaganda stressed the entanglement aspect. Looking at the question that way, why not simply give the stuff to the British? To take the raw edge off giveaway, Roosevelt cleverly hit on "lend-lease"—it all still belonged to America; the British merely had it for the duration of the war. Afterward they could return the leftover. He bemused a press conference with the metaphor of a garden hose one lent to a neighbor whose house was on fire.

In taking his garden-hose parable to the nation via a Fireside Chat, Roosevelt seized the opportunity to knock Colonel McCormick's (and America First's) suggestion of a negotiated peace:

> Is it a negotiated peace if a gang of outlaws surrounds your community and on threat of extermination makes you pay tribute . . . ?

Whatever they thought of Roosevelt's hyperbolic rhetoric, few listeners or readers in December 1940 could take seriously the idea of a negotiated peace. The gravity of Britain's plight was not understood. Roosevelt took care not to quote Churchill's revelations of weakness even indirectly, but was at pains to assure the country that no American expeditionary force would be necessary: "You can . . . nail any talk about sending armies to Europe as a deliberate untruth." Rather, he said, America's role would be that of "the arsenal of democracy," a phrase that rang with militance while staying safely behind the lines. Finally, he promised that "the Axis powers are not going to win this war. I base that on the latest and best information."

That took cheek. The information he was talking about could only be Churchill's December 8 letter, expressing a confidence in victory through British air power that Roosevelt's military people were far from sharing.

The White Committee once more spearheaded the interventionist offensive, though this time minus the services of William Allen White. The old

Kansas editor had gotten word of a story the moderate neutralist Scripps-Howard papers were planning on him and his committee, and had written Roy Howard a long letter making the point, with what proved to be an excess of eloquence, that his committee was bent solely on keeping America out of war. Howard cleverly got permission from White to convert the letter into an interview. Its publication brought into the open the ideological split in the White Committee. Some hawks threatened to resign, others proposed that White resign. White might have weathered his friends' anger, but he was put out of countenance by the embrace of his enemies. Colonel Charles A. Lindbergh, a late but star addition to the America First lineup, commended his indorsement of the slogan "The Yanks Are Not Coming" (invented by the Communists), and General Wood invited White to join America First. Baffled, White resigned from his own committee, which passed into the hands of the nonsqueamish all-outers.

The Communists and other Leftists attacking the White Committee in its most embarrassing moment stressed its Wall Street connections (four Morgan partners). Colonel McCormick took a more sophisticated view. Recollecting Roosevelt's one-time stigmatization of the "economic royalists," the *Tribune* employed its usual irony to observe that the White Committee's Wall Streeters were doubtless among those FDR had been talking about, but their royalist character in the present context was something else—"They are the Wiswells [Tories] of another 1776."

> We never accepted the theory that they got us into the last war to make money. We do not believe their kind will get us into this war just to make money. The great bankers of the east do have international stakes of great importance, but above that they have international social connections and friendships to which they are loyal.
> . . . Mr. Morgan himself enjoys the friendship of the Archbishop of Canterbury and may and does invite distinguished people to shoot grouse with him.

After identifying the Morgan types as committed anglophiles, the editorial mentioned two Jewish Wall Streeters, James Warburg and Frank Altschul, and without using the word *Jewish* pointed out that they had many European connections, that their European properties had been confiscated, and that their coreligionists had been subjected to an oppression "greater than that which the Irish suffered." A second category of committee members consisted of luminaries of stage and screen—the Lunts, Tallulah Bankhead, Clare Boothe, Melvin Douglas, Archibald MacLeish, and others who "live in the characters of emotion and sentiment. The drama of the great struggle enlists their sympathy, and when their sentimentality is dynamic their reason is static."

Then there were the anglophile clerics, especially such orotund Episcopalians as Bishop Manning of New York.

Religion and racial ties, even subconsciously operating upon the minds of persons who possess influence in American life, should be seen for what they are when national safety requires that the predominating and governing thought be unselfish devotion to the good of the American people.

The editorial predicted a new Nye investigation after the coming war, which would at least be better than another possible alternative, "some violent retaliation" by the deluded American people "outside the processes of orderly government."

In the flood of material published by the interventionists, one theme in particular caught Colonel McCormick's eye and aroused his indignation. Despite the tide of emotion generated by the Battle of Britain, the White Committee felt that lend-lease demanded something more in the nature of American self-interest, as in the case of the destroyers-for-bases swap. An argument was found in the danger Roosevelt had cited in abstract form in his quarantine speech, imaginatively elaborated by War Department generals and leaked to the White Committee and the interventionist press. Reminiscent of the German invasion scares of 1916, the 1940–1941 version pictured the Germans as arriving on American soil via Dakar (West Africa), Brazil, and Mexico, or in an alternative version, via Newfoundland. The fantasy had first been unfurled in support of the draft act the year before, but though shot down by military experts (Hanson Baldwin, *New York Times;* Major George Fielding Eliot, *New York Herald Tribune;* Marine General Smedley Butler), it was now revived with fresh touches, such as Nazi-inspired risings in Latin America.

A sixteen-page pamphlet titled "The Atlantic Is Not 3,000 Miles Wide," put out by the Chicago chapter of the White Committee, chaired by Adlai Stevenson, seemed to be specifically designed to stir up Colonel McCormick. When the Colonel received an invitation from Senator Hiram Johnson of California, an old Progressive isolationist, to testify on the Lend-Lease bill, he accepted, stipulating that he sought only the opportunity to refute this part of the interventionist argument, not to comment on the merits of the bill.

Meantime the *Tribune* was joined in its attack on the Lend-Lease bill by Joe Patterson's *New York Daily News.* For Patterson, who had stoutly supported Roosevelt against Willkie, it was a painful break. His sister, Eleanor (Cissy) Patterson, followed his lead with her *Washington Times-Herald,* creating what the interventionist press dubbed "the Patterson-McCormick Axis."

Yet the thrust of the argument against the bill, especially in the *Tribune*, was not aid to Britain but the wide discretionary powers given the president. An Orr cartoon (February 3) showed an Uncle Sam in flying togs about to take off in a plane, "Aid Short of War," while a small officious figure labeled "New Deal Dictators" refused to give him a parachute, labeled "Amendments and Safeguards to the Lease-Lend Dictator Bill."

Colonel McCormick's turn to testify in the Senate committee hearing came on February 7. By that time the committee had listened to the objections of Joe Kennedy, who had quit his ambassadorial post in London; Socialist Norman Thomas, who feared that U.S. entry into the war would finish off America's sick democracy; and Colonel Lindbergh. Lindbergh took up Churchill's air-power argument (articulately voiced in the *New York Herald Tribune* and other papers by Major Alexander P. de Seversky, another self-made military expert, with a self-made "de"). Much as he desired a British victory, said Lindbergh, it could only be obtained by an invasion of the Continent at enormous cost in blood. Further, America's defenses were being weakened rather than strengthened by the continuing war because of the priority given to aircraft for Britain. Therefore Lindbergh concluded with McCormick that the only good solution for the United States was a negotiated peace.

That brought Colonel McCormick to the stand. He began by explaining that he had decided to accept Senator Johnson's invitation, not to voice opposition to the bill, but because of the recent scare talk about a Nazi invasion of the United States via Dakar and Brazil or Newfoundland. He stated that he had "personal knowledge of a considerable part of the ground over which such attack [Dakar-Brazil] would come, and second-hand information of the most reliable kind about the rest of it. I have also traveled extensively in eastern Canada, in Newfoundland, and Labrador."

He cited the serious geographical barriers in the way of the advance even of a German air contingent through Africa, to Brazil and up to the West Indies, and concluded:

I cannot conceive of any one having the slightest fear of an attack along this line, if he has any respect at all for our own air force.

Therefore, an attack on the United States could only come via the North Atlantic. Noting that "Iceland is now held by Canadian troops," that "south Greenland and Labrador would be of no use to an invader because of their rough character," that a Canadian-British air base defended Newfoundland and that U.S. soldiers now manned the new U.S. base there, he expressed the opinion that

It is an hysterical imagination which can conceive of our being driven from Newfoundland. Even if we were, the enemy would find no supplies in that barren land. There would be Cabot Strait to cross. . . . Nova Scotia is a peninsula with a narrow neck, and New Brunswick largely forest and muskeg.

Can anyone dream of an enemy forcing his way through this country in face of one or two million trained American and Canadian troops?

Senator Tom Connally (D.-Tex.) raised the question of how the Atlantic military geography would be affected if "the attacking power had naval power so as to be able to establish bases in South America." McCormick asserted that the United States should acquire a base in the Azores, where American commercial aviation flew now (the Pan American Clipper). Acquisition would be politically feasible, since the British had leverage with Portugal.

> SENATOR CONNALLY: They could give us a great deal of trouble if they had the British fleet, could they not?
> MCCORMICK: Senator, I have known Winston Churchill for twenty-five years. A more thoroughly honorable man never lived. He would not have made that promise [not to surrender the British fleet] if he had not intended to keep it.

Pressed on whether he was "hinging the whole safety of the United States" on Churchill's promise, McCormick stated that "we could stop the [hostile] fleet anyway," that a defending U.S. fleet did not need even to be as large as an attacking enemy, and that the Panama Canal made a "one-ocean" navy effective in both oceans. Connally asked if he wished to express an opinion on "the bill as such," and McCormick again declined.

After a bland and friendly question from Senator Arthur H. Vandenberg (R.-Mich.), who was also on record as favoring a negotiated peace, Senator Claude Pepper (D.-Fla.) took over the interrogation. A red-hot interventionist, Senator Pepper had been somewhat discomfited when he had opened his interrogation of Lindbergh with the query "When did you first go to Europe?" to which the response "In 1927" brought the day's biggest laugh from the gallery. Pepper began more carefully with Colonel McCormick. "What would be your attitude," he demanded, "as to the policy of this country if Hitler should conquer England and proceed to take over and occupy the British bases in what is regarded as this hemisphere?"

"I would not let him do it," McCormick answered promptly.

Senator Pepper raised the hypothetical question of Hitler's getting control of the French fleet and French West Indies bases, to which McCormick replied again, "I would not let him," and added that he favored acquiring

French bases in advance, but if necessary would take them by force. (Neither the Colonel nor the senator was aware that the Vichy government had expressly offered to arrange for a U.S. presence in Martinique, a proposal toward which the State Department was for some reason cold.) Pepper raised the same hypothetical question about Bermuda, and McCormick reminded him that the United States already had a base there. Perhaps a little rattled, Pepper then asked the witness, "To whom do the Azores belong?"

MCCORMICK: To Portugal.

PEPPER: Suppose Hitler should capture and occupy Portugal and set up a puppet government in Portugal. What would you recommend this country to do about the Azores?

MCCORMICK: I would get there first.

PEPPER *(getting sarcastic):* You think that would be a policy calculated to keep the peace of the United States?

MCCORMICK: Yes, I think so.

PEPPER: Wouldn't Hitler do anything to resist?

MCCORMICK: I think England will make an arrangement with us to occupy the Azores. You understand that England has the right. [Two years later Britain exercised the right and established a base of its own in the Azores, and in 1944 the United States acquired one.]

PEPPER: If Hitler conquered both England and Portugal and decided there should be a Hitler base at the Azores, what would you do?

MCCORMICK: Get there first. Just as General Jackson did in Florida [Pepper's home state]. I would go right in and take them. That is how we got Florida.

PEPPER: Suppose Hitler declared war on us for occupying the Azores?

MCCORMICK: Then we should have a fight. Those Germans are not so tough. I have been up against them and there is no use being scared of them.

At this doughty response Senator Pepper pronounced himself "somewhat encouraged by your testimony. You would then protect American interests whether Hitler liked it or not?" to which McCormick answered, "I would."

Pepper raised the question of an Axis force "heading for Dakar to occupy it," to which McCormick replied that it was difficult to say whether Dakar would be an appropriate point to dispute militarily, since "on getting farther away from home it is harder to hold . . . positions."

Senator Pepper then hypothesized Hitler's laying hands on the combined fleets of Italy, France, and Britain. McCormick pointed out that all those fleets had suffered losses, and he "did not believe your naval advisers will say" that even the combination would be stronger than the U.S. fleet. Senator Pepper added the Japanese navy, to which McCormick riposted with the Panama Canal—"I can hardly believe the Japanese would send their fleet to the Atlantic."

McCormick's equanimity, as well as the common sense of his answers, apparently had a disarming effect, leading to an exchange of pleasantries at the expense of the Italians, recently defeated in North Africa. Pepper asked if McCormick had heard the one about Mussolini promising Hitler "all aid short of war," and McCormick said no, but he had heard that "the Italians have a new secret weapon—the German army."

They reverted to the naval question and McCormick expressed the opinion that if the U.S. Navy were to occupy the Azores it could defend them against any combination. "I would like to get to the Azores right away," he asserted. "The British would be glad to have us." He reiterated the British treaty right in the islands and recalled that "we based our navy on the Azores in the war of 1917–1918."

The senator then turned to Britain.

SENATOR PEPPER: You said England was not going to be conquered. Do you think she has the means of producing enough materials of war to continue to defend herself against Hitler without aid from this country?

McCORMICK: I am certain of it.

PEPPER: You do not think Britain, then, needs to buy or acquire any more war materials from the United States in order to defend herself?

McCORMICK: If Britain were in any serious danger of invasion, can you imagine her sending a huge motorized army corps to Libya? Would she not keep those machines in England? That is the evidence to me.

PEPPER: So you think it would be all right for us to cut now the arteries of supply to England?

McCORMICK: If there is to be an invasion of the continent she will need many munitions from this country and several million men—and I am against that. I am willing to furnish material to Britain for her own defense but not to carry a great and terrible war to the continent of Europe. She should have whatever she needs for defense—and I do not think she needs anything.

PEPPER: Would you put your judgment as a criterion on that matter or would you take the British idea of their own need as the criterion?

McCORMICK: I would use my own judgment.

Senator Pepper gave over the questioning to isolationist Bennett Champ Clark (D.-Mo.), who asked the witness if he did not think it would be fair of the British to give up island bases in return for cancellation of World War I debts—an old *Tribune* proposal. McCormick merely replied, "I think it would be very nice if they would." To another question he answered, "I would not want to take them from England by force, no."

Senator Carter Glass (D.-Va.), a Wilson administration veteran, anti-New Deal reactionary, and unapologetic proponent of going all the way to war, was asked if he had any questions. He ended the session with dry humor: "I think that if things are as serene as Colonel McCormick imagines, the congress ought to pass the normal appropriations and go home."

CHAPTER SEVENTEEN

The Argument Turns Bitter

DESPITE the narrow substantive gap between proponents and opponents of lend-lease (America First announced at the outset that it would not oppose credit to Britain, and Senator Taft introduced a substitute proposal for $2 billion worth), and despite the level of civility maintained in Congress, of which Colonel McCormick's treatment on the witness stand was a sample, the atmosphere of the national debate grew steadily harsher. Their sincere protestations to the contrary could not keep those opposing the bill from getting labeled "anti-British," the 1941 equivalent of 1917's "pro-German." Where the emotional focus of World War I was on the alleged crimes of the Germans, that of World War II was on the role of Britain as courageous underdog. The "pro-Germans" had been perceived as countenancing the kaiser's Belgian atrocities; the opponents of lend-lease were seen as hostile to the people with whom most Americans identified. In retrospect, much irony is apparent, but in 1941 Hitler was regarded as little if any worse than Mussolini or Franco, and Churchill's preoccupation with the imperialist-colonialist side of the war was too fine a point to attract attention.

In the prevailing atmosphere, even McCormick's protest against the irrationality of the Dakar-Brazil invasion scare was treated as a sort of anti-British treachery. A lengthy *Tribune* editorial of April 1, 1941, repeated the argument while protesting a new major naval escalation by Roosevelt, the extension of patrolling to the twenty-fifth meridian (Iceland-Azores), and warning against a rumored proposal to use the navy to convoy cargoes to Britain:

> . . . If that happens . . . the United States navy will be in the war. . . . That will end the talk of aiding Britain short of war. . . . Sooner or later some of our sailors will be blown up or drowned after a torpedo attack. . . . The American people will be told they must avenge this taking of American lives. . . .

The editorial concluded, "America is being urged to sacrifice the lives of a million of its sons to avert nonexistent dangers."

The objectionable thing about such a minority view was, not so much that it contradicted the majority, but that it stated aloud things that the majority preferred not to talk about.

As acrimony deepened, the Chicago interventionist papers, the *Daily News* and *Times,* departed from traditional journalistic abstinence to directly attack the *Tribune*'s stand on the war. Colonel McCormick rejoined with a biting, arrogant editorial titled "These Jackals Grow Too Bold," in which derisive reference was made to the *Times*'s and *Daily News*'s alleged financial problems:

> These newspapers are so deeply in debt that whoever may be held up as the editor or manager is little more than an office boy for the creditors.

Just three years earlier when a fire had damaged the *Times* pressroom, Colonel McCormick had put aside political differences and offered the *Tribune*'s presses to the afternoon paper, which came out with the headline "Hot off the Press (the Tribune's)." But now Samuel Emory Thomason dictated an editorial answering the Colonel's in which he observed, "Bertie McCormick is yapping like a feisty dog." To John McPhaul, later author of an entertaining history of Chicago journalism *(Deadlines and Monkeyshines),* Thomason explained that "feisty" meant "a puppy that's always barking." Thomason's charges that the *Tribune* was not sufficiently anti-Hitler stung McCormick and put an end to a friendship dating back to law school.

The lend-lease rancor also removed whatever restraints McCormick had felt about personally attacking Roosevelt, Ickes, and the rest of the New Deal crew who were now characterized as "fat old men, senile hysterics . . . able bodied men in bombproof public positions who devote their every energy to stirring up wars for other men to fight." The *Tribune* even recalled erroneously that James Roosevelt, FDR's great-grandfather, had been a Tory in the Revolution (the Tory was James's father-in-law, Abram Walton, FDR's great-great-grandfather).

Whatever the merits of his position on the war, McCormick was painting himself into an embattled corner, stirring up enemies on all sides. The *Montreal Daily Star,* far from expressing gratitude for his support for the U.S.-Canada alliance, told its readers that

> In Canada Colonel McCormick [owns] newsprint mills, vast timber limits, and water power . . . [which] are actually being utilized by this man in his nefarious efforts to mislead his countrymen and slander the British people in their hour of sore trial. . . .

When other English-Canadian papers joined in the attack, Arthur Schmon took alarm. To McCormick he reported rumors that the campaign was inspired by "publishers who are competitors in Chicago or New York, and by the New Deal administration." Several other U.S. publishers grew concerned at the Canadian threat to the *Tribune,* and Roy Howard, head of the large Scripps-Howard chain, warned the Newsprint Association of Canada that "ninety-five percent of the American press would object strenuously to any attempt to influence the free editorial expression of a U.S. newspaper." Cranston Williams, general manager of the American Newspaper Publishers Association, also spoke up, and the *Toronto Globe & Mail* warned that Canada could not afford to yield to the temptation of trying to cut off the *Tribune*'s newsprint supply.

In Chicago a more legitimate anti-*Tribune* move, and one destined to have a far more tangible and lasting effect, was afoot that spring. Marshall Field III invited William Benton to lunch and sought the advice of the former Madison Avenue genius on starting a rival morning paper. Field's biographer, Stephen Becker, reports that Field told Benton that "Chicago needs a liberal newspaper," though it already had the pro-Roosevelt *Times.* What Field meant was a morning liberal paper, and by liberal he meant interventionist. He had recently come to the rescue of *PM,* the new mid-morning New York tabloid, which was both four-square liberal and red-hot interventionist, and had the two ideologies thoroughly mixed.

Though many New Yorkers, perceiving him through *PM,* thought Field was Jewish (a liberal department-store king), he was a super-Wasp, with strong British connections—among other things, his aunt had been married to Earl Beatty, hero of the Battle of Jutland.

Benton had gone to Chicago to help out his old college chum (Yale again) Robert Maynard Hutchins, president of the University of Chicago. Hutchins, an iconoclast in and out of the academic world, had drawn fire from the *Tribune* and *Daily News* over his Left-leaning politics, and Benton had idealistically quit his Madison Avenue gold mine to become Hutchins's PR man. He had succeeded in disarming the suspicions of both the morning and afternoon colonels, and in 1941 the University of Chicago no longer had a pressing PR problem. Field was a University of Chicago trustee. Yet Benton was an odd choice to be mentor for a publisher seeking to do battle with the wrongheaded isolationist Colonel McCormick, because Benton himself was as isolationist as McCormick (so was Hutchins), and in fact was in the very top echelon of the America First Committee.

This oddity was perhaps less obtrusive in the context of the larger oddity of Marshall Field's entry into the newspaper business. His family had had a single prior connection with it: the loan his grandfather had made to Joseph Medill to buy the *Tribune* in 1874. Between grandfather and grandson came Marshall Field II, who had created a front-page scandal by committing suicide in 1905. The tragedy had clouded the life of Field III until his psychoanalysis in New York by a colorful Russian Jew named Gregory Zilboorg. Despite having served in his youth as a minister in the Kerenski government, Zilboorg had remained an undisillusioned idealist, and under his sunny influence Field saw the error of his Republican ways, voted for Roosevelt in 1936 and 1940, cut down on drinking, gave money to clinics to aid disturbed children, and finally allowed himself to be captivated by Ralph Ingersoll, the ex-*New Yorker,* ex-*Fortune* brains behind innovative, precarious *PM.*

Colonel McCormick was well aware of the New York publishing venture of his fellow Chicagoan (Ingersoll had had the nerve to ask Joe Patterson for help) and from the outset disapproved of everything about *PM,* especially its tax-write-off advantages for Marshall Field. The novelty of *PM,* which shocked fellow publications not only by its liberalism but by not selling advertising, had already brought a flurry of potshots. The fact that Ingersoll had been through analysis with the same Dr. Zilboorg as Marshall Field inspired the *Saturday Evening Post* to speculate, in the third person: "The extent to which Doctor Zilboorg has influenced PM's editorial policy, if at all, is a popular topic of argument in New York newspaper circles."

Field's newspaper plans for Chicago were less daring than *PM,* in whose conception he had had no part. Through Benton he approached Thomason at the *Chicago Times* and Knox in Washington. Thomason was willing to sell him the *Times* cheap, Knox was willing to rent his underused presses, and discussions were soon under way.

At this moment, while Marshall Field dickered, while McCormick and his current newspaper rivals exchanged jeers, and while the English Canadians threatened the *Tribune*'s newsprint, the larger war took its most dramatic and significant turn.

The *Tribune* was one of the few papers to forecast the invasion of the Soviet Union. Donald Day, who had been expelled from Latvia after the Soviet takeover, reported from Stockholm in April 1941:

> Most [German informants] say the attack will not be made until next autumn when the campaign against England is expected to be completed. Others believe it may come very soon and admit the German high command has virtually completed its plans.

The story was played prominently on page one. McCormick, despite his anti-Soviet bias, was not among those who mistook the Nazi-Soviet pact for an alliance, and had sharply rebuked Edmond Taylor for a story forecasting joint German-Russian action in Romania and the Near East.

Day's Stockholm rumors included Soviet transport of machinery east-ward from the threatened Baltic states and discussions of U.S. aid between Molotov and Ambassador Steinhardt.

The *Chicago Daily News*'s Leland Stowe had already broken a sensational story (February 27): "Stalin Biding Time—Feels War with Nazis Inevitable," and a few other European correspondents were picking up rumors. None of their Washington colleagues guessed that the biggest story of the war lay hidden under their noses. Since January the State Department had possessed a copy of Hitler's order to his army activating Plan Barbarossa. The document had been slipped to a U.S. Embassy attaché in a darkened Berlin movie theater and the news passed along, as evidently intended by the German informant, to the Soviet ambassador in Washington.

On June 15 the *Tribune* front-page banner read:

HITLER-STALIN CRISIS NEAR

Day, now in Finland, reported that diplomatic sources were predicting that Stalin would give in to Hitler's requests for material, but added that Tass "admitted that a vast force of Germans was massed on the Russian border," and cited rumored German demands so extravagant as to make clear that the crisis was real. Dispatches from London, Berne, and Ankara added confirmation.

A week later a lengthy editorial summarized the war, taking off from a Churchill quote to the effect that though confident of victory, he could not as yet "see how deliverance will come or when it will come." The *Tribune*'s editorial expressed sensible doubts about an early end to the stalemate in the West:

> The time when the bomber can win the war seems to be as remote as the prospect of ending it by invasion, by one side or the other.

Turning to the "renewed rumor of friction between Hitler and Stalin," the *Tribune* thought

> If any war could be regarded as containing the possibility of a benefit to the world [,] one between the Nazi and Red dictatorships would seem to be that war, particularly if it could offer the promise of the overthrow of both systems. . . .
>
> With Russia extending the German lines the continental situation might brighten up, but hopes built upon such an event may be very illusory. . . .
>
> Mr. Churchill is dealing with actualities as he sees them when he says that he does not know when or how deliverance will come.

Written before that day's news broke, the editorial anticipated the page-one banner:

NAZIS-REDS AT WAR!

Hitler Orders His Army to Invade Russia

The next day's editorial expressed jubilation:

The Heat Is Off

The German declaration of war against Russia has cut the ground from under the war party in this country.

They said we must go to war to save Britain from invasion. Britain is no longer threatened with invasion. German air power must be concentrated against the new enemy. So must German land power. Hitler can now have no panzer divisions, no mechanized divisions, no parachute troops to spare for an assault upon the British Isles. . . .

The military conquest of Russia, or only of Russia's western provinces, is a stupendous undertaking calling for the maximum of exertion. . . . The Russians command an immense army, by far the largest which Germany has yet faced and in many respects a better equipped army than any which the Germans have conquered in this war. . . .

The news is hardly less welcome in this country than in Britain, for it means that if there ever was any justification for our intervention in arms that justification no longer exists. The heat is off . . . Even if the Germans knife through to Moscow . . . the most favorable season for invading England will have passed. . . .

Once again, as in the case of the fall of France, McCormick's logic was sound but his psychology all wrong.

From Washington Arthur Sears Henning reported a disquieting note: While at first all officials had characterized the German-Soviet war as "a much to be desired case of dog eat dog," Winston Churchill's broadcast promising assistance to Russia and appealing to his "friends and allies" to do the same had brought a change of tune, "in the expectation that the President will adopt the policy laid down by the British prime minister."

Next day the *Tribune* took note of the unexpected turn:

Our war birds . . . may try . . . to welcome [the invasion] as reason for getting into war. To other Americans, to the majority of them, it presents the final reason for remaining out. . . . Should we aid Stalin to extend his brutalities to all of Finland, to maintain his grip on the Baltic states, or to keep what he has of Poland and Rumania? Should we enter the war to extend his rule over more of Europe or, having helped him to win, should we then have to rescue the continent from him?

Stark, Knox, Stimson, Ickes, and the rest of the flock of war birds in fact saw in Hitler's invasion of Russia a good opportunity for America to declare war. Ickes in his diary came closest to giving a sensible reason, that if the country waited any longer it might find itself alone in the world with Hitler and the Japanese. Yet this viewpoint could scarcely have weighed with Ickes's more military colleagues, since they were all certain that Hitler would finish the Russians off in two to three months. Nobody suggested anything like a second front. Knox talked of "a smashing blow" that would, anticlimactically, "clear the path across the Atlantic." The *Christian Science Monitor* and the *New York Times,* taking cues from Washington, clamored ambiguously for "throwing every weight into the scales on the Western front" and throwing "into the Western front, on Britain's side, every plane that we can spare."

The *Monitor, Times,* and others expressing similar sentiments were not proposing to help the Soviet Union defeat Hitler. So remote were they from any such thought that many interventionist editors and commentators made common cause with isolationists in opposing lend-lease to the Soviets. The *New York Times* raised the specter of Stalin making

a sudden treacherous peace. . . . We should be in a fine state of affairs if we landed a hundred bombers on Russian soil just in time for this reconciliation.

Colonel McCormick, after an early favorable appraisal of Russian resistance that would have enhanced his reputation as a military expert had he stuck to it, turned around and joined the *Times* in predicting collapse or treachery. He indorsed a bill Illinois Republican Congressman Stephen Day introduced to forbid sending Stalin any lend-lease.

To the surprise of Colonel McCormick, Congressman Day, the *New York Times,* and the pundits, the public took a different view. It welcomed godless, Communist, dictator-ruled Russia onto the battlefield with a rousing American cheer. Gallup reported that even though his respondents strongly opposed convoying to Britain—Knox, Stimson, Stark, and Roosevelt notwithstanding—they were glad to lend and lease to the Reds.

The unexpected popularity of the Soviets, together with the explosion of zeal for the war on the far Left, had a distinct effect on the political division in U.S. opinion. The small American Communist party dominated most Left thinking, and as several top labor leaders and intellectuals (such as Hollywood writer Dalton Trumbo whose *The Remarkable Andrew* had just been excerpted serially for the *Tribune*'s page one) did an about-face, the moderate liberals and conservatives still holding the isolationist fort became more isolated.

Interventionist liberals and Communists, embracing like estranged but passionate marriage partners, felt the need for somebody they could agree to be mad at. Nowhere did they find a more ideal target than in Chicago. Word of Marshall Field's new journalistic enterprise had spread, though up to June 22 the far Left had taken only a tepid interest in it. Now old and new allies for all-out war got together. Against the "reactionary, isolationist *Chicago Tribune*" the Fight for Freedom Committee organized a mass meeting at Orchestra Hall on South Michigan. On July 29 a noisy throng jammed the auditorium (oddly, the *Daily News* estimated 3,000 people, the *Tribune* 3,500) to applaud anti-*Tribune* invective that brought back memories of Big Bill Thompson. While pro- and antiwar pickets paraded outside, ex-*Tribune* foreign correspondent Edmond Taylor delivered the principal address, "What Is Wrong with the Chicago Tribune?" Though he accused the *Tribune* of "Nazi tactics," Taylor was a good deal more temperate than the crowd. Asking the rhetorical question "Is it fair to consider the *Chicago Tribune* as an agency of propaganda even if only an unconscious agency?" he confessed that it was "a very hard question," and that the answer was "both yes and no. Yes if you mean that the *Chicago Tribune* is playing exactly the role Hitler would like to see it play. No—if you mean that the *Tribune* is taking orders or even wittingly accepting support from the German government."

Taylor thought the *Tribune,* along with Senator Wheeler and Colonel Lindbergh, guilty of contributing to national disunity in the face of the fascist danger. As for Colonel McCormick personally, Taylor called him a "loyal and patriotic American" and asserted that his own service with the *Tribune* had lasted as long as it did because of "the sense of fairness which distinguished Colonel McCormick as an employer as much as its absence distinguished him as an editor. He certainly leaned over backwards to be fair to me," a reference to the generous sick-leave pay the *Tribune* had twice given him, including severance pay when his second illness forced his resignation.

The other two speakers offered the crowd redder meat. Episcopal Bishop Henry W. Hobson of Cincinnati, a twice-wounded veteran of 1918, called for "immediate use of every resource of the country" to win Britain's battle of the Atlantic, and did not shrink from admitting that "this means war." The third speaker, a member of the Chicago chapter of the committee named Frank J. Gagen, introduced a resolution to "end the un-American monopoly now enjoyed by the *Chicago Tribune* and in the interests of freedom of enterprise, freedom of speech, truth, fairness and justice, give positive encouragement and cooperation to those individuals who are

. . . now contemplating to provide Chicago and the Middle West with another morning newspaper." The crowd cheered, and streamed out to buy early *Tribune*s and build a bonfire in Michigan Avenue by way of driving home its anti-Nazi sentiments.

While the *Tribune* struck back with a series of Washington stories accusing the Roosevelt administration of attempting to manipulate the press, the Fight for Freedom Committee promoted a boycott of the *Tribune* by a direct-mail campaign. It had little impact. In a full-page ad melodramatically headed THE TRIBUNE ACCEPTS THE CHALLENGE, the paper boasted of its dominant circulation position (1,064,342 daily, 1,220,962 Sunday), far ahead of the *Daily News* and *Times.* The *Trib*'s news stories on its assailants sarcastically depicted a coalition of "communists [and] fighters of the marshmallow set." The Red-baiting was not without basis; on August 20 the paper reported on an inside page:

COMRADE FOSTER ARRIVES
TO LEAD DRIVE ON TRIBUNE

Comrade (William Z.) Foster was credited in the story with consistency in having always "damned the Tribune," but the paper pointed out that "his speech tonight . . . will reverse what he said here last fall. He now wants the United States to enter the war."

All the same, Foster was given a fair shake in an interview and allowed to make his points, which, as wartime quotes go, do not read too badly today:

> Germany's invasion of the soviet has "basically changed the character of the war and increased the threat to the United States." . . . He contended that the only reason Hitler did not invade England was that Russia could then have struck a weakened Germany.
>
> "The job of defeating Hitler is not the job of the soviet union alone, but of the United States and Great Britain, with the help of the rebellious peoples of Europe," he said . . .
>
> The meeting at which Foster will speak tonight will be held in the outdoor arena that adjoins the Chicago Stadium. Admission prices range from 25 cents to $1.10.

The meeting was duly covered, including the speech of local Communist Morris Childs, who identified America's Quislings as Herbert Hoover, Norman Thomas, Charles A. Lindbergh, Burton Wheeler, and Colonel Robert R. McCormick.

"Chicago is cursed with a landmark, Tribune Tower, built to disseminate lies," Childs declaimed. "The boycott is assuming momentum."

He declared that this newspaper was the "patron saint" of Al Capone, that it echoes Goebbels, the German propaganda minister, and "reeks with espionage and defeat." . . .

It was a better break than the *Daily Worker,* or even some other papers, would have given Colonel McCormick.

CHAPTER EIGHTEEN

"FDR's War Plan!"

BETWEEN denunciations by its enemies, the *Tribune* scored a small beat by getting out a midmorning extra on the Roosevelt-Churchill "Atlantic Charter" meeting, news of which was released following a five-day press blackout on August 14. Next day the *Tribune* interpreted the meeting:

PACT PUSHES U.S. NEAR WAR

Arthur Sears Henning reported that official Washington rocked today under the impact of the announcement of an Anglo-American alliance to conquer and disarm Germany, Italy, and Japan, and thereafter police the world.

From London Larry Rue reported that Britain saw in the historic meeting "the prelude to a message to the American congress calling for a formal declaration of war."

In its editorial, titled "What Has Roosevelt Promised Churchill?" the paper waxed mordantly ironic:

. . . That interchange [the Atlantic Charter] didn't require any meeting of the minds at sea. Mr. Churchill wouldn't have felt justified in making a lunch date merely to talk over a bit of rhetoric.
   . . . His business is to preserve Britain, preserve the British Empire, its dominant position in the world, and to knock off Hitler. . . .
   . . . His job is to win the war, if he can, and he has been told by his generals that he will need all the American soldiers he can get. Without them he was not able to take advantage of Germany's war with Russia. He wants soldiers.
   Churchill could humor Mr. Roosevelt and treat his grandiloquence and moral excursions with the patience required to get something important out of a talkative man. . . . What he wanted to know of Mr. Roosevelt was: When are you coming across? And it is the answer to that question that concerns the American people who have voted 4 to 1 that they are not going across at all unless their government drags them in against their will.

Referring to the phrase in the communiqué, "after final destruction of the Nazi tyranny," the *Tribune* predicted that Churchill would regard that as

179

"the pledge of a government, binding upon the country," and asserted, "The country repudiates it. Mr. Roosevelt had no authority and can find none for making such a pledge." Subsequent stories by Chesly Manly and Walter Trohan of the Washington bureau pursued the subject to such effect that Roosevelt told his press conference that he had been reading "vicious rumors, distortions of facts [and] just plain dirty falsehoods" about his meeting with Churchill.

Most of his listeners sympathized, yet few of them thought Manly and Trohan were wrong in substance. Privately, correspondents, columnists, and editors assumed that Churchill must have asked for American troops —what else?—even though they were indignant at anybody telling the public as much.

Strangely enough, they were all, prowar and antiwar, mistaken. Churchill had indeed asked Roosevelt when America was "coming across." He had in fact first asked for an American declaration of war back in May, as well as implied the demand in many messages, and in the meeting off Newfoundland he had put it with all his persuasive force (the *Tribune* was far wrong in thinking Roosevelt had done most of the talking). Roosevelt had stubbornly refused to make a promise and had tossed in the "after final destruction of the Nazi tyranny" phrase as a sop. Yet though he wanted an American declaration of war, Churchill did not seek a large American manpower commitment. That he had been "told by his generals that he will need all the American soldiers he can get" was a reference to a couple of injudicious interviews British generals Wavell and Auchinleck had given Harold Denny of the *New York Times* in the wake of British defeats in Africa and Greece. Nevertheless, Churchill still did not believe he needed troops to defeat Hitler, and expressed no such need in the Atlantic conference. He still placed his faith in city bombing (he placed none in the Russians; his public speeches notwithstanding, he argued vehemently against Harry Hopkins on lend-lease to Stalin, which he was sure would all fall into Hitler's hands), and there were even recondite political reasons why he was reluctant to see any large number of American troops get involved in Europe.

What Churchill wanted from America was still a guarantee of the Atlantic lifeline, plenty of bombing planes, and a block against the Japanese threat to Singapore and Malaya. The whole program had been spelled out before the conference in a British "General Strategic Review" forwarded to Washington in early July.

But even while the British insistently reiterated their futile bombing-plane-and-colonial-war strategy, America's own military high command was laying down an opposite blueprint, one far more realistic, and carrying a credibly ominous designation of America's role. Therein lay one of the news sensations of the war, the *Chicago Tribune*'s greatest single scoop ever, and some breathtaking historic irony.

Senator Burton K. Wheeler, old Progressive party leader, Teapot Dome investigator, Fighting Bob LaFollette's running mate in 1924, and real-life original of Jimmy Stewart in *Mr. Smith Goes to Washington,* was one of the liberal pacifists who had stayed with the neutralist doctrine as the war clouds turned into war. An enthusiastic New Dealer, he had had hopes of the vice-presidential spot on the third-term ticket in 1940, on the theory that Roosevelt might want to balance his own hawkish image with an outspoken dove. (Roosevelt had gone instead for interventionist liberal Henry Wallace and Wheeler had wound up voting for socialist Norman Thomas.) Wheeler had helped get America First started and had embraced its policy line that aid to Britain endangered America's own defense buildup. As a result he had become a useful congressional contact for a disaffected element in the buildup, the Army Air Corps. General Henry H. (Hap) Arnold, jolly, ambitious chief of the corps who wanted to turn it into an "Air Force," that is, an independent outfit on equal footing with army and navy, apparently caused a certain anonymous captain to leak to Senator Wheeler news of alleged short-changings of the Air Corps.

On a visit to Wheeler's office sometime in September, the captain let slip what should have been a provocative tidbit—that under the direction of General Marshall something had just been drawn up called a "Victory Program," outlining future strategy and procurement needs. The genesis of the Victory Program lay in the appointment of General Motors head William S. Knudsen as boss of defense production. Knudsen had raised the question of the approximate parameters of the task, that is, how much of what items had to be produced over the next few years to meet the combined needs of lend-lease and America's buildup. Roosevelt had turned the question over to Marshall, who had put a task force to work on it.

Wheeler evidently missed the potential implications in the captain's hint, and for the time being nothing happened.

Meantime the country edged nearer war. On his return to London from the Atlantic conference, Churchill told Parliament that the United States had undertaken diplomatic containment of Japan, which was the first real news the meeting had produced. In case of a Pacific war, according to Churchill, a British-U.S. alliance had been pledged. Shortly thereafter (September 1) Arthur Sears Henning reported from Washington the opening of a "spectacular and momentous diplomatic fencing match" between Roosevelt and Prince Konoye of Japan, the outcome of which "bids fair to influence profoundly the course of the wars now raging in Europe, Africa, and Asia." Henning speculated about the effect of Pacific diplomacy on the war in Europe and listed the major issues at stake: Japan's invasion of

China, Manchuria, and Indochina; the cutoff of American oil shipments; and the Japanese "co-prosperity sphere" that shut the open door in east Asia. Henning closed his dispatch with a pair of hypotheses:

> Thus the negotiations may have been initiated by Mr. Roosevelt, springing from the necessity of the British to get Japan neutralized in order to permit the withdrawal of the American fleet to the Atlantic for a grand assault on Germany.
>
> On the other hand, the negotiations may have been sought by Japan, which has been hard hit by the American economic sanctions and may have been convinced by the formation of the Anglo-American alliance and by the Nazis' slow progress against Russia that the axis is doomed to defeat.

In that last thought, Henning was way ahead of the military experts, British, American, or Japanese, who were all sure the Soviets were sunk.

Henning's belief that Roosevelt might be trying to arrange a Pacific peace in order to give Britain maximum help against Hitler reflected Colonel McCormick's thinking as well as his own, and was widely shared among interventionists as well as isolationists. They were all mistaken. Roosevelt had told Churchill he thought he could "baby the Japs" along for another few months, but conceded that ultimately the string would play out. As for Churchill, far from wanting peace in the Pacific in order to concentrate against Hitler, he was ready and eager for war with Japan, provided that America undertook to do most of the fighting. Had the press been able to penetrate the true attitude of either of the two leaders it would have made startling news.

But the most urgent problem facing Roosevelt, or the one that he conceived to be most urgent, was Britain's Atlantic lifeline, and the *Tribune* and other papers were not mistaken in suspecting that he was seeking an "incident" to justify expansion of the navy's role. The one he got on September 4 was less than ideal for his purpose, and he had to do some stretching, not to say downright prevaricating, to make it work. The *Tribune* indicated its own skepticism by enclosing its banner in quotes:

'SUB FIRES ON U.S. WARSHIP'

Destroyer Then Releases
Depth Bombs, Says Navy

A shooting incident of the sort which interventionists have long predicted would bring America into active participation in the European war was announced tonight by the navy department.

The Navy Department's announcement in fact concealed important details, making it appear that the destroyer *Greer* had been attacked without warning while going about its business. The truth was that the *Greer,* en route to the new American base in Iceland, had received a signal from a British patrol plane—such was the degree of unannounced military cooperation—that a submerged U-boat lay ten miles dead ahead. The *Greer* located the submarine and trailed it, broadcasting its position to guide British aircraft and naval units in hunting it down. In self-defense the harassed U-boat skipper fired two torpedoes, both of which missed, and the *Greer* retaliated with depth bombs.

That was the way it happened, but Roosevelt seized the opportunity with both hands. The death of his mother postponed his radio address to September 11, when he gave a highly flavored account:

> The Navy Department of the United States has reported to me that on the morning of September fourth the United States destroyer *Greer,* proceeding in full daylight toward Iceland, had reached a point southeast of Greenland. She was carrying American mail to Iceland. She was flying the American flag. Her identity as an American ship was unmistakable.
>
> She was then and there attacked by a submarine. Germany admits that it was a German submarine. The submarine deliberately fired a torpedo at the *Greer,* followed later by another torpedo attack. In spite of what Hitler's propaganda bureau has invented, and in spite of what any American obstructionist organization may prefer to believe, I tell you the blunt fact that the German submarine fired first upon this American destroyer without warning, and with deliberate design to sink her.

It was a clear case of "piracy," according to Roosevelt, and he did not stop there:

> . . . The incident is not isolated, but is part of a general plan. . . . Hitler's advance guards—not only his avowed agents but also his dupes among us— have sought to make ready for him footholds in the New World, to be used as soon as he has gained control of the oceans.

And though nobody was looking for war, "when you see a rattlesnake poised to strike, you do not wait until he has struck before you crush him."

After talk like that it was almost anticlimactic when he announced that the navy had been given orders to attack German warships entering waters "the protection of which is necessary for American defense." In the order implementing the decision he added a postscript very helpful to Britain— the U.S. Navy would convoy all shipping, American or other, to Iceland, shooting U-boats on sight. The British navy would only have to take over at Iceland.

Admiral Raeder read Roosevelt's speech and flew to Hitler's command post in Russia to plead for letting the U-boats loose against U.S. shipping —no idle threat, as the U.S. Navy presently learned—but Hitler said no, not yet. He wanted to keep America from a declaration of war until after he had defeated the Russians, which he now figured to take one more month —to mid-October.

The *Tribune* gave Roosevelt's speech straightforward coverage under the banner FDR GIVES SHOOTING ORDER—U.S. MUST DRIVE AXIS FROM SEA, SAYS PRESIDENT. In column three a story was headed "FDR Creating War Incidents, Lindbergh Says." Far down in the Lindbergh text, which jumped with Roosevelt's to page ten, came a passage that caused more press furor over the next several days than Roosevelt's shooting order. Lindbergh named as "the three most important groups who have been pressing this country toward war . . . the British, the Jewish, and the Roosevelt administration." Lindbergh added mention of "a number of capitalists, Anglophiles, and intellectuals" who favored the British Empire, and "the communistic groups" newly joined to the war party, but the only culprit in his list who got any attention was the Jews. According to Lindbergh, American Jews would really be better off opposing the war because "they will be among the first to feel its consequences. Tolerance is a virtue that depends on peace and strength." That sounded like a threat, and he coupled it with identification of the "greatest danger" the Jews posed as being "their large ownership and influence in our motion pictures, our press, our radio, and our government."

Lindbergh spoke in Des Moines, home of the *Des Moines Register,* which asserted that the speech disqualified him for any leadership role in the country—and that was one of the more moderate press comments. New York resounded with outrage. The *Chicago Tribune* was embarrassingly stuck with an upcoming Sunday color feature, already off the press, showing Lindbergh's collection of medals, and could only express a hopeful confidence that "none of our readers will assume that the publication of this page at this time is to be regarded as in any sense an evidence of approval."

On the speech itself the *Tribune* said something that Lindbergh might better have read before he spoke:

> Jews, as Col. Lindbergh said, have every reason to hate and fear Hitler. . . . But . . . other Americans no more wish to be treated as Hitler has treated the Germans than American Jews wish to be treated as he has treated the Jews. The case for American participation in the war does not rest on detestation of Hitler. If it did, our navy, with the consent of the whole nation, would have started across the Atlantic the day Poland was invaded.

In the context of 1941 it was natural for the editorial to mention that the proportion of Jewish employees on the *Tribune* was ("we imagine") roughly parallel to their proportion in the Chicago population, and included "two of the writers for this page." Hitler's anti-Semitism was generally regarded as only worse in degree from garden-variety U.S. anti-Semitism. Neither Colonel McCormick, Lindbergh nor anybody else had the slightest inkling that Hitler's treatment of the Jews was at that very moment undergoing a diabolical progression, with the shelving of a Nazi plan for resettlement in Madagascar and substitution of the satanic "Final Solution."

What that meant the outside world was amazingly slow in discovering, but meanwhile Lindbergh's speech gave isolationism a black eye. The violence of the reaction was compounded partly of hypocrisy and embarrassment. America in 1941 was a distinctly anti-Semitic country, and as Socialist leader Norman Thomas pointed out, Lindbergh was "not as anti-Semitic as some who seize the opportunity to criticize him." The Jews had actually kept a low profile on the war. Contrary to Lindbergh's allegation, they were by no means prominent among the war hawks, for example, those in the Century Group. In fact, such clubs as the Century either excluded Jews entirely or, like Yale and the other Ivy-type colleges, had tight quotas for their admission. Speeches and editorials inveighing against Hitler's persecutions invariably brought in the Catholics and Protestants, not because anybody really thought they were coequal victims with the Jews, but because they were more respectable. In the gentleman's-agreement atmosphere of elitist anti-Semitism (rather notoriously present in the State Department), mention of the Jews' stake in the war was felt to be tasteless. At the same time, the newly galvanized prowar Left saw in Lindbergh's speech just what was to be anticipated from the opponents of the war. Anti-Semitism fitted right in and completed the pattern—America First was a fascist outfit, Lindbergh was a Hitler stooge, Colonel McCormick was a Nazi, and that explained why they acted the way they did.

Through September and into October, as the titanic battles raged in Russia, while the navy's destroyers convoyed British cargoes to Iceland and the negotiations between Washington and Tokyo continued behind a news curtain, tension mounted and the isolationist-interventionist debate, less argument than mutual polemic, raged. When another destroyer was damaged by a torpedo Roosevelt pulled out all stops (October 16), even though admitting the vessel was engaged in defending a British convoy:

America has been attacked. The U.S.S. Kearney is not just a Navy ship. She belongs to every man, woman, and child in this nation. . . .

Whatever in the world that meant.

Meantime Congress began debating virtually the final step in going to war, revision of the Neutrality Act to permit U.S. cargo ships to go to Britain, in other words, what Churchill had asked for in his letter of December 8, 1940.

Four days after Roosevelt's speech the *Wall Street Journal* published an article by the chief of its Washington bureau (Eugene Duffield, an old *Tribune* hand) under the stock head "The Week in Washington" and subtitled " 'Victory' Arms Plan Foreshadows America's Military, Personal, Financial History." The story began:

> During the past seven days the shadow of coming events fell across Washington with a clarity and unity which make the week remarkable.
>
> Sharpest and most revealing is the shadow cast by the "Victory Program," the newly evolved munitions schedule which Washington and London expect to beat Hitler. . . .
>
> The "Victory Program"—what it takes to lick Hitler—is understood here to be actually on paper. It embraces many predictions about which officials have been talking publicly for two or three weeks.

The story went on to detail figures on production—65 percent of the nation's economy to be devoted to war by 1943, tank production of 2,000 to 3,000 a month, production of 77,000 or 80,000 aircraft, doubling and tripling of ordnance and shipping production. Then it rambled off into what all this would do to the civilian sector of the economy, raw materials shortages, the danger of inflation, and the prospect of higher income taxes.

At last, in its fourteenth paragraph, the *Journal* story began getting to a point that should have waked up any reader who made it that far: Military opinion in Washington concluded that Russia could not hold out, and therefore the army to man the Victory Program's vast armaments had to come from the United States and Britain. The strength of the German army was put at "9 to 10 million," and an attacking army needed a 50-percent to 100-percent numerical advantage:

> An attacking army is contemplated. By its emphasis on tanks and ordnance, the "Victory Program" reveals that long-range bombing and ocean blockade no longer are counted on to subdue Germany.
>
> That Britain cannot raise more than a third of the necessary army is shown by parliamentary debates within the past two weeks. Raising of the rest of the force—an army far bigger than has been contemplated by anything but the "Victory Program"—may fall on the United States, taking one of every three men between the age of 18 and 45.

This extraordinary and ominous revelation, buried far down in a story that appeared on page four of a specialized though widely read national newspaper, apparently passed completely unnoticed, a silent news event, like the tree that crashes deep within the forest.

A few days later Roosevelt opened a press conference by announcing that he planned to tell Congress in January all about an enormous increase in the arms production program. Once more newsmen and editors failed to react. Evidently they were bemused by the vagueness of the announcement and by the fact that the arms program was already giant size; Roosevelt seemed to be merely promising more of the same. Nobody had the wit to perceive that the presidential statement confirmed the *Wall Street Journal*'s deduction.

Meantime Arthur Sears Henning reported (October 24) that the talks with Tokyo had broken down as a result of a too intransigent stand by Roosevelt. The thrust of the *Tribune* view of the negotiations was that Roosevelt, in trying to satisfy Churchill's pleas for help in defending the British Empire, might be committing the country to declaring war if the Japanese attacked Malaya or Singapore.

That the Japanese might begin the war themselves did not enter McCormick's head any more than it did anyone else's, for the good reason that such an act by Japan would be incredibly stupid. McCormick's assumption that if war came in the Pacific it would be by American decision, that is, by act of Congress, led him into an editorial expression much ridiculed later: "Japan cannot attack Hawaii. That is a physical impossibility."

The ridicule was unmerited. The phrase "attack Hawaii" meant carry out an assault landing, which, as Colonel McCormick had occasion to point out later, was what the army garrison stationed in Hawaii was there to guard against. Nobody thought Hawaii, or for that matter California, was immune to air raid and the *Tribune*'s appreciation of the value and limitation of air power, expressed in many editorials, was exceptionally sophisticated.

On December 2, under a column-one, page-one head, Henning reported that the renewed ambassadorial talks were bringing "no expectation . . . of a settlement of the questions at issue. . . ."

All signs indicate that whether there is to be war between the Anglo-American alliance and Japan is going to be determined not by the negotiations in Washington but by events in Indo-China and Thailand. . . .

The British are relying upon the United States to take the lead in halting further aggression by Japan. . . .

The editorial page took up this theme with an effective argument. Pointing out the "strangeness of this situation" in which the main parties to the

potential conflict, the British and Dutch, were leaving the burden of negoti-
ation entirely to the United States, which had little material interest at
stake, the *Tribune* commented that although Churchill had said that the
Atlantic Charter did not include the Pacific, nevertheless, "the only talking
point Mr. Roosevelt and Mr. Hull can have with the Japanese government
is derived from that charter."

> It should be apparent that Mr. Roosevelt's government is the only one which
> is talking in terms of international justice and is the only one declaring that
> Japan is morally wrong in its attacks upon other peoples. The [British and
> Dutch] imperial interests do not even give that doctrine lip service.

The *Tribune*'s conclusion was that while Britain and the Netherlands could
easily come to terms with Japan if Japan stopped threatening Malaya,
Singapore, and the Indies, "America is doing the talking and America may
find itself doing the fighting."

> We are facing the possibility that the American navy will come to grips with
> the Japanese in the far east and American bombers will be destroying the
> populous Japanese cities, whose flimsy construction would invite disaster. No
> doubt there are many people who would think this a just retaliation for the
> fury the Japanese have expended on China, but some undoubtedly will not
> regard it as the noblest work of American military power. . . .

Next day, December 3, a page-one head reported:

President Asks Japs to
Explain Massing Troops

Henning called Roosevelt's query to Tokyo about the troop concentration on the border of Thailand "a new and sensational turn" in the stale-
mated negotiations.

Meantime something more sensational than that was developing. Senator
Wheeler's Air Corps captain called Wheeler and advanced a startling offer.
Did Wheeler recall the Victory Program that he had mentioned in September? The captain could actually obtain for a brief time a copy of the
document itself. Would Wheeler be interested in seeing it? Wheeler, who
like so many others had missed the *Wall Street Journal* story, said he would.

That evening the captain brought to Wheeler's house on Joslyn Street
a huge book-size typescript wrapped in brown paper. According to the
captain, only five copies existed, and this one had to be returned to its
place in the War Department by morning. As Wheeler leafed through it
his "blood pressure rose. . . . The document undercut the repeated

statements of Roosevelt . . ." that aid to Britain would keep the United States out of the war.

He debated turning it over to the Senate Foreign Relations Committee, but figuring that the interventionists on the committee would succeed in burying it, he decided to take the other traditional course and leak it to the press. Wheeler's Senate leadership of the antiwar bloc had made the *Chicago Tribune* overlook his lifelong career as a prolabor liberal to give prominence to his combative speeches for America First. Wheeler telephoned Chesly Manly, who covered the Senate for the *Tribune*.

Together Manly and Wheeler set to work scanning the pages, and Manly, who saw in the document corroboration of his Atlantic Charter coverage, was soon typing out his lead:

A confidential report prepared by the joint army and navy high command by direction of President Roosevelt calls for American expeditionary forces aggregating 5,000,000 men for a full land offensive against Germany and her satellites. It contemplates total armed forces of 10,045,658.

One of the few existing copies of this astounding document, which represents decisions and commitments affecting the destinies of peoples thruout the civilized world, became available to The Tribune today.

It is a blueprint for total war on a scale unprecedented in at least two oceans and three continents, Europe, Africa and Asia.

The report expresses the considered opinion of the army and navy strategists that "Germany and her European satellites cannot be defeated by the European powers now fighting against her." Therefore, it concludes, "if our European enemies are to be defeated it will be necessary for the United States to enter the war, and to employ a part of its armed forces offensively in the eastern Atlantic and in Europe and Africa."

July 1, 1943, is fixed as the date for the beginning of the final supreme effort by American land forces to defeat the mighty German army in Europe.

In the meantime, however, increasingly active participation is prescribed for the United States, to consist of the gradual encirclement of Germany by the establishment of military bases, an American air offensive against Germany from bases in the British Isles and in the near east, and possible action by American expeditionary forces in Africa and the near east.

For the ultimate supreme effort the war prospectus calling for 10,045,658 in the armed forces would give the navy 1,100,000, including the naval air forces, and would place 150,000 in the marine corps, 6,745,658 in the army ground force, and 2,050,000 in the army air force.

The report states that the forces deemed necessary to defeat the potential enemies of the United States total five field armies, consisting of approximately 215 divisions (infantry, armored, motorized, air borne, mountain, and cavalry) and approximate supporting service elements.

The estimate that 5,000,000 will be sent overseas to European areas is contained in the section of the report that deals with shipping. . . .

Quoting directly from the document, Manly reported the authors' opinion that since the situation confronting the United States in 1943 could not be predicted, "We may require much larger forces" even than the estimates given. Little help was anticipated from allies; the Soviet Union was expected to be "militarily impotent" by July 1, 1942, whereas the new U.S. Army would not be ready until July 1, 1943.

In his memoirs Senator Wheeler states that he turned the Victory Program over to Manly on December 3. Walter Trohan, however, says that their meeting was earlier, and that the story was held up in Chicago. It seemed almost too hot to handle; Trohan himself opposed publication on the grounds that given Colonel McCormick's military background and rank "it did not behoove the *Tribune* to publish" it. But managing editor Pat Maloney had been searching for a major scoop to use on December 4, because that was the scheduled publication date for the first issue of Marshall Field's *Chicago Sun*. By accident or design, the *Trib*'s superscoop appeared on December 4. It had no effect on the *Sun*, which sold out its press run as first issues always do, but it had plenty of other effect. The 144-point banner read:

FDR'S WAR PLANS!

Two-column subheads proclaimed:

Goal Is 10 Million Armed
Men: Half to Fight in AEF

Proposes Land Drive by July 1, 1943, to Smash Nazis;
President Told of Equipment Shortage

The *Tribune*'s sister, or cousin, papers in New York and Washington were given the story, which Cissy's *Times-Herald* used but Joe Patterson's *Daily News,* for some reason, passed up till next day. In Washington the *Times-Herald* achieved dramatic impact, selling out instantly and practically stopping work in many government departments.

Correspondents thronged the White House, whence they were shunted to the War Department. There they were tersely informed that the leak was under investigation, which indeed it was—Chesly Manly was being hectored by the FBI and was stoutly maintaining the freedom of the press by refusing to divulge his sources. Senator Wheeler, whom nobody suspected of having a connection with the leak, promised to introduce a resolution calling for an investigation of the origins and meaning of the Victory Program.

Not till next day, December 5, did Secretary Stimson allow the press in, and then only to listen to him read a statement improbably claiming that the Victory Program was merely "unfinished studies of production requirements for national defense," and asserting that it was the army's duty to "investigate and study every conceivable type of emergency which may confront this country and every possible method of meeting the emergency." Stimson had the effrontery to demand rhetorically, "What do you think of the patriotism of a man or a newspaper that would take these confidential studies and make them public to the enemies of this country?" He then ended the conference, refusing to answer questions.

Despite freely tapping *Tribune* telephones (a Washington police lieutenant who checked Walter Trohan's lead box found four bugs—FBI, army intelligence, navy intelligence, and the Anti-Defamation League), the FBI never did find out where the leak came from. Its suspicions fixed on Lieutenant Colonel Albert C. Wedemeyer of the army's War Plans Division. Wedemeyer had done the actual drafting of the army's part of the plan and had custody of the original copy. Years later, as a famous (and controversial) general writing his memoirs Wedemeyer still denied the charge, but freely admitted that he had felt gratification at the exposé, which he said showed "that President Roosevelt's promises to keep us out of the war were only campaign oratory" (a phrase Wendell Willkie had made memorable by so characterizing for a Senate committee his own charges that Roosevelt was leading the country into war).

To this day the source of the leak remains shrouded. A recent tale that the whole thing was a plant by British intelligence is bereft of all verisimilitude; Stimson after the war admitted frankly that the Victory Program was "the chief work of the [General] Staff in fulfillment of its highest and most important duty." The probability that Hap Arnold was behind the leak is strengthened by internal evidence of the document. The section prepared by the army's air intelligence stated that it was unlikely that an invasion of German-occupied Europe could be undertaken within three years, and expressed the belief that "if an air offensive is successful, a land offensive may not be necessary." Out of enthusiasm or self-interest, General Arnold was joining the British in their airpower argument.

Behind the tight-lipped silence in the White House some fairly violent talk went on. Administrative assistant Ben Cohen told Ickes that McCormick could be indicted for conspiracy and suggested that "an outstanding Republican, whom no one could charge with having a New Deal taint, should be appointed as a special assistant to the Attorney General and given charge of the case." In the Cabinet meeting on December 4 Attorney

General Francis Biddle said that besides conspiracy, an indictment could be drawn under the Espionage Act of 1917. Ickes asked if McCormick was still a reserve officer and if he could be court-martialed. Stimson didn't know and Roosevelt asked him to look it up, though Stimson said that even if he was he could not be court-martialed. Roosevelt liked the Cohen-Ickes suggestion of a special prosecutor. In the end, though, Roosevelt recovered his cool and sensibly instructed press secretary Steve Early to kill rumors of prosecution by a statement that American newspapers were free and that "the right to print the news is unchallenged."

On December 5 the *Tribune* was filled with follow-up—

NATION STIRRED BY AEF PLAN

House in Uproar over FDR War`Aims;
Delays Debate on 8 Billion Arms Bill

Two stories from Washington were supplemented by a Larry Rue wire from London, where the press was ecstatic over the Victory Program. In Tokyo there was an intriguing press reaction that drew no particular attention. *Yomiuri* headlined (according to the AP), "United States Lack of Preparedness Exposed by American Paper . . . United States Wholly Unprepared for Military Operations." Somebody might reasonably have wondered why the Japanese were so interested in that angle of the story. In Berlin an official comment declared the plan for the invasion of Europe "fantastic," and expressed doubt that the world's shipping could carry 5,000,000 American soldiers to Europe. In the light of the shipment of the AEF of 1917–1918 that seemed like whistling in the dark, but again, no one noticed the indication of significant Axis concern.

At home the prowar press reacted in mortified concert with the White House, playing the revelation way down. The *New York Times* used a one-column head above the fold on page one (December 5) to give its readers an elliptical view more suited to the *Wall Street Journal:*

PUT VICTORY COST AT 120 BILLIONS

Under the by-line of James Reston, the story, without ever mentioning the *Chicago Tribune,* blandly credited "a report scheduled to be sent to President Roosevelt within the next few days" with the estimate in the head. On the jump (page 19) Reston reported that Roosevelt and Churchill had agreed at the Atlantic Charter meeting that an expeditionary force would have to be equipped to fight on the European continent, but making no mention of the Victory Program's conclusion that Britain could not defeat

Hitler alone and that a United States army of 10 million was needed, Reston left *Times* readers with the impression that the United States might merely equip a British army to invade Europe. The very different truth was, the substance of the Victory Program had been transmitted to the British six weeks after the Atlantic Charter meeting, as a resoundingly negative commentary on Britain's air war strategy. (The *Times* was not counting on the Russians either; an editorial of December 3 again referred to the invasion of the Soviet Union as a "breathing spell" for Britain.)

The Hearst papers and some others aggressively pursued the *Tribune*'s exposé, but even the neutrally inclined press was a little bemused by what seemed an altogether too shocking discrepancy between Roosevelt's public pronouncements and his evident real plans. The Scripps-Howard *New York World-Telegram* published the day-old story, but editorialized that "the public should and will withhold judgment" on a charge that the President had "repeatedly disavowed," that is, an expeditionary force to Europe. (The *World-Telegram* editors were also among those who did not read the *Wall Street Journal.*)

A lengthy *Tribune* editorial that day recalled that the paper's many earlier predictions of offensive warfare had been denounced by government spokesmen as lies, and repeated Colonel McCormick's estimate of a million dead American soldiers.

Next day, December 6, Chesly Manly did a follow-up on Stimson's tardy response, while the editorial page ridiculed the claim that the Victory Program was a mere routine contingency plan.

The prowar press continued to downplay the *Tribune*'s revelation (though the *New York Times* gave page-three space to "Stimson Assails Telling War Plan," which must have mystified its readers). It was aided by the mounting Washington-Tokyo crisis, which it may have emphasized by way of muting the Victory Program revelation. The *Tribune*'s preoccupation with its scoop, on the other hand, may have led it to neglect the Far East danger, which momentarily vanished from its page one. On December 7 the top banner reported the navy's seizure of Finnish ships in U.S. ports, with an italic streamer below, "FDR Sends Note to Mikado as Japs Move Toward Thailand." On the editorial page, under the headline THE STINGING TRUTH, the paper took up the big story again, comparing it to the 1919 scoop on the Versailles treaty and stating with satisfaction that this time the scoop "has not come too late."

On that point it was mistaken.

The shock of Pearl Harbor—as incredible to readers of the prowar as the antiwar press—abruptly deflated the Victory Program. Isolationists of all stations and persuasions whipped off their coats and roared for a fight to the finish. The *Tribune* began its lead editorial on page one, under a boxed head, WE ALL HAVE ONLY ONE TASK:

> War has been forced on America by an insane clique of Japanese militarists. . . .
> . . . The thing that we all feared, that so many of us have worked with all our hearts to avert, has happened. That is all that counts. It has happened. America faces war thru no volition of any American.
> Recriminations are useless and we doubt that they will be indulged in. Certainly not by us. . . . All of us, from this day forth, have only one task. That is to strike with all our might to protect and preserve the American freedom that we all hold dear.

Next day another editorial beginning on page one, "Japan's Perfidy Unites the American People," joined Roosevelt in saying unkind things about the sportsmanship of Pearl Harbor, and a second unbylined but very McCormick-style piece on the editorial page recalled other American wars that had started with defeats and ended in triumphs. Still another front-pager next day (December 9) urged young men to join the armed forces. Suitable cartoons reinforced the calls for national unity, determination, and all-out effort, while on the editorial page masthead Stephen Decatur's toast reappeared.

On the subject of the Pearl Harbor battle, the *Tribune* was (for the moment) surprisingly calm, even though McCormick had sent his Washington bureau a message on December 8: "The Japanese attack couldn't have taken place if the Hawaiian commanders had been alerted. Why weren't they?" An editorial noted that information already revealed showed that losses were far heavier than they would have been if the defense had been adequately alerted, but nonetheless expressed the conviction that the main lesson was the superiority of airplanes over battleships (a familiar *Tribune* theme):

> . . . When all that can be said on this point has been said it will still be true that the outstanding lesson of the disaster for us is the fact that the battleship is obsolete and that the men in charge of the navy didn't know it.

As for the British role in getting America into the war, it was forgiven in a page-one Orr cartoon on December 12 showing Uncle Sam telling John Bull, as the figure of World War II arose from the grave of World War I, "This time, John, we must bury the monster deeper!" A story inside told of Colonel McCormick interrupting the program at the *Tribune*'s annual advertising convention at the Palmer House to announce a piece of news and propose a toast: "To the gallant young aviator who sank a Japanese battleship today."

Yet if the *Tribune* was willing to forget the Victory Program, its enemies were not. To the prowar party, once the initial shock was over, Pearl Harbor came as vindication of all the dire warnings they had hardly believed themselves. Hitler had not actually invaded Texas by way of Brazil, but to the all-out hawks that seemed a technicality. The claim that the Axis represented a threat to America seemed to have been resoundingly demonstrated.

For three days an acute interventionist embarrassment, the Victory Program suddenly needed no apology, and when Hitler, declaring war on the United States on December 11, cited it, the McCormick-Patterson papers were converted into Axis Fifth Columnists. Joe Patterson called at the White House to make peace and Roosevelt, triumphantly censorious, first kept him standing for five minutes while he signed papers, then gave him a lecture on the *Daily News*'s conduct during 1941, which he said had slowed "the effort" by sixty to ninety days (without, as Patterson ruefully observed, specifying whether he meant war preparation or getting into the war).

A long generation later, the interventionists' logic seems to gallop off in all directions. Something Colonel McCormick did not himself notice in his immediate emotional response to Pearl Harbor was that the mere form in which the war with Japan came said nothing about what had caused it, let alone about Hitler's joining in. (This truth eventually dawned on him and the *Tribune* earned fresh opprobrium by referring to December 7 as the moment when "our undeclared war became a reality.") If one focused simply on Pearl Harbor and asked oneself the question, had America pursued the policies advocated by Colonel McCormick, would Pearl Harbor have happened, one would have to conclude that the answer was no. Logic would have dictated that answer at the time, and postwar knowledge of the struggle inside the Tokyo government confirms it.

Even more interesting is the reaction to Hitler's citation of the Victory Program. Without its publication, would Hitler not have gone to war? Nobody thought that even at the time. The accusation against McCormick and the *Tribune* was not that they had helped bring Hitler's declaration of war, but that they had made it possible for him to offer an extra excuse, something he hardly needed.

But the main thing Pearl Harbor and Hitler's speech did to the Victory Program was to give it a sort of backward psychological justification. If Hitler was getting ready to go to war with America, then there was nothing wrong with working up a plan for fighting him.

That, however, ignored completely the reason Hitler was declaring war, though everybody on both sides of the controversy knew perfectly well why he was doing it—because America's aid to Britain had gone entirely beyond neutrality into open belligerence, and far from being masked by pretensions of neutrality, was accompanied by a ceaseless barrage of verbal bellicosity by Roosevelt, his advisers, and the prowar press. America had committed warlike acts reinforced by threats and promises to do worse, soon.

In short, there was no way the events of December 7–11 could be used to demonstrate that Colonel McCormick and the isolationists were wrong, and, narrowly viewed, could only be used to show that they were right. Neutrality would have prevented Pearl Harbor and averted Hitler's declaration.

No one offered this observation at the time, and had anyone done so, the interventionist answer would have been that the Axis attack would have come sooner or later anyway. That brings up two real questions about December 7–11. Could America have pursued a policy that would have resulted in decisive aid to the Allies without active American participation? And, if America had to get into the war, was December 7–11 the optimum moment for it?

The first question is hardly answerable without some kind of computer-simulation-game study, but it at least seems possible that the answer could be yes. The second, though, is the interesting one.

General Marshall had predicated his Victory Program on the assumption of America and Britain fighting Germany and Japan without other allies of importance. Unlike Churchill (and Hap Arnold), he did not believe air power could do the job, and so postulated a 215-division American army, nearly all earmarked for Europe, with an unspoken but inescapable implication of immense casualties.

The actual American expeditionary force that Eisenhower led into Europe two and a half years later numbered at its peak sixty divisions. That represented a major American military effort, and in nine months fighting plenty of casualties were taken. Yet the difference between Marshall's estimate and the actuality resulted in not only enormous savings in American lives, but also in a far greater assurance of victory.

The difference, of course, was made by the continued participation of the Soviet Union in the war. Therein lay the supreme irony of the juxtaposition of the *Tribune*'s December 4 exposé and the events of December 7–11. The furious but indecisive fighting on the eastern front had been gradually moved off the front pages by the crises in both oceans. In the *Tribune*, the Victory Program scoop contributed to pushing the Russians inside even before Pearl Harbor shoved them still farther back. A reader of the December 9 issue therefore had to go through sixteen pages of coverage of the Pacific war before coming to the one-column head:

Moscow Beyond
Reach This Year,
Germans Admit

Two days later, a column head on page ten announced:

Germans Routed
Before Moscow,
Russians Claim

Suppose those heads had announced not the German retreat from Moscow but the fall of the city and the collapse of the Red Army? How would the Victory Program have sounded to Americans as the realization dawned that they were going to have to assume the main burden of bloodshed in a very large war?

Roosevelt, Stimson, Knox, Marshall, and the interventionist press were saved from the consequences of their policy by a Soviet victory they had discounted throughout the summer and fall.

On the other hand, American neutrality would hardly have solved the problem of Hitler loose in the world. McCormick, Lindbergh, and the isolationists were also rescued, perhaps even more ironically, by the rascally Reds.

CHAPTER NINETEEN

Colonel McCormick Becomes Hated but Happy

IN late March 1942, a meeting of the Overseas Writers Association at the Willard Hotel in Washington, attended by several top government officials, heard a number of speakers, including three former correspondents of the *Chicago Tribune,* talk about Colonel McCormick and his Patterson cousins in language that astonishes today:

> Roosevelt advisors . . . applauded lustily such declarations as: The American Senate must be taught the facts of life. . . . The important thing is to put an end (to criticism of the Roosevelt Administration) by whatever means may be necessary—be as ruthless as the enemy. . . . Get him on his income tax or the Mann Act. . . . Hang him, shoot him or lock him up in a concentration camp.

The report of the meeting is from John O'Donnell's column in the *New York Daily News* (March 30, 1942). George Seldes, one of the ex-*Trib* correspondents who spoke, found fault with O'Donnell's reporting, asserting that his parenthetical interpolation did not fairly represent what the correspondents meant, that they were thinking not of mere criticism of the Roosevelt administration but of "treason, sabotage, etc." But Seldes not only otherwise confirmed the story in detail, but made a point of the fact that the men designated for hanging, shooting, or concentration camp were Colonel McCormick and Captain Patterson. The attack, Seldes said, was made, not because of the two publishers' opposition to intervention before Pearl Harbor, but because since Pearl Harbor the two had continued to publish "news, editorials, and cartoons which must please Hitler." Furthermore, the correspondents meant what they said. William L. Shirer, who was apparently one of the three (the third was probably Edmond Taylor), visited Attorney-General Francis Biddle shortly after and urged him to find grounds for indicting McCormick, Patterson, and Hearst. Biddle was cordial to the proposal, but pointed to the legal difficulty.

One's first thought might be that the disaffected correspondents had personal grievances against Colonel McCormick, but such was not the case. Their eagerness to see Colonel McCormick (and Patterson, for whom none

COL. McCORMICK, HATED BUT HAPPY

of them had worked) shot or hanged stemmed entirely from their senti- ments about the war.

Then the news, editorials, and cartoons that would have pleased Hitler must have been treasonable, or at least vicious? Not as one scans them thirty-seven years later. In the months between Pearl Harbor and the corre- spondents' oratory at the Willard, the *Tribune*'s editorial strictures on the government were mild. The truth was, the correspondents and their audi- ence were carried away by an ardor for the Allied cause that brooked no cavil or appearance of cavil. They would have been indignant at the accusa- tion, but nevertheless they were guilty of what John McCutcheon had feared a return to in his cartoon, the martial enthusiasm of 1917 that they themselves had often referred to as "war hysteria." A week earlier the Republican superhawk *New York Herald Tribune* had accused the *Chicago Tribune* of "blanketing great areas of the middle west with every sort of suspicion of the government." The *Tribune* had tartly rejoined that its circulation area was "in the forefront in enlistments, in subscriptions to government loans, and in every other significant aspect of the war effort— the place the middle west has always held in times of national danger," but in New York and many other places the *Chicago Tribune* was honestly believed to be pro-Axis.

Only a few months earlier Seldes himself had been denying *PM*'s accusa- tion that his own isolationism made him a Communist. Now he wanted to hang Colonel McCormick as a Nazi. The very breadth of the new prowar frontage—antifascists, anglophiles, old-fashioned U.S. patriots—seemed to contribute to the emotional zest on behalf of the "war effort." Seldes' characterization of journalistic treason as printing something that would "please Hitler" caught the mood. Substitute "the kaiser" and the whole episode could have occurred in World War I. The fact that, historically speaking, Hitler and the kaiser are not really to be confused is irrelevant; contemporary perception of the two was very similar and the emotional reaction identical.

Congressman Elmer Holland (D.-Pa.) called Cissy and Joe Patterson "America's No. 1 and No. 2 exponents of the Nazi propaganda line . . . doing their best to bring about a fascist victory, hoping that in the victory they were to be rewarded." Patterson for the first and only time signed an editorial, titled "You're a Liar, Congressman Holland." Archibald Mac- Leish, who as Roosevelt-appointed Librarian of Congress was known as "the poet laureate of the New Deal," told the ANPA that some of its members were guilty of treason (though he had the same difficulty as Stimson with the Victory Program, calling it "a secret document of vital importance" but turning on a dime to re-label it "one of several tentative war plans"). Fatherly, tolerant William Allen White only regretted that

MacLeish had failed to name names, "Coughlin, McCormick, Patterson, Pelley, et al.," thus bracketing McCormick and Patterson with semifascist Coughlin and outright fascist William Dudley Pelley, leader of the Nazi-emulating Silver Shirts.

At such childish games two could naturally play, and Colonel McCormick, not one to back away from a fight, promptly labeled Glencoe-born MacLeish a Communist (he was only a slight fellow traveler). William Gropper, a real Communist and a cartoon genius, did a drawing whose powerful simplicity made Carey Orr look like an amateur. Gropper depicted a Hitler with four snake's-tongues: Hearst, McCormick, Patterson, and Roy Howard. In his book *Facts and Fascism,* Seldes called the four men "native Fascists," explaining, "Hitler, Mussolini, Hirohito represent the enemies we have to fight with guns; Hearst, Howard, McCormick and Patterson represent the enemy within."

The only specific charge against the four publishers was their publication of the Victory Program, though the critics continued to have trouble in satisfactorily framing their criticism. Seldes asserted that McCormick's military background permitted him to "know better than any layman that the publication of the secret war plans of any nation is right next to treason, if not treason itself. . . . Colonel McCormick, however, was too interested in fighting the New Deal and working with fascist appeasers to care whether or not he betrayed his country." Seldes then repeated Stimson's and MacLeish's acrobatics, somersaulting to, "He published one of the many war plans which his country had made to protect itself."

The truth was, McCormick was absolutely sincere in backing the war, just as he had been when he switched over in 1917. Then he had given the navy a boat; now he gave the army his private plane. He wanted to go all out, fight to the finish, knock off Hitler, Mussolini, and Tojo, exactly like everybody else. His criticisms of defense planning and production could be read as constructive, or picky, or merely boring, but they could by no stretch be construed as treasonable. It may be that without the Victory Program exposé, his isolationism would have been forgiven. The story, obliterated from discussion by Pearl Harbor, remained a sort of hidden wound, even while its major premise, the American Expeditionary Force of 215 divisions, was slowly receiving a drastic revision from the battlefield victories of the Red Army and the lobbying victories of Hap Arnold's Air Corps.

The tactical aspect of Pearl Harbor also soon contributed to exacerbation. That the Japanese did the attacking suited everybody, interventionists and isolationists, but the startling success of the attack inevitably created new friction, despite the *Tribune*'s early editorial restraint. Colonel Knox admitted the loss of only one battleship, the *Arizona,* while Walter Trohan told

Tribune readers that, according to "unimpeachable sources," six had gone down. They were both right. Six went down, but since Pearl Harbor is shallow, five could be raised (and were, four rejoining the fleet, making the Japanese Navy's own claim of two destroyed and four severely damaged an exceptionally good assessment). That explanation of the discrepancy in accounts (Trohan was not the only correspondent to get word from "unimpeachable sources") was lost in the welter of claims, charges, defenses, and countercharges over the adequacy of the warning given by Washington to Admiral Kimmel and General Short. The whole controversy should have been left to the military, but in the context of Roosevelt's skillfully dishonest maneuverings in the Atlantic war it was not really surprising that the suspicion rose of something sinister behind the Pacific disaster, a suspicion that in turn fueled furious rebuttal on the part of Roosevelt's defenders.

In the charged atmosphere, strange, painful, and comic incidents abounded. Colonel McCormick, frustrated at being called a traitor instead of being thanked for everything he thought he had done for the country, wrote (February 1942) the letter to Jacob Sawyer that the *Chicago Daily News* published with such glee:

Dear Mr. Sawyer:

Thank you for your very temperate letter.

What the most powerful propaganda organization in the world has misled you into believing was a campaign of hatred, has really been a constructive campaign without which this country would be lost.

You do not know it, but the fact is that I introduced the R.O.T.C. into the schools; that I introduced machine guns into the army; that I introduced mechanization; that I introduced automatic rifles; that I was the first ground officer to go up in the air and observe artillery fire. Now I have succeeded in making that the regular practice in the army. I was the first to advocate an alliance with Canada. I forced the acquiring of the bases in the Atlantic Ocean.

On the other hand, I was unsuccessful in obtaining the fortification of Guam; in preventing the division of the navy into two oceans. I was unable to persuade the navy and the administration that airplanes could destroy battleships. I did get the marines out of Shanghai, but was unsuccessful in trying to get the army out of the Philippines.

Campaigns such as I have carried on inevitably meet resistance, and great persistence is necessary to achieve results. The opposition resorts to such tactics as charging me with hatred and so forth, but in view of the accomplishment, I can bear up under it.

Yours sincerely,

Robert R. McCormick

The Colonel's regal style—"I introduced," "I was the first," "I have succeeded," and so forth—gave the letter a pomposity that malice readily interpreted as megalomania. That he was under some stress when he dictated it is suggested by an odd slip—far from having advocated the fortification of Guam, the *Tribune* had sensibly opposed it as a useless provocation to Japan. The whole or partial validity of several of the claims passed unnoticed as forthwith on the *News* editorial page appeared "Colonel McCosmic," drawn by cartoonist Cecil Jensen. From a perch astride a horse borne in the rear of a truck (reminiscent of the horse-van tale) the new cartoon hero, a bland caricature of McCormick, announced, "I was the first to mechanize the cavalry." Administering a vigorous kick in the seat of the pants to Uncle Sam, McCosmic asserted, "A powerful man like you can be of considerable assistance to me in winning the war." Seated behind Grant on an equestrian statue, McCosmic observed, "You know, General, I like bad news because it shows up bungling." Extending a glove on the end of a pole, he explained, "After mature consideration I am reluctantly extending the hand of friendship to my brave ally, Josef Stalin." The concept of Colonel McCosmic may have owed something to "Colonel Blimp," the inspiration of talented British cartoonist David Low.

Joe and Cissy Patterson shared the abuse. A *New Yorker* profile of Patterson outrageously garbled an incident from his childhood—he was depicted as "wringing the neck of a canary whose trilling he resented." Cissy wrote publisher Harold Ross an emotional letter—what she had told the interviewer was that the bird had died a natural death and Joe had held it in his hand and wept. Patterson wrote Ross to please not publish Cissy's letter—he was embarrassed enough already—and Ross wrote him back a fairly half-witted note saying, "The general theory here [meaning apparently within the office of *The New Yorker*] is that all small boys go through a period of killing things."

Next McCormick again went off half-cocked, with a salvo aimed at Marshall Field. The provocation was the Ralph Ingersoll case. Ingersoll, the founder of *PM,* had sought a draft deferment under a provision that exempted persons indispensable to certain industries, including communications. Other New York editors took advantage of the clause without stirring a furor, and Ingersoll was forty-one years old, but because *PM* was liberal as well as prowar, he was treated to the national spotlight. The *Chicago Tribune* was only one of a national chorus of critics, but when Ingersoll enlisted as a private, McCormick's reaction startled Chicago:

> Ralph Ingersoll, editor of PM, has been shamed into entering the army as a volunteer after his draft board refused to grant him a deferment requested by his boss. It remains to be seen whether Ingersoll's friends in Washington will

obtain a commission and a nice safe berth for him. Whatever his value as an editor, and it isn't much, he has had a real value to his owner. The publicity given to Ingersoll as a draft dodger has detracted attention from Marshall Field as a slacker. Field is of an age to volunteer. He cried for war before it came. Now that it has come, he lets men like MacNider and O'Hare do the fighting while he skulks in his clubs. . . . No one would suggest that he is indispensable to PM or to anything else. The term to fit to him and to all the herd of hysterical effeminates is coward.

McCormick had totally forgotten, and nobody apparently had the alertness to remind him, that Field had served with distinction in World War I, the *Tribune* of 1918 commending in text and pictures his battlefield rise from private to captain. (Ingersoll topped that, going from private to colonel.) One might wonder how come the Colonel himself now failed to volunteer, even at sixty-plus. The truth was, he would have loved to, and his frustration at not being invited may have contributed to the editorial. When an exchange of messages with MacArthur misled him into thinking he at last had an invitation, his editors had to restrain him, in Walter Trohan's words, from "getting his uniform out of moth balls."

Field, who must have been astonished at the attack on him, permitted his editors only a very terse rejoinder. Under the title "Editorial of the Day," the *Chicago Sun* said simply: "You are getting rattled, Colonel McCormick."

He was, and he had no excuse, but he did have some reason. Besides the rain of brickbats in Chicago and elsewhere (the *Wilmington* [Del.] *Star* ran a full-page ad on March 16, 1942, saying he should be either "interned or interred," which adless *PM* solemnly reprinted as an editorial feature "because we think it's something to think about"), he had for the past year drawn an extraordinary attention from the Roosevelt administration. Strangely enough, the *Chicago Tribune* was one of the half dozen papers FDR read daily ("He wanted to know the worst being said about him," was Robert Sherwood's explanation). FDR had taken a personal interest in Marshall Field's project, the *Sun,* had passed along encouragement, and had undertaken to do more. Field found himself in the position of Hearst in World War I. He needed an Associated Press franchise but could not get one because the AP granted monopoly service to the first comer. Later arrivals could only join the club by getting a waiver from a competitor, not easy to do, or by buying a paper that already had the franchise (which Joe Patterson had done in New York).

Roosevelt, according to Kent Cooper, head of AP, called in Attorney General Biddle (another Groton alumnus) and told him: "We have a friend in Chicago for whom we must get the AP service. We have also got an enemy of the New Deal in Chicago who has the AP service and won't let our friend have it. Is the law such that we can make the Associated Press serve our friend?" Biddle (who did not deny the story in his own subsequent memoirs) checked it out with his assistant, Thurman Arnold, who was making a career of trust-busting as a prelude to a career as a Washington-based corporation lawyer.

Arnold found himself in the middle of a funny coincidence. The AP's franchise system had long been under attack on antitrust grounds, and recently a major Washington publisher had been hectoring Arnold about it. The publisher was Cissy Patterson, whose *Times-Herald,* acquired from Hearst, was denied AP service by its morning rival the *Post.* Cissy, who had gone along with brother Joe rather than cousin Bertie in the 1936 and 1940 elections, had good friends inside the New Deal, notably, of all people, Harold Ickes, but her defection over lend-lease had cooled the relationship and left her AP complaint dangling. In 1941 Arnold and Biddle, after doing nothing for Cissy, turned on the heat for Marshall Field, the more zestfully since it was against Colonel McCormick. FBI men fanned out over the country to ask publishers how they stood on the *Sun*'s AP application. Some of McCormick's fellow wheels in the AP asked him if he wouldn't let Field have the franchise to avoid a Justice Department suit that was likely to end the whole clubby system. McCormick told them he would be glad to, provided they did the same and invited their own competitors to share their franchises.

Kent Cooper remembered that McCormick had once told him that he did not like the fact that the *Tribune* was the only morning paper in Chicago and would prefer having a competitor. Cooper reminded the Colonel and asked him why he did not waive his franchise right. McCormick's reply, according to Cooper:

> I would have been glad to have waived had Field asked me. He never did. Instead, the President of the United States intervened with the power of his office to bring it about. Yet the grandson of a man who was an ardent supporter of my grandfather's *Chicago Tribune* in its early days could have had an AP membership if he had asked me to propose it.

Why had Field not asked him? McCormick's guess was that Field was afraid he might offend Roosevelt by seeking a favor from one of his chief critics. McCormick added that Field had never even told him his intention of starting a new paper, though he had been at Field's house for cocktails only a few days before the public announcement.

There is some verisimilitude in the Colonel's account. Field, like McCormick, was a shy man. His *Sun* staffers smiled behind his back at his jolly

British accolade, "Oh, well done, you!" He may have found McCormick's personality forbidding, and may too have felt embarrassed by his role as a sort of amateur intruder in Chicago journalism. It does seem at least odd that he made no attempt to get McCormick's consent to a franchise before appealing to the government.

The AP case reached court the following year (1943) and ended with a Supreme Court decision in June 1945 that canceled the franchise system, a result that had hardly any effect apart from the local Chicago and Washington situations.

But a year before the AP case came to trial the Colonel and his *Tribune* plunged themselves into water a hundred degrees hotter. Frank Knox had surprised some of his old newspaper colleagues by demanding a "voluntary censorship" from the press—"an unprecedented request," in Oswald Garrison Villard's words, "and one that should never have been listened to short of an act of Congress." The post-Pearl Harbor atmosphere stifled nearly all such objections, but not quite all, and a very few publications, notably the *Chicago Tribune,* refused to be bound.

Since despite its refusal the *Tribune*'s correspondents followed the rules, the question seemed academic. Then on June 7, 1942, the *Tribune* came up with another scoop, one much less sensational to the public than Chesly Manly's, but of an interest to the U.S. Navy that Colonel McCormick hardly dreamed of.

The two-line banner on June 7, 1942, trumpeting the U.S. Navy's great victory in the Battle of Midway (June 3–5) led into an AP story from Pearl Harbor stating that "13 to 15 warships and transports of the repulsed Japanese invasion fleet" had been sunk or damaged, with "two, and possibly three, aircraft carriers" sunk.

"Adm. Nimitz's Own Story" was played in boldface, oversize type across two columns. Next to it was a one-column head:

Navy Had Word Of Jap Plan
To Strike at Sea

Knew Dutch Harbor Was a Feint

The story carried no by-line but a Washington dateline, and began:

The strength of the Japanese forces with which the American navy is battling somewhere west of Midway Island . . . was well known in American naval circles several days before the battle began, reliable sources in the naval intelligence disclosed here tonight. . . .

The advance information enabled the American navy to make full use of air attacks on the approaching Japanese ships, turning the struggle into an air battle along the modern lines of naval warfare so often predicted in Tribune editorials. . . .

Describing the Japanese fleet as divided into three parts, a striking force, a support force, and an occupation force, the story proceeded to give astonishing details of the makeup of all three. The striking force was credited with four aircraft carriers, "the Akaga and Kaga of 26,900 tons each, and the Hiryu and Soryu of 10,000 tons each; 2 battleships of the Kirishima class . . . 2 cruisers of the Tone class . . . 12 destroyers," and so on through the support and occupation forces.

No other newspaper had anything like such identification of the enemy fleet units, for the good reason that the navy had given out no such information.

June 7 was a Sunday. The Navy Department's reaction to reading the Tribune's story (in the Washington Times-Herald) was vividly recorded for the Naval Institute's oral history division by a staff officer named Arthur H. McCollum:

> I came down to the Navy Department . . . and my goodness, the place was shaking.

The identification of the Japanese ships in the story, amazing in itself, had an absolutely sinister look in navy eyes, because the information was closely parallel to a secret dispatch of Admiral Nimitz, sent May 31, on the eve of the Midway battle (CINC PACIFIC FLEET ESTIMATE MIDWAY FORCE ORGANIZATION X STRIKING FORCE 4 CARRIERS (AKAGI KAGA HIRYU SORYU) 2 KIRISHIMAS 2 TONE CLASS CRUISERS 12 DESTROYERS SCREEN, etc.). Nimitz's message, to his Pacific commanders, was based on intelligence gained through a sensational triumph of cryptographical warfare, the breaking of the Japanese naval code. The fact of the code breaking was a top secret that the Tribune's story seemed to the navy to give away—"The strength of the Japanese forces . . . was well known in American naval circles," etc.

The dateline implied that the leak had sprung in Washington, and McCollum briefly found himself under suspicion because he happened to have in his desk a "bootlegged" copy of Nimitz's dispatch. Seeking to explain, he took the dispatch and a clipping of the story to show another superior, Admiral Wilkinson. Wilkinson

> grabbed the secret dispatch out of my hand and the newspaper clipping out of the other and he went charging down the hall toward [navy commander-in-chief] Admiral King's office with me behind him hollering "Wait, wait, wait,

don't take that down." He paid no damned attention—he was a little deaf anyway. He went charging through the outer office, into King's office, and Carl Holden, who was King's communication officer—I got into the office just in time to hear Carl Holden say, "Well, they can't point the finger at me. There are only five copies of that dispatch in existence [in Washington], and I've got all five of them." Well, here was Wilkinson going in there with Number Six.

The first word the *Tribune* got of trouble was mild—a notification that Sunday to Arthur Sears Henning that the paper was being cited for censorship violation. Henning may have been taken by surprise, because despite the Washington dateline, the story had actually been written in Chicago. Its author, as the *Tribune* readily disclosed, was Stanley Johnston, an outstanding correspondent just returned from the Pacific with a great eyewitness account of the Battle of the Coral Sea (May 7–8, 1942). The only correspondent present, Johnston had distinguished himself by his heroism in helping rescue wounded men as the aircraft carrier *Lexington* sank under him. His recommendation for a Navy Cross was at this moment on Admiral King's desk.

Henning's explanation seemed to mollify the censor's office, which informed him that it was "adequate." But that evening Admiral King called a press conference to warn all Washington correspondents against even "inadvertently" giving "aid and comfort to the enemy," and mentioned that the morning's "leak" might involve "very serious consequences." He also rather baffled the newsmen by being at some pains to explain that the happy outcome at Midway was merely the result of routine navy preparation.

The navy would have been well advised to let the whole thing go at that, but the navy was no freer from war hysteria than anybody else. Colonel Knox was in a froth, along with his admirals, and when he took his complaint to the White House he drew immediate support. Roosevelt, Ickes, and the rest, still seething over the Victory Program exposé, saw a great chance to nail Colonel McCormick. Monday was spent in discussions, and on Tuesday (June 9) Knox signed a letter to Biddle formally calling on the attorney-general to take

immediate action . . . under the Espionage Act . . . against Mr. Stanley Johnston . . . Mr. J. L. Maloney and such other individuals as are implicated in the unauthorized publication of a newspaper article which appeared on June 7, 1942.

J. Loy (Pat) Maloney was the *Tribune*'s managing editor. In the absence of information, Colonel McCormick was for the time being merely included as "such other individuals," but everybody knew who the real target was.

At the Navy Department Admiral Cooke called McCormick "a god-damn traitor" and exulted that "the President is buying this thing and we're going to hang this guy higher than Haman."

The government's intentions toward McCormick were not long concealed from the world at large. Walter Winchell, father of the gossip column and radio's noisiest voice, declaimed over the national air that the hated *Chicago Tribune* had betrayed a military secret to the Axis. Other *Trib* enemies repeated the accusation until millions believed the paper had deliberately committed treason, though exactly how remained very unclear.

In Chicago Colonel McCormick was groping. He knew neither Stanley Johnston nor Pat Maloney would dream of compromising a navy secret for the mere gratification of a scoop. As the meaning of the case—the fact of code-breaking—spread among Washington newsmen, he became aware of the potential seriousness of the problem, and sent first Maloney and then Johnston to Washington to try to explain to the navy. Maloney did his best to argue that it had been possible to arrive innocently at the conclusion that the navy had had "advance information," citing a story in Colonel Knox's *Chicago Daily News* that could be interpreted as crediting the navy with foreknowledge of Japanese movements. The admirals refused to be convinced by that or by Stanley Johnston's claim that he had deduced the Japanese fleet makeup from *Jane's Fighting Ships* and the Coral Sea battle. By the time Johnston came to Washington the navy had figured out how he had gotten hold of Nimitz's dispatch (to nail down the fact that he had copied the dispatch, the admirals could point to some of his spellings of Japanese ship names, which corresponded to Nimitz but not to *Jane's*).

Along with other survivors of the *Lexington,* Johnston had been brought to San Diego after the Coral Sea battle by the navy transport *Barnett.* Not being a combat ship, the *Barnett* normally ignored most radio traffic, and decoded messages only when its own name was mentioned at the beginning. But the senior officer among the *Lexington* survivors, Commander Morton T. Seligman, had requested full message decoding for the information of himself and his fellow combat officers. Johnston, as it happened, had shared quarters aboard the *Barnett* with Seligman and two other officers.

From San Diego Johnston had proceeded to Chicago, where on the Saturday night the Midway story broke he was writing up his Coral Sea adventure in the *Tribune* newsroom. Reading the AP flash, he realized that he had a scoop on Midway, and promptly notified Pat Maloney. Since copying the Nimitz dispatch was a technical violation of the Espionage Act, they hit on the unlucky expedient of crediting navy intelligence and giving the story its Washington dateline.

After Maloney's and Johnston's visits to Washington nearly a month went by with nothing happening. Then suddenly on August 7 Biddle announced that a grand jury would be convened in Chicago to investigate a story the *Chicago Tribune* had printed on June 7. The government's case would be handled by William D. Mitchell, a Wall Street lawyer who had been Hoover's attorney-general, Biddle and Roosevelt having adopted the suggestion Ickes and Ben Cohen made at the time of the Victory Program story of hiring a Republican to prosecute a Republican. Mitchell spent a fortnight studying the case and put his finger on the crux: Was the navy really willing to tell the grand jury about the code-breaking? If it was, the navy's secret would be out; if it wasn't, the grand jury would refuse to indict, because there would be no demonstrable injury to national security. Biddle checked back with Knox, and Knox assured him the navy backed Mitchell all the way, code-breaking included.

At the *Tribune,* Colonel McCormick could hardly fail to see in the investigation the enmity of the Roosevelt administration, though not over-looking that of Colonel Knox. The announcement from Washington was presented in an AP story that was coupled on the right side of page one with the beginning of a very long unsigned piece, half article, half editorial, giving the background of the case from the *Tribune*'s point of view:

> That Washington would attack the *Tribune* and other newspapers which
> have demanded an all-out war effort and the removal of high officials who
> have been fumbling the ball . . . came as no surprise.

Besides denouncing Colonel Knox as a vindictive and none-too-princi-pled competitor, the story revealed that agents of the FBI and naval intelli-gence had been "hounding" the *Tribune.* It explained about Stanley John-ston writing his story out of his vast knowledge of world naval affairs (he had even had an office neighboring that of the *Jane's* top editor in London) and his Coral Sea experience, and went so far as to admit that he had had some discussions with navy officers en route home.

On the lengthy turn it emphasized the patriotic credentials of Maloney (grandson of an Illinois pioneer, alumnus of Dartmouth and Columbia, a flyer in Eddie Rickenbacker's squadron in 1918) and Johnston (an Aus-tralian veteran of Gallipoli and France, a correspondent in the London blitz, and a freshly naturalized American citizen), and by way of biting comparison cited Attorney-General Biddle's war record: "According to *Who's Who* [he] served in the United States Army from Oct. 23 to Nov. 29, 1918."

To most readers of the *Tribune,* and of other papers reporting the grand jury investigation, the affair must have seemed highly mysterious. It got more mysterious as the jury conducted its hearing. The government, it turned out, had practically no case. Maloney and Johnston reiterated their version, Mitchell claimed Johnston must have copied Admiral Nimitz's dispatch, the jury could see no harm done, and the indictment was dismissed.

What had happened was that the navy had executed a 180-degree turn and steamed off, leaving Mitchell and Biddle high and dry and the *Tribune* and Colonel McCormick unscathed. Mitchell had been forced to go through the travesty of an investigation in the very circumstances he had warned everybody against. The *Tribune* front page chortled, and the public was more bewildered than ever.

Behind the navy's strange behavior lay unexpected fresh intelligence. The cryptographers reported that the Japanese code had remained unchanged, and still readily decipherable. The navy, which had assumed without stopping to think about it that the enemy was sure to learn about the code-breaking from a sidebar story in three newspapers, had suddenly found itself obligated to announce in plain English to the whole world the secret it had wanted to hang Colonel McCormick for disclosing.

Knox explained to Biddle, and Biddle explained to Mitchell, but the public never got any word at all. And to the navy's horror, the press, once alerted, wasn't easy to shut up. *Newsweek* announced that the navy's big secret had been bandied in Washington "pressrooms and cocktail bars" while still tantalizing its readers with the question of what the secret was. Samuel Thomason's *Chicago Times,* commenting on the jury verdict, let the cat out of the bag, and *Time,* as if to make sure no Japanese agent in the country missed it, quoted the fatal passage:

> If anyone in our naval intelligence had disclosed the makeup of the Japanese attacking force, which presumably our profound scholars in Washington cubbyholes had identified by deciphering the secret Japanese code, there would have been a violation of the Espionage Act. . . . Of course the Japs would immediately change their code and that would hinder our war effort and endanger our fighters until we cracked the new code.

A couple of days later (August 31) Representative Holland of Pennsylvania, the congressman who had slandered Joe and Cissy Patterson, spelled it all out even more unmistakably, though less accurately:

> It is public knowledge that the *Tribune* story . . . tipped off the Japanese high command that somehow our Navy had secured and broken the secret code of the Japanese Navy. . . . Three days after the *Tribune* story was published the Japs changed their code.

The congressman was crazy, but what was more incredible was that even after his statement Tokyo still did not change its code. Everybody in America knew the Japanese code was broken, and millions continued to blame the *Chicago Tribune* for spilling the secret (some still do), but in defiance of all credulity the Japanese never discovered it, or if they did, refused to believe it. The navy's secret continued to be of value throughout the war, among other things facilitating an aerial ambush that shot down Admiral Yamamoto.

Had the navy not defected, Mitchell would doubtless have gotten an indictment of Colonel McCormick along with Johnston and Maloney. How long everybody would have been happy with that outcome is not very certain. Indictment was one thing, a conviction would have been something else. The evident innocence with which the *Tribune* had acted would have become clear, and at least some of McCormick's fellow publishers would have come round to perceiving the freedom of the press issue, as they had in the case of the Canadian newsprint threat. Colonel McCormick in the bar as a latter-day Peter Zenger sounds a little fantastic, but it could have happened (if anyone doubted his willingness to go to jail for freedom of the press they didn't know him).

The day of the grand jury's dismissal of the case, a nice little drama was enacted in the *Trib* newsroom. The Colonel had been in daily attendance at the hearing, and when the finish came he varied his routine by stopping off at the fourth floor en route to his office. Typewriters stopped in mid-clack. "There was electricity in the air," recalled an editor. As the tall figure approached the city desk the tense staff broke into spontaneous applause.

The drama's phlegmatic hero could not conceal his emotion, and for a moment could not speak. Then he said, "I had no fear of this investigation. I had the utmost confidence in Pat Maloney and Stanley Johnston." He looked around him and added, "There never has been a bunch like the *Tribune* bunch. As I have told you before, every member of the *Tribune* is a member of my family."

Once more the *Tribune* promised to let bygones be bygones:

> We shall not seek reprisals or indulge in factional politics, but shall continue to devote ourselves to winning the war. So far as we are concerned the chapter is closed.

Once more its enemies were not ready for peace. Very few saw the conflict in the terms of Oswald Garrison Villard (who, high-principled as he was, may have been just a bit influenced by his own prewar isolationism). No admirer of the *Tribune,* Villard nevertheless thought that Colonel McCormick has been placed in the position of defending the rights and liberties of the American press. This will not be conceded by the many who are demanding, in the name of the Four Freedoms, that the *Chicago Tribune* be forthwith suppressed. . . .

If they couldn't suppress, they could still slander, and the collapse of the grand jury's frontal assault on the *Tribune* was followed by a furious renewal of guerrilla warfare.

In Washington a mean falsehood was circulated that Colonel McCormick had been a coward in World War I and that Arthur Schmon had covered up for him, while in New York fantastic tales were repeated of secret security devices his paranoia had elaborated for his Tower office. The *Chicago Sun* ran an ad that the *New York Times* and *Herald Tribune* turned down accusing McCormick of treason, and the Chicago chapter of the Union for Democratic Action published a grossly libelous seventy-two-page brochure claiming that "The Tribune Betrays Military Secrets" (the Victory Program and Midway), "Tribune Delights the Axis" (its skepticism of the *Greer* incident), "Tribune Adopts Home-Grown Fascists" (mainly Elizabeth Dilling, a witch-hunter whom McCormick briefly patronized but soon tired of), "The Tribune Endangers the Winning of the War and the Peace." Under the rubric "What Shall We Do?" the brochure recommended not buying the *Tribune* and instead buying its competitors, and encouraging "all justified legal steps" against anyone injuring the war effort.

The *Trib* naturally called the Union for Democratic Action Communist, an especially irritating counter-slander, since the UDA (forerunner of Americans for Democratic Action) took pride in its anti-Communism.

"The People vs. the Chicago Tribune" was a passing irritant, the *Chicago Sun* an enduring one. What bothered McCormick most about the *Sun* was the fact that Marshall Field was losing so much money (about twice as much as he had expected) without having it hurt, because of his 80 percent write-off. As a newspaper the *Sun* was, so far, a flop, partly because its efforts to hire people from the *Tribune* had failed, partly because it still lacked AP service, and partly because it could not get its hands on competitive comics and other features, but Field showed no inclination to quit. To the *Tribune*'s frequent biting allusions (and McCormick's comments in speeches and interviews) Field answered by pointing out that the *Trib* was not unacquainted with the art of tax write-offs, having taken them on the *New York Daily News*'s early days, on *Liberty*'s heavy losses, on WGN, and on the short-lived *Detroit Mirror*.

It was a measure of the editorial atmosphere that the *Sun* could express indignation over Radio Tokyo's picking up a *Tribune* editorial sharply criticizing the ineffectual defense of Burma by the Allies and calling for replacement of British Lord Mountbatten with American General Joseph W. Stilwell. If Tokyo liked it, the reasoning went, the editorial must be treason. To the liberal-internationalist war climate Colonel McCormick made no concession. The "States Across the Sea" editorial (April 25, 1943) that outraged anglophiles and internationalists sounded the characteristic *Tribune* tone: nationalist, superior, ironic, a Yankee Doodle crow.

Liberal instincts on the war were more rationally offended by the *Tribune*'s emphasis on the Pacific theater as against the European. The *Daily News*'s Jensen drew a busy Colonel McCosmic sending messages by phone, voice, and carrier pigeon in support of his strategy: "Admiral Nimitz, congratulations on successful execution of my orders. . . . General Marshall, stop worrying about Hitler. . . . Admiral King, press home the attack." On his opposition to the "second front" in Europe, rooted partly in a perception of America's interests and partly in his hostility to the Soviets, McCormick once more had a variety of bedfellows, including Norman Thomas, the *New York Times,* and the really effective one, Winston Churchill. Churchill's covert but powerful resistance did his image no harm, even on the American Left, while McCormick's open opposition, to which nobody in Washington paid any attention, brought renewed suspicions of Nazi sympathy. That charge got an embarrassing boost from Donald Day, who in 1944 had the harebrained idea of enlisting in the Finnish army, and later took up broadcasting for Radio Berlin. By that time the *Tribune* had publicly disowned its old Soviet expert.

Among all the fresh wounds dealt and received, McCormick found an opportunity to heal an old one, writing a friendly letter to Henry Ford, who was shifting gears from pacifist isolationism to building the world's longest four-motored bomber assembly line.

In the summer of 1944, after the second front, scaled to one fourth the size of the Victory Program, had finally been opened, Ralph McGill, the liberal editor of the *Atlanta Constitution,* took advantage of his presence in Chicago for the Democratic National Convention to meet Colonel McCormick. The result was a remarkable interview in which McGill did not disguise his sentiments of large, even historic apprehension, beginning by recalling the circumstances under which he had first heard of the *Chicago Tribune.* It was back in his childhood, on the front porch of a farmhouse in Tennessee, where an old country doctor read aloud, in deep anger, an article—perhaps a Joseph Medill editorial—on the crimes of the South. When he finished there was a silence, broken by the minister: "God have mercy on the *Chicago Tribune* for its sins!"

"In the years that followed," McGill wrote, "I have heard many persons mention the *Chicago Tribune,* but never another to ask God's mercy on it." Interestingly enough, in McGill's eyes, the *Tribune*'s anti-South posture had continued, though softened, up to the present—"or so it seems to the South."

Consequently, "to a Democrat from Atlanta, Georgia, and a believer in some form of postwar association of nations . . . [Colonel McCormick] is a fabulous and rather fearful character." About the Tribune Tower swirled "controversial clouds of fire . . . lightning flashes of hate and fear and the clashing of partisan swords." Colonel McCormick arrived for the interview. Surprise: "He is friendly, charming, quick with repartee."

The southern editor told the northern publisher about his feelings in respect to the *Tribune* and the South. McCormick made no denial. He explained his grandfather's hostility by the loss of two brothers in the Civil War—"the iron entered into his soul." McGill reflected reasonably that if such was the case with victorious Medill, it must have been doubly so for many defeated southerners.

As McCormick talked freely in answer to questions, McGill was struck by an odd insight: McCormick's Midwest patriotism sounded much like his own feelings about the South—the problem of absentee ownership of industry, the fact that communications and finance were so centered in New York. McGill in fact exaggerated this aspect of McCormick's views for the very reason that it echoed his own. McCormick was well aware that the highly industrialized and urban Midwest had no such dependence on New York as did the still agrarian South. Asked what he would do if he owned a newspaper in the South, he unhesitatingly replied that he would crusade against "all interests which kept the South in a position of economic peonage. . . . Don't worry about advertising," he told McGill. "Let the people see you fight and they will stay with your paper and the advertisers will stay with you, too, even though you may step on their toes."

On the "Negro problem," McGill found McCormick, "oddly enough," espousing the very viewpoint he held himself: "He would seek decent housing, equal educational facilities, equal pay for equal work, adequate health facilities, and he would denounce those demagogues who sought to inject the social equality issue into what, to him, should be a readily acceptable plan. Also, he would let them vote"—which in McGill's eyes was certainly going the whole route.

In fact, not only did McGill's Colonel McCormick turn out to be a perfectly decent fellow, but it was none too easy even to convict him of being a reactionary. Nevertheless, McGill had the courage and candor to question the slanted treatment the Democratic National Convention was receiving in the *Tribune,* and McCormick, with equal candor, admitted that, "yes, certainly, we do use every weapon we can find [in a fight]. My one rule is never to print anything obviously untrue. That is what I tell my editors."

That, reflected McGill, was "a good loose rule, and a convenient one."

In fact, it made "a good pair of journalistic brass knucks." In a word, frankly partisan political coverage was in McGill's eyes the one great defect of McCormick's *Tribune*. McGill would have been very surprised to learn of certain exceptions to the "every weapon" rule. The Colonel's Washington bureau wanted to do a story on Franklin D. Roosevelt's relationships with Lucy Rutherfurd and Missy LeHand, but Colonel McCormick turned down all such proposals, saying, "The *Tribune* doesn't fight that way." The tales were left to liberal Democratic writers of a later era.

Others continued to be less accepting than McGill. The prowar liberals were now wrapping FDR in the flag as "our commander-in-chief," to the irritation not only of old isolationists but of prowar conservatives. Had Willkie or Dewey been president during the war, the *Tribune* would doubtless have had plenty of criticizing to do, but probably would have outraged liberals somewhat less.

Tribune coverage of the military side of the war was extensive and of high quality. Large maps, with plenty of color, kept readers oriented on the torrent of copy the paper's correspondents cabled across both oceans. Stanley Johnston's unique Coral Sea experience had won him a generous bonus from Colonel McCormick (who furnished the story gratis to other papers) and also supplied the material for Johnston's best-selling book, *Queen of the Flattops*. On the other hand, he never got his Navy Cross, Admiral King pettishly refusing it after the Midway furor (Commander Seligman, Johnston's presumed informant, was permanently deprived of promotion).

Trib correspondent Seymour Korman made the D-day landing in southern France and Tom Morrow those on Iwo Jima and Okinawa. Robert Cromie covered Guadalcanal and Patton's Third Army in Europe. Larry Rue, who had flown in World War I and had won the roving correspondent job by his ignorance of foreign languages, covered London in the blitz (which the *Tribune* helped dramatize with the first colorphoto of the bombing) and afterward Eisenhower's headquarters. William Strand survived a wound on the Anzio beachhead to cover the Battle of the Bulge. Harold Smith made ten assault landings in the Pacific. Walter Simmons got a citation for his entry into Manila with the first liberating troops; Jack Thompson jumped into Tunisia and Sicily with the paratroops, survived a Purple Heart, and covered D day in Normandy. Arthur Veysey covered New Guinea and Luzon landings, flew in Pacific bombing raids, and covered the kamikaze attacks. Al Noderer, among other adventures, escaped from Singapore to Australia on a river ferry.

Don Starr had a special assignment—the *Overseas Tribune*. This time no fewer than eight editions were published, starting with Honolulu and adding offshoots in the Canal Zone, Sydney, Britain (printed in New York), Manila, New Delhi, Bremerhaven (after V-E day), and aboard the cruiser

Chicago. Starr and other *Trib* correspondents ferreted out printers and paper sources and sometimes located *Trib* mechanical hands in the armed forces who could be reverse drafted. The *Overseas Tribune*s were twelve-page tabloids printed from plastic plates flown from Chicago.

On the political front the Colonel got good news and bad news in 1944. The good news was the debacle of Wendell Willkie in the presidential primaries, ending his odd political career. The bad news was Dewey's defeat in November despite a good run. The McCormick and Patterson papers were for once united on a candidate, and all three drew very pained expressions from liberals for their open allusions to the possibility that Roosevelt might not live out a fourth term. (That danger short-circuited the old alarm over a Roosevelt dictatorship, of which little was heard in 1944. Instead, Harold Ickes confided to his diary fears of a Tom Dewey dictatorship.) Yet despite slanted coverage and the usual forecasts of victory, the *Trib*'s 1944 effort seemed perfunctory. For one thing the heavy war coverage crowded domestic politics for page-one space. For another the isolationist-interventionist debate, revived over plans for American participation in a postwar world organization, did not excite anybody very much. The "United Nations," sidling on stage as a docile assemblage of American allies, seemed harmless, and the Republican Platform, after much argument, settled on a mere stipulation that the Senate should keep checking out all treaties. The *Tribune*'s foreboding over Roosevelt's alleged intention to "pledge the power of the American nation, in perpetuity, to the service of other nations" did not trouble most readers. The real problems involved in America's postwar role were not yet visible. Roosevelt got a big laugh from a Soldiers Field crowd by saying the Republicans were promising to keep everything his administration had done, but would manage "to satisfy the *Chicago Tribune.*"

Despite his disappointments, late in 1944 Colonel McCormick found a new measure of genuine happiness. Since Amy's death five years earlier he had cut down on social life, habitually dining alone, entertaining only occasional parties of close friends or servicemen. It came as a surprise to most when he remarried on December 21, 1944. His bride was Maryland Mathison Hooper, a belle of Baltimore who in Chicago had become a friend of Amy McCormick. Like Amy she divorced a husband to marry the Colonel. The Hoopers had been suburban neighbors and during Amy's lifetime the two couples had socialized in town and country. In May 1944, the Hoopers had separated and later divorced.

The marriage ceremony took place in the Lake View Avenue apartment of Chauncey McCormick, president of the Art Institute, like the Colonel a grandson of William Sanderson McCormick, and a Wheaton neighbor. *Life* covered the ceremony, emphasizing the gathering of the McCormick and Patterson cousins (Joe Patterson was best man) and describing the Colonel as "excited and misty-eyed as any young swain." The *Sun* and *Daily News,* putting aside old rancors (Colonel Knox had died at his post in Washington earlier that year), gave friendly and straightforward coverage to the wedding and reception, which was memorialized for Chicago journalism by a briefly embarrassing prank. The photographer for the *Chicago Times,* a hearty fellow named Bill Bender, was part owner of a tavern. Bender was having fun ordering the fearsome Colonel McCormick to move this way and that and say cheese (the Colonel didn't) when some of his colleagues surreptitiously packed six champagne glasses in his camera-equipment bag. When Bender found them he put them on display in his bar, until the *Times* city desk got a polite call from the Colonel's butler. The glasses were "rather valuable"—they had belonged to Napoleon. Bender hastened to his tavern and returned the goblets unharmed to the McCormick Astor Street house.

CHAPTER TWENTY

Colonel McCormick
Becomes a Legend

A LIFELONG travel addict, Colonel McCormick was prompted by postwar air transport and marriage to a vivacious traveling companion to become a latter-day Ibn Batuta. His journeys over the final decade of his life ranged the globe from Canada to Latin America, from Europe and Africa to easternmost Asia. In 1948 he seized an opportunity to buy a nearly new surplus B-17 Flying Fortress at the knockdown price of $15,000, had the machine guns removed, the bomb bays floored over, bunks and reclining chairs installed, and the nose gunner's perch converted to an observation post. Though the auxiliary fuel tanks were jettisoned, the four-engine ex-bomber, renamed the *Chicago Tribune,* made possible transatlantic and other long-distance over-water flying to places where Pan Am could not take him. Only on his last trip abroad (1953), a sentimental journey to Europe and especially to England, did he revert to the airlines.

Everywhere he was accorded VIP treatment. U.S. ambassadors met him at airports, cabinet ministers, presidents, dictators, and Emperor Hirohito welcomed him to audience. AP and Reuters joined the *Tribune* correspondents in jotting down his quotes. The *Trib* people frequently had other assignments in connection with the travels: scheduling interviews, alerting the ambassadors, making airport reservations. Usually all went smoothly, but Washington bureau chief Walter Trohan recalled one case of extraordinary imposition for which McCormick gave a characteristic explanation. Alerted at the very last minute by a telegram concluding ABSOLUTE MUST, Trohan and W. D. Maxwell, managing editor in Chicago, turned cartwheels to get the traveling party accommodations in Tripoli, Libya. When he had a chance to ask why he had been given so unreasonable an assignment, Trohan drew this answer: "Arthur Veysey [the *Tribune*'s London correspondent] said it was too late to change reservations and I wanted to show him what *Tribune* people can do."

Air travel in the late forties and early fifties involved other hazards besides uncertainty of hotel reservations: storms, loss of radio contact, fogbound airports, especially in Iceland and Spain, an engine fluttering over Communist territory in China, another quitting on takeoff in Belgium. A particularly unsettling experience was an electrical fire that broke out in the

218

lavatory of the B-17 over the Andes. They managed to extinguish it and could even laugh at the American Club in Bogota next day, where they were kidded with the joke: "Altitude 14,000 feet. Fire aboard plane. No place to land. What should we do? Tower: There is only one thing to do. Repeat slowly, Our Father Who Art in Heaven . . ."

An equally alarming experience took place at home in Chicago, where they often commuted in a small plane from Northerly Island (Meigs Field) in Lake Michigan two miles south of the Tribune Tower. From there to Wheaton was a twelve-minute flight. One evening the pilot thought they could beat a cold-front fog moving in, but they didn't quite, and (in Maryland's words) "shaken . . . like a terrier shakes a rat" they moved from closed airport to closed airport before finally landing farther from home than they had been when they started out.

The Colonel reveled in the adventures of flying and enjoyed the VIP treatment, but perhaps most of all he profited in extraordinary measure from that favorite gratification of the traveler, the opportunity to tell others about the trip. Just as the *Tribune* staff in some measure took the place of children and grandchildren, so also did the entire city of Chicago, or at least that part of it that happened to enjoy light opera. In his ten-minute spot on WGN (and its offshoot, the Mutual network) he rambled freely, mixing travelogue with history and the current political scene. On Sunday morning those who missed the broadcast could read the script on the *Trib*'s edit page (and in the *Washington Times-Herald*).

His first trip took him to the Panama Canal Zone in early 1947. There he announced that he was speaking from the most important spot in the world in the new atomic age, explaining that neither New York nor Chicago was equally indispensable, and in fact destruction of the former would pay a dividend in the elimination of subversive elements, while Chicago could be replaced by Pittsburgh and Birmingham. From Canada he quoted William Cullen Bryant's panegyric on birchbark canoes and reminisced about timber-cruising with his Indian guides thirty years earlier. He threw in a folksy touch ("On the ferry I saw a car with a North Carolina license. Those Tar Heels were a long way from home") and a bright idea ("Half of [all old newspapers] are not recovered. A de-inking process, if somebody could invent one, would save paper and ink" [somebody has, since]). He gave Canada a salute with a pungent postscript: "The Canadian customs and immigration authorities were, as always, courteous . . . The *Times-Journal* of Fort William [ran] an editorial about the Dutch outrages in Indonesia. The Canadian newspapers are believed always to follow the imperial line [but they don't]. It is only among the seaboard snobs of both countries that sycophancy to the aristocracy is the leading incentive in life."

From San Francisco he gave a political twist to the shots the party had to take before heading across the Pacific—typhoid, typhus, yellow fever, cholera, smallpox, and the plague: "So low is the standard of sanitation all over the world, which proposes to apply its standards of all kinds to us." Looking ahead to Hawaii, he commented on Pearl Harbor, pointing out something few who had joined in the interminable debate on the disaster had observed, that the army garrison, several of whose commanders he had known, had conceived its mission strictly in terms of defending Hawaii from invasion, without assuming responsibility for the safety of the navy's battle-ships. The navy, meantime, "thought that the battleships could neither be bombed nor torpedoed in the harbor. It would not occur to the army to question this belief. The only soldier who ever did question it was General [Billy] Mitchell, and we know he was forced out of the army for expressing his opinion. . . ." As for Hawaiian statehood, he was cautious: "There are those who think that such racial strains . . . are not capable of self-govern-ment. That is something I must look into."

When he arrived in Honolulu (via Pan American Clipper) he turned up a new detail on Pearl Harbor: "Three weeks before the attack . . . the American carriers at sea sent up planes which were detected by the army's radar set at a distance which would have permitted the planes on the island to have shot them down a hundred miles from there. The experiments were not continued, apparently because the navy felt that airplanes could not injure battleships and because the army was only interested in preventing a landing. That seems to have been the reason why they kept the radar going all night, when a fleet might approach unseen, and shut it down as soon as ample warning could be received from the signal corps on various moun-taintops." He added that despite U.S. blunders, the Japanese raiders had blundered more in not following up their advantage by renewing the attack and perhaps sinking the carrier *Enterprise.*

The Colonel's observations conflicted somewhat with the official *Tribune* Pearl Harbor line, which was, naturally, to blame Roosevelt ("John T. Flynn Traces Blame in Pearl Harbor Disaster to Roosevelt"), a theory in which it was joined by Arthur Krock of the *New York Times* and a substan-tial part of the press. McCormick was right in finding the navy guilty of underestimating air power, especially that represented by torpedo planes, though he might have made an allowance—up to Pearl Harbor even tor-pedo planes had not really proved effective against surface warships.

A week later McCormick reported on his audience with Hirohito, who had extended the invitation "because my father, when ambassador to Russia during the Japanese-Russian war, represented Japan and looked out for the Japanese nationals in Russia. He also was the originator of the first move that led to the peace conference." The interview reminded the Colonel of his earlier encounters with royalty, from Queen Victoria, the kaiser, and the czar to the kings of Italy and Spain. The next Saturday he described flying over Hiroshima, where the destruction was immense but less than at either Tokyo or Osaka, to Korea, where he visited the thirty-eighth parallel and "surprised our people by reading the Russian sign. . . . The Russian characters resemble the Greek alphabet which I learned in school." A visit to MacArthur was rewarded by an illuminating exposition of the tactics and methods of future warfare, "imparted to me as from one soldier to another," and apparently a little too esoteric to be shared with the WGN audience.

Next week: "I've now been in Asia three weeks and this is what I've learned: A Japanese cook told me how to make ice cream—one whiskey bottle of mix, one whiskey bottle of water, three eggs, and two spoons of vanilla. If the eggs smell bad, five spoons of vanilla." He digressed to the United Nations, whose sessions at Lake Success reminded him of the Tower of Babel; what was needed was a universal language, and Esperanto being ridiculous, English had a good chance of becoming it. One advantage of the triumph of English would be the availability to all mankind of the great works written by Americans; although he did not specify, most of his listeners knew him well enough to realize he was talking about the Declaration of Independence, the Constitution, the Federalist papers, the Northwest Ordinance, and the rest of the national canon of statecraft, including several judicial opinions on the freedom of the press.

The following Saturday night, having just flown over Communist-held territory between Shanghai and Peking, his thoughts turned to communism. Like many observers with better China credentials than his, Colonel McCormick found it hard to believe that the individualistic Chinese would succumb to collectivism, which he characterized as "the most primitive form of property ownership . . . practiced by the Indians" and other early people, to their detriment. From medieval feudalism in England and the enclosures that (he said) created private ownership and stimulated technological advance, he slid back and forth between modern England, modern Russia, Marx, Lenin, and "smart alecks like Laski" in a fairly bewildering summation that must have sent much of his audience to the kitchen for a snack. (The Colonel's feelings about University of London professor Harold Laski's socialism had not prevented him from admiring the same British "smart aleck's" sentiments on freedom of the press, which the *Tribune* had quoted in a three-part editorial series at the time of the Midway crisis in 1942.) On the danger of communism in America, he was reassuring: It had only infected "a few pinko professors, the free lovers, New Deal politicians, and newspaper millionaires who look up to Laski and who hope to become a socialist American upper class." How Marshall Field planned to retain his department store holdings under socialism the Colonel did not specify. The rapidity of his transitions at least once baffled the Colonel himself.

Rereading a passage to be reprinted in the Sunday *Trib*, he checked with Trohan in Washington: "This is a paragraph from my radio broadcast. What do I mean?"

Sometimes he stuck pretty closely to one subject, such as the Panama Canal, but even there, after reminiscing about his own 1903 trip and criticizing the Hay-Pauncefote Treaty and Teddy Roosevelt's attempt to intimidate the *Indianapolis Star* and *New York World*, he digressed into an anecdote about the sculptor Rodin, told to him by Bunau-Varilla, French founder of the Panama republic.

The first flight in the B-17, in 1948, took him to Britain via Quebec, Labrador, Greenland, and Iceland, to learn "what the Labor party was all about." He discovered that "the key to everything in Britain was that there 'ANCESTRY is more important than ACCOMPLISHMENT.' " Again he was in tune with G. B. Shaw and other British socialists, as well as with Grandfather Medill, who had knocked the class structure of Queen Victoria's day. Yet he had no use for the Labor government either, asserting that it had "done much harm to the haves without doing anything for the have-nots."

In early 1949 the B-17 was off for South America, with the cadre augmented by a "fotografer" to shoot movies for WGN-TV. It was on this flight that a short circuit caused the alarming fire. In Bogota the president of Colombia bragged to McCormick about how he had thwarted the Reds, and in São Paulo, where the B-17 was the first four-motored plane ever to land, the Colonel made a big hit by paraphrasing Patrick Henry: "I am not a North American. I am not a South American. I am an American."

In Buenos Aires he interviewed Peron, who made a favorable impression by his openness, lack of pomp, and preference for trade over aid. "Why all the outcry about him?" McCormick wondered aloud. "I don't know. He has a clear majority of the population with him. . . . His domestic policies closely approximate the New Deal, with political success and economic collapse."

In 1950 the hegira returned to Europe, this time targeting Spain and Greece. He described General Franco's hunting-lodge residence ("about the size of the late Potter Palmer's mansion"), compared Franco's Moorish honor guard with the Scots archers of Louis XI and the French guards of Mary Queen of Scots, recalled his earlier visit to King Alfonso, and knocked bullfighting. Nobody minded all that, but his reported belief that Franco might yet turn out to have been a great statesman brought pained cries from liberals who still bracketed Franco with Hitler. Even McCormick's crediting Franco as a military innovator for his airborne invasion of Spain from Morocco stirred indignation.

In Greece the Colonel was unexpectedly disarmed by the U.S. aid personnel and even the aid program itself, which was building roads and railroads in Greece "paid for by money which the pork seeking states of the south and southwest will have to forgo." He thought the monarchically inclined State Department was being properly frustrated by the advance of republicanism in Europe, just as foretold by the *Tribune*'s 1914 editorial, and the British Empire was visibly waning.

The McCormick tours also received news coverage in the *Tribune* (and often in other papers). Under the head "Colonel McCormick Confers with Mexico's Chief," he was quoted as offering President Aleman the *Tribune*'s expertise in developing Mexico's forest preserves and assuring him that "as long as the *Tribune* has existed, and that's one hundred years, we have always been pro-Mexico," forgetting among other things Joe Patterson's 1916 advocacy of the annexation of the whole country down to the isthmus. The AP quoted him in Tokyo as telling some MacArthur-for-president army officers that there was widespread sentiment at home in the general's favor but no national organization. The Japanese press front-paged his suggestion that the alleged surplus population problem in Japan could be mitigated by permitting emigration to sparsely settled regions (though he stopped short of suggesting that either the United States or Australia drop their discriminatory immigration policies). He thought the Japanese peace treaty should be postponed until Russia agreed to participate: "I just don't want to kick up a row with Russia if it can be avoided."

In Cairo in 1950, the Colonel told Egyptian reporters that a proposed Truman-Stalin conference could not guarantee the world against war because "no statesman ever keeps his word," but that the United States "can lick everyone, including Russia." The last war he attributed to "Hitler and Roosevelt; maybe the next one will be brought about by Truman and Stalin." On economic prospects in the United States he observed, "Our technological knowledge is so enormous that it looks like we can overcome the asininities of the government." The new Egyptian constitution of King Farouk he pronounced a phony, lacking in guarantees of liberty.

Amid the travels, he still found some time to devote to the *Tribune*, the Republican party, and even his Wheaton neighbors. With Maryland, Cantigny recovered its old social liveliness, absent since Amy's death. It was the scene of one of the parties thrown to celebrate the *Tribune*'s centennial in 1947, the others including one for 2,000 guests at the Stevens Hotel, one for 3,500 at the Tower, and one for a crowd in Burnham Park estimated at no less than 300,000, who were treated to 25 tons of the fireworks the *Tribune* had succeeded in removing from the hands of the nation's children. *Time* and *Life* covered the centennial, seasoning their reportage with spite, though *Time* gave credit where it thought credit due:

The big reason for his Tribune's success is that McCormick has simply made it indispensable. No paper in all Chicagoland can match its overwhelming coverage of the news. When a big story breaks, the Trib can throw a score of men on it to outreport and outwrite the opposition. . . . It is the housewife's guide, the politician's breakfast food. . . . A classless paper, it is read on the commuter trains from swank Lake Forest, and on the dirty "El" cars taking workers to the stockyards.

Time quoted Louisville publisher Mark Ethridge: "I have always felt that those who said [the *Tribune*'s] great hold came from comic strips and other features were wrong: it possesses an animal vigor." *Time* converted this notion into something more usable on the cover, which portrayed Colonel McCormick wearing a triangular admiral's hat fashioned from a *Tribune,* by attributing a more *Time*-type quote to an anonymous *Trib* editor: "It ain't Little Orphan Annie, it's the hair on our chest."

Behind *Time*'s acknowledgment of the *Tribune*'s success lay the continuing failure of Marshall Field's *Sun,* despite acquisition of the AP franchise and absorption of the *Chicago Times* (resulting in a new logo, *Chicago Sun-Times*), to do more by 1947 than keep hanging on. Some of what *Time* said of the *Trib*'s success was true, and more could be said of the staff's all-around ability, but a deeper truth was probably the steeply rising cost of starting a new newspaper. Nevertheless, Marshall Field heroically persevered and in the 1950s the *Sun-Times* gradually developed its own features, solidified its circulation, increased its ad linage, and established its reputation.

On the subject of the centennial, *Life,* itself barely ten years old, waxed malicious under the title "A Newspaper Congratulates Itself":

> The Tribune's readers take a view somewhere between that of Colonel McCormick and that of the colonel's chosen enemies: England, Russia, and the U.S. east (to which he sometimes sends "foreign correspondents") and most things beyond "Chicagoland." Rare is the Tribune reader who does not like the Tribune's crisp, thorough reporting, its chatty columns and the famous comics. . . . Rare also is the Tribune reader who mistakes these assets for true greatness. For he knows that the Tribune has been made into a worldwide symbol of reaction, isolation and prejudice by a man capable of real hate.

Possibly a foreknowledge that in a generation *Life* would be gone and the *Tribune* still there might have mitigated the judgmental tone a bit. The conviction that Colonel McCormick was capable of "real hate" may have reflected a touch of the personal antagonism between McCormick and Henry Luce, whose anglophile-imperialist patriotism collided with McCormick's neutralist-isolationist brand. If so, Chiang Kai-Shek admirer and "American century" proponent Luce had a bit of nerve calling McCormick a reactionary.

The attribution of "real hatred" by McCormick toward "England, Russia and the U.S. east" was slanderous fantasy, though widely credited. *Time* cited a late 1941 head in the *Tribune:* FIGHT JAPS. BRITONS TO U.S. Six years after Pearl Harbor, *Time* apparently had no awareness that the head was accurate, and in fact one of the best insights expressed in the press in those days of wrath and confusion. *Time* was on a better track in its use of the term *hate* in the opposite sense, calling McCormick "the most bitterly hated press lord of his time." He wasn't, as long as Hearst was alive, but he may have been the runner-up. Yet in the postwar world, with the save-England vs. keep-out-of-war debate softened and diffused into arguments over NATO and the Marshall Plan, the old fury was damped down. (On NATO the Colonel found himself in bed with Henry A. Wallace, who had as recently as 1944 called him a fascist.) Colonel McCormick flying around the world and sending back pontifications was not really hatable. Also, as the travels wound on, and despite some evidence of hostile reportage, it was difficult to miss a detail that contradicted *Life*'s depiction of the *Tribune* as "a worldwide symbol of reaction, isolation and prejudice." In India and Pakistan, which the McCormicks visited in 1950, the *Tribune* proved to be a symbol of something quite different. Deputy Prime Minister Vallabhbhai Patel, No. 2 to Nehru in India, told McCormick that during his years of imprisonment by the British he had "gained great comfort from reading the *Chicago Tribune* editorials demanding the end of English rule." Pakistan Prime Minister Liaquat Ali Khan was equally well disposed, accepting a counterinvitation from the McCormicks in Karachi and paying a visit with his family to Cantigny. Among other emerging leaders who found McCormick's reputation sympathetic was Left-oriented Kwame Nkrumah of Ghana, who waxed so enthusiastic over their presumably shared feelings about the British (he had just gotten out of a British jail) that the Colonel felt constrained to correct him. The truth was, in much of the world, a reputation for being quote anti-British unquote was a badge of quote liberalism unquote.

Not that the Colonel limited his strictures on imperialism to the British: "The history of the European people in China is murder, rapine, and robbery. Beginning with the Portuguese, the Dutch, the English, French, and later the Russians and Japanese: the history has been one of such turpitude that no words are strong enough to condemn." To which he added perceptively, "Our own history has been pretty fair until the last three or four years, but now the influence of the United States government is everywhere supporting those European monarchies that are oppressing the peoples of the Orient."

He mistrusted the activist foreign policy he saw shaping up under Truman as he had that of Roosevelt (and Hoover) and put his faith in the political prospects of Senator Robert A. Taft. He told a reporter that after Taft he didn't mind MacArthur, Senator Bricker, Senator Martin, or House Speaker Martin, but had doubts about Eisenhower and waxed bitterly whimsical on committed internationalists Dewey and Stassen: "I don't know what those foreigners would do coming to Chicago [for the convention]. Wall Street forced Dewey and Wendell Willkie on the Republicans before. I don't think Wall Street can do it again." The Colonel, no great detractor of Wall Street, may have been thinking of a sensational disclosure made by George Seldes in his newsletter *In Fact,* that a small coterie headed by Morgan partner Thomas W. Lamont had handpicked Willkie to guide the United States into the war, not that it was exactly news that both Willkie and Dewey (dubbed by the *Daily Worker* "Wall Street's fig leaf") had backing in the financial community—LaSalle Street as well as Wall Street.

The Colonel's least favorite postwar politician, however, was unquestionably Harry Truman. When Maryland found a wallpaper in Hong Kong she thought would be perfect for the Cantigny dining room because of its motif of horses, the Colonel demurred; pointing to a horse prominently facing away from the viewer, he said he didn't want to have to look at Harry Truman every night at the dinner table (Maryland bought the wallpaper anyway).

The feeling between McCormick and Truman was mutual. Whistle-stopping to California in June 1948, Truman seized on the *Tribune* as a target to go with the "do-nothing, good-for-nothing Republican Eightieth Congress." On June 11, 1948, a long editorial starting on page one welcomed Truman's attack: "Mr. Truman has added his name to the long list of political crooks and incompetents who have regarded The Tribune as first among their foes." Truman's political origins as a creation of the Kansas City Democratic machine whose boss, Tom Pendergast, had been sent to prison for taking bribes from Chicago insurance companies, caused McCormick to confuse him with Bill Thompson and Boss Lorimer, both of whom were mentioned in the editorial. Beyond that, he blamed Truman for giving too much to the Russians at Potsdam.

Both notions were widely held, even by Truman's friends, though neither had validity, as time eventually proved. Truman was no crook and no bad diplomat. The *Trib*'s June 11 editorial also took note of the fact that Colonel Jacob Arvey, Chicago Democratic boss, was trying hard to dump Truman, as were many other Democratic bosses. (They wanted to draft Eisenhower, who was coyly not saying which party he belonged to.) When Truman used his presidential clout to take the nomination, the *Tribune* joined the entire press of the country in a conviction that there was no way he could win. Toward Republican nominee Dewey, chosen over his own favorite Taft, Colonel McCormick maintained some discernible reserve, but on election night the *Tribune*'s early edition came out with the banner DEWEY DEFEATS TRUMAN, a forecast the scanty available returns hardly justified. McCormick had been on better ground in an earlier prediction that if Dewey got the nomination, the Republicans were licked. Next morning Truman had his picture taken holding up the *Tribune* with the rash headline, and it passed into folklore. Colonel McCormick was not personally responsible for the head, and the *Tribune* was far from alone in embarrassment. The radio networks had held back for hours from admitting Dewey's defeat; as late as 4 A.M., when Truman had an insurmountable lead, H. V. Kaltenborn, dean of commentators, insisted Dewey was in. The print press had nothing to congratulate itself on either. Besides the spectacular blunders of the three national polling organizations (Gallup, Roper, Crosley), then at the height of their prestige, the *New York Times* had done its own nationwide study and announced a Truman victory impossible. The *Washington Post* hopefully headlined its FINAL edition, **Dewey Gaining on Early Truman Lead**, while Washington columnists Joseph and Stewart Alsop appeared the morning after election with a big scoop—the names of Dewey's cabinet. *Time,* caught with its cover and everything else down, went to fantastic lengths in a search-and-destroy mission that converted the unrecovered copies into collector's items. Nevertheless, everybody remembered Truman holding up the *Chicago Tribune*.

The episode added another embellishment, along with the fabled descent from the horse van, the rumored trappings of the Tower office, the Sawyer letter, the anglophobia, and the funny spelling, to the legend of Colonel McCormick.

People who had read and heard about him and happened to find themselves in his presence continued to be taken aback, like Ralph McGill, at the discrepancy between image and reality. A striking example was David Lilienthal, a top New Deal official (head of TVA) who in 1948 was Truman's chairman of the Atomic Energy Commission. Ernest Lawrence, nuclear physicist and Nobel laureate who had worked on the Manhattan Project headquartered at the University of Chicago, had gotten acquainted socially with the McCormicks and hit it off so well that he became a frequent visitor to Cantigny. One evening he expansively suggested that his peripatetic hosts drop in on the national atomic installations at Hanford and Los Alamos. The Colonel expressed interest, and Lawrence suggested to

Lilienthal that he stop by to see McCormick on his next visit to Chicago. New Dealer (and old Gary, Indiana boy) Lilienthal recorded the resulting meeting:

> I ascended the Tribune Tower this noon, and was swept at once into the Sanctum Sanctorum and before the Presence, the Colonel Himself. His office is high-ceilinged, with papers scattered about the leather lounges, dark and Gothic. Col. McCormick was older-appearing than I expected [he was nearing sixty-eight] but rather courtly, courteous in the extreme, and with no slight hint that I was one of the devils that for years and years he had been whamming vigorously. . . .
>
> Dr. Zinn . . . and I were greeted not only by the Colonel, but with no little exuberance by a waddling, gallumping English bull, the kind that is terrifying to see but actually very friendly. (When we left for the Argonne Laboratory later, after luncheon, the Colonel put a chain-leash of huge links on "Buster," who pulled the Colonel along through the corridors where people gawked and guards straightened up, passed a double column of pickets—the Typo Union has been on strike since last November—and into his car, manned by the most obvious tough-guy driver I have ever seen. Buster sat in the front seat with the driver, and stuck his ugly but much excited phiz around every so often. An *English* bull.)

Lilienthal may have been the more taken aback by the *English* bull if he had chanced to read two recent writers on McCormick who had employed the baleful, almost fascist designation of "German wolfhound" to classify the bull's predecessor, an elderly and benign German shepherd bitch named Lottie.

Lilienthal was astonished three separate times. The first was at the Colonel's lighthearted reference to the hotel elevators in Philadelphia, where the Republican convention had just nominated Tom Dewey contrary to McCormick's wishes. Lilienthal apparently thought Philadelphia would be too touchy a subject to mention. The second was by McCormick's pleasant laugh when Lilienthal essayed a small joke of his own about the demonstration of radioactive phosphorus in roses. The third was when Zinn, in the course of his description of plans for a new laboratory at Du Page, reiterated that it would be plain, modern, with "no Gothic." Lilienthal was sure the Colonel would huff at the slight to Gothic, in the light of the Tribune Tower's "gargoyles, flying buttresses, and all the rest, but the Colonel didn't bat an eyelash!" Unbelievable! "A strange chapter in my acquaintance," was Lilienthal's final note on Colonel McCormick.

The British, who learned all they knew about America from New York and Washington, were repeatedly surprised to discover the real Colonel McCormick. A 1948 interview by a British reporter named Frank Walker, while failing to get the name of the paper right, expressed characteristic surprise at the discrepancy between the real and the reputed McCormick:

> Colonel "Bertie" Rutherford McCormick, millionaire owner of the *Chicago Herald-Tribune,* which has said more unkind things about Britain than probably any other newspaper in America, stepped from his converted Flying Fortress at Prestwick yesterday and raised a big, fleshy hand (he's 6 ft. 4 in., weighs 18 st.).
>
> "No politics," he said. "I'm here on vacation. Just give me a cup of coffee and I'll talk to anybody. But nothing controversial. I am no emissary of my Government. If I can't agree with it, I'll hold my peace.
>
> "Isolationist? Anglophobe?" His ice-blue eyes flashed. "No, I'm a patriot."
>
> He apologised for nothing. Polite and on the defensive at first, he later relaxed mentally during a 12-hour hustle tour, seeing just the things that any other American visitor would see.
>
> The fire-breathing colonel who has many times complained of British Imperial lust stood bareheaded when—by chance—he witnessed a proclamation from Edinburgh's Mercat Cross in which George VI announced the casting off of his title Emperor of India. . . .
>
> The man whose paper has spoken of the degenerate aristocracy of Britain drank whisky and soda and chatted pleasantly for half an hour with Scotland's premier nobleman, the Duke of Hamilton, in his private apartments in the Palace of Holyroodhouse.
>
> The man to whom "English gentleman" is anathema is in appearance the squire himself—silver-haired, neat-mustached, with un-American horned-rimmed glasses and not much of an accent [meaning not much of an American accent]. . . .

Like many others, the interviewer found it "difficult to believe" that this "distinguished figure" in military raincoat, with "old-world courtesy" and "quiet and undemonstrative speech" was the ferocious Colonel McCormick with whom British children had been frightened.

In 1951 a London magazine editor named Sidney Moseley told his readers that he had tried to find out "when we were in New York" why Colonel McCormick was so prejudiced against England. When his New York contacts failed to supply a definitive explanation for the phenomenon, Mosely hit on the idea of asking the subject himself, which he did, not by visiting Chicago, but by writing a letter from London. McCormick wrote back, and made a gaffe: "My hatred for the English originated with the British Foreign Office, who wish to set down my just criticism to prejudice."

As he realized afterward, he should have stuck quotes around "hatred," but the sense was not really hard to fathom if one brought reasonably good intentions to the interpretation. Either Sidney Moseley didn't, or was none too bright, and *Time* definitely did not. Alert like

Walter Burns to all the trouble it could find or create, *Time* picked up the letter to offer as proof that McCormick himself admitted he hated the English. The rest of the letter hardly supported the interpretation. As examples of what he felt critical about, McCormick named the fatuous rhetoric that made Dunkirk out to be some sort of victory; the tame surrenders of Hong Kong and Singapore ("the generals should have been shot"); the British "retention of troops in Egypt and the Sudan," which he characterized as "aggression and tyranny"; and finally, the "bribing of the American administration to get the Marshall dole," which he thought "a disgrace to both countries."

Characteristically, the Colonel had dashed off his letter as he departed for a trip—this time to Haiti. After *Time* had had its chortle, another British magazine, *People Today,* undertook a clarification, with a resulting McCormick letter that was composed in less haste, explained about the missing quotes, defended his criticisms, and added the very thing he should have mentioned to Moseley:

> My years at Ludgrove School in England were among the pleasantest of my life. I still correspond and exchange visits with my surviving schoolmates. I remember with admiration how patriotism was taught in the school, as it was not taught in our eastern schools.

Still another Englishman who discovered the real McCormick was Berkeley Gage, the British consul in Chicago in the 1950s, who became a regular guest at Astor Street and Cantigny. Not to wonder—Gage was another old Ludgrovean, and he and the Colonel entertained Maryland and other company with renditions of old school songs.

Through the early fifties, the Colonel continued to alternate travel with stays in the Tower, losing none of his zest for the paper. As ever, he was an early riser at Cantigny, where gifts and sales had reduced the acreage to a mere five hundred and where he no longer fox-hunted, though he still rode. His daily routine still included clipping the *Tribune* at breakfast, and usually he telephoned his secretary to dictate a few memos and letters even before leaving home. His office hours were generally limited to eleven-thirty to four-thirty, but not his working day, which continued as he entered the waiting limo with a briefcase full of homework.

The Washington bureau and the editorial page remained his favorite concerns, though he did not neglect any part of the paper. Claudia Cassidy, a talented critic he hired away from the *Sun-Times,* recalled a visit from him. He was on his way out of the building with the English bulldog, and stopping in her office he inquired in his usual direct way: "Don't you think opera is too long?"

"Not when it's good," said Claudia promptly.

"Well," said the Colonel meekly, "I just thought I'd ask," and sauntered out.

He maintained his interest in the foreign bureau, but continued his policy of restraint in command decisions. Arthur Veysey in London got a message tipping him off to a story the *Tribune* had heard in Chicago, that members of the Labour government were passing up the nationalized hospitals for their own medical care in favor of private hospitals. Veysey looked into it and found it wasn't true. After that the Colonel always added a modifier to his requests to Veysey—"after you have investigated."

At home in Chicago he kept up pressure for two favorite engineering projects: elevated highways and a lakefront airport. The elevated highways came after his death, at a cost many times what they would have been when McCormick first proposed them in the 1920s and 1930s, and the new international airport was built inland, northwest of the city. Its naming created another Colonel McCormick story, perhaps apocryphal. At a committee meeting the Colonel is said to have nodded approval of a suggestion that the facility be named for George C. Marshall, until someone pointed out that in that case it would be known as Marshall Field. Consequently the world's largest airport honors a somewhat obscure navy flying hero, son of a Chicago racetrack owner who was bumped off by gangsters.

The flow of memos to the staff and to the Washington bureau did not abate. Among those Walter Trohan received in the postwar years:

Is Saltonstall descended from the Saltonstall who left Boston with Gage in the Revolutionary War?

From whom must I obtain permission to land at Fernando Noronha?

In view of the enormous expense, is the *Missouri* still being kept in commission?

What does Acheson propose to do to get the British army of conquest out of Egypt?

My file of correspondence with General Willoughby is missing. Did we send it to you?

I don't like the expression "young turks." Stick to New Deal Republicans.

He was also a constant visitor to New York and Washington. In New York he stayed at the Ritz or at the Waldorf Tower, but in Washington he complained that there was no good hotel, and until Cissy's death put up at 15 Dupont Circle, even though her parties sometimes disturbed his early-to-bed habits. When Joe Patterson died suddenly in 1946 (on the eve of his fiftieth Groton reunion), the Colonel persuaded Cissy to accept the post of chairman of the *Daily News* board, but they had begun to have friction over the corporate management when Cissy herself died suddenly in 1948. McCormick received the news at the Ritz in Paris, and the *Tribune* gave her an editorial salute as "the most effective woman publisher this country has ever known." Sentiment aside, Cissy's death created much more of a problem than Joe's. Her *Times-Herald* was losing money and the seven top executives to whom she had willed it did not want to keep it. McCormick took it off their hands at a good price (creating a slight furor in some circles —Vandenberg exaggerated that "the whole town seems to dread" his arrival). He tinkered with the paper's format, restored some features Cissy had pared for economy, and appointed his bright niece Basie McCormick (Medill's and Ruth Hanna's daughter) editor, and even took charge himself for a while, but nothing worked, and the *Times-Herald* remained a loser.

A 1951 visit to Washington was the result of a different matter. The *Tribune* had inadvertently caused General MacArthur some hurt by getting early word of Truman's decision to fire him and so triggering an abrupt public announcement rather than a personal visit to MacArthur by the Secretary of the Army. The ANPA invited MacArthur to come home and address their annual meeting, and McCormick thought the general should instead be invited to address Congress. Several members of Congress had the idea, too, but McCormick could claim credit for helping bring about the memorable joint session. Walter Trohan, who did the spadework, also had to get the McCormicks seats for the performance, a difficult feat in light of the demand, which he nonetheless managed to accomplish. The day came, the House was packed, MacArthur spoke. As he reached his peroration about old soldiers never dying, "there was not a dry eye in the place," Trohan noted, or an empty seat—save one. Well as he knew the Colonel, Trohan was flabbergasted to see him get up, make his way down the row, and head for the exit. Waiting for his hero's windup he had run out of patience.

Politically, the Colonel gravitated further to the right in his last years, something the whole country was doing. The *Tribune* gave prominence to the revelations of real spy networks and the fabrications of imagined ones. Inadvertently the Washington bureau helped Joe McCarthy get started when the then-obscure senator phoned for help on a Lincoln's Birthday speech he was scheduled to give the Republican Women's Club of Wheeling. Willard Edwards clued him on past investigations of State Department employees' loyalty that McCarthy turned into the magic formula, "I have here in my hand a list of two hundred and five known members of the Communist party," etc. The AP put it on the wire and McCarthy was launched into orbit.

Though the new star seemed made to order for McCormick, with his

COLONEL McCORMICK BECOMES A LEGEND 233

choice of targets as "Communists, traitors and homosexuals" in the State Department—McCormick had never dared call them anything worse than "pantywaists"—the Wisconsin senator was a little gamy for the Colonel. In McCarthy's four years in the spotlight, they met only twice, and in answer to a reporter's question McCormick brushed aside the notion that the fellow might be presidential timber.

The Colonel's favorite candidate remained Robert Taft, admired for his integrity as well as his orthodoxy and resistance to foreign adventure. When North Korea invaded South Korea, even the *Tribune* joined in approving Truman's prompt decision to send help, but later appreciated Taft's historic demur over a president's making war without consulting Congress. The Colonel distrusted Eisenhower's NATO-related Europeanism and had no use for Ike's foreign-policy mentor, John Foster Dulles, a one-time isolationist. Asked if he would support Dulles for vice-president the Colonel replied that he would "just as soon support Judas Iscariot." (When Senator Vandenberg, another ex-isolationist, found himself labeled "Judas" by a *Tribune* editorial he meditated on "whether that is 'progress' or not—the last time I was 'Benedict Arnold.' ") Maryland didn't agree with the Colonel on Ike. According to one story, when they called on Eisenhower in Paris McCormick refused to commit himself to support the general's candidacy, but as they left Maryland flipped back her lapel to display an "I Like Ike" button. On WGN the Colonel broached the idea of a third party dedicated to American independence, stimulating the largest mail response he ever got to a Saturday night broadcast. He even thought he had found a candidate, wiring Trohan in Washington, "I have found my Fremont." The new Fremont, coincidentally enough, was Albert C. Wedemeyer, the officer suspected of giving the *Tribune* its Victory Program scoop, now an outspoken general who favored a tougher anti-Communist foreign policy. McCormick, however, had neglected to first ascertain Wedemeyer's sentiments on being a Fremont, and it turned out they were negative. In the end, and characteristically, the Colonel came around to Eisenhower after all, accepting the general's Morningside Heights promise to Taft that he wouldn't do anything dangerously internationalist. The *Tribune* campaigned for him and was pleased with his victory over Adlai Stevenson, who in 1941 had been chairman of the Chicago chapter of the White Committee.

Its editorial congratulations were restrained, however, and sounded rather like the *New York Times,* stressing the fact that people seemed to like nice-guy Ike, with a condescending implication that his intellectual equipment for the White House was not exactly that of Lincoln or Jefferson.

In 1953 the Colonel and Maryland made their last overseas trip, a sentimental journey to England, France, Germany, and Italy. In London they were met at the airport by correspondents Arthur and Gwen Morgan

Veysey, and given lunch at the country house of their friends Lord and Lady Kemsley, whose gardens had a view of Windsor Castle. After lunch they drove to Ludgrove. Headmaster A. T. Barber, alerted by Veysey, was on hand to greet the Colonel, perhaps the school's oldest surviving old boy, and to reassure him over tea that British patriotism was still taught at Ludgrove.

They were late getting back to London, but before returning to the Claridge stopped off to see a little house on Brook Street where the McCormicks had lived sixty years earlier.

Again he was interviewed by a dozen British reporters, but not to his satisfaction. They "omitted to say that I considered communist infestation even more prevalent than we have suspected in our state department, in the left wing of the British Labor party, and in Canada. . . . They all failed to report my explanation that I was not anti-British, that I greatly admired the personnel of their colonial office, but that it was faced with a changing world and had . . . sooner or later to free [the colonial] peoples."

By 1954 the Colonel was becoming less active. His WGN broadcasts, in which at the suggestion of *Times-Herald* executive Frank Waldrop he had launched his oral memoirs, ceased, though he had covered only the early part of his life. His by-line vanished from the Sunday editorial page. On the other hand, Maryland's by-line appeared, first in the *Washington Times-Herald*, where she began writing a weekly column, succeeding Austine Hearst, then in the Sunday *Trib* and several other papers.

One column, in which she waxed frivolous over the Colonel's English bulldog and her own four dogs, got her in trouble—with *Trib* editors. Maryland was given to understand that she had made fun of the Colonel and herself, that the copy was "too intimate," that she should keep her stuff on a higher plane. So she wrote a column about that, picturing the editors as getting together over her dog column and asking themselves, "Why do publishers ever marry?" and concluding that they must marry aggressive women who

> kidnap these noble lords of the press. . . . Why, O why do so many consorts of the fourth estate try to convince their husbands that they are backing the wrong candidate? These women should all stay home and cook good, hot, nourishing meals, and perhaps do a little laundry, instead of infringing on their husbands' territory. . . . It would be a much happier world for the editors if publishers would only take a vow of celibacy.

During 1954 the Colonel experienced a long illness, which induced him to give up on the *Washington Times-Herald*. With Kent Cooper as intermediary, he sold the paper to Eugene Meyer, publisher of the *Washington Post*, a fellow Yale man and one who had stood with him in the AP fight in 1942. McCormick's fellow conservatives were taken aback at sale of the *Times-*

Herald to Meyer, a pronounced liberal, but the Colonel simply said that Meyer was a good professional newspaperman, and he did not want to sell to an amateur. As he doubtless foresaw, Meyer closed down the *Times-Herald,* taking to the *Post* several of its features, including Maryland's column. When Meyer telephoned her to ask her to keep on with it, the Colonel took the phone to tell Meyer, "Be careful, she has had no experience and has never written anything beyond a check, and her signature on that is illegible," and to wish him the best of luck with the *Washington Post.* Later Walter Trohan, wondering out loud how Maryland could write a column for the liberal *Post* and conservative *Tribune,* told her, "Lady, you are either awfully dumb or very clever."

The Colonel's illness inspired a rumor that the *Tribune* was going to be sold to John S. Knight, who had bought the *Daily News* after Colonel Knox's death in 1944. The *Tribune* denied the rumor, which was partly grounded in its recent circulation decline—from a high of 1,047,000 in 1947 to 885,000. All big-city papers were being hurt by TV and the flight to the suburbs, but the *Trib* did not push any panic buttons, although it introduced some new features—"adult" comics, "The Other Side" (contrary editorial opinions from other papers), some new typefaces and makeup devices. The "hot wire" remained connected, and still buzzed on the city desk. Back in Chicago after a stay in Florida, the Colonel for a while returned to his old routine, driving in daily, reading the *Trib* and the opposition papers, and making notes for the staff. To those with whom he exchanged greetings in the Tower and who gathered in the Overset Club, he looked gaunt.

In December he summoned Weymouth Kirkland, the legal lion who had fought the Henry Ford and Bill Thompson battles over forty years earlier, to give his will its final amendments. The Robert R. McCormick Foundation had already been established two years earlier to put his philanthropic donations on a permanent basis. Essentially, he gave everything to charity, and through the eventual liquidation of the McCormick-Patterson Trust left the *Tribune* in the hands of its top executives.

He delivered his last broadcast over WGN-Mutual on Christmas evening. The next week, on New Year's Day, the announcer read the Colonel's talk, and the Saturday night audience never heard him again. His last months were spent at Cantigny, where he died early in the morning of April 1, 1955, on the eve of the prairie spring, and where he was buried next to Amy in his old 1918 uniform. In accordance with his instructions, the funeral was kept simple, no flowers and only "Onward Christian Soldiers" for music. The Fifth Army sent a squad to fire a salute and a bugler to blow "Taps."

He had lived seventy-five years, by a nice coincidence the same span as grandfather Joseph Medill.

CHAPTER TWENTY-ONE

Looking Back on the Colonel

COLONEL McCORMICK sleeps in peace at Cantigny, his tomb (and Amy's) enclosed in an exedra, an open marble structure modeled on the ancient rendezvous where Athenians met to exchange the news. Not far off are the ten acres of formal gardens designed in response to the Colonel's wish that Cantigny be made a place of beauty for the people of Illinois. In the Rose Garden blooms the famed "Chicago Peace," developed by the estate's first caretaker, Stanley Johnston, the war correspondent whose Midway scoop caused all the furor in 1942.

Even before the Colonel's death, peace descended on the embattled Chicago newspaper business, where of all the fabled city rooms of the *Front Page* era only the *Tribune* is left, facing the latecomer *Sun-Times* across North Michigan Avenue. Though the two survivors compete in news gathering and ad soliciting, neither ever sends out a truckload of armed thugs to beat up the other's circulation men, or vilifies the opposing publisher in editorial and cartoon. John S. Knight quietly retired "Colonel McCosmic" from the *Daily News* in 1944 and three years later, for the *Trib*'s centennial, wrote a tribute extolling Colonel McCormick's "courage and singleness of purpose" while admitting that his views were frequently "unpalatable." When the Colonel died, Knight wrote a piece recalling how McCormick had opposed a reform of the AP board of directors that Knight had sponsored and then afterward, when it passed, "accepted the decision gracefully" and finally urged Knight to take his own seat on the board.

In a like spirit of reconciliation was the suggestion emanating from Field Enterprises that Chicago's new exhibition hall be named McCormick Place. The Colonel was already officially memorialized in McCormick Boulevard, dating from 1919, and in many other reminders besides the brick in the Tribune Tower.

But Cantigny remains his special and personal memorial, preserving side by side his spirit and that of his model, Grandfather Joseph Medill. In line with an expression in his will, the Museum of the First Division was established on the grounds, southwest of the house, where the riding stables once stood, a repository for memorabilia of America's most famous military unit, membership in which meant so much to him.

Inside the house, some changes have been made. The red-and-white marble desk that Amy brought from Paris, with Grandfather Medill's long-bladed shears and fixed magnifying glass, now stands in the Colonel's bedroom. So does Medill's own rolltop, and the globe. Nearby are busts of both Medill and McCormick, the Colonel's mounted at his standing height of six feet four. The dining room is still papered with the Chinese horses that inspired the pleasantry at Harry Truman's expense. Among the paintings are portraits of Maryland and the Colonel done by Amy. That of the Colonel shows him aboard a favorite horse, in the act of jumping; a silhouette of the same decorates a fire screen in the library. In the theater downstairs the walls are covered with photos and cartoons—two slight surprises are the *Time* cover of the Colonel in a paper admiral's hat and one of Eleanor Roosevelt.

Despite the Sawyer letter, the Colonel was not a braggart, and despite his editorial assault on Marshall Field III, he was not a bully. His was an innocent ego, as proud of having fought for his country as of anything he ever did on the *Tribune*. The fact that so many of the Colonel's old subordinates remember him with respect and affection suggests that he was perhaps less corrupted than most by the seductions of power. George Seldes had the honesty as well as insight to deny to fellow liberals that his old boss suffered "one of the Roy Howard, Paul Block, Hearst and Northcliffe complexes. . . . Power, money, fame, egotism, do not seem to be the Colonel's motives in making his newspaper what it is . . ." Another old *Trib* correspondent, Waverley Root, says cheerfully, "He had his megalomaniac side, but that only made his reign one of grandeur."

More to the point in assessing his place in the history of journalism and public affairs, he was not a demagogue. Interviewed, he was frank and to the point, and despite the famous impatience, little given to anger. His hostility to Roosevelt and the New Deal expressed less fury than fear. His businessman's bias made the economic experimentation suspect, and the breadth and sweep of New Deal legislation, even apart from such provocative specifics as the Supreme Court bill, Lend-Lease, and the third-term candidacy, stimulated apprehensions of a Roosevelt design for dictatorship. The notion seems fantastic today, but in the 1930s and 1940s many sane people worried along such lines, as they watched dictatorship surface in one place after another, with no very clear indication of what caused it. Despite the *Tribune*'s arrogant and, to Roosevelt supporters, maddening tone of contempt and disdain for a great liberal president locked in a war against fascism, Oswald Garrison Villard was dead right in commending the *Tribune* for "keeping alive the historic American right of press dissent even in war-time." The truth was, as Villard almost alone at the time said, "Colonel McCormick . . . has in his stubborn way steadfastly fought for the right of the press to live up in fullest degree to that one of the Four Freedoms which pertains to it."

Demagoguery was not to the Colonel's taste. The characteristic *Tribune* editorial style was antidemagogic—rational, ironic, articulate, and long-winded—the reverse of the Hearst-Brisbane formula of short, declarative, and supersimple. Quite apart from his direct contributions to the preservation and strengthening of the First Amendment guarantees (which several of his contemporaries remembered at the moment of his death, though perhaps forgetting about them later), Colonel McCormick had a reverence for the history of democracy. True, he somewhat exaggerated America's role, but he did not minimize Britain's, and in overlooking the contributions of some others, such as France and Italy, he merely reflected the general historical egotism and ignorance of his American generation.

His real prejudices were those of his class and group. The prejudices that separated him out—the anti-British and anti-East Coast—were in the eyes of his beholders, who only discovered them under exceptional circumstances. In the 1920s a Chicago columnist, not on the *Tribune*, expressed the opinion that Colonel McCormick would make an ideal ambassador to the Court of St. James. Westbrook Pegler, the *Tribune* sportswriter who turned conservative political columnist for Scripps-Howard en route to becoming a reactionary one for Hearst, did a column on his former boss in 1944 that made a nice point: McCormick, he said, believed that "any alliance between the U.S.A. and Britain should be made on our terms with Britain in the inferior position and as a favor to Britain, not to us." That was McCormick's anti-Britishness in a nutshell, and it bothered anglophiles because it exalted their new fatherland at the expense of their old. They could hardly contradict the sense, but they objected to the taste, of asserting that the Empire had no clothes on. Walter Lippmann, Henry Luce, the *New York Times* editors, all would have preferred to keep the two "English-speaking countries" coequal on top of the world, as for a moment they were, at least in anglophile perception. A generation later another truth seems to be dawning, that the imperial American dominance perceived by McCormick after World War II had some of the illusory character of the British Empire. McCormick's perception of an independent American power and glory was perhaps as erroneous as Walter Lippmann's of an America long protected by benevolent British sea power, but the historical view from today seems to leave Colonel McCormick looking better than he once did, and Lippmann, among others, looking not as good.

The Colonel's reputed bias against the East Coast, especially New York, carried an infinitely smaller emotional charge than the anti-British accusation. Even parochial, and slightly paranoid, New Yorkers hardly took it seriously. Contrary to *Life*'s claim, the Colonel had no need to send "foreign correspondents to New York from time to time," since the *Trib* maintained a bureau there. Contrary to A. J. Liebling he never thought of New York as "Gomorrah," that is, Sin City. Few did in the years when Mayor La Guardia was shutting down the Times Square burlesque theaters and the Legion of Decency was picketing foreign movies. What the Colonel indicted New York for was harboring most, if not all, of the country's subversives (he overlooked some closer to home), nurturing an affluent, snobbish Tory international set, and exercising a dominant influence on communications and corporate finance, something many have accused the city of, and something New York has often boasted about. In a broadcast recorded by BBC in 1949, he explained the political "geografy" of America on historical grounds: New York had been occupied by the British and Tories in the Revolution, and retained a Tory coloration—powerful elements had wanted to secede in 1861, and it was the only city to have draft riots in 1863. Elsewhere in the East similar influence was evident, as in New England's secessionist Hartford Convention. The Midwest in contrast had received "the most enlightened government devised by man up to that time" in Jefferson's Northwest Ordinance, whose provisions were too liberal for most of the country until after the Civil War. The Midwest had been settled by Revolutionary veterans, imbued with democratic patriotism, and though it had had plenty of immigrants, in the Colonel's view they got more democratized and Americanized by coming that far west. McCormick's Midwest blurred imperceptibly into the West, with an exception—California, settled by easterners sailing around the Horn in 1849, had always remained a little weird. Otherwise, he did not admire New York architecture and pitied the city for not having a lakefront, but gave it credit—New Yorkers might have been surprised—for cleaning up its litter better than Chicago did.

McCormick's Midwest patriotism was a sort of reverse image of the eastern elitist's condescension toward the region. What the eastern snob saw as plebeian mediocrity, McCormick saw as democratic egalitarianism. Though he himself was a product of prep school and rich man's college, and though his habits were patrician verging on seigneurial, he was a firm believer in merit and the common man, as expressed in the Midwest aphorism "One man's just as good as another, and probably a damn sight better." He romanticized the Midwest as "the center of the American spirit" and exaggerated its role as "the decisive force in holding the nation together thruout our history." During the war he liked to think of the Midwest as isolationist, just as the eastern interventionists did, and pointed to the frequent votes of Midwest congressmen against measures tending toward war. But on such critical decisions as the extension of the service term for drafted men in 1941, eastern congressmen showed themselves no less reluctant than midwesterners, and the unpopular measure was passed solely thanks to the overwhelming martial enthusiasm of the old Confederacy.

The South got no applause from anybody for that or anything else. Northern liberals never tired of reciting its conservative sins while McCormick blamed its Democratic politics for Roosevelt's success. His choice of the vicinity of Grand Rapids as the ideal site for the national capital reflected objection to Washington's southern as much as to its eastern geography. But the *Tribune*'s decades of gibing at the South's revivalists, moonshiners, and Kluxers, wounding to Ralph McGill, passed unnoticed by *Life* magazine. Like other McCormick prejudices, these were too generally shared to draw criticism. Throughout his life his opinions on nearly any political issue would have won cordial agreement from any group of conservatives, say a gathering of his Yale classmates.

The one thing that marked him as different was his isolationism in World War II. Not his neutralism before the war—practically everybody to the right of the Communist party (and some people to the left of it) joined him in that. But on September 1, 1939, he found himself leading only a corporal's guard as he continued marching in the same direction while the principal mass of his fellow conservatives did a sharp by-the-right-flank wheel. Had McCormick fallen in step with that maneuver his image and memory would have been very different. Not inconceivably, he might have served in or out of uniform in a Washington war job.

To see why he and a few others did not flip-flop with the crowd seems to require as much analysis of the majority who did as of the minority who did not. Setting aside the rhetoric of war hysteria, the parting between isolationists and interventionists seems to have reflected two things: an honest difference of opinion on the war and the psychological inertia induced by a high level of political involvement. A doctor or dentist who in 1937 recalled his service in the AEF and swore, "Never again," could in September 1939 with little sense of inconsistency exclaim, "Now Hitler's gone too far!" The changeover was different for a newspaper publisher who over the years had formed, refined, elaborated, and reiterated a neutralist stance. The papers that hailed Roosevelt's quarantine speech were those that had hawked the war in 1916, had remained discreet for many years, and now with the sounding of the new alarm seemed to paw the ground once more. With the first great shift of American public opinion in September 1939, the *Chicago Daily News, New York Times,* and *New York Herald Tribune* found themselves suddenly again at the head of the mainstream. The *Chicago Tribune, St. Louis Post-Dispatch,* and other confirmed neutralists sought comfort from the polls that showed nobody eager to go to war, but the parade was moving away from them all the same. Newspapers that

had articulated their position less categorically could slide over from neutrality to aid-to-Britain along with their readers. The majority of the press,
like the majority of its readers, resembled the man in Auden's poem—
"When there was peace he was for peace./ When there was war he went."

The eastern stereotype of the Midwest isolationist was a small-towner
with limited information about the outside world and no great interest in
it. Colonel McCormick was the very opposite—an educated cosmopolitan
intensely interested in foreign affairs and armed with all the information he
could get his hands on. There is no way to explain his and Joe Patterson's
neutralism in 1916, as contrasted with the hawk ardor of Teddy and Franklin Roosevelt, save as a matter of conviction, and looking back today it is
difficult to argue the superior common sense of the Roosevelt-Roosevelt
position over the McCormick-Patterson. Hence the widespread, if not prevailing, assumption today that America's World War I intervention was
dubious in contrast to that of World War II. Yet the vindication of the
nation's World War II role seems to be rooted less in the arguments actually
used by the debaters of 1940–1941 than in events and perceptions that came
later. Dakar-Brazil was a fantasy, but Hitler a genuine monster.

History is typically in no hurry to say its final word. From an American
perspective World War II was such a smash success—out of the Great
Depression into world power and affluence—that nobody has prodded the
historians to tell us where we made our mistakes. The "internationalism"
that came out of it, however, no longer shines untarnished. For a long time
we were sure that the ideal promoted by FDR, Willkie, and Ralph McGill
was a Good Thing, with its United Nations, Marshall Plan, Point Four, and
Peace Corps. Yet the UN, despite many good works, has proved as power-
less a peacekeeper as the old League of Nations, and America's foreign aid
has turned into an arms supply program. Colonel McCormick's and Henry
A. Wallace's negative view of NATO does not look quite as wrongheaded
or simpleminded as the high-riding internationalists of the 1940s—Luce,
the Alsop brothers, the *New York Times,* and the *Herald Tribune*—
thought. McCormick may have remembered better than they that America's history in international relations has had its ugly chapters, and as a
result they contributed to adding another, the ugliest of all. For a time the
phrase "foreign entanglement" was employed mainly in the form of deroga-
tory wit. Since Vietnam less laughter has been heard over the conviction of
George Washington and Colonel McCormick, not to mention Lincoln,
whom McCormick admired, and Bryan, whom he didn't, that the proper
place for America's armed forces was inside America's own defense perime-
ter. The superior scorn lavished by the internationalists of the 1940s and
1950s for such prudent doctrine has come to sound a little like *Time*'s
amusement at McCormick's use of an automobile seat belt.

Many wheels unexpectedly come full circle. Who would have guessed that forty years later college presidents would be protesting government regulation while liberal columnists echoed the *Chicago Tribune*'s calls for gun control and objections to government dam-building? Or that just as the press extended a gingerly recognition to John Maynard Keynes, Milton Friedman would come along (and find an early forum for his "Chicago school" economics in the *Chicago Tribune*)? Liberals of the 1930s and 1940s have experienced many surprises. Again to quote Auden, poet of the 1930s Left, "Who nurtured in that fine tradition/ predicted the result," that Alf Landon would win our respect and even our admission that he may have been in some ways a better man than FDR? Or that we would look back on 1940 and be embarrassed for both Roosevelt and Willkie?

True, the conservative ideology that dominated the 1930s–1940s press looks, if anything, even worse from here. One might paraphrase Oswald Garrison Villard and say, "You can never be certain whether the press's opinions are going to turn out later to have been reactionary and vicious, or whether they will accidentally be found on the side of progress and enlightenment."

Colonel McCormick was as stubborn, opinionated, and partisan as his adversaries, and could have profited as much as they from meditation on the words of the British parliamentarian: "I beseech you, in the name of Jesus Christ, conceive that you might be wrong." But the fact that a reactionary can sometimes be right is perhaps a little less recognized than the fact that a liberal can be, and Colonel McCormick, for all his impatience and prejudice, had a streak of something not too common among editors and commentators, the engineer's taste for problem-solving. Besides his own inventions, patented and unpatented—printing improvements, an electric-motor regulator, an electric self-starter—he had a good appreciation of the role of technology in history, once entertaining, or lulling to sleep, his WGN audience with a competent exposition of history's energy sources and conversion devices. His testimony on the Lend-Lease bill represented a problem-solving approach, and if the country had been able to agree that the Dakar-Brazil scenario was a fake threat, the problem of overcoming Hitler might have received better definition.

Another point on which attitudes seem to have changed in an unexpected way is toward the philosophy of news presentation. Despite some lip service to objective political reportage, McCormick clearly followed the example of Joseph Medill rather than the precepts of James Keeley and Robert Patterson. As he told the Washington courtroom, what some people called news slanting he called "news evaluation."

Marshall Field III stated an alternative philosophy: "All shades of opinion, all significant versions of the facts, should have representation, and be

given free access to the channels of communication." In his time Field
would have been drowned in "Hear, hears," and doubtless we still believe
in the principle of diversity, but with the reduction in the number of
newspaper voices, the growth of the chains, and above all with the mon-
strous intrusion of network television, the news actually presented to us
contains fewer "significant versions of the facts" than it did in the days of
Field and McCormick. The reduction of the number of channels of communication seems to impose a heightened obligation on each surviving channel
to present diversity, and some honest attempts have been made (e.g., the
latter-day *Chicago Tribune* hiring liberal columnists). Yet TV news has a
malign unanimity, while in the print press the flowering of the opinion
column has helped to blur the demarcation between news and opinion.
Harold Ickes, Irving Brant, Oswald Garrison Villard, and other old-time
liberal critics might be shocked at some of the common practices of modern
journalism, both print and electronic.

A year before his death Colonel McCormick strolled out of the Tribune
Tower in the company of General Levin Campbell, retired chief of army
ordnance. The two old gentlemen paused on Michigan Avenue and General
Campbell remarked politely that the Colonel must be proud of the lasting
memorial he had created in the *Tribune*. Characteristically, the Colonel
thought it over a moment, then pursed his lips and said, "I suppose it will
last about the way I leave it for about ten years."

In the eyes of most observers, the *Tribune* lasted much the way the
Colonel left it for longer than ten years, and some thought its law-and-order
conservatism even hardened a bit in the 1960s. Inevitably, the pendulum
swung, new leadership came in, and the *Tribune* modernized its look and
its outlook. One element was the melancholy alteration in the Chicago
newspaper scene. The Colonel's successors had bought the faltering Hearst
afternoon paper, the *American*, at a price some believe the Colonel would
not have been foolish enough to pay, and for a while competed in the
afternoon with the *Daily News*, purchased earlier by Marshall Field. But
the *American* lost money for the *Tribune* as it long had for Hearst and when
such palliatives as changing its name failed it was shut down. A greater loss
to journalism was the *Daily News*, which in 1977 succumbed to shifting
metropolitan demographics and television, leaving Chicago without an afternoon paper. By that time the *Tribune* had successfully experimented
with round-the-clock publication, which the *Sun-Times* also adopted, so
that the two papers are on Chicago streets twenty-four hours starting with
early-bird editions at 5 P.M. the day before dateline. The *Sun-Times* remains
a tabloid (probably the best imitator of Joe Patterson's New York venture)
and the *Tribune* full-size (but six columns, with some new typefaces), and
there is still a discernible though hardly obtrusive liberal-conservative

schism between them. The *Tribune* no longer claims to be the World's Greatest Newspaper ("constructive impudence," somebody once called the slogan), but is at least, as the *Sun-Times* has said, one of the world's greatest, and so is the *Sun-Times.* True to its traditions, the *Tribune* still writes and edits smartly, but dropping one of the traditions, spells according to Webster's. It has won several Pulitzer Prizes since McCormick's death, something it did not do during the last nineteen years of his life (could there have been a slight case of bias by the Pulitzer committee?). It remains one of the few dailies with its own foreign service, and does an outstanding reader-service job in food, style, recreation, the arts. Its sports pages rank among the brightest. It was one of the original homes of two classic latter-day comic strips, "Peanuts" and "Doonesbury." (But the cartoon is gone from page one.) To the journalistic extravaganza of Watergate it contributed a triumph of technical virtuosity: The entire transcript of the tapes, introduced by President Nixon on TV in the evening, was published in a special section in next morning's *Tribune,* which certainly gave the Chicago and Northwestern commuters enough to occupy them for the ride.

Possibly, as John Knight predicted at the time of Colonel McCormick's death, the paper has become "a little duller" with his loss. Nevertheless, if the Colonel were to return to his Tower he would surely still be proud of the *Tribune,* though he would doubtless have a few memos to dictate to the staff.

The *Tribune* owes its life to McCormick's far-sighted Canadian newsprint enterprise, and owes much of its success and most of its reputation, good and bad, to his guidance. The news industry owes him something too. He has been called "an original," apparently in the sense of a creature interesting because unusual, but in a world of chains, syndication, network news, and all the glib and shallow mental uniformity conjured up by the phrase "mass media," he stands out as an independent thinker. "One of the finest minds of the fourteenth century" no longer looks like one of the worst ones of the twentieth. True, he didn't always know what was going on, or perhaps more accurately he seldom knew completely what was going on— Schlieffen Plan, Capone mob, Hitler's intentions, Churchill's needs—but groping amid ignorance is a basic of the "demented profession," however knowing its practitioners like to sound.

If one quotes some of the things McCormick said over his lifetime, he can be, and has been, made to sound like a fool, but so can anybody who expressed himself freely during the era of two world wars and the depression —Roosevelt, Hoover, H. L. Mencken, Norman Thomas. Being wrong out loud or in print is an inevitable privilege of the leaders of opinion. In a democracy we need Marshall Field's diversity in order to make our choice, but twenty, thirty, or forty years later we still may make a different one.

A reasonably careful look at Colonel McCormick's life dissipates much of the mystery his personality and character held for contemporaries, especially those who never met him. His imposing physical stature, which to stubby Ickes made him appear a bully, seems rather, as Waverley Root intimates, to have conferred a confident majesty, perhaps a little overconfident. With his boss role at the *Tribune,* it may have contributed both to his remoteness and his artless egotism. Walter Howey thought him a Quixote tilting at windmills that none but he could see. In longer retrospect than Howey had, he seems rather a large, impatient Candide or Zadig, journeying through life and history unafraid, confident in his own perceptions but curious, at once worldly and naïve.

His ideas and attitudes, whether in harmony or in conflict with those of the majority, were indisputably his own, though the tenacity with which he stuck to them may have been his grandfather's. James O'Donnell Bennett, his favorite newspaper writer, could have written of McCormick what he wrote of Joseph Medill: "He believed that the United States was the finest country on earth, that Chicago—despite Democrats—was the finest city in that country, and that the *Tribune* had more character and sense of service than any other newspaper in the world."

Similarly, what John Knight said of McCormick at the time of his death was probably true of Medill: "He had a full life, and I doubt that he would have changed any of it."

Walter Trohan, who worked for him for four decades, recalls the Colonel's once confiding that all the McCormicks except himself were crazy, and then adding shrewdly, "You wouldn't agree with that, would you, Walter?"

Trohan had to answer that in all honesty there were times when he wouldn't. That did not prevent him from recording for the Illinois Historical Society a difficult-to-improve-on epitaph:

> Certainly he had his idiosyncrasies, but they became our idiosyncrasies and we loved him for them, even when we smarted most under them. He was the greater editor for being human and having faults common to all. With all his faults he was a better editor and a better man than those who mocked and derided him.

BIBLIOGRAPHY

A NOTE ON THE BIBLIOGRAPHY

THE *Chicago Tribune* has reserved Colonel McCormick's private papers for an authorized biography. Fortunately other sources, including the Colonel's published works, furnish ample material for an appraisal of his career as a publisher and figure of controversy in twentieth-century American history.

Principal sources, in addition to those listed below, include Colonel McCormick's radio memoirs, broadcast and printed in the *Tribune,* but never published in book form; interviews and correspondence with persons who knew the Colonel, including his widow, Maryland McCormick; and, most important, the microfilm files of the *Chicago Tribune* and other newspapers in the Library of Congress.

Alexander, Jack. "The Duke of Chicago," *Saturday Evening Post,* July 19, 1941.

———. "The World's Greatest Newspaper," *Saturday Evening Post,* July 26, 1941.

Allen, Frederick Lewis. *Only Yesterday, an Informal History of the Nineteen-Twenties.* New York, 1931.

Allsop, Kenneth. *The Bootleggers, the Story of Prohibition.* New Rochelle, N.Y., 1961.

Andrews, Wayne. *Battle for Chicago.* New York, 1946.

Beard, Charles. *President Roosevelt and the Coming of War.* New Haven, Conn., 1948.

Becker, Stephen. *Marshall Field III.* New York, 1964.

Biddle, Francis. *In Brief Authority.* Garden City, N.Y., 1962.

Bloom, John Morton, ed. *The Diary of Henry A. Wallace, 1942–1946.* Boston, 1973.

Bright, John. *Hizzoner Big Bill Thompson, an Idyll of Chicago.* New York, 1930.

Burns, James MacGregor. *Roosevelt, the Soldier of Freedom.* New York, 1970.

A Century of Tribune Editorials. 1947. Reprint. Freeport, N.Y., 1970.

Childs, Marquis. *I Write from Washington.* New York, 1940.

Cohen, Bernard C. *The Press and Foreign Policy.* Princeton, 1963.

Cole, Wayne S. *America First, the Battle Against Intervention, 1940–41.* 1953. Reprint. New York, 1971.

"The Colonel's Century," *Time,* June 9, 1947.

Cooper, Kent. *Kent Cooper and the Associated Press, an Autobiography.* New York, 1959.

Crozier, Emmet. *American Reporters on the Western Front, 1914–1918.* New York, 1959.

Daniels, Jonathan, ed. *Complete Presidential Press Conferences of Franklin D. Roosevelt,* Vols. 1–2, 1933. New York, 1972.

Demaris, Ovid. *Captive City, Chicago in Chains.* New York, 1969.

Dennis, Charles. *Victor Lawson, His Time and His Work.* Chicago, 1935.

Department of State, U.S. *Peace and War. United States Foreign Policy, 1931–1941.* Washington, D.C., 1943.

Duroselle, Jean-Baptiste. *From Wilson to Roosevelt, Foreign Policy in the United States 1913–1945.* New York, 1968.

Edwards, Jerome E. *The Foreign Policy of Colonel McCormick's Chicago Tribune, 1929–1941.* Reno, Nev., 1971.

Eisenhower, Dwight D. *Crusade in Europe.* Garden City, N.Y., 1948.

Farr, Finis. *Chicago, a Personal History of America's Most American City.* New Rochelle, N.Y., 1973.

Flynn, J. T. *The Roosevelt Myth.* New York, 1956.

Freidel, Frank. *Franklin D. Roosevelt: the Apprenticeship; the Ordeal; the Triumph; Launching the New Deal.* Boston, 1952, 1954, 1956, 1973.

Gertz, Elmer. "Eccentric Titan, McCormick of the Tribune," *Nation,* April 30, 1955.

Gibbons, Edward. *Floyd Gibbons, Your Headline Hunter.* New York, 1953.

Gies, Joseph. *Crisis 1918.* New York, 1974.

———. *Franklin D. Roosevelt, Portrait of a President.* Garden City, N.Y., 1971.

Goren, Dina. "Communication Intelligence and the Freedom of the Press; the Chicago Tribune's Battle of Midway Dispatch and the Breaking of the Japanese Naval Code." Unpublished Thesis, Yale Law School, May 1978.

Gregory, Barry. *Argonne 1918, the AEF in France.* New York, 1972.

Gunther, John. *Inside U.S.A.* New York, 1947.

———. *Taken at the Flood, the Story of Albert D. Lasker.* New York, 1960.

Healy, Paul F. *Cissy, the Biography of Eleanor M. "Cissy" Patterson.* Garden City, N.Y., 1966.

Hecht, Ben, and MacArthur, Charles. *The Front Page.* New York, 1928.

Hoge, Alice Albright. *Cissy Patterson, the Life of Eleanor Medill Patterson, Publisher and Editor of the Washington Times-Herald.* New York, 1966.

Hunt, Frazier. *One American and His Attempt at Education.* New York, 1938.

Hutchinson, W. T. *Cyrus Hall McCormick.* 2 vols. New York, 1930.

Hyman, Sidney. *The Lives of William Benton.* Chicago, 1969.

Ickes, Harold L. *America's House of Lords.* New York, 1939.

————. *Freedom of the Press Today, a Clinical Examination by 28 Specialists.* New York, 1941.

————. *The Secret Diary of Harold Ickes.* 3 vols. New York, 1953–1954.

In Fact, 1940–1942.

Ingersoll, Ralph. *Top Secret.* New York, 1946.

Johnson, Walter. *The Battle Against Isolation.* Chicago, 1944.

Kahn, E. J., Jr. "Democracy's Friend: II. Smears, Sneers, Snarls, Snorts, and Snaps," *The New Yorker,* August 2, 1951.

Kennan, George F. *American Diplomacy 1900–1950.* New York, 1951.

Langer, William L., and Gleason, S. Everett. *The Challenge to Isolation, 1937–1940.* New York, 1952.

————. *The Undeclared War, 1940–41.* New York, 1953.

Lasch, Robert. "Chicago Patriot," *Atlantic Monthly,* June 1942.

Leuchtenberg, William E. *Franklin D. Roosevelt and the New Deal, 1932–1940.* New York, 1963.

Liebling, A. J. *The Press.* New York, 1975.

————. *The Wayward Pressman.* 1945. Reprint. Westport, Conn., 1973.

Lilienthal, David E. *The Atomic Energy Years: 1948.* The Journals of David E. Lilienthal. Vol. 2. New York, 1964–1971.

Linn, James Weber. *James Keeley, Newspaperman.* Indianapolis, 1937.

Lowe, David. *Lost Chicago.* Boston, 1975.

Lundberg, Ferdinand. *Imperial Hearst, a Social Biography.* New York, 1936.

Martin, Harold H. *Ralph McGill, Reporter.* Boston, 1973.

McCormick, Cyrus III. *The Century of the Reaper.* Boston, 1931.

McCormick, Robert R. *The Army of 1918.* New York, 1920.

————. *The Case for the Freedom of the Press.* Address before the New York State Chamber of Commerce, New York, November 16, 1933.

————. *How We Acquired Our National Territory.* Chicago, 1942.

————. *The Freedom of the Press.* New York, 1936.

————. *Ulysses S. Grant, the Great Soldier of America.* New York, 1934.

————. *The War Without Grant.* New York, 1950.

————. *With the Russian Army.* New York, 1915.

McCutcheon, John T. *Drawn from Memory.* Indianapolis, 1950.

McPhaul, John J. *Deadlines and Monkeyshines, the Fabled World of Chicago Journalism.* 1962. Reprint. Westport, Conn., 1973.

Manchester, William. *The Glory and the Dream, a Narrative History of America, 1932–1972.* Boston, 1974.

Martin, John Bartlow. *Adlai Stevenson.* New York, 1952.

———. "Colonel McCormick of the Tribune," *Harper's Magazine,* October 1944.

Mencken, H. L. *The Bathtub Hoax and Other Blasts and Bravos from the Chicago Tribune.* New York, 1958.

Miers, Earl Schenck, ed. *The American Story from Columbus to the Atom.* Great Neck, N.Y., 1956.

Millis, Walter. *Road to War, America 1914–1917.* Boston, 1935.

Moore, William T. *Dateline Chicago, a Veteran Newsman Recalls Its Heyday.* New York, 1973.

Mott, Frank Luther. *American Journalism, a History, 1690–1960.* New York, 1962.

Murray, George. *The Madhouse on Madison Street.* Chicago, 1965.

"A Newspaper Congratulates Itself," *Life,* June 23, 1947.

Pasley, Fred D. *Al Capone, the Biography of a Self-Made Man.* 1930. Reprint. Freeport, N.Y., 1971.

Patterson, Joseph. *A Little Brother of the Rich.* Chicago, 1908.

———. *The Notebook of a Neutral.* New York, 1916.

———. *Rebellion.* Chicago, 1911.

Philipps, Cabell. *The 1940s, Decade of Triumph and Trouble.* New York, 1975.

Pictured Encyclopedia of the World's Greatest Newspaper. Chicago, 1928.

Public Opinion Quarterly, 1941, 1942.

Rascoe, Burton. *Before I Forget.* New York, 1937.

Roper, Elmo. *You and Your Leaders, Their Actions and Your Reactions.* New York, 1957.

Rue, Larry. *I Fly for News.* New York, 1932.

Schultz, Sigrid. *Germany Will Try It Again.* New York, 1944.

Seldes, George. *Even the Gods Can't Change History.* Secaucus, N.J., 1976.

———. *Facts and Fascism.* New York, 1943.

———. *Lords of the Press.* New York, 1946.

———. *One Thousand Americans.* New York, 1947.

———. "Portrait of a Press Lord: My Decade with Col. McCormick," *Lost Generation Journal,* Fall 1974.

———. *Tell the Truth and Run, My 44 Year Fight for a Free Press.* New York, 1953.

————. *You Can't Print That! The Truth Behind the News, 1918–1928.* Garden City, N.Y., 1929.

Sheean, Vincent. *Personal History.* Garden City, N.Y., 1934.

Soule, George. *Prosperity Decade from War to Depression, 1917–1929.* New York, 1968.

Stimson, Henry L., and Bundy, McGeorge. *On Active Service in Peace and War.* New York, 1947.

Stallings, Laurence. *The Doughboys, the Story of the AEF, 1917–1918.* New York, 1963.

Stuart, William H. *The Twenty Incredible Years.* Chicago, 1935.

Sturm, Paul W. "Is There an Exorcist in the House?" *Forbes Magazine,* September 1, 1977.

Swanberg, W. A. *Citizen Hearst, a Biography of William Randolph Hearst.* New York, 1961.

————. *Political Animals.* Garden City, N.Y., 1975.

Tebbel, John W. *An American Dynasty, the Story of the McCormicks, Medills and Pattersons.* Garden City, N.Y., 1947.

————. *The Compact History of the American Newspaper.* New York, 1963.

————. *The Life and Good Times of William Randolph Hearst.* New York, 1952.

Terrall, Robert. "Meet the Colonel," *U.S. Week,* September 27, 1941.

Trohan, Walter. "My Life with the Colonel," *Journal of the Illinois State Historical Society,* Winter 1959.

Union for Democratic Action, *The People vs. the Chicago Tribune.* Chicago, 1942.

Vandenberg, Arthur. *The Private Papers of Senator Vandenberg.* Edited by Arthur H. Vandenberg, Jr., with the collaboration of Joe Alex Morris. Boston, 1962.

Villard, Oswald Garrison. *The Disappearing Daily.* New York, 1941.

————. "The Press Today: I. The Associated Press," *Nation,* April 16, 1930.

————. "The World's Greatest Newspaper," *Nation,* February 1, 1922.

The W.G.N. Chicago, 1922.

Waldrop, Frank C. *McCormick of Chicago.* Englewood Cliffs, N.J., 1966.

Wedemeyer, Albert C. *Wedemeyer Reports!* New York, 1958.

Wendt, Lloyd, and Kogan, Herman. *Big Bill of Chicago.* Indianapolis, 1953.

Wheeler, Burton K. (with Paul F. Healy). *Yankee from the West.* New York, 1962.

White, David Manning, ed., and Abel, Robert H. *The Funnies, an American Idiom.* New York, 1963.

Wiegman, Carl. *Trees to News.* Toronto, 1953.

Williams, Greer. "I Worked for McCormick," *Nation,* October 10, 1953.

Zorbaugh, Harvey W. *The Gold Coast and the Slum, a Sociological Study of Chicago's Near North Side.* 1929. Reprint. Chicago, 1976.

Wilson, Woodrow, 43, 55, 57, 59, 61, 62, 63–64, 78, 80, 84, 144, 148, 151, 157, 161, 168
Winchell, Walter, 159, 208
"Winnie Winkle," 105
Wisner, George W., 30, 42
With the Russian Army, 59–61
Wolf, Otto, 103
Wood, General Leonard, 59–60
Wood, General Robert E., 156, 162
Woolley, Robert W., 63
Works Progress Administration (WPA), 127, 133
World Court, 111, 113

WGN, 7, 104–105, 150, 153, 157, 212, 216, 221, 233, 234, 235, 242
Wright, Orville and Wilbur, 25

Yale University, 2, 16–19, 20, 22, 24, 26, 27, 58, 111, 125, 156, 171, 185, 234
Yamamoto, Admiral Isoruku, 211
Yerkes, Charles, 23
Yetter, John, 103

Zangara, Giuseppe, 116
Zilboorg, Gregory, 172
Zinn, Walter H., 228
Zuta, Jack, 98–99

ABOUT THE AUTHOR

JOSEPH GIES has worked as an editor for *This Week* magazine and for Doubleday in New York, for the Encyclopedia Britannica in Chicago, and is presently employed by the Association of Governing Boards in Washington, D.C.

He is the author of ten books, including biographies of Truman and Roosevelt. He lives in Oakton, Virginia.